Pride Publishing books by
K. Evan Coles and Brigham Vaughn:

Wake

I0611635

CALM

K. EVAN COLES &
BRIGHAM VAUGHN

Calm
ISBN # 978-1-78686-318-8
©Copyright K. Evan Coles and Brigham Vaughn 2017
Cover Art by Posh Gosh ©Copyright September 2017
Interior text design by Claire Siemaszkiewicz
Pride Publishing

Published in 2017 by Pride Publishing, Think Tank, Ruston Way, Lincoln, LN6 7FL, United Kingdom.

Pride Publishing is an imprint of Totally Entwined Group Limited.

CALM

Dedication

Calm was part of an almost four-year journey. It wouldn't have been possible without the incredibly supportive people in our lives.

For my husband, who is patient (usually) and encouraging (always) of my endless scribbling.
For my son, who makes me laugh every single day.

For the people in and around my life who inspire me, let me be weird and make me feel brave.

And for Brigham Vaughn, who puts up with my thousands of questions, listens to my rants, never complains when I occasionally fall off the face of the planet and is always ready to put pen to paper when our stars align.
— K. Evan Coles

This book is for my friends who were patient when I was too busy writing or editing to spend time with them. For the people who cheered me on and had faith in my writing long before I did. For my parents who are the best patrons of the arts a writer could ask for.

And mostly, for K. Evan Coles, who got me into reading and writing gay romance in the first place. I wouldn't be here without you! It's been a wonderful — and occasionally frustrating — journey. There's no one would rather have done it with.
— Brigham Vaughn

K. and Brigham would also like to thank their patient beta readers: Shell Taylor, Jayme Yesenofski, Rebecca Spence and Kade Boehme. You slogged through two hundred thousand words, multiple times, to help us mold it into the story you see before you today. We could not have done it without you.

Chapter One

Riley Porter-Wright whistled as he let himself into his West Village apartment on a warm Thursday night in April. He'd left work with a spring in his step. He had a date with Will Martin—his boyfriend—that night, and a three-day weekend ahead of him.

As senior vice president and head of the e-pub division of his family's publishing house, Riley had been delighted to share the year's first quarter data for his division at the board meeting that afternoon. The numbers had been high enough to impress even Jonathon Porter-Wright, the CEO of the company and Riley's father. He was a demanding man under the best of circumstances and the flicker of pleased surprise that had crossed his face during Riley's presentation had been gratifying.

Although completely estranged from his parents since his coming out and divorce the previous fall, Riley still had to deal with his father at work. He was no longer concerned with living up to his father's expectations, but Riley felt perversely pleased that the better he performed, the more of an ass his father appeared to be. There was a certain measure of satisfaction in proving to his father that being an openly bisexual man hadn't done a thing to affect his career. If anything, finally feeling content with his life had *improved* Riley's performance.

He'd left the office immediately after the board meeting and hurried home. He hastily dressed in a tux, then checked his watch to be sure he wasn't late as he dashed out of the door. Why the Metropolitan Opera held premieres on a weeknight, he didn't know, but thankfully, Will didn't have any classes to teach at NYU that evening.

Riley texted Will on the way to his building. He came out to meet Riley after the town car pulled up. The driver held the door while Will slid inside and gave Riley a brief, warm kiss. "Hey, good to see you."

"You, too." They'd both been busy in the past few weeks and hadn't been able to spend much time together. Riley smiled at him, struck again by Will's high cheekbones and classic good looks. Riley hadn't seen him in a tuxedo before, but he wore it well. "How was your day?"

"Mmm, faculty meeting this afternoon and most of my students seem to have spring fever, so I'm glad it's over," Will replied with an easy grin, his blue eyes brightening. "Getting better now, though. Yours?"

"Great, actually, and I'm looking forward to tonight."

They kept the discussion light while the car crossed Manhattan, but Riley's anxiety rose as they neared the Lincoln Center. He straightened his bow tie for the umpteenth time. Will set a hand on his thigh, the touch warm and heavy.

"Are you *sure* you want to do this tonight?" Will asked softly. "You seem jittery."

"Of course." Riley gave Will a reassuring smile. "I'll admit I'm...anxious about how it will go, but I refuse to let anyone keep me from living my life. I love opera and I want to share that with you."

That night was the gala premier of *Giulio Cesare* and Riley had spent the better part of a week debating if he should invite Will to be his date. Riley had done little socializing with anyone from his past since his abrupt coming-out the previous November and subsequent divorce from his now ex-wife Alex. The possibility of seeing his parents was nerve-racking. Even worse was the thought of seeing his former best friend, Carter, and Carter's wife, Kate. Carter had been shocked by Riley's coming out and Riley's confession that he loved Carter had driven a wedge between them. Riley hadn't had any contact with Kate and, other than a brief and awkward run-in during the holidays at Serendipity when Carter had been out with the kids, Riley hadn't seen Carter, either.

Will knew enough about his past that he wouldn't be caught off-guard if an awkward situation arose, but that didn't make it any easier. The thought of Will and Carter in the same room caused his anxiety to rise.

In the three months Riley and Will had been seeing each other, Will had more than lived up to Riley's first impression of him. Not only gorgeous, he was thoughtful and well-read. Patient, too, while Riley shook off the hang-ups from his past and struggled to figure out the new path he was on. In fact, he'd been more than patient.

Although they'd been intimate in every other way, Riley hadn't reached a point where he was ready to let Will penetrate him or vice versa. Will assured Riley he shouldn't feel rushed and reminded him some men never wanted anal sex, but, still, it bothered Riley.

They'd decided not to see other people, but sometimes Riley held Will at arm's length when he should have been pulling him closer. Taking him to the opera tonight was one way to include Will in another part of his life. He genuinely cared for Will and thought maybe, in time, he could fall for him.

Riley could hardly say he was *over* Carter, but thoughts of Carter had grown less and less frequent. As time passed, the acute pain of losing him had faded to a dull ache. Time certainly did heal wounds, but, unfortunately, it did nothing to lessen the feeling that something important was missing from his life.

"I'm glad you invited me," Will said, bringing him back to the moment.

Riley smiled warmly at him. "I'm glad you were willing to come. I don't think my ex-wife will be there — she really only bothered with the events here to network — but I can't promise anything. Let's just hope we can make it through the night without any drama."

"If there is, we'll either ignore it or cut out early." Will shrugged and slid his hand a little higher. He leaned in to whisper in Riley's ear. "No matter what happens, the night can end in my bed with your dick in my mouth and you coming so hard you see stars."

"Promises, promises," Riley teased, his voice more breathless than he intended. He closed his eyes for a brief moment as Will feathered kisses against his jaw, then glanced at the driver in front of him. He was grateful for the man's discretion and that he hadn't once glanced at them in the rearview mirror. Although finally at ease with showing affection with Will in public, Riley didn't want to make the driver uncomfortable.

Will pulled back when the car slowed to a stop and Riley looked up in surprise, realizing they were already in front of Lincoln Center. He stepped onto the sidewalk and waited for Will to follow, nodding at a few people mingling outside the entrance whom he recognized. He couldn't resist a peek at the fountain, half-expecting to see Carter standing beside it. But the familiar silhouette was nowhere in sight, so he turned back to Will.

"Still nervous?" Will asked quietly as they walked through the lobby, with its endless red-carpeted floors and the mid-century Sputnik-style chandeliers that had been a gift from the Austrian government.

"A little," Riley replied. "Mostly trying not to think too much about your comment in the car. I'm afraid these pants don't hide much." He grinned wryly and Will laughed.

"Sorry."

"As long as you follow through, I have no complaints." Riley's grin faded when they stepped into the cocktail reception. He glanced around anxiously. To his relief, the only familiar faces in sight were distant acquaintances and he and his date were able to get a drink and mingle. People stared, of course—he'd expected that—and there were a few who gave him and Will a suspiciously wide berth, but frankly, it went better than he'd anticipated.

Riley had just begun to relax when he spotted his parents. His good mood immediately plummeted, replaced by an increasing tightness in his chest. "That's my parents ahead," he murmured. "Brace yourself."

The woman standing next to his mother noticed him. "Oh, look, Geneva, it's *Riley*." Her tone held a nasty note, as if she merely wanted to make a jab at his mother. Riley didn't know Helena Finch well but enough to remember she was someone who should be aware of the current situation. Perhaps she disliked his mother, or maybe she just wanted to catch a bit of the gossip. He smiled thinly when he approached them, hoping for Will's sake that the typical Porter-Wright way of handling difficult situations would hold out tonight. Ignoring the situation and acting politely in front of company sounded good to him.

"Will, this is Jonathon and Geneva Porter-Wright." He nodded to his parents. "Jonathon, Geneva, this is William Martin." He didn't see any point in elaborating on Will's part in his life. "Will's a law professor at NYU."

His mother nodded frostily and his father put out his hand. The gesture seemed hesitant and begrudging.

"Nice to meet you both." Will's tone came across as polite, but there was little of his usual warmth.

"Likewise." His father didn't try to hide his disdain.

A rotund gentleman who looked as if he might pop the buttons on his jacket at any moment held out his hand to Will. "Marcus Finch. I went to NYU law myself back in the day."

Riley glanced at his mother, but she wouldn't meet his eye. Outwardly, she appeared cool and composed, but Riley would bet agitation churned under the surface.

Helena gave Riley a knowing smile. "And Will is here *with* you? How *interesting*." Her voice dripped with innuendo.

"We've been seeing each other for a while." Riley kept his tone polite but cool. "On top of being a law professor, Will is a writer. We have a great deal in common."

Will made small talk with Marcus while Riley remained silent.

"It appears they're seating for dinner," Geneva said after a few minutes, her voice brittle. "Come, Jonathon, we should find our seats. Nice seeing you, Marcus and Helena. Riley. Mr. Martin." She disappeared before they could reply and Riley made polite excuses to the Finches. He and Will found their table, grateful to end the encounter. His parents would make sure their paths didn't cross again that evening.

Riley didn't relax until dinner had concluded and Will followed him to his box for the beginning of act one. He took a seat next to Will, relieved that dinner had been calm and uneventful.

"I'm glad you came with me tonight," Riley told him with a smile. Will briefly touched Riley's knee.

"I am, too."

The final knot of worry in Riley's chest dissipated and he got comfortable, eager to see the production. Unfortunately, the good mood only lasted until intermission.

Riley and Will were enjoying the champagne and dessert when a blonde in an ice-blue dress crossed his field of vision. Riley tensed at the sight of Kate Hamilton. He glanced around, trying to be casual as he searched for Carter, but found him nowhere in sight. Riley frowned. The crowd was thick, but Carter stood tall enough to be seen in any group. Perhaps he was in the restroom or had stepped outside to take a call. Kate headed toward him, although she hadn't made eye contact yet.

Riley set down his champagne glass, his hands suddenly nerveless and clumsy when Kate spotted him. Her eyes went wide and she came to an abrupt stop. "Riley."

"How are you, Kate?"

"I'm fine." Her smile seemed automatic, forced. Riley paused, really looking at Kate. She appeared to have lost weight and her normally bright eyes and smile were dimmer than usual. Although beautifully made up as always, something was off.

"Will, I'd like to introduce you to Kate Hamilton, a good friend of mine. Kate, this is Will Martin, law professor, writer and my date this evening."

The corners of Kate's mouth briefly tightened before she smiled at Will and held out her hand. "It's nice to meet you, Will."

"Likewise." Will, in turn, appeared relaxed and comfortable. Clearly, whatever was obvious to Riley wasn't to someone who had never met Kate before.

"Are you as big of a fan of opera as Riley is?" Kate asked.

Will grinned. "I'm not sure anyone's as big of a fan as Riley, but I do enjoy it." Will brushed his fingertips across Riley's back. "I'm glad he wanted to share it with me."

"Oh, I've been known to give Riley a run for his money," Kate said lightly.

A little more warmth appeared in her eyes, but she still seemed off and Riley turned to Will, laying a hand on his arm.

"Would you get me another glass of champagne? I'd like a moment to talk to Kate, if you don't mind."

"Of course," Will reassured him.

"Thank you. I'll try not to be long." Riley squeezed Will's arm.

"Take your time. I'll be over by the bar when you're done." He nodded at Kate. "Very nice to meet you, Kate."

"You, too."

Will left with a smile and Riley felt grateful for his understanding. He turned back to Kate, growing serious. "Are you sure everything's okay? You don't seem…" He wasn't sure how to finish. Kate seemed unhappy, stressed. "Is it that Carter's around and you're worried about us running into each other?"

She shook her head. "No. Carter's…Carter's not here with me."

Kate's fingers trembled as she smoothed them over her pale blue dress and, although it took him a moment, Riley finally registered what was wrong with the picture. A faint stripe of lighter skin adorned the third finger of her left hand instead of the glittering diamond ring Riley had carried in the breast pocket of his tux the morning of Carter's wedding. He wanted to ask her about it but realized there were too many people around. "Can we talk? Privately?"

She nodded, the motion tense and jerky. Riley steered them toward a secluded alcove, reminded of the night he and Carter had discussed finding a woman to join them. It seemed like it had been a lifetime ago, rather than just over a year. "What's going on, Kate? I know you well enough to know you're not okay."

She let out a shaky breath. "Riley, a lot has happened since we last saw each other."

He bit back a disbelieving laugh. "I'm well-aware."

Her expression softened. "I know. You've been dealing with…well, more than any man should. I'm sorry to hear about your parents. They're completely out of line."

"It wasn't unexpected."

"That doesn't mean it doesn't hurt."

"And what about you? Is something going on with you and Carter? I noticed you aren't wearing your ring."

She glanced down at her left hand with a wistful glance. "Carter and I are separated. We're in the process of filing for divorce."

Riley blinked at her. "You *what*? Christ, what happened, Kate?"

The sad smile was trained on him, her tone gentle, but the words barbed. "You came out."

Blanching, Riley tried to make sense of what she'd said. "I don't understand."

Her gaze remained unflinching, but her voice became so quiet he could barely hear it. "Carter told me the truth, Riley. The girls in college, the escort...your feelings for him."

The news hit him like a ton of bricks. "I'm so fucking sorry, Kate." His voice grew raw. "We never meant to—"

"I know. But it hurts deeply to know my husband and a man I considered a good friend betrayed me that way." Kate's voice shook. Riley saw the strain on her face as she struggled to keep it together. She looked away and he gave her a moment to compose herself before she continued. "How long, Riley?"

"What do you mean?"

"How long have you loved him?"

"Since college," he admitted. "Probably since the moment I met him."

She shook her head and dropped her voice to a whisper. "The whole time. Long before Carter and I met."

Riley swallowed, his throat suddenly tight.

"How could you let him marry me?" she continued. "How could you stand beside him at the altar and hand him the ring when you loved him?"

"Because I truly believed it was the right thing to do. I couldn't tell him how I felt—I could hardly even admit it to myself. He loved you—he really did—and I thought if he married you, the feelings I had for him wouldn't matter. Asking Carter to divorce you to be with me last November was out of line. I shouldn't have done it, but I couldn't cope with hiding my feelings for him anymore. I thought he needed to know the truth. I've never loved anyone the way I love Carter, but I understand he doesn't feel the same way about me. I know that now." His voice sounded strained, even to him. "I wish it hadn't taken the end of both our marriages and our friendship to prove that, though."

"Me, too." She stared him straight in the eye. "You know, he's been a wreck since then, Riley. And when he ran into you before New Year's, he became so depressed. He barely slept or ate—he just...wasn't himself. He couldn't live with the lies anymore and it all fell apart after that."

"It kills me to know I hurt both of you." He looked down, unable to meet her gaze. "I've come to terms with the fact I've lost Carter. I'm moving on now. Figuring out my life."

"And Will?"

"We're seeing each other. I care about him, but we're—we're taking things slow. He doesn't know the exact details, but he knows there's someone else I still have feelings for."

"As long as you're being honest with him."

"I am." Riley shoved his hands in his pockets. "I won't live a lie like that again. I never should have done it in the first place."

"I think the worst part is, I didn't know I was," Kate said softly, tears shimmering in her eyes. "I think somewhere deep down, I knew there was something between you and Carter, but I truly didn't want to believe it. I wanted to believe the happy marriage and family were real."

"Carter loves you and the kids. I know he does," he whispered, his voice raw. "There are so many things I wish I'd done differently. Hurting you and the kids...I hope you know how much I regret it. Although I hoped Carter would want to be with me, I don't think I ever believed he'd leave you. I *know* he didn't want to tear apart your marriage or your family."

"We can't always predict the outcome of these things." She laid a hand on his forearm, her smile wistful. "Besides, you coming out may have precipitated this, but it became inevitable. Once Carter stopped being honest with me, this was bound to happen. I am so, so angry at both of you, but I am trying to understand it. I can't imagine what keeping your feelings a secret must have been like. Maybe once the hurt passes, I'll be able to forgive you."

He nodded, his heart aching. "It's more than I deserve."

Before she could reply, the lights dimmed briefly, indicating intermission had ended. She offered him a small, sympathetic smile. "I need to head back to my seat, but, Riley, I'm glad we talked."

"So am I. Take care of yourself, Kate."

"You, too."

He stood staring after Kate until someone gently touched his upper back. He turned to see Will staring at him with a worried frown.

"Are you all right?" Will asked.

Riley shook his head to clear it. "Yeah. We should get back to our seats, though."

Will nodded and fell into step beside him, his gaze worried. Riley couldn't blame him. The conversation with Kate had completely thrown him and he knew he was acting oddly. He needed some time to process it.

Throughout the second half of the performance, Riley felt grateful for Will's silent presence. He hadn't asked Riley to explain, had merely sat beside him and laid a comforting hand on his knee. Riley didn't know what to think of the conversation with Kate. Despite having wanted Carter to end his marriage, the news that Kate and Carter were no longer together felt like an unexpected blow. It would be difficult to come to terms with his partial responsibility for it. He'd never wanted to hurt Carter or Kate and his heart ached for their children, Sadie and Dylan.

He instinctively wanted to reach out to Carter and see if he needed to talk, but Riley wondered if Carter would welcome it or not. Would he blame Riley for the end of his marriage? Was there any hope of repairing their friendship?

* * * *

The car pulled up in front of Will's building and Riley turned to look at him. "You're not going to come up, are you?" Will asked gently. Riley gave him a small, apologetic smile.

"I'd like to, but, no. I have a lot on my mind tonight."

Will brushed a thumb across his cheekbone and nodded. "Okay."

"I'm sorry tonight didn't go the way we hoped."

Will shrugged. "Considering what I'd prepared myself for, I think it went remarkably well."

Riley kissed Will goodbye, then spent the ride to his place in the West Village staring at his phone, typing and retyping messages to Carter. Later that night, in bed, he finally worked up the courage to send it.

I spoke to Kate tonight and she told me what's going on. I'm sorry. I'm here if you need to talk.

* * * *

With no response from Carter, Riley headed to his beach house on Long Island the following morning. He eagerly anticipated a few days of relaxation. After the staggering revelation from Kate the night before, the timing couldn't have been better. Some time alone to sort through his thoughts — that was what he sorely needed.

The pleasant drive put him in a good mood by the time he pulled into the garage. He dropped his bag onto the floor near the entryway, headed straight through the house and made a beeline for the doors that led out onto the deck. With the remodeling completed, the place looked absolutely fantastic. All traces of his parents and Alex were gone. For the first time in years, Riley felt like he belonged there.

He flung the doors open and stepped outside, breathing in the salty air as he tilted his face up to the sun. Although it was early April and still on the cool side, the fresh air and sunshine were incredible. He went for a long jog on the beach, pleasantly windblown and tired when he returned. After his shower, hunger prompted him to throw together a quick meal. He had just finished eating and was lounging on the deck with a cup of coffee when his phone rang.

His heart rate sped up. He was hoping to see Carter's name flash across his screen. The sight of Will's name was bittersweet.

"Will," he answered, pleasure at hearing his voice mingling with disappointment that it wasn't Carter.

"Hey, Riley. Any interest in going to an art show at NYU with me tonight?"

"I'd love to, but I'm actually at my beach house in Southampton." He wondered why it hadn't occurred to him to invite Will to join him. Odd. Although he cared about Will, it didn't feel right to bring him to a place with so much history, especially involving Carter.

"No problem. A colleague mentioned it today and I thought you might be interested." Will sounded unconcerned and Riley knew Will could find a friend to go with him if he wanted. "What are you doing at the beach house? It's a little early for swimming, isn't it?"

"Far too early, but I love being near the water. I figured I'd enjoy a long weekend here and unwind. Get some running and yoga in. I brought work with me, but it's always more enjoyable with the ocean in front of me," he explained.

They kept the conversation light until Will broached the subject of the opera gala. "Feel free to tell me it's none of my business, but do you want to talk about last night?" he asked quietly.

Riley took a sip of his coffee and set the mug down, toying with the handle for a moment before he answered. "Well, seeing my parents was difficult. I deal with my father at work every day, but somehow that's different. I can compartmentalize it. And I hadn't seen my mother since they told me I was no longer their son."

"They reminded me of my family. My condolences." Will's voice sounded grim.

Riley chuckled. "I have low expectations of them, but I suppose I should be grateful they weren't outwardly rude, although that's never been the Porter-Wright way." His tone turned mocking. "Appearances above all else."

"I'm familiar with the motto."

"I appreciate you coming with me, knowing it might be a difficult situation," Riley said, shifting to get more comfortable in the deck chair.

"I'm glad you asked me to be there." Will fell silent for a brief moment. "Can I be blunt, though? I don't think the interaction with your parents is what really bothered you."

"No, it wasn't." Riley noticed he'd been tracing circles on his thigh and sighed, forcing himself to stop. "Kate is the wife of the man I told you about. The one I was in love with. I-I feel like I should tell you more about my history with him."

"Okay."

"A lot of what I'm about to tell you could have lasting repercussions for a lot of people, so I'm trusting you to keep this between us."

"Of course."

"Carter and I met at Harvard our freshman year. We hit it off right away and were pretty much inseparable. I didn't realize it at the time, but I fell in love with him then. We started these threesomes with girls we met. I'm sure it made sense at the time, but in hindsight it's pretty fucked up." Riley exhaled heavily. "I think we wanted to be together but knew our families wouldn't accept it. Somehow if there was a girl involved and we didn't fuck each other, it meant we were still straight."

"Oh, Riley."

"Yeah," Riley agreed. "It wasn't exactly logical. But when you're twenty, in love with your best friend and know being anything *but* straight will get you disinherited…"

"You did the best you could," Will said. Riley smiled, because he thought Will really believed that about him.

"I tried, anyway. Carter and I both returned to Manhattan after grad school and we were nothing more than friends for about ten years. Then Carter got it into his head that we should start the threesomes again. He worked out this plan where we'd hire an escort. I resisted for a while, but I loved him and it seemed like my only chance to be close to him. I'm not proud of it, but I thought it was the only chance I'd ever have."

"So, *that's* how you know Natalie," Will said.

"Ahh, you know, then?" Riley asked, a little taken aback. He'd been wondering if Will knew about their mutual friend's former profession and how he could dance around the subject without letting her secret out.

"That Natalie worked as an escort? Yes." Will's tone was laced with amusement. "Natalie and I are close. Although clearly not as close as you two were. I never availed myself of her services."

Riley chuckled. "Well, for about six months Carter and I had an arrangement with her."

"The same rules as when you were in college?"

"Yes." He swallowed. "We had these stupid unspoken lines we never crossed. It got more and more difficult for me to hide my feelings, though, and I just kinda snapped last November and told Carter I wanted to be with him."

"And he didn't return your feelings?"

Riley hesitated. "I think he did, but he certainly wasn't at a point where he wanted to break up his marriage and family for me. I basically ended up cutting all ties to everyone from that social circle after that."

"So, you hadn't seen Kate in a while?"

"No, I hadn't seen her since I came out. Last night, she informed me that Carter told her at least some of what happened between us. I also learned they're getting a divorce."

"No wonder you seemed so rattled." The surprise was clear in Will's voice.

"It was a shock," Riley admitted. "When I came out to him in November, a part of me wanted him to leave her, of course, but now that it's actually happened...I feel terrible." He pushed away his mug, no longer interested in the coffee. "I never meant for any of this to happen this way."

Will grew quieter. "Does it change anything between you and him?"

Taken aback by how perceptive Will was about his feelings for Carter, Riley struggled to respond. "I can't imagine why it would. He's not married now, but as far as I know, he's still unwilling to explore any interest in men—and he still has a career and children to consider."

"But you still love him?"

"I can't imagine not loving him," Riley replied quietly. "I suppose I always will. But I've accepted that he either can't or won't return those feelings. I sent him a text message telling him I heard what happened and I'm here if he wants to talk. I haven't heard back from him. I'd like to repair our friendship, but I think that's out of the question."

Will hummed thoughtfully and they changed the subject, but the conversation lingered in Riley's mind. Even as he ran on the beach, did yoga on the deck and worked his way through the never-ending list of tasks on his agenda, thoughts of Will and Carter danced through his brain.

On Sunday afternoon, as he stared out over the water, he let out a heavy sigh and acknowledged that Carter clearly had no intention of rebuilding their friendship. He hadn't had a reply in three days and that told him everything he needed to know. *How much longer should I pine over a man who wants nothing to do with me?*

It was time to let Carter go and fully invest in a relationship with Will.

* * * *

"Riley," Will said after he answered the door later that evening. A surprised but pleased expression crossed his face. He was dressed casually in a comfortable-looking pair of pajama pants and a long-sleeved T-shirt that clung to his torso. His jaw was scruffy with a couple of days' worth of stubble and Riley had a sudden urge to feel it against his lips. "I didn't expect you to drop by."

"I hope that's okay," Riley said, jamming his hands into his pockets. "I've been thinking about you all weekend and when I got back from the beach house, I had this impulse to see you."

Will's face lit up and he reached out to pull Riley toward him. "That's more than okay. I was researching Professor Bernard Schwartz's work as Chief Counsel of the House Legislative Oversight subcommittee in the late 1950s."

Riley raised an eyebrow at him. "Well, I'd hate to interrupt what sounds like a very exciting evening."

Chuckling, Will drew Riley flush against his body and kissed him. "I think I'll put Professor Schwartz to bed for the night."

"I'd rather you put me to bed," Riley replied, feeling bold. He backed Will into the apartment and let the door close behind him.

Will gave him a searching glance. "I could read a lot into that statement."

"Maybe you should." Riley snaked a hand under Will's shirt, smoothing over hot skin and hard muscle. "I've been holding back, Will, but our phone conversation made me think. A lot. I know Carter's been kind of a shadow over our relationship this whole time, but I think it's time I let that go. I have a gorgeous, amazing man in front of me who *is* interested in me and I shouldn't be taking that for granted."

Will didn't try to hide his surprise. "I'm glad to hear that, but are you sure?"

Nodding, Riley slid both hands up Will's back to remove his shirt. "I'm sure."

After Will's shirt landed on the floor, their lips met in a heated kiss. A surge of nervous anticipation went through Riley's body as they grappled with each other's clothing and stripped there in the hall. Will's body was lean and toned, his skin more tan than Riley's, his torso longer. "I don't remember any of my professors in college looking like this," Riley murmured.

Chuckling, Will took his hand and tugged him in the direction of the bedroom. "You slept with a lot of professors, did you?"

"No. I might have if they looked like you, though," he admitted, trailing behind. Will's ass was a thing of beauty.

"Well, I'm happy to tell you I am fully qualified to teach more than law history," Will said with a teasing grin. He yanked back the covers and sprawled on the bed. "If you're interested. Although I'm perfectly content with what we've been doing so far."

Riley's mouth went dry as he knelt on the edge of the bed and crawled over Will. "I'm interested in learning something new." He hesitated for a moment. "But..."

Will raised an eyebrow. "But? Oh, but now we're at the awkward stage where we have to negotiate things. Top, bottom or versatile?"

"I-I don't know," Riley admitted. "Curious, I guess?"

Will grinned and smoothed a hand along Riley's back, pressing him down until their bodies were fully aligned. "Then why don't I make it easy? I'm versatile, happy to bottom for you and we can go from there."

Riley relaxed, propping himself up on one elbow so he could look Will in the eye. "Sounds good to me."

They didn't talk much after that, but they did kiss and Riley was half out of his mind by the time Will flipped onto his hands and knees. Fingers slick with the lube he'd used to prep Will, Riley fumbled with the condom wrapper. His pulse beat in his throat and his cock as he rolled the condom on, anxiety and desire mingling in a confusing tangle of emotions. It wasn't so much the act that made him nervous, but the significance of what he was doing. Maybe he shouldn't attach so much importance to something he'd done numerous times with women, but somehow, it seemed different with Will. He'd never imagined being in a relationship like this with anyone but Carter. Considering how hidden he'd kept his feelings from Carter and from Alex, no matter what he did with Will, he was already closer to Will than he'd ever been to anyone else.

He rested a hand on Will's hip and squeezed once before he gently pushed in. Will shuddered and Riley went even more slowly, draping his torso over Will's back when he finally bottomed out. He threaded a hand through Will's thick brown hair and pressed a kiss to his scruffy jaw. "Thanks for being patient with me," he whispered against Will's skin.

Will smiled, craning his neck to brush his lips across Riley's. "You're worth it."

Riley moved with slow, steady strokes. Since Will was taller than him, with a longer torso, kissing proved awkward. Instead, he grasped Will's shoulder and straightened, rolling his hips forward smoothly. Will shuddered under him and Riley watched the muscles in Will's back move. They settled into a rhythm and Riley lost himself in Will's body. The snug heat sent tingling pleasure surging through him. Will was responsive, reaching back to clutch Riley's hip, groaning with pleasure when Riley changed the angle, begging Riley to go faster when he got closer to orgasm.

He reached down to grasp Will's cock, jacking him with short, hard strokes as he tried to keep a grip on Will's sweaty shoulder and not come too soon.

Will came with a strangled sounding, "Riley!" on his lips.

Riley carefully pulled out, then stripped the condom off. It only took a few jerks of his hand before he came all over Will's back and hip, dizzy and sweating from the pleasure. Will collapsed and Riley fell onto the bed, curling around him.

The bed was already a mess, so he took the corner of the top sheet and cleaned the cum from Will's skin before stroking his fingers through Will's hair. They were silent for a few minutes, both breathing harshly in the otherwise quiet room.

"How'd I do, Professor?" Riley asked eventually.

Will turned to look at him with a heavy-lidded gaze and content smile. "I think that earned an A. I'll give you extra credit if you help me change the sheets before you leave, though," he said with a wink.

"Kicking me out?" Riley asked teasingly.

Propping himself up on one elbow, Will grew serious. "Not at all. I just figured you were planning to head home tonight."

Riley hadn't stayed in the past, so he could hardly blame Will for assuming he'd leave. "I thought we could shower before we change the sheets, then I could stick around until my alarm goes off at some ungodly hour and I have to rush home and change before work."

Will curved his lips up in a smile. "Or we could sleep in and I could loan you a suit. We're close enough in build, I think."

"Hmm, I can just picture my father's reaction if I show up to work in another man's suit. That would almost be worth it." He leaned in and kissed Will. "I'll decide that in the morning."

Later that night, as Riley lay next to a sleeping Will, thoughts of Carter passed through his mind. He felt a sense of profound sadness that he'd never had a chance to be with Carter this way—fully and without apology—and he draped an arm over Will's waist to pull him closer.

Chapter Two

Carter Hamilton had half-emptied the washing machine in his new apartment before he noticed the entire load of white T-shirts, socks and underwear was stained bright pink. Groaning, he pulled the rest of the clothes out of the machine's tub and pawed through the wet pile. Near its bottom, he found a small, red sock.

The sock belonged to Dylan, his five-year-old son. It had gone missing earlier that day, just before Carter took Dylan and his sister, Sadie, back uptown to their mother's. Dylan had been grumpy as they searched the apartment, but Carter knew his son was upset about more than a misplaced sock. Both kids hated living apart from their father. Even after almost three months, taking them home to their mother's on East 63rd hadn't gotten easier.

Carter ran his fingers over the sock, the silence around him growing steadily more oppressive. He stuck it into his pocket, finished loading the stained clothes back into the washer, then pulled it back out of his pocket along with his phone. He snapped a photo of the offending garment and sent it to his almost-ex, Kate, with a six-word message.

All of my underwear is pink.

He started when the phone chimed almost immediately and nearly dropped it in his haste to answer.

"Yeah, hi?"

"Did I catch you at a bad time, Carter?" Kate sounded amused.

"No, no. Just wasn't expecting a call." He smiled at her dry tone. "What's up?"

"Call it women's intuition, but I'm thinking you need help getting your whites back to white again. Unless you want to wear pink underwear, which is totally your call, of course."

Carter slumped against the side of the washer with a grunt. "I don't want pink underwear. And I really don't understand how one tiny sock fucked up the whole load."

"Rookie mistake."

"I never saw the goddamned thing, I swear!" Carter protested, turning his head to stare down at the washer's contents. "It must have been rolled up in a towel or T-shirt or something."

"I can tell you how to get the pink out," Kate told him, "but it'll cost you."

Carter frowned and stood up straight. "What are your terms?"

After agreeing to take the kids again the following weekend, he followed Kate's instructions dutifully. With the washer humming again, he walked through the apartment to the terrace and stood outside, watching the sky turn purple.

Not long ago, the tub of ruined laundry would have put Carter on his ass emotionally, probably driving him to bed. He wasn't freaking out, though. He was dealing with it instead and it felt good to acknowledge that.

Carter and his family had been through a lot in the last few months. One panicked evening, Carter had called one of his oldest friends, Dan Conley, and had spilled his guts of over a decade of secrets. He had told Dan about his secret, very sexual history with Riley Porter-Wright, the third member in their long friendship. Carter had talked about the girls he'd shared with Riley back at school and the affair they'd had the year before in New York with an escort named Natalie.

Natalie had been everything they'd wanted in a shared partner — she'd been discreet, professional and very, very hot. Carter and Riley had had some of the most intense shared sex of their lives with her. And those experiences had proved to be a catalyst for feelings Carter hadn't known how to handle.

He'd come to understand he no longer loved Riley only as a friend, but had no idea how to make those feelings work within his life. So, he had said nothing, even after Riley had confessed his own feelings for him. Unable to choose his best friend over his family, Carter had walked away.

'I know you're hurting over this thing with Ri," Dan had told him that night on the phone. "And you're hurting because you lied to your wife. I think — no, I know — that you're going to have to make all of this right before you do anything else, Carter. Do you honestly think you can go back to the way things were before you called me tonight?"

"No," Carter had whispered. "There's no making this right, though, Danny."

"Maybe not. Some people are comfortable living a double life, but that's not who you are. So, don't be that guy, Car.'

Carter stared at the skyline before him now, his chest aching. *How the fuck did this happen?* he wondered. How had his life had gone from seeing his kids every day to blocking off Tuesday and Thursday mornings and every other weekend?

He'd felt lost for a long time after Kate had kicked him out of their apartment. Most of the things he'd taken for granted in his life were gone or unrecognizable—his marriage, home, friendships, family. Carter's parents had sided with Kate after he'd told them about the affair with Natalie, and he'd been careful to leave out any mention of the part Riley had played. Carter's face still burned with shame whenever he recalled the look of disgust on his mother's face. Worse still was knowing that while lies had killed his marriage, Carter had continued to tell them to protect Riley.

Overwhelmed, he'd withdrawn into himself. When he hadn't been working or visiting the kids, he'd holed up in Audrey and Max's guest room. Finally, his sister had forced him to see a therapist and that had proved to be a turning point.

Carter's therapy regimen had included a low-dose prescription for antidepressants and, after months of coming undone, things had begun to turn around. He'd worked fewer hours and spent as much time with the kids as Kate allowed. He'd started visiting the athletic club again and had gone out with Audrey and Max, building up his social circle bit by bit.

These days, Carter felt better connected to the world around him. He spent more time trying to figure out how to live with the changes in his life and less time hiding from them. He'd rented a place of his own on East 34th Street, near Audrey and Max, and his relationship with Kate had improved enough they were able to spend short periods together and simple things like talking on the phone had become less fraught.

As Carter watched the city's lights come up, he could admit he wasn't happy. Things were better, though, and he'd grudgingly accepted his 'new' life. He'd begun rebuilding himself from the ground up—now he needed to figure out what the hell came next.

* * * *

At the end of the week, Carter went uptown to pick up the kids. Kate looked stressed and tired as she opened the door and Carter frowned, wondering if her plans had changed.

"Something wrong?"

The kids, who'd streaked through the apartment to greet Carter, drowned out Kate's reply. She seemed more relaxed after he'd shooed them off to get their overnight bags, though.

"Thanks again for doing this. They're really excited to hang out with you two weekends in a row."

Carter shrugged. "I promised them we'd go see the new Disney Pixar movie and get pizza—of course they're excited. And you know I'm happy to take them anytime."

"Be careful what you wish for." Kate's tone was dry. "I *will* take you up on that offer."

"I hope you do, Katie. I love having them."

Kate's smile faltered slightly at Carter's use of her nickname. "I know you do." Pushing off the front door, she tilted her head toward the kitchen and stepped past him. "C'mon, I'll pour you a glass of wine."

Carter followed, working the knot on his tie loose. Leaning against the counter, he popped the top button of his shirt and watched Kate pull a bottle of rosé from the refrigerator.

"You never answered my question," he reminded, accepting the glass. "Everything okay? Are the kids giving you a hard time?"

Kate took a healthy sip of wine. "Oh, I'm okay," she replied, even as her brow creased. "The kids have been bouncing off the walls since getting home from school, but nothing out of the ordinary."

"So, what's with the frowny face and the bottle of wine? It's like you were waiting for me to show up so you had someone to clink glasses with."

"Hey, you gave me that wine. I figured I'd butter you up a little for taking the kids again for the weekend." Kate sounded grumbly, but her eyes were twinkling. "You know, I'd almost forgotten how very annoying your super-powers of perception can be."

"Uh-huh." Carter narrowed his eyes at her. "So, are you gonna tell me what's up in the next" — he checked his watch — "ninety seconds before the kids come screaming back in here?"

Kate set her glass down. "I'm going to a dinner party tonight with people from the opera planning committee. This will be the first time I've seen some of those people since you and I split up," she added. "I mean other than last Thursday, which was my first time *at* the opera since you moved out."

Carter dragged a hand through his hair. "Well, shit."

"Yeah. It was weird. I kept thinking of the way people gossiped when Alex and Riley broke up."

"Was it *that* bad?" He shrugged after Kate raised her brows. "There's not much for people to talk about, Kate. The lawyers have kept things quiet and it's not as if you and I are openly fighting. I know my parents have been close-lipped, too—they're still hoping their fuck-up son figures out a way to fix everything."

He winced as Kate made a face. "Sorry, that was rude of me. I'm just so pissed at them. I know this is all my fault, but, Jesus, you'd think they could at least offer some kind of support to their only son."

"Still nothing?"

"My father hardly looks at me when we're at work. He sends his assistant in with messages if he has to communicate with me." Carter sipped his wine. "And my mother won't answer my calls, so I can only assume she's even more pissed at me than Brad."

Kate sighed. "If it makes you feel any better, neither of them has said anything negative about you to the kids."

"That's because they're trying to pretend nothing's actually wrong."

"Oh, they know something's wrong," Kate replied. "They were pretty unhappy when I told them we're ready to file the divorce papers. They're not taking it out on Sadie or Dylan, though."

"That's something. Also, good to know they save all of their displeasure for me," Carter joked, though he thought Kate also recognized the truth in his words.

"Anyway. You're right. People didn't have a lot to talk about last week," Kate told him. "That certainly didn't stop them from speculating."

Carter studied her for a moment. Kate's cheeks were flushed and the light from the kitchen windows struck her hair, burnishing the golden strands. She hadn't dressed to go out yet and stood tall and sleek in a navy sweater and dark jeans that highlighted her slim figure. Carter knew it was only a matter of time before she started dating again, and what that meant for their little family he could only guess. The surge of protectiveness he also felt surprised him.

"Do you *have* to go tonight?" he hedged, swirling the wine in his glass.

"No. I'd like to, though." Kate's voice was quiet. "I miss it. I miss going out and I haven't been doing a lot of that recently."

"You're taking someone with you, right?"

"Your sister kindly agreed to be my date," Kate replied with a faint smile, "though I suspect she knows less about opera than you. I actually considered calling Alex, if you can believe it." She had the good grace to look slightly embarrassed after Carter groaned. "I thought maybe having her there would neutralize the gossip about you and me."

"Didn't peg you as someone who'd use a friend as a human shield, Kate."

"Yeah, well, the impulse passed after all of fifteen seconds," she told him, turning toward the kitchen door at the sounds of pounding feet. "And if I had to hazard a guess, Alex is probably the least likely Porter-Wright to show up this evening."

Carter nodded numbly, his gaze on his glass. "You think Riley and his friend will be there?"

"I don't know," Kate replied over the sound of the kids dumping their bags by the door. "Riley was the only member of that family who really wanted to be at the opera and genuinely enjoyed the music."

Carter considered Kate's comments as they walked to the hallway to help the kids gather their gear. There had been plenty of photos of Riley in the gossip columns, all taken at the Met the previous Thursday. He'd been in the company of a handsome, dark-haired man and both of them had appeared happy.

The children crowded around Carter, clamoring that they were ready to go, and he snapped back to the present. Pushing down his envy, he assumed a fearsome scowl that never failed to make Sadie and Dylan laugh.

"You creeps ready for a movie?" he growled.

"Ready!" Sadie shouted while Dylan doubled over laughing.

"Then say goodbye to Mommy and let's hit the road!"

* * * *

Later, after the children had gone to bed, Carter walked through his apartment, tidying up their toys and possessions. He visited the kitchen for a glass of water, then sprawled out on the sofa in front of the TV. He sank against the cushions with a grunt and let the sound of a movie he wasn't really watching wash over him. His thoughts turned again to Riley and the message of support he'd sent the week before.

Carter pressed a hand against his chest, emotions swirling through him. Why would Riley reach out now? Should he talk to Riley? *Could* he?

"Fuck if I know," Carter muttered. He had no idea how Riley could be sympathetic or understand his frame of mind — Carter hardly knew what to make of his own life. He did know that he didn't feel prepared to talk to Riley, though.

The message continued to hover in the back of Carter's mind for the rest of the weekend. The kids kept him occupied during the day, but the evening hours were a different story, when the apartment was quiet and his thoughts free to wander. He finally forced himself to reply on Sunday while making sandwiches for lunch.

It took me a while to figure out how to say thanks, Ri. I appreciate the offer. Want to meet for coffee some time?

Carter read through the words, unsure if he'd said too little or too much, before he tapped Send. Several hours passed before he had time to check his phone again and his stomach warmed as he read Riley's reply.

I'd like that. Can you get away Wednesday, say 7pm?

Carter knew he should reply with a 'no.' He had a busy week filled with deadlines and Brad would be sure to notice Carter leaving early. Carter trusted his staff to manage themselves, though, and he no longer cared what his father thought. Brad's now customary expression of disappointment flitted through Carter's head while he typed out a reply.

Sounds good — you pick the place and I'll meet you there.

* * * *

Oddly, Carter didn't feel nervous about meeting Riley again until Wednesday rolled around. He made his way out of the office at six-fifteen anyway, Brad's stare burning a hole in the back of his suit jacket. The unease in Carter's gut slowly intensified during the cab ride to Chelsea and he was breathless by the time they pulled up to a storefront on West 16th. He paid the driver and forced himself to get out of the cab, only realizing he'd arrived nearly ten minutes early as he approached the red-painted door.

He snagged one of the few remaining open tables and worked at quelling his anxiety by reading every item on the menu. He'd almost decided to order a beer to settle his nerves when a shadow fell across the table.

"You're early."

The familiar voice made Carter's throat ache, but he managed a half-smile. "Early is kind of my default setting these days." He glanced up and folded his hands over the menu while Riley pulled back a chair and sat. "It's good to see you, Riley."

"Good to see you, too, Car." Riley demeanor was friendly, if not exactly smiling, and the warmth that flushed over Carter's body shocked him.

Oh, fuck.

"You look well," Carter managed after a pause that lasted a beat too long, and Riley gave him a lazy smile.

"Thanks, I think. I could say the same for you," Riley offered before his expression shifted. "I don't really know how well you are, though, other than the little Kate told me the other night. Are you okay?"

Carter considered the question for a moment before replying. "I'm…mostly okay. Coping, I guess you'd call it." He gestured toward Riley with one hand. "You probably know what I mean by that."

"More than your other friends, maybe," Riley agreed. He ran a thumb thoughtfully over his right eyebrow.

"I'm really sorry, Ri," Carter blurted. Riley pressed his lips tightly together. "I'm sorrier than you can imagine for the way I disappeared after you came out. I didn't know what else to do...how else to keep everything together. But I should have been a better friend to you."

The tips of Riley's ears turned red as he stared at Carter. A server approached then and Riley changed gears instantly, smiling as he ordered a large macchiato.

Carter ordered the same, aware of Riley's gaze, and cursed himself for becoming so flustered.

"I've never been here before," he began when they were alone again, striving to keep his voice light. "Come here often?"

Riley nodded. "Often enough to know what's good without really needing to think about it. I have friends in the neighborhood and this is one place everyone agrees on when we're craving different kinds of food."

Carter dropped his gaze to the tabletop while Riley spoke. He imagined the man from the photographs to be one of the friends Riley had mentioned. Riley looked relaxed tonight, impossibly handsome and put together in his beautiful blue suit. Whatever difficulties he'd experienced since coming out, he was clearly flourishing now. And wasn't Carter a god-awful mess in comparison?

"Carter?" Riley's gaze had thawed slightly when Carter glanced up. "I was asking how you've been."

"I'm...still trying to figure stuff out." Carter gave him a weak smile. "I wasn't lying earlier when I said that I was coping. I still have my job, though, see the kids and sometimes get together with friends. I do okay."

Riley gave him a knowing glance. "But nothing's the same. Everything in your life—"

"Is different," Carter finished. "Pretty much everything outside of my job is *radically* different. And figuring it all out is fucking tiring."

"I understand," Riley replied.

"I know you do." Carter clasped his hands together in his lap. "Dan's been pushing me to talk to you...told me if anyone would understand how I'm feeling, it would be you."

"Why haven't you? I know we didn't part on the best of terms and you asked for some time...but you could have called me at any point."

"I didn't know how after the way I treated you." Carter sighed. "At first, I stayed away to keep our arrangement with Natalie a secret. Alex wanted ammunition to use against you and there were Kate and the kids to consider. After I told Kate...well, you had your hands full with your own shit. I couldn't see adding my drama to yours."

They paused their conversation after the server returned with their coffees and a basket of cornbread. A hush fell between them for a few minutes, cut only by the sounds of Riley adding sugar to his cup and Carter's knife against his plate.

"Was it because I told you I'm attracted to men?" Riley looked at him, his face unreadable. "Or because I told you I had feelings for you?"

Carter shook his head even before Riley had finished speaking. "I don't care who you're attracted to. It *did* throw me that you'd never told me you were bisexual. Obviously, I knew you liked fooling around with guys"—he paused, his brow furrowed—"or with me, anyway. I didn't know you *preferred* guys, though. You dated a good portion of Harvard University's female student body, you got married... In all those years, I never guessed." Carter worried his lower lip with his teeth. "You're a really good actor, Ri."

Riley's face flushed dark red. "It wasn't an act. I didn't know, either, not really. I didn't know enough about myself to understand that what I felt when you and I were fooling around was more than curiosity. And when I finally figured it out, I couldn't do anything about it."

Carter frowned as he chewed a mouthful of cornbread. "What do you mean?"

"Our families expected a lot of us. Hell, *we* expected a lot of ourselves and I think it was pretty clear to both of us you were straight." Riley waved a hand between them. "What could I do, stand up at your wedding and not forever hold my peace?"

"My wedding?" Carter swallowed, feeling sick. "You knew you had feelings for me before I got married?"

Riley didn't hesitate to reply. "Carter, I started having feelings for you the first summer after we met. You came to visit me in the Hamptons and by the time we went back to school, things had changed for me."

Carter pressed his hands together tightly under the table to control their shaking. Riley had no idea that Carter's own feelings had begun to change and deepen over the last year and perhaps even before. With a few casual words, Riley had also fundamentally changed the friendship they'd shared in Carter's eyes, and possibly the relationship they would share going forward.

"So is this where you're going to get up and walk away again?"

Startled, Carter glanced at Riley, taking in his smirk. "I—no, that's not—"

"I guess I wouldn't blame you, after everything," Riley cut in, his voice hard. "I'd be pissed that you ran again, maybe even more than I am that you ran the first time, but I'd understand."

"I'm not going anywhere, Riley." Carter met Riley's gaze for a full minute before Riley spoke again.

"What's different about this time?"

"I told you—everything is different. You're not the same man you were six months ago, and neither am I." Carter turned his coffee cup slowly in its saucer, wishing he could be candid about his feelings. The timing was all wrong, though.

"I was scared after you came out. I knew that if anyone found out what you and I had been doing with Natalie…" He pressed his lips into a thin line. "Those secrets had the potential to make a lot of lives difficult."

"Was it worth it?" Riley's expression was cold. "Hiding and lying, pretending to be someone you weren't to protect your reputation?"

"It wasn't just about me." Carter swallowed against the lump that had risen in his throat. "I don't think you understand. I worried about Kate and the kids, about my family and yours. About *you*, Riley. And, no, it wasn't worth it. Everything I told you I felt afraid would happen did, and I hurt everyone."

Riley's face softened. "Shit, I'm sorry."

"I fucked up my own life," Carter told him. "I'm just trying to get back to a point where things are maybe a little less fucked up."

"So, you're hoping to reconcile with Kate?" He frowned after Carter shook his head.

"There's no going back—reconciliation's off the table."

"You sure about that?"

"Oh, I'm sure." Carter met Riley's questioning gaze evenly. "Kate and I can't go back to what we were. We don't want to. We had a good thing, but…it wasn't the right thing."

"You sound awfully certain."

"As I said, I'm not the man I used to be." Carter shrugged. "Or the man you used to know."

"I could say the same about myself." Riley looked both curious and troubled. "Well then, who are you, Carter?

After several long moments, Carter made himself answer. "I'm not sure yet. Part of me doesn't truly know, I suppose, and I'm scared shitless." His laugh was low but not harsh. "I'm done lying, though, to myself and everyone else."

"It's not so hard once you get used to it," Riley told him, "but it can be rough on the people in your life."

"So I've noticed."

Riley cocked his head. "Are things that bad for you?"

"About what you'd expect, maybe. I see the kids a couple of times a week and have them at my place every other weekend." Carter rubbed the stubble on his chin with one hand. "Sadie and Dylan hate that I'm not at home with them and things with Kate were pretty bad for a while."

"She told me things have been difficult."

"She was telling the truth. We're working on it, and it's getting better."

"And your parents?"

"Yeah, that's not getting better. They blame me for everything and they're not wrong to. They know I had an affair with Natalie. They don't know about you, though," Carter added quickly, "or about you and Natalie and me."

Riley said nothing for a moment. "You didn't tell them?"

"No. It's none of their business." Carter exhaled through his nose. "Anyway. Audrey and Max were pissed at first, but they were always there when I needed them. They've been good to me and made sure I didn't completely unravel. They're even trying to organize my social life now." He smiled and Riley let out a weak laugh.

"Oh, Jesus, your *sister*'s setting you up on dates?"

"No, nothing like that." Carter's chest grew tight at the mere thought of going out with a stranger. "Just, you know, getting me out of the apartment, making sure I do more than work, that kind of thing."

"Not ready for a love life yet?" Riley's teasing smile faded as Carter's cheeks flushed.

"No."

"Smart idea," Riley replied earnestly. "Don't rush anything if you don't need to. Besides, I'm sure the single women of Manhattan will wait as long as it takes for you to feel comfortable."

Carter nodded absently, dropping his gaze again to the tabletop before him. The silence lingered long enough to become awkward, but he tried not to squirm. When he finally looked up, Riley was watching him.

"Something you want to tell me?" Riley asked and Carter couldn't decipher the undercurrent in his voice.

"Well…you're not the only one to come to terms with understanding the line between curiosity and something else when it comes to being with men." He held up a hand when Riley made to speak. "I don't really know anything yet, Riley. Just that the times I spent with you...there was something there," he hedged, his insides twisting with nerves. "Something about being with you stayed with me, and I need to know what that means."

The server's approach cut short anything Riley wanted to say. "Can I get you both another cup of coffee?" he asked, "or perhaps you'd like to order some dinner?"

Carter and Riley eyed each other for a moment before Riley smiled and shook his head. "Just the check, please."

Riley stared at Carter for a long moment once they were alone again. "I have to go—I'm meeting my boyfriend for dinner on Christopher Street in half an hour."

Carter nodded, ignoring the sting in those words. He blinked in surprise when Riley spoke again.

"You wanna do this again sometime? Maybe grab a sandwich when you don't have the kids or something?"

Carter nodded without even thinking and relief flitted through him at Riley's unguarded smile. "Yeah. Yeah, I would."

Chapter Three

'Well…I guess you could say that you're not the only one who's had to come to terms with understanding the line between curiosity and something else when it comes to being with men. I don't really know anything, Riley. Just that the times I spent with you…there was something there. Something about being with you stayed with me, and I need to know what that means.'

Carter's words echoed through Riley's mind as he left the bistro on West 16th and strolled to L'Artusi, the Italian restaurant where he'd made a date to meet Will.

What *did* that mean? Clearly, Carter didn't know, so how was Riley supposed to figure it out? He stuffed his hands into his pockets and shook his head. Christ, leave it to Carter to make his head spin with confusion for the umpteenth time in their lives. Not that Riley blamed him—if Carter was questioning his sexuality, Riley could imagine how he felt right now.

A part of him had gone into the bistro expecting his friend to disappear on him again—hell, he'd been sure he would bolt when Riley revealed how long he'd had feelings for him. Riley had been surprised by the promise that he wasn't going anywhere.

During their conversation, he'd waffled between worry about his friend and vague resentment for Carter's disappearing act since their falling out. But the more they'd talked, the faster the resentment had faded. Carter *wasn't* the man he'd been six months prior, but he was still someone Riley had nearly a decade and a half of history with. He seemed to be struggling just as much — maybe more — than Riley had been. Before he'd left, Riley had realized he didn't want to let the opportunity slip by. He wanted to repair their friendship.

Carter still made his heart race, but there had been too many wasted moments in Riley's life so far. He'd put his entire adult life on hold, hoping Carter would come around. Even if he was ready to admit his attraction to Riley, it was too little, too late. It would be easy to get sucked into Carter's orbit again, but Riley couldn't take that risk.

Along with everything he'd been through in the past six months, his feelings for Will were too strong for him to throw it all aside. He wanted to continue to see Will and build the life he'd been working toward when he'd come out. A life where he didn't have to pretend to be anyone but himself. He hoped Carter would be a part of that life as a friend, but either way, he'd keep moving forward. He would let his friendship with Carter unfold naturally and, in the meantime, he looked forward to spending the evening with Will.

He felt calm and content with his decision by the time he pushed open the door to L'Artusi and spotted Will just inside the entrance. He greeted Will with an easy smile and a warm, lingering kiss before they checked in for their reservation. The restaurant was packed and they threaded through the seating area, past the bar and up to the second floor. The dark walls and floors were offset by the lighter tables and chairs. Riley held the chair for Will and slid into the banquette across from him. "So, what sounds good tonight?"

They'd been to L'Artusi several times before, so they quickly made their choices about which wine and small plates they wanted. Once they'd placed their order, Will reached out and took Riley's hand. "How did things go with Carter? That was tonight, right?" Will's question appeared casual, but the shadow of something lurked behind it and Riley squeezed his hand to reassure him.

"It was strange, but I think it went well. We have a long way to go before we are able to repair our friendship, but we'd both like to try."

Will nodded. "I'm glad. I know how important his friendship is to you."

Riley gave him a long, searching gaze. "You do know that's all it is, though, right?"

"You were in love with him for half your life. I hardly expect that you don't have any feelings for him now."

"True. I'm not going to pretend I'm completely over Carter, either, but our timing was awful and I'm tired of living my life hoping that'll magically be fixed. I'm with you for a reason."

Shoulders relaxing, Will squeezed Riley's hand and sat back. "I know. But thank you. That is nice to hear."

A few moments later, the waiter arrived bearing the bottle they'd ordered. "The Vitovska, 2010."

After the waiter had uncorked the bottle and poured the honey-colored wine into their glasses, Riley changed the subject. "How was your day?"

A dazzling smile lit up Will's face. "Fantastic. I had lunch with Charles and he gave me some good news."

Charles Barrett—an Intellectual Property and Cyberlaw professor at NYU—had briefly dated Will. He had a golden skin tone, blondish-brown hair, vibrant blue eyes and, if Riley had been any less secure in his relationship with Will, he might have been uneasy about their friendship.

He smiled at Will while he gently swirled the wine in his glass. "What's the good news?"

Will beamed. "He and Gabe got engaged."

"That's fantastic!" Riley said, his enthusiasm entirely genuine. Charles' boyfriend—now fiancé—Gabriel Rivera was a gorgeous Hispanic man with light brown eyes, thick, dark hair and a neatly cropped beard. He owned a French-Vietnamese fusion restaurant in Manhattan and Riley and Will had eaten there several times. They'd socialized with the other couple often and Riley liked them both. "I'll have to congratulate them."

Will leaned forward. "A small group of us typically go to Provincetown over Memorial Day weekend. It sounds like the guys are planning to celebrate their engagement party there this year. We'd all love it if you came."

"That sounds great. When do you plan to leave?" Riley slid his phone out of his pocket and thumbed through his calendar.

"Probably Friday morning and we'd return on Monday evening."

Riley hummed while he considered it. "Let me see if I can move around the meeting I have scheduled on Friday morning. Assuming I can, then, yeah, I'd love to go."

"We can leave midday on Friday if you can't," Will said.

"Sounds good. I'm sure we can figure something out." Riley took a small sip of the flavorful wine and allowed himself to ask the question that had been nagging at him for the last few minutes. "If this is an annual thing, you must have made reservations for the trip already. Why did you wait until now to mention it to me?"

Will hesitated, then gave Riley an apologetic smile. "To be honest, I wanted to see how we were doing. Last month, when you said you wanted to see where this would go if we dated exclusively, I was happy, but a part of me wondered if you were really ready for it."

The truth stung, but Riley could hardly deny that Will had every reason to be wary. Riley had spent fifteen years hiding the truth about his sexuality, was recently divorced and had been in love with Carter that whole time. He sighed and nodded. "Fair enough."

The waiter arrived with several dishes and Riley was grateful for the interruption. Riley and Will sat back while he set the plates on the table. "First we have the scallops with sea salt, olive oil, lemon and espelette pepper." He set another plate down. "This is the spring pea salad, with English peas, snap peas, yogurt, poppy seed and walnuts, and finally, the gnocchi with rabbit cacciatore and parmesan."

"Thank you," Riley murmured.

Once the waiter had left, he focused on Will again. "It's been a difficult year for me. I understand why you're a little wary."

Will gave him an apologetic smile. "It's not that I don't think you can commit, Riley. I just needed to be sure you were ready to."

Riley sipped his wine, savoring it as much for an excuse to pause and gather his thoughts as for his own enjoyment. "I mean it. I don't blame you for not entirely being sure. But I hope that from here on out I can prove to you that I am serious about our relationship. You've made me very happy and I want you to know how much I appreciate your patience."

Will reached out, stroking his fingertips across the back of Riley's hand. "You're welcome. It's been more than worth it."

* * * *

A week passed before Riley and Carter were able to meet again. Riley wanted to be sure he didn't infringe on the limited time Carter had with Sadie and Dylan. The weather was too beautiful to stay inside, so they took the sandwiches Riley had purchased to the park. They stripped out of their suit jackets and rolled up their sleeves before they took a seat on a bench. Carter unwrapped his turkey and brie and shook his head at Riley's Reuben. "How the hell do you manage to stay so fit when you eat like that?"

Riley laughed. "Because I *don't* eat like this often. It just sounded good tonight. I worked through lunch. I'm *starved*. Besides, I work out. I've been running and doing yoga."

"You do look good."

"Thanks. I feel good." Riley glanced away and he continued, wondering if he'd imagined the heat in Carter's eyes. "When Natalie suggested I try yoga, I scoffed at first, but it's been…therapeutic in a way. It helped with my stress and it's a good workout." He smiled to himself at the thought of the bendy men Natalie had promised. There had been a couple of those, too, although that had been before things got serious with Will.

"You stayed in contact with Natalie?" Carter sounded surprised.

Riley's tone became a little defensive. "Well, who else did I have? You and Kate were gone and I'd left Alex. My parents weren't speaking to me." Carter winced. "I talked to Dan when I could, but he's halfway across the country, so Natalie was about the only person I had left in my life who already knew the situation. I trusted her and I need *someone* to talk to."

"Ri. I didn't think…"

"No, I know."

"It just took me by surprise. How's she doing?"

"Really well. Her dance studio is taking off and she's dating a choreographer."

"Good. I'm glad to hear it." Carter took a sip of his drink, not meeting Riley's gaze. "You said yoga was therapeutic. I went to a therapist."

Riley paused, his sandwich mid-way to his mouth. "You did?"

Carter leaned forward, clenching his hands and making the paper wrapper on the turkey and brie crinkle as he stared down at it. "Yeah. I wasn't…coping."

"With what?"

"My *life*. I'm not blaming you, please don't think that, but you coming out, it really messed with my head. It shattered everything I thought I knew about our friendship and made me question everything in our past. I didn't know how to cope. I was depressed."

"I'm glad you got help." Riley took a bite of the Reuben and they sat in silence for a few moments while they ate. He wiped his mouth with a napkin and spoke. "I was depressed, too. Christmas was my low point. I went to the beach house and drank myself stupid on Christmas Eve. I'd never felt so totally alone before. It hit me hard."

Carter swallowed, visibly stricken, and Riley held up a hand to stop him.

"Don't, Carter, don't go there. It was good for me."

"How can that be good?" Carter asked roughly. "Jesus, that mental image…" He shook his head.

"It was good," Riley argued, "because it made me realize that I needed to figure out what made me happy. It simplified things for me. I spent the rest of the week getting my head on straight while I repainted the whole damn beach house. It occurred to me that I had the opportunity to be who I always wanted to be. Not the guy living in his father's shadow and basing every decision on what would please him. Suddenly, the sky was the limit." He shifted to face Carter. "It feels good to be my own man."

Carter regarded him for a long moment. "It looks good on you. Being happy, that is. I don't think I've seen you so relaxed since Harvard."

"I haven't been this relaxed since then. I'm happy. Making these changes in my life is the hardest thing I've ever done, but it was so worth it."

They were silent while they finished their sandwiches, but neither made any move to leave.

"Do you have plans for the three-day weekend?" Carter asked eventually. "I thought maybe we could catch a baseball game. The Sox are playing the Yankees and Malcolm managed to snag us some tickets. The seats will be shit, but it would be a blast even if we're in the nosebleed section." His enthusiasm made Riley smile.

"I'd love that, Carter, but I have plans. I'm not going to be in the city this weekend."

"Oh." Carter sounded disappointed and Riley bit back a smile. "Going to the beach house?"

"Uh, no. I'm going to Provincetown with Will. Friends of his are having an engagement party."

"Ahh, okay. Well, maybe we can figure out another time to go to a game."

"Absolutely."

"You know, I miss the beach house," Carter added.

Riley's first instinct was to tell Carter he was welcome there any time, but he held his tongue. The beach house contained too much history with Carter. If they were going to focus on their friendship, he didn't need to muddy it with residual feelings from the past.

He chose another response instead. "I didn't fight for anything else in the divorce. Paid for it through the nose, of course, but it saved Alex's pride, I think."

"Do you speak to her at all?"

"No. Unlike you and Kate, there's nothing to give us any reason to."

Carter shifted, straightening his pant leg. "Yeah, kids have a way of binding you to someone, even when the rest falls apart. I hope someday Kate and I can be friends. We're working at it."

"I miss Kate," Riley admitted.

"I think she'll come around. Give her some more time someday you two will be back to your old habits of talking opera until everyone else in the room falls asleep from boredom."

Riley laughed. "Let's hope so." He grew more serious again. "How are the kids doing? I've thought a lot about how this is affecting Sadie and Dylan."

Carter gave him a half-smile. "They're hanging in there. It's been rough on them. Dylan seems to be taking it the hardest, but they're adjusting. In the long run, it's better for them to have two parents who are apart and honest with each other and themselves than what they had before."

"I'm glad they're doing better. I know your time with them is limited and I don't want to intrude, but maybe some time we could do this again? Meet at the park and you could bring them."

"Really?" Carter's glance seemed full of surprise. "I didn't think you liked kids that much."

"I like *your* kids," Riley protested. "Just because some children are...intolerable doesn't mean I don't want to spend time with Sadie and Dylan. Christ, I've been around since they were born and I'm Dylan's godfather. Of *course*, I miss them."

"You made it sound like you were dreading having kids yourself."

Riley shrugged. "I was. With Alex. I wasn't about to let her treat them like my parents treated me. With the right partner, I might feel differently."

Carter's response was slow to come. "I don't know that I ever realized that about you."

Riley reached out and touched his elbow. "I think there's quite a lot we didn't know about each other, but there's no reason we can't fix it now."

"I'd like that." The glance Carter gave Riley warmed him all the way to his toes.

* * * *

"This is gorgeous, Will," Riley said after he set his bags down. He glanced around the suite Will had reserved for them at the bed and breakfast. It was light and open, with a roomy bed, fireplace, lofted area with a jetted tub and a balcony with a view of the water below.

They'd flown from LaGuardia to Boston, Massachusetts, and taken the high-speed ferry to Provincetown. Reports promised ideal weather and Riley was eager to enjoy the long holiday weekend.

Will smiled. "I thought you'd like it. This is Gabe and Charles' favorite place and I've stayed a few times before."

"You guys come to P-town every Memorial Day?" Riley asked, peering out of the window at the pool below. There were several half-naked men sunning themselves beside the pool and several more swimming. He could hardly complain about the view.

"For the last four — no, five — years."

"Do you usually bring someone?"

Will shrugged. "Yes, although not always someone I care about the way I care for you."

Riley turned and crossed the room to where Will stood at the foot of the bed. "I care for you, too, Will," he said huskily. "I feel very lucky that I decided to go to Natalie's New Year's Eve party."

Smiling, Will trailed his fingertips down Riley's cheek and leaned in for a kiss. "I do, too. Although, I suspect if we hadn't, she would have found a way to introduce us at some point."

"I suspect you're right." Riley smiled back, then changed the subject. "So, what's the plan for the afternoon?"

Will glanced at his watch. "How about a little bit of shopping, then we can meet Gabe and Charles and everyone else for dinner?"

"Sounds good to me."

It was a glorious, sunny day and the smell of the salt air and fresh breeze made Riley glad to be away from the noise and chaos of Manhattan. He loved Manhattan — couldn't imagine living anywhere else — but the sunshine and salty breezes on the coast made him wonder why he didn't spend more time outside the city on his days off.

Small shops lined the main streets that ran parallel to the water and Riley and Will wandered aimlessly, stopping wherever something struck their fancy. They browsed gift shops and galleries and, at the second gallery, Will purchased a stunning contemporary abstract painted by a local artist and arranged to have them ship it to Manhattan for him.

"That'll look great in your dining room," Riley commented as the salesperson tapped Will's information into the computer.

Will turned to him with a surprised glance. "You're right, it will. I hadn't decided exactly where to hang it, but the colors are just right for the dining area, aren't they?"

Riley nodded. "Over the sideboard, maybe?"

"I'll try it there first." Will beamed at him, raking a hand through his thick brown hair. Riley's mouth went dry at the sight of Will's lean muscles bunching under the sleeves of his pale watermelon-colored shirt. He was tanned and gorgeous, sleek despite the casual T-shirt and shorts he wore.

Will stepped closer to him as the sales clerk calculated the shipping cost of the painting, giving him a crooked grin. "What was that look for?"

Apparently, Riley's heated glance had not gone unnoticed. "Just admiring the view."

"Well, admire away, then," Will teased, turning back to the clerk, who had finished ringing up his total. Riley did, trailing his gaze down from the breadth of Will's shoulders to the narrowness of his waist and lingering on the firm curve of his well-toned ass.

Will signed the receipt with a flourish and turned back to face Riley. "What next?"

Riley shrugged. "I'm not searching for anything in particular. Let's keep wandering."

Will nodded and held out his hand to Riley, who took it, surprised to realize it was the first time he'd ever held a man's hand in public. Will must have noticed something, because he gave Riley a searching glance after they stepped out onto the sidewalk. "This not okay?" He held up their joined hands and Riley shook his head.

"It's okay. Just…new."

"Ahh. Well, it all takes time and it depends on where you are. Geographically, I mean. Nothing to worry about in P-town and Manhattan's fine—"

"Assuming my father isn't around," Riley interjected in a dry tone.

Will's grin was sardonic. "Depending on who's around, Manhattan's typically fine. But otherwise, just trust your instinct."

As they strolled down the street hand-in-hand, Riley regretted that he'd never had this kind of relationship before. The easy camaraderie was something he'd always had with Carter, but they'd always been scrupulously careful about any casual affection in public. He'd had neither the camaraderie nor the fondness with his ex-wife. The thought saddened him. He'd grown up with parents who were only demonstrative for show. They'd had separate bedrooms since his childhood and he doubted they'd been intimate in years. He wondered if either of them ever regretted marrying and the direction their relationship had taken. Or maybe that had always been the plan. He wasn't sure which was worse.

"Do your parents love each other?" Riley asked and Will blinked at him.

"What?"

Riley chuckled softly and shot Will an apologetic grin. "My mind wandered to my parents' relationship and it made me wonder about yours."

"Oh." Will shrugged. "I think so, yes. They married for political expediency. I am sure even if they were unhappy they'd never divorce—it would damage my father's career, after all—but from what I can tell, they care for each other. I think the relationship is more pragmatic than passionate, but when my mother was in a serious car accident years ago, my father was genuinely distraught. He seemed…extremely lost without her."

Riley nodded. "That's a hell of a lot more than my parents have or than I ever had with Alex."

Will's sad smile and reassuring squeeze of his hand did more for Riley than words could and they walked in silence for a few minutes. When they passed a gourmet grocery store, Riley tugged Will into it.

"You don't cook for me nearly enough," Will teased as they wandered the aisles of exotic spices and infused oils.

"You don't cook for me at all," Riley teased back, reaching for a package of wild mushroom pasta and putting it in his basket.

"Trust me, you don't want me to cook for you," Will replied, his tone dry. They continued down the aisle. "Scrambled eggs are the best I can manage."

"What is it with me and guys who can't cook?" he joked, the words leaving his mouth before he could stop them. He froze with his hand on a jar of blueberry lavender jam. He cleared his throat and offered Will an apologetic smile. "Sorry."

"Carter doesn't cook, either?" Will's expression was placid.

Shaking his head, Riley reached for a jar of rhubarb-ginger jam he intended to bring back for Natalie. "Not well. I gave him so much shit about that over the years. I shouldn't have brought it up, though."

Will gently grasped his upper arm when Riley turned away. "Hey, above everything else, Carter was your best friend for the better part of your adult lives, right?" Riley nodded. "And you guys are working to get back to that point, yes? Please, don't worry so much about mentioning him. He's a big part of your life. I don't want you to erase that. What we have is something different. Now, I'd really prefer it if you never call out his name in bed, but I'm trying very hard to not feel threatened by who Carter was to you. In fact, I'd like to meet him someday."

Riley tried to hide his immediate urge to wince at the thought. "We'll see," he said quietly. "I am not sure it's a great idea at this point."

Will brushed his thumb against Riley's biceps for a moment before he let go. "Well, I'm not going anywhere," he said lightly. "We have time. Now, I was thinking about putting together a gift basket for my sister. Would you help me pick some things out?"

"Sure," Riley replied easily. He listened intently as Will described his sister, Olivia, and her tastes and Riley enjoyed slowly browsing the store to collect the products. That was what he should be doing — getting to know Will and the people in his life more. After all, he was committed to being with Will and they would be slowly incorporating each other into their lives, like Will had included him by inviting him to come to P-town with his friends. *Maybe I should introduce Will and Carter at some point,* he mused.

"We ought to head back to the bed and breakfast," Will coaxed. Riley reluctantly moved toward the register to pay for his purchases. Will's basket was equally laden with gifts for Olivia. "We don't want to be late for dinner."

Riley glanced at his watch. "Dinner's at seven, right? We have two hours. Even if we both shower and shave, we should have plenty of time to dress before dinner. I thought you said the restaurant was right here in town."

Will's crooked grin made a tingle run down Riley's spine. "Oh, it is. But who knows how long it'll take to shower."

Riley laughed. "Well, when you put it that way..."

* * * *

The engagement dinner was held in a small restaurant with minimalist decor, a seasonal menu and a wine list that made Riley salivate. "This looks fantastic," he murmured to Will after he perused the menu. Will chuckled.

"What did you expect? Gabe is a restaurateur. Do you think he'd hold his engagement dinner just anywhere?"

Riley laughed. "You have a point."

Will stood when Gabe and Charles approached and Riley followed suit. "Congratulations!" Will said, hugging Charles. "I couldn't be happier for you guys."

Riley shook Gabe's hand, smiling at him. "I am, too. And thank you for including me in your celebration."

"Of course." Gabe smiled warmly. "Will cares for you and Charles and I feel like you're a great fit for him and for our group of friends as a whole."

"Well, thank you," Riley said, a wash of affection for the men in front of him and how warmly they'd welcomed him into the group filling him. It had never been easy for Riley to make genuine friends and he was grateful to all of them for helping him change that.

Charles leaned in to shake his hand as he stood with the other on Gabe's shoulder. The skin around his blue eyes crinkled when he smiled at Riley. "Gabe's right. We're thrilled you came this weekend. How do you like P-town?"

"It's fantastic," Riley said honestly. He'd spent a decent amount of time along the Eastern seaboard and he liked the feel of Provincetown. It lacked the pretentiousness of the Hamptons but still had plenty of charm. "I am sure I'll come back."

Gabe smiled warmly. "Well, we come every year and I am sure you'll be welcome to join us." Of course, that was dependent on whether Riley and Will were still together next year. Riley glanced over at him. Will flashed him a distracted smile, immersed in conversation with someone Riley had yet to be introduced to. *Can I see myself with Will a year from now?* he wondered as they took seats at the table.

Could he picture himself with Will five or ten years from now? Living together? Maybe getting engaged like Gabe and Charles? He'd assumed, after his divorce from Alex, that he'd never marry again, but he supposed there was no reason not to consider the idea. His father would have apoplexies at seeing Riley's name linked to another man's in the engagement announcements in the *New York Times*, but what else was new? Riley no longer lived his life according to his father's wishes, so if he wanted to remarry, why shouldn't he?

The thoughts lingered in his mind as more people joined the table and they ate dinner and celebrated the engagement. He watched Gabe and Charles share a slow, tender kiss after their friends toasted the happy couple and Riley felt a flicker of the longing he'd always had for a relationship. More than the sham he'd had with Alex. The one he'd always envisioned with Carter but never thought would come to pass.

Will rested his arm on the back of his chair and Riley caught a whiff of his cologne when he leaned in to whisper in Riley's ear. As Riley took a bite of flan, Carter wasn't the man forefront in his mind. It was Will. He listened to the banter around the table as the guests teased Gabe and Charles about their bachelor party and honeymoon plans, and he reached out to grip

Will's thigh, squeezing it gently. Will turned to him with a brilliant smile, and something about it made Riley's heart race when he remembered seeing a similar expression on Charles' face as he'd looked at Gabe earlier. Riley smiled back, wishing he knew how to tell Will what he meant to him. How to put into words the way Will had opened up a whole new world. It was more than a chance to visit P-town and enjoy a weekend away together.

It was the potential for a whole new life.

Chapter Four

A knock on his office door drew Carter's attention away from the files he'd been studying and he glanced up with a surge of gratitude for the interruption. Waving his assistant in, he laid his pen down on the desk then watched Malcolm cross the room.

"What have I forgotten this time?"

Malcolm smiled and handed Carter a document over the desk. "Nothing, sir, other than having asked me to follow up with you on this quarter's prospective-clients list."

Carter ran a hand over his head with a sigh, then gestured to one of the guest chairs in front of his desk. "I did, didn't I?"

"Yes, sir." Unbuttoning the jacket of his navy cotton suit, Malcolm sat, his gaze on the pad and documents in his hand. "I read through your comments and believe you should start with the clients you've noted we stand the best chance of signing."

"Agreed." Carter straightened his glasses and picked up his pen. "Have you received my father's notes on the list already?"

"Janet assured me Mr. Hamilton's comments would be ready later this afternoon," Malcolm replied. "He was in Newport during the long weekend and did not review the list until late Sunday evening."

Carter raised a brow. "Does Janet always give you such detailed information about how my father spends his time away from the office?" He watched the tips of Malcolm's ears redden with a pang of satisfaction.

"Not always, no." Malcolm's voice was quiet. "It...surprised me to receive comments from *you* this weekend, sir, and not from Mr. Hamilton—"

"—so you followed up with Janet to find out what the old man had been doing over the weekend besides working?"

Malcolm's shoulders moved in a small shrug. "Yes."

Carter exhaled through the little twist in his chest. He'd removed his own gray suit jacket earlier in the day and allowed himself a moment now to fidget with his cufflinks. "I was in town over the weekend, Malcolm. Sadie and Dylan were out of town visiting their cousins and my plans with friends didn't pan out. So, I caught up on some work and assumed my father's comments would follow whenever he had time."

"I see."

Carter blinked, slightly bewildered at the disappointment he recognized in his assistant's face. "Is that a problem? I don't expect you to be working during off hours, too, unless I specifically request you do so."

"I understand, sir." Malcolm's cheeks flushed to match his ears. "I just...well, I wondered."

"Wondered what, Malcolm?" Carter pressed, trying and failing to quash his irritation. "And, please, if we're going to be dissecting how I spend my off hours, I insist you call me by my given name."

Malcolm pressed the things in his hands to his lap, distress clear on his face. "I'm going about this all wrong."

Carter forced himself to draw in a breath and let it out slowly before he spoke again. "Going about what wrong?"

"We don't discuss your personal life in great detail, sir—"

"Carter, *please*."

"—but, of course, I can't help being aware of the changes that have taken place in the last six months." Malcolm licked his lips.

Carter fought not to wince at the multitude of things his assistant left unsaid. Outside of Kate, only Audrey, Max and Malcolm knew exactly how much his life had changed since the New Year.

"You've made concerted efforts to work less, sir," Malcolm continued, "particularly during weekends and off hours. That said, there were forty-three messages from you in my inbox this morning, time stamped at all hours of the day." His blue-gray gaze was serious. "You haven't pulled hours like these in a long time."

Carter took off his glasses and tossed them onto the desk, unable to feel annoyed at being called out. He'd spent most of the Memorial Day weekend working because he'd been alone. The kids had been in Maine with Kate, Audrey and Max had gone to Iceland for their anniversary and Riley had been God knew where with Will Martin.

"You're right," Carter told Malcolm. "It *has* been a while since I worked through a weekend. I didn't expect to feel at such loose ends over the three days and I had no idea what to do with myself. So, I worked." Malcolm's demeanor turned sympathetic but Carter managed a grin, though heat crept up the back of his neck. "I think it's safe to say I'm still getting used to being a single man."

"You're doing fine, sir." Malcolm told him kindly. "And I realize I'm overstepping all sorts of boundaries here, but—"

"—you're doing it because you care." Carter finished. "I know that, Malcolm. I realize I haven't been the easiest person to work for this year. I appreciate all your efforts—inside and outside the office—to keep me on the straight and narrow."

Malcolm seemed about to protest and Carter held up a hand. "If this were a movie, we'd sit down and talk about what amazing people we are over coffee and a plate of perfect cheese Danish. Seeing as this is real life, I'd settle for you accepting my clumsy attempts at gratitude while we go over the forty-two email messages I sent."

"Forty-three, sir."

"Oh, fine, forty-*three* messages."

Malcolm's lips twitched. "And while there are no cheese Danish on the premises, there are some lemon bars in the executive lounge I'd be happy to liberate."

"Good man." Carter clapped his hands together with a smile. "I'll look these notes over again while you're off storming the castle."

* * * *

Carter was packing up his briefcase at the end of his day when his desk phone trilled. The muscles in his shoulders tightened as an extension from his father's suite flashed across the display, but he quickly hit the hands-free button.

"Hello, Janet."

"Hello, Carter," Janet replied, her voice mellow. "Mr. Hamilton would like to discuss the client prospectus with you before close of business."

Carter eyed the clock and reached for another folder. "It's nearly quarter to five."

"I am aware of that, sir."

"Then can it wait? I have a hot date at six with a tuna noodle casserole prepared by Chefs Sadie and Dylan Hamilton." Janet's quiet laughter made Carter smile.

"I appreciate that, sir, and I'm sure Mr. Hamilton will be happy to schedule a longer discussion tomorrow. He was adamant that you receive his responses to your notes today, however."

Dropping his head in defeat, Carter stifled a sigh. "I understand. I'll be there in a moment."

Carter crossed the office and nodded cheerfully to Janet, an elegant middle-aged woman who waved him in with an indulgent smile. The twinkle in her brown eyes did nothing to lessen Carter's dread as he opened his father's office door. Every meeting he'd had with his parents in the last six months had left him feeling emotionally bereft. Dealing with Bradley alone was even more difficult.

Pausing for a moment on the threshold, Carter inhaled then stepped inside the massive room. Brad had situated himself in a seating area by the windows, files and legal pads arranged in neat piles on the low table before him. If he noticed Carter's presence, he gave no sign.

Carter stood silent for a moment, watching his father ignore him before he spoke. "You asked to see me about the client prospectus." A shiver of discomfort crawled up his spine when Bradley finally looked up.

"I read through the summary you prepared." Like his expression, Bradley's tone was cool. Glancing down at the table again, he selected a document from one of the piles and scanned it, his brow furrowing. "I concur with the majority of your observations, save one. You're wrong about the Murtagh Media Conglomerate. They're a good fit for this firm."

Carter allowed himself a frown. "With all due respect, I disagree. They're family owned and run, without an oversight committee. Several of the family members sit on the company's Board of Directors and the politics that could occur are a potential nightmare."

"Acknowledged," Bradley replied. "But while Murtagh Media may not be our typical client, I see no reason this firm can't stretch its capabilities to fit their needs." Bradley's gaze grew sharp. "If anyone understands the mechanics behind a family owned and run company, it's Hamilton Advertising. I want a meeting on the books as soon as possible and I want that account."

"Fine. I'll start making phone calls tomorrow." Carter stiffened when his father curled his lip in a sneer.

"Keeping banker's hours, are we?"

Carter hitched the strap of his briefcase a bit higher on his shoulder. "I'm having dinner with Sadie and Dylan," he replied, holding his father's stare. "They were out of town with Kate over the weekend and this is the first chance we've had to catch up."

Bradley nodded. "How does that work?" he asked suddenly. "Do you split the time evenly with Kate?" The honest curiosity on his face made Carter's heart pound.

"Not quite. The kids stay at Kate's more than they do mine. Her place is closer to their school and all of their things are there."

"So, what, they sleep on the couch at your place?"

Carter pursed his lips. "No. Sadie and Dylan have rooms of their own when they stay with me. My apartment isn't as large as Kate's, but there's plenty of—"

"Have they met her?" Anger made Brad's gaze cold.

Carter blinked. "Have they met—?"

"That woman. The one you were sleeping with while still married to your wife."

"No." Carter swallowed, dismay and anger roiling in his belly. "Of course, they haven't met her. I don't see Natalie any more—that all ended before I ever told Kate."

Bradley sneered. "I can't think why you called it off at all, considering you broke your wedding vows for some piece of ass in the first place."

"Oh, for God's sake, would you shut the hell up?" Not even the shock on his father's face could keep Carter there a moment longer. "You have no idea what you're talking about," he threw out and turned to leave. "If I thought you cared about what really happened, I'd try to explain. Since we both know you don't, I'll spare us both the trouble and the time."

"Where the hell do you think you're going?" Bradley had gotten to his feet when Carter looked back, and anger mottled his face. "We're not *done* here."

"That's where you're wrong—we've been done for months." Carter paused with his hand on the doorknob, aware of the frantic pounding of his heart.

"Have Janet send me your outline on the prospectus." He kept his voice low to hide their argument from the rest of the office. "I'll read it over and have my comments to you by tomorrow morning."

Carter was out of the building and halfway down the block before he really felt the side effects of the adrenaline in his system. Slowing his steps, he moved out of the flow of pedestrian traffic and came to a stop in front of a boutique. He stood under the bright orange awning, sweating under his suit, and concentrated on breathing.

The idea of Natalie in his life—that Natalie would even *want* to spend time with Carter, never mind his children—had him on the verge of hysterical laughter. That was what his father thought, Carter understood, and probably his mother, too. That his marriage had imploded over someone he'd *hired* to give him an excuse to be close to Riley.

"God, Ri," Carter murmured, "what the fuck am I supposed to do?"

He pulled out his phone with trembling hands, desperate to hear his friend's voice, even if only so Riley could call him a melodramatic ass and talk Carter down from one hell of an anxiety spike.

Then Carter remembered he couldn't dump problems on Riley—he'd forfeited that right months ago, after he'd left Riley alone to deal with coming out. Now, Carter had been left to pick up the pieces and he knew he was lucky Riley had been willing to remain friends, if nothing else.

"Christ." Swallowing hard, Carter silently counted to ten before he shoved his phone back into his pocket and forced himself to keep moving.

Oddly enough, Riley messaged him that evening, proposing they have a drink on Thursday after work. While eager to see Riley again, Carter hesitated in accepting, though he wasn't sure why. They sent messages back and forth again on Wednesday and it was late evening before Carter finally agreed to meet.

It's about time. I was starting to get a complex, Riley replied. *Because I'm such a nice guy, I'll come to you this time.*

Carter shook his head at Riley's unspoken reluctance to cross 5th Avenue onto the East Side.

Will you be okay? Your cool quotient won't plummet slumming around Murray Hill?

Riley fired back a moment later.

You're an ass. Tell me where and I'll do my best to blend in with the unwashed masses.

Carter thought a moment, considering the places he'd been to in Murray Hill and Kips Bay with Audrey and Max. He'd made an effort to explore his new neighborhood, but hadn't yet found a regular hangout. Riley's snarky comment about unwashed masses rang a bell, however, and Carter grinned as he tapped out a reply.

The Ginger Man. Prepare to get in touch with your inner hipster.

* * * *

"I feel very old in this place." Riley grimaced and took the glass of Corsendonk Abbey Brown Ale Carter handed him. "And you don't need to look so goddamned happy about it."

Carter glanced around at the Ginger Man's interior, which was buzzing with the energy and conversations of its many patrons. "You're only a few months older than me, Ri. There's a pretty heavy after-work crowd in here, along with the students and assorted riff raff."

Riley snorted. "Lord, you sound like an old geezer right now. I have such a hard time imagining you here and kicking back with Max."

"It's not like that," Carter protested. "Max likes the crowd, I like the music and it's close to where we live, so…" He shrugged, feeling a bit foolish when his friend raised his eyebrows. Riley cut an elegant figure in his dark summer-wool suit, his shirt and tie crisp and immaculate even after the long day.

"So, what, you listen to Max talk about books and authors we haven't read since we were in school? Do you wear rock band T-shirts so no one discovers your not-very-secret Ad Man identity?"

Carter frowned at his friend's mostly playful words. "I…might have some T-shirts, but they're all plain — no band names. And, sure, Max talks a lot about books, but he's recommended a couple I enjoyed, so it's not like he bores me."

Genuine surprise filtered over Riley's face. "Since when do you have time to read anything that isn't ad copy?"

"Since I've made it a point to stop working twelve and fourteen-hour days. I told you last Christmas when we ran into each other that I've been trying to work less."

"How's that going?"

"It's okay." Carter shrugged and loosened his tie. "I still pull long hours now and again, but I do pretty well." He gave Riley a crooked smile. "My visitation arrangement with Kate and the kids helps, believe it or not. I can't fuck around with the limited time I have to see them. Plus, Max has made it a personal mission to get me to relax, too."

"You've always liked him." Riley's gaze was so bright, Carter could hardly look at him. "And for what it's worth, I'm glad you're not killing yourself at the office. I know you like the job, but—"

"The job's fine," Carter agreed. "I'm good at it and the work can be interesting, but I've always put a lot into it because it was expected. Brad demands one-hundred-percent commitment from all his employees, and even more from me."

"Still?"

"Of course. He didn't take it well when I told him I wanted to make a change. That firm is everything to him."

Riley scoffed. "So, if I placed bets your old man does not approve of Carter Hamilton version 2.0...?"

"You'd rake in the winnings," Carter finished. He grimaced at his own bitter tone, then sipped his beer. "Brad's not a fan of any version of Carter these days."

"I'll bet Sadie and Dylan are."

Carter shook his head. "Not quite yet. But that's mostly down to my living in another apartment and making their mother cry a lot. They seem to like the new-ish me otherwise."

Riley's face fell. "They'll get there, I suppose."

"I know." Carter laughed softly. "They're actually doing better than their parents a lot of the time."

"How's that?"

"Sadie and Dylan are more adaptable to change. They're young and don't have to handle the responsibilities behind the changes. They just take everything in and move on." Carter focused his gaze on the ruby-brown beer in his glass. "I wish I could say the same about myself. I'm still working on the moving-on part, even with simple things, like the job." He blushed when he met Riley's narrowed gaze.

"Carter…what did you do?"

"I spent Memorial Day weekend working."

"What? Why?"

"Everyone went out of town." Carter made a face. "God, that sounds weak now that I've said it out loud. Anyway, the kids were in Maine with Kate, Audrey and Max were in Iceland and I sort of forgot to make plans for myself. By the time the weekend rolled around, it seemed too late to do much of anything but stick around the city."

He fought to hold Riley's gaze as Riley watched him, his face blank. "You know what they say about old habits dying hard. I started working without even thinking about it and the next thing I knew, it was Monday night."

"Damn." Riley frowned. "Tell me you at least took a break to go to the Sox game."

Carter gave a strained chuckle. "I gave Malcolm the tickets, actually. He and his brother had a blast — posted photos of themselves all over Facebook and tagged me in a couple. They even bought me a Yankees hat as a thank-you," he added and grinned at Riley's groaning laugh.

"Oh, God. Bless his heart. I know Brad hassled you about hiring Malcolm on as your assistant, but that kid really is a gem."

"He's twenty-six years old, hardly a kid."

"Oh, please, he's almost a decade younger than either of us, which makes him a kid. I don't care what you say." Riley smiled. "I'll have to have a word with him about the importance of maintaining the Carter 2.0 project."

Carter held up a hand. "Unnecessary. Malcolm is on board with the effort."

Riley cocked his head. "Is he, now?"

"Oh, yes. He chewed me out for working over the weekend. Well, you know — in that very mild-mannered way of his, where it's like light scolding, but you still feel like shit." Carter laughed before noticing Riley's furrowed brow. "What?"

"Don't take this the wrong way, but letting an employee into your personal life at that level could get complicated."

"Malcolm's not in my personal life," Carter replied. "Or at least not at the level I think you're implying."

"You just said he commented on how you spent your time over the weekend. He's either keeping tabs on you, or you're actively inviting him into your life away from the office."

Anger welled up in Carter's gut. Carefully, he set down his beer before staring at Riley. "My assistant doesn't keep tabs on me outside of doing his job and doing it well. Malcolm saw the dates and times on the emails I'd sent him and correctly inferred that I'd spent the weekend working."

Riley held up a hand. "Okay — I was out of line."

"And while I haven't *invited* Malcolm into my personal life, he could hardly help noticing a lot of that life has changed," Carter pressed. "My marriage broke up and I moved twice in a six-month period. I also have a weekly appointment with my shrink during business hours." He licked his lips and hated Riley a little for looking at him with pity.

"So, yes, my assistant is aware of my life outside of the office — he'd be an idiot otherwise. We don't discuss it in detail, but he's intelligent and I trust him. If I weren't Malcolm's employer, I like to think we'd be friends. That's probably unlikely given the age difference, but still."

Riley reached over to cover Carter's hand with one of his own. "I'm sorry, man. What I meant to say came out wrong. I apologize for making it sound like your relationship with Malcolm is anything but professional."

The earnest light in Riley's gaze immediately defused Carter's irritation.

"It's fine. You're not entirely wrong — Malcolm knows a lot about my life outside of the office, but primarily because he pays attention. He's been great, in spite of everything." Carter tried and failed to bite back a sigh — the warmth of Riley's skin on his own made him ache. It had been so long since someone had touched him.

"Honestly, it's my respect for Malcolm that keeps me from dumping my entire personal life into his lap. He doesn't deserve that and I'd hate to lose him. He's always done a lot to keep me sane on the job." Carter's laugh lodged in his throat. "It's...hard finding people I'm comfortable talking to about what's going on. Outside of my shrink, of course, and he's great, don't get me wrong. I can't talk to Kate, obviously. Audrey and Max are always willing to listen, but I try not to burden them with too much."

"Hey." Riley's handsome features were pinched. "You can talk to me, too. I am always willing to listen. I hope you know that."

Carter bit his lip and slowly nodded. "I know, but there are some things I can't talk to you about." His heart twisted at the hurt on Riley's face.

"We said no more secrets, Carter."

Without thinking, Carter flipped his hand up, wrapping his fingers around Riley's when their palms met. "I know." Riley's grip tightened and Carter drew their hands even closer together, his throat aching.

"So, why do you feel like you can't tell me things? You never felt like that in the past, did you?" Riley's rough voice sent arousal prickling through Carter and he wanted to roll his eyes at himself in frustration.

"I don't even know how to answer that—" Carter broke off with a soft, pained laugh. "Jesus, this is weird. *You*, Riley, are one of the things I can't talk about with you. I really, *really* appreciate how supportive you're being, but it also makes me feel more than a little awkward."

Riley swallowed before clearing his throat. "*I'm* something you need to talk about. To other people, like your shrink. Me."

"Yep. You're quite the topic of conversation."

"Oh, good." Riley wrinkled his nose. "Do I want to know *why* I'm a topic of conversation?"

"Probably not, but I'll tell you if that's what you want." Carter pasted on a smile and turned to flag down a barman.

"I do," Riley replied. His eyes were wide when Carter glanced back at him. "I'd like that, very much. I'd like another beer, too, if you're buying another round."

Carter nodded, gently releasing Riley's hand and shifting his gaze back to the space behind the bar to catch the barman's attention. He ordered a beer for Riley and water for himself, ignoring his pounding heart while he pulled out his wallet. The silence between him and Riley lasted only a few minutes, but it was long enough for panic to begin creeping in. By the time Carter had paid for the drinks, his hands were shaky.

"I'm not sure how to start," he admitted, running the fingers of his left hand over his lips. "But I suppose the easiest thing to do is start with Natalie."

Riley frowned. He clearly hadn't expected to hear Natalie's name. "What about her?"

"I wasn't entirely honest with you about why I wanted to hire her, or someone like her." Carter drank deeply from his glass. "I know I made it sound like I missed the threesomes you and I had with all those different girls—"

"And you're saying you didn't miss them?"

"No, I did," Carter replied, "but not the way you probably think. I missed being with you more than I missed being with the girls." He shrugged when his friend's face went blank.

"It was never about Natalie or the girls and what we did with them. I...wanted to get closer to you. To be with you. Sexually, I mean, and more than we were doing with the girls."

"Jesus...I wish I'd known." A wistful look fell over Riley's face. "We could have helped each other get through everything, instead of struggling alone."

"I should have told you, but I didn't know what to do—we were both married, for Christ's sake, to women. At the time, I wasn't even sure of what I was feeling. I just knew I couldn't ignore it, no matter how hard I tried. And I *did* try." He laughed, nodding at Riley's crooked smile.

"I had no idea how to deal with it." Carter closed his eyes, focusing on keeping his breaths slow and even. "I didn't know how to handle myself around you, how to get back to a place where it wasn't so complicated. I only knew I wanted it, so, *so* badly." When he opened his eyes again, his friend was pale.

"So we hired Natalie," Riley ventured.

Carter nodded, his chest tight. "I went back to the formula that had worked for us in the past. The threesomes with the girls were easy. I always felt good. We had fun...I thought they were a way to get what I needed without messing up the rest of our lives." He stared down at the beer in his glass. "It was perfect for a while, too. I could justify lying to Kate and balance everything to keep everyone happy. Of course, it turns out you were never happy with the arrangement."

"It wasn't enough for me," Riley agreed, his words sharp but his voice soft. "And you should have told me how you felt."

"Do you really think anything would have changed? That either of us would have been ready at that point to leave the lives we'd built?" Carter knocked back the last of his beer and placed his glass on the bartop before him. "I don't think so."

"I'm not sure." Riley seemed pained at his own admission. "Maybe not. I definitely needed time to come to terms with my feelings for you. That's why I agreed to hire Natalie in the first place and why I kept up those Thursday appointments. But at least then we would have known the truth about ourselves and each other."

Carter nodded. "True. Doesn't mean anything would have been better or easier, though."

They sat for a time, lost in thought as they sipped their drinks, surrounded by the noise of the crowd and the music in the bar. Carter felt painfully aware of the space separating him from Riley. He nearly laughed to find himself wishing he could rewind the night thirty minutes, just to feel Riley's warm fingers wrapped around his own. He glanced up when Riley shifted in his seat, looking troubled.

"You said earlier that I'm something you need to talk about with other people. As if I were some kind of problem to you."

Carter's cheeks went hot. "That's not what I meant. If anything, I'm the problem because I'm still figuring out how to get my head around the way I feel about you."

"I don't understand what you mean."

"Think about it. I'm finally free to explore a side of my sexuality that I've been ignoring for years, probably my entire adult life. Sadly for me, the one person I'd like to go exploring with is now otherwise engaged." Carter's heart panged at the sudden sorrow that crossed Riley's expression.

"Oh, Carter. I don't know what to say."

"You don't have to say anything." He forced a smile. "After everything I put you through, you have to admit, there's a certain kind of symmetry there."

Riley scoffed. "What, you think I'm enjoying this? Enjoying knowing that you're struggling because of me?"

"Don't be such a drama queen. My struggles are not because of you," Carter chided. "I'm entirely responsible for the shitfest that is my life—we both know that. I don't think you're enjoying knowing that I'm a mess. But you had to go and pull the No Secrets Card and now we're practically crying into our drinks."

Riley laughed. "God, you're sick. How are you able to joke about this?"

Carter sipped his water. "I can joke today," he said at last, "but tomorrow may be a different story. So, I'll wake up, take my meds, go to work, talk to my kids, maybe go out on a date with some hipster friend of Max's."

Riley's brows rose. "Really?"

"I'm thinking about it." Carter tried not to flinch at Riley's dubious expression.

"Are we talking about dating men or women here?"

"Men. I'm pretty sure, anyway." Carter clenched his hands tightly for a moment to fight off his nerves. "The only man I've ever been remotely sexual with is you, but I'm done ignoring how much I enjoyed the times we spent together."

Riley nodded, though he seemed oddly uncertain. "I understand what you mean. And I hope you find what you're looking for." His eyes widened at Carter's burst of nervous laughter.

"Yeah, me, too. I'm, ah, pretty freaked out. It's been a long time since I went on a date with anyone, let alone a *guy*."

Riley threw back his head and laughed. "You know, I really can sympathize."

"I'm selfish enough to be glad someone knows what I'm going through." Carter's grin was rueful. "And as scared as I am, I have to figure myself out. Figure out who I am, now that everything's so different."

"I think you're absolutely right. And you can *always* talk to me about it, if you want." He gave Carter a small, sweet smile. "You'll be okay."

"I'm working on it." Gently, Carter knocked his shoulder against Riley's and huffed out a laugh. "Just like I'm working on everything else."

Chapter Five

"I can't believe I let you talk me into this," Carter grumbled as he lowered himself to the mat beside Riley's.

Riley grinned and sank forward in a wide-legged seated fold, his back and hips twinging in protest when he stretched his arms forward. "Too late to back out now," Riley muttered, nose and forehead a few inches from the mat.

"Too early, you mean. I didn't even know they offered classes at this time on a weekday morning."

"It's convenient," Riley countered. "We can get a class in before work."

In an attempt to rebuild their friendship, they'd decided to work out together once a week. Carter had suggested a cycling class, which Riley hated. This week they were trying hot yoga. So far, Carter seemed skeptical.

"How do you do that?" Carter sounded baffled and Riley lifted his head and turned it so he could look at

Carter, who was obviously attempting to mimic him. Painfully.

Riley winced at the sight and sat up. "Uh, maybe not so wide, buddy. That'll take practice."

Carter straightened, the pained grimace on his face smoothing out into an expression of intense concentration as he brought his legs closer together. "Now you tell me."

Chuckling, Riley lowered his torso again, breathing into the stretch. "I don't remember you being this much of a grumpy bastard when you had to get up early for crew."

"I was twenty, Ri. *Twenty*. Now I'm an old man with creaky joints."

Riley snorted. "Well, this will help with that."

An hour later, Carter hobbled to the locker where he'd stored his clothes and Riley conceded that he appeared wrecked. "You didn't have to push yourself so hard, you know," he gently chastised his friend.

Carter glared as he stripped out of his T-shirt, tossing it onto the bench with a sodden plop. "What kind of masochist are you that you enjoy this shit? This isn't therapeutic, Ri, it's *punishment*."

Riley snorted and tried not to stare. Carter's hair was damp with sweat and beads of it dotted the tops of his broad shoulders. Riley shuddered and turned away, gripping the metal locker door until it bit into his palm. What was *wrong* with him? He had been trying to focus on his friendship with Carter, not find excuses to ogle him, but ever since Carter's confession about his interest in dating men, Riley had been struggling not to think of Carter in a sexual way.

With a guilty start, he thought about his boyfriend. Will deserved better than Riley ogling Carter in the locker room. His voice came out gruffer than he intended.

"I don't know what you're talking about, Carter. Just because you're a wuss."

Riley yelped when a towel snapped against the back of his thighs.

"I am not a wuss. I'm just not a glutton for the torture that is hot yoga. I'll stick to my cycling and you can enjoy this sweaty pretzel-making punishment you call yoga."

Throwing a genuine glance of amusement over his shoulder at Carter, Riley shook his head. "Fine, but we need to come up with something we can both agree on. Tuesday morning workouts together are fun" —*if I can keep my eyes to myself*, Riley thought with a wince he tried to hide—"and we should be able to find something we agree on."

"What about running?" Carter asked. He hooked his thumbs in the waistband of his shorts. Riley turned away again and took a deep breath.

"Running? Sure, that might work," Riley agreed, trying to ignore the little skip in his heart rate at the brief glimpse he'd gotten of the soft brown trail of hair that disappeared into Carter's waistband.

Being friends with Carter is going to be a lot more difficult than I'd imagined. Maybe exercising together isn't such a great idea if I'm going to spend the time thinking about Carter's fit, sweaty body.

"Dude, are you going to stand there all day staring at your locker?" Carter asked, his tone teasing. "I'm headed to the shower."

Riley cleared his throat. "Yeah, be right there."

He resisted the urge to bang his head against the locker door after Carter walked away. *Fuck, I'm in trouble.*

* * * *

Three weeks later, as Riley snuck glances at Carter's lean thigh muscles flexing with every step forward, he came to the conclusion that he'd never stop checking Carter out. The sight of Carter sweaty from exertion pushed all of his buttons. Fine, he was attracted to his friend. He was resigned to it. It didn't have to mean anything, though. It wasn't like he was going to act on it or anything.

"How's Will?" Carter asked. Riley jerked, his foot catching on a rough edge of the concrete path beneath him.

Righting himself, Riley cleared his throat. "Uh, Will's good. Thanks. It's going well." It was true, but Riley couldn't shake his sense of unease whenever he spoke with either man about the other. "What about you? How's dating going?"

Carter made a strange noise in the back of his throat.

"What does that mean?" Riley asked with a laugh.

"Fuck, I don't know! I don't know what the hell I'm doing." Carter snorted. "It's…going."

"Well, that's vague."

"I know. I know."

"You don't have to talk to me about it if you don't want to," Riley said eventually when Carter didn't continue. "I thought maybe it would help to have someone to talk to, is all."

"No, no, I appreciate it." Carter was silent again for a few moments, the only sound coming from their feet thudding on the pavement and their labored breaths. "I've been on a couple of dates. With guys."

Riley laughed softly. "From what you said the last time we talked about it, I assumed as much. And…did you like it? Hate it?"

"Mostly it just seemed awkward. I'm not sure how I'm supposed to act."

"I think it only has to be complicated if you make it that way," Riley said gently. "Just act like your normal charming, funny self and it'll be fine."

Carter let out a huffing laugh. "I know *that*. It's just… Fuck, I don't know. It's different somehow."

"It'll get easier."

"I know. And one guy…I guess we hit it off fairly well. Well enough that I think I can unequivocally say, 'hey, I *do* like dudes.'"

Riley's laugh was loud and genuine. "Well, good. That's something then."

"I suppose."

"Are you planning to go out with him again?"

"Yeah. We have plans on Thursday."

"Good," Riley said, despite the sudden twinge of jealousy at the thought of Carter dating a man. That was what he wanted, right? He was happy with Will and he wanted Carter to be happy, too. Riley's steps faltered when he imagined Carter passionately kissing another man. The image morphed into memory and a sudden rush of heat went through him at the memory of Carter kissing him. The recollection was vivid and yet he regretted the fact that he couldn't remember what Carter's mouth tasted like, or what the texture of his hair felt like between his fingers. It made him want to reach out and grab Carter. Shove him against a tree and devour his mouth. Riley shuddered.

"You okay, Ri?" The sight of Carter peering at him with a concerned expression snapped him out of his trance. "Did you drink enough water? It's hellishly hot even at this ungodly hour. You sure you're feeling all right?"

Riley let out an uncomfortable laugh, realizing he'd stopped in his tracks. "Yeah, I'm okay. Just got lost in my thoughts." He shook his head and took off at a jog, settling into the rhythm they'd had before.

Carter followed, easily matching his pace, but he kept sneaking concerned glances over at Riley as they finished their run. Riley had a sinking in the pit of his stomach that ignoring his attraction to Carter was only going to get more difficult.

* * * *

"I can't believe how quickly Gabe and Charles put this wedding together," Riley commented as Will set the beautifully wrapped gift they'd purchased for the happy couple on the table near the entrance of Gabe's restaurant. It was mid-July and they'd done a remarkable amount of work to plan the wedding in the short time since Memorial Day.

"Well, he does have experience with event planning," Will pointed out. "Not to mention having the venue and food prep taken care of already."

Riley chuckled and glanced over at his date, who fiddled with his tie. "True."

Damn, Will looked good. The pale blue suit wasn't an easy style to pull off, but he kept it modern with an even lighter blue shirt and a contrasting orange tie that he kept tugging at. Riley reached out, gently knocking Will's hand aside. He twisted the cross knot Will had tied in the silk, loosening it a fraction and smoothing out the length of the tie until it lay better.

Will glanced down with a rueful smile after Riley stepped back. "Thanks. I thought I'd try a different style of knot, but I couldn't seem to get it to lie right."

"That's what you have me here for," Riley said lightly.

Will's smile blinded Riley. "It's a little bit more than that."

"I'm glad to hear it."

Will brushed his fingertips against Riley's lower back as they walked toward the rows of chairs set up at one end of the restaurant. The wedding was relatively small, with what appeared to be a few dozen guests. His own wedding had been unmanageably large and he'd been exhausted by the time the reception had wrapped up. He hadn't known the majority of the guests. Most had been friends of his parents or people Alex or her family had invited. He'd never crossed the line into drunk, but he'd kept a drink in his hand most of the night. He winced at the thought. That should have been one of many clues that he'd made a massive mistake marrying Alex, but he supposed that was easy to say in hindsight.

"Time for me to perform my best man duties," Will said. Riley gave him a smile and nod. He pulled his phone out of his pocket as Will crossed the room to stand with the grooms and a man who resembled Gabriel closely enough that he could be his brother, or at the very least his cousin. A photographer snapped some photos while the men laughed and joked.

Riley checked his watch and stifled a groan when he realized they still had at least half an hour before the ceremony was due to start. They'd arrived early because of Will's duties in the wedding party, although Riley was grateful this wedding was much less extravagant than his or Carter's, which had both lasted all day.

He fiddled with his phone while he waited for the ceremony to start, bringing up a word game he and Carter had started playing recently. They texted each other as they played and Riley grinned at Carter's trash talking. He was completely absorbed in it when someone sat beside him. He glanced up to see one of the guys from the trip to P-town.

"Hi, Riley."

"Hey, Blake." Riley smiled at him. "How have you been?"

"Great. Excited for Gabe and Charles." Blake nodded toward the grooms.

Riley and Blake made small talk until an officiant took her place and the ceremony began. It was brief but heartfelt and there was a lump in Riley's throat when the men exchanged vows. He tried to focus, but his thoughts drifted to Carter. He was so frustrated that he couldn't shake his reaction to Carter's coming out. He knew he'd done the right thing by focusing on his relationship with Will, but there were times he wondered what would have happened if he'd made a different decision. Knowing that both he and Carter were finally admitting their attraction to men made him wonder where things would go if they did pursue a relationship. It was what he'd wanted for the majority of his adult life. It wasn't so easy to brush off the idea.

At Carter's wedding, and his own, he'd had the fleeting image of making those vows with Carter. At the time, he'd been so sure it would never happen. *And look where they are now.* He and Carter had both divorced their wives and gay marriage was legal in the state of New York.

After a brief but passionate kiss, the ceremony ended and Riley stood to clap and celebrate the happy couple. He forced himself out of the weird mood he was in. He was here at Gabe and Charles' wedding with Will, not Carter.

Will made a beeline for him with Charles just a few steps behind. Riley stuck out his hand to congratulate the new groom.

"Congratulations! I am so happy for you both," he said.

Charles grinned. "We are, too. It wasn't an easy road to get here, but I couldn't be happier."

Gabe and Charles had alluded to how difficult the beginning of their relationship had been before, but Riley didn't know the whole story and he made a mental note to ask Will about it some time. They mingled for a while, making small talk as they sipped cocktails and munched on an array of appetizers.

"Where are you going on your honeymoon?" Riley asked a while later, when he and Gabe were talking.

"Vietnam, actually." Gabe gave him a sheepish grin. "The hazards of being a restauranteur, I guess, but it's a honeymoon combined with a working trip. We're going to eat our way through the country, which isn't all bad, and Charles sounded interested in going."

Riley's phone buzzed in his pocket and he slipped it out. Will chuckled at Gabe's comment. "Well, I am sure we'll all benefit from your trip."

"That's the plan. I hope to bring home some new recipes and try some authentic cooking techniques while we're there."

Riley had a message from Carter teasing him about his latest play in their game and he'd dismissed it and tucked his phone back into his jacket. Will shot him a glance out of the corner of his eye as he listened intently to Gabe's enthusiastic conversation about their honeymoon plans.

"C'mere, Gabe, Will," Charles called, interrupting his new husband. "We need you both in a few more photos. Dinner's about to start, but the photographer needs a couple more shots."

"Be right there." Will leaned in and brushed his lips against Riley's cheek. "Photo time. Grab our seats and I'll join you at the table shortly."

"Sounds good."

Riley sat down at the table and had just taken a bite of shrimp dumplings dipped in a ginger scallion sauce when his phone buzzed again. He pulled it out to see a message from Carter.

Are you ever going to play or I am going to grow old and gray waiting?

You are already old and gray, he responded.

Fuck you. Old, maybe, not graying yet.

I am starting to.

Riley had noticed an increase in the number of silver strands at his temples and in his beard when he didn't shave on the weekends.

Hmm, there's something I hadn't considered. Riley Porter-Wright – silver fox. Wonder if you'll look like Jonathon.

Gross. Are you calling my father a silver fox?

Maybe.

Riley let out a huffing laugh and responded.

I'm not sure I like this side of you, Carter.

"Man, lots of work crises tonight, huh?" Will said as he sat next to Riley. Guilt swamped Riley and he slipped his phone into his jacket.

"Oh, it's not work. Carter and I are giving each other shit."

"Ahh." There was tightness around the corners of Will's mouth and his smile didn't quite reach his eyes. "Glad you're keeping yourself entertained at least, since I'm so busy."

"Sorry." Riley touched Will's thigh and ignored the buzzing in his pocket.

Will opened his mouth to respond, but they were interrupted by the waiter bringing food. They were both drawn into conversations around their table while they ate. Always delicious, the food that night was particularly good, as if the chefs in Gabe's restaurant had outdone themselves for the boss. The dinner was peppered with distractions though. After half a dozen notifications on his phone, he pulled it out to tell Carter he was busy and turn it to silent when he read the last one from Carter.

Want to grab drinks tonight?

Can't. At a wedding with Will, he replied.

Riley snorted quietly when he read the response from Carter. *Not yours, I hope.*

Uh, no, if I ever take that leap again, I plan for you to be an important part of it.

He winced, knowing that hadn't quite come out the way he'd meant it. What he'd meant was that Carter would be his best man, again, should that day ever come.

Carter's response didn't ease his mind.

And what part would that be?

Best man, of course. He paused for a moment, debating if he should ask the question that lingered in his mind. He typed it out and hit Send, regretting it almost immediately.

What were you thinking?

Had Carter, like Riley, imagined Carter and Riley as grooms?

His phone was silent for a while and he was most of the way through his pan-roasted salmon with lemongrass sauce when his phone rang. He let out a short exhalation of frustration. "Give me a few, Will, I need to answer this. I'll make it brief, though."

Will tightened his lips and nodded toward the grooms, who had finished their meal already. "They're about to cut the cake."

Riley smiled reassuringly. "Save me a piece. I heard it's filled with passion fruit curd and I'm dying to try it."

Nodding, Will glanced down at his five-spice duck, but there was no disguising the look of irritation on his face. Shit, Riley was going to have to figure out a way to make it up to Will. He had been pretty distracted tonight and he could hardly blame Will for being annoyed.

Riley wove his way through the tables of guests as he thumbed through his phone to call Carter back. "Hey. I told you I'm at a wedding," he said when Carter answered. "I'm finishing up dinner."

"I know. I just wanted to make sure things hadn't gotten weird."

"Why would they be?" Riley asked. He pushed open the door to the street and Carter huffed.

"You know why."

Riley propped himself against the side of the building near the door. It was hot and humid, the scents of the city hanging heavy in the air. Behind the towering buildings, the clouds were orange-red, reflecting the setting sun. "I didn't mean anything by my comment."

"I know, I'm just... Fuck, never mind. I'm the one making things weird and I'm interrupting your evening."

"No, talk to me, Carter," Riley coaxed. "I want to clear up any weirdness."

"Will won't be pissed?"

Riley snorted. "Will's already pissed."

"Shit, I didn't mean to cause problems. I'm just in a strange mood tonight, I guess. I don't have the kids and when I threw on one of my old Harvard sweatshirts, I started thinking about our summers at the beach house in college and…" Carter's voice grew softer, lower. "Thinking about when we used to swim late at night, then rinse off and sit by the bonfire. Just drinking and talking and listening to the waves and it was so damn perfect, Ri."

Riley felt a lump in his throat. "Yeah, it was."

"And I just wonder what it would be like if we did that now."

Riley closed his eyes and leaned his head back against the rough stone. "I think you know the answer to that question. There's a reason I haven't invited you to the beach house since my divorce."

"I wondered about that."

"I've just been worried that it would be crossing a line. There are so many memories there and I…" The truth was, Riley wasn't sure he trusted himself to be alone with Carter like that. It would seem perfectly natural for them to skinny dip or even shower together, and Riley knew he wouldn't be able to keep his hands off Carter. Not now that he knew they were both being honest about their attraction to men and each other.

"Shit, I know."

"I feel guilty enough that I'm with Will and spend half my time thinking about you. I'm already crossing lines I shouldn't and I don't know what I should do. I care about Will, but you know my feelings for you haven't changed."

Carter drew in a sharp breath. "They haven't?"

Riley laughed softly. Sadly. "Did you really think I'd stopped?" Neither of them mentioned the 'L' word, but it hung in the air nonetheless.

"No. Maybe."

"Oh, Carter. I-I don't think I could stop if I tried. I just feel like I need to give this thing with Will a real chance.

You know how hard it is for me to open up to anyone and I wonder if I'm sabotaging it deliberately because I'm scared to let him in. You're the only one I've ever let get that close to me and I feel like I need to do this."

Carter's sigh was heavy, even through the phone, and Riley could picture the furrow he probably had on his forehead. "I know. And I'm an asshole for getting in the way. I'm trying to date, too, and all I can think about when I'm out with these guys is that none of them are you."

Riley sucked in a breath sharply. "Fuck. This is getting complicated."

"Hasn't it always been?"

"Yeah, you have a point." Riley smiled sadly to himself. Was that part of the allure? He really didn't know anymore. He just knew he felt guilty no matter what he was doing. Like he was betraying both men, somehow, despite the fact that this was the first time he wasn't sneaking around or hiding his feelings.

He'd been tracing patterns on his thigh with his fingertips like he always did when he was anxious, and forced himself to stop. He jammed that hand into his pocket instead.

"I'm sorry."

"You don't have to be sorry about anything. I'm the one who needs to get my priorities straight and put more into this relationship with Will."

"Let me know if there's anything I can do to help," Carter said. The sincerity in his tone made a lump rise in Riley's throat.

"Thanks." There was little Carter could do, short of ceasing to exist, and Riley couldn't imagine his life without Carter in it. Even when they hadn't talked at all, it had been comforting to know that somewhere in the city of nearly eight million people, Carter was near.

"I'm gonna let you go. Hope you have a good night with Will. Enjoy the wedding."

"Thanks," Riley said, still lost in the thought. "Have a good night."

"Night, Ri." The call ended and Riley lowered his hand to his thigh as thoughts swirled through his brain. The restaurant door flew open. Startled, he straightened and turned to see a scowling Will Martin.

"What the hell, Riley?" his date snarled. "I thought you were going to be right back. You missed my best man speech, cutting the cake and their first dance. I had planned to ask you to dance, but you've been out here talking to Carter. Or ignoring me, I'm not sure which."

"Shit. I feel terrible, Will, I didn't mean to take so long…"

"This is getting ridiculous. I've done my best to be understanding about your relationship with him. You're good friends and I respect that. Hell, I respect that you still have some lingering romantic feelings for him. But this has got to *stop*."

"Will…" Riley said weakly, hating that he'd hurt someone who had been so good to him, but unable to deny that he didn't really know where things stood with Carter. "I never meant…"

"I know you didn't, but it doesn't change the fact that I feel like I have to compete with your best friend for your affection. Not to mention your attention."

"I told Carter that I know I need to focus more on my relationship with you. That I need to make it more of a priority."

"It shouldn't be so damn hard to want to spend time with me." Will smiled sadly. "You left me, at one of my closest friend's weddings, to talk to him. I need you to make a decision about your priorities. Because right now, I feel like I rate pretty low."

"I am honestly, sincerely sorry. I made a mistake and I want to fix it." Riley stepped closer. "Please, let me make it up to you."

But Will shook his head and stepped back. "I need some space. Spend a couple of days figuring your shit out with Carter. Then we'll talk." He reached for the door to the restaurant and Riley went to stop him, then hesitated. Although he wanted to chase after Will and apologize again, Will had a point. Riley wasn't sure about his feelings for Carter and maybe he needed to make that decision before he did anything else.

Long after Will had disappeared, Riley stood and stared at the door of the restaurant, deep in thought.

Chapter Six

Carter bit back a curse as his office phone trilled. He'd been in meetings with one of his project teams all day and knew his assistant would interrupt at the request of only one person. Leaning to pick up the handset, Carter gestured to the others to continue.

"Something I can do for you, Malcolm?"

"Sir, Mr. Hamilton is requesting a status report on the Abello account by four p.m. this afternoon," Malcolm replied. "He also asked I remind you about dinner this evening with the Murtagh Media Group at Gramercy Tavern. Cocktails are scheduled for seven-thirty."

Carter mulled over Malcolm's words, the muscles in his shoulders and neck tightening. *A meeting and dinner with Brad – wonderful.*

"Thank you, Malcolm," he replied, then glanced up at the figures clustered around his conference table. "Would you send in some lunch around noon? We'll need feeding and watering if we want to wrap up before four." He grinned after one of his project managers mooed for effect. "The usual selection from the kosher deli on 7th will be fine."

"Yes, sir."

"Be sure to order something for yourself, too."

"Thank you, sir."

"I'm sure no one would complain if a cookie platter made its way into the order," he added and bowed as the team burst into applause.

"I'll see what I can do, sir." Carter heard the smile in Malcolm's voice before he cut the call.

"I've got a meeting at four p.m. today, ladies and gentlemen," he told his team. "Let's get these design issues with the subcontractor in Chicago straightened out as quickly as we can."

* * * *

Carter arrived early to the restaurant that evening and went directly to the bar. His meeting with Brad had gone poorly and now, faced with an evening of charming people while his father watched, Carter craved a few moments to recharge. He kept his gaze on his drink when a figure slid into the next seat, and tried not to react to the deep voice directed his way.

"Now that's a sight I can appreciate."

Carter allowed himself a small smile—so much for non-verbal cues to be left alone. "You're a whiskey fan?"

"Sure. Though from what I see, there's more to appreciate here than a good drink."

Carter looked up then—he'd been on enough dates in the last few weeks to recognize a pick-up line when he heard one. He didn't react as he recognized his seatmate, though. Jesse Murtagh was even more attractive in person than online photos had led Carter to expect. His features were strong and handsome and a slate-blue suit set off his fair skin nicely. He'd gone tieless and the unbuttoned collar of his white dress shirt lent him a casual air. His startlingly blue eyes held Carter's gaze, however.

"Does a line like that usually work?" Carter asked, faintly surprised by his own lazy drawl.

"Yes." Murtagh shrugged. "It's the first time I've used that particular line, though, so I'll have to get back to you." He smiled and extended a hand in greeting. "Jesse Murtagh. Upstart media mogul. Scotch drinker."

Carter shook the hand with a grin. "Carter Hamilton. Ad wrangler. Bourbon man, generally."

Murtagh hummed before releasing Carter's hand. "I was afraid you'd say that."

"That I prefer a different type of whiskey?"

"That you're a guy I might have to hire," Murtagh clarified, eyes gleaming. "I'd hoped you were just a hot random I could chat up while I waited. Now I know I should behave myself around you."

Carter felt a little breathless to realize Murtagh's blatant flirting didn't bother him in the least. "No rules against my buying you a drink, Mr. Murtagh," he pointed out and nodded at the glass on the bar before him.

"None whatsoever." Murtagh eyed the contents of his glass. "As I said, I'm generally a Scotch drinker, but I'll give whatever you suggest a shot if you tell me it's worth trying."

"Definitely worth it." Carter signaled the bartender for a second glass. "We're drinking Bulleit. The high rye content gives it a spicy flavor even a life-long Scotch drinker like my father can appreciate."

"Speaking of fathers, mine should be here shortly, along with my brother, Eric," Murtagh added. "They called from the car with some crazy story about getting held up in cross-town traffic. They were stuck behind a parade, from what I could make out."

He shook his head, looking baffled. The bartender set a second glass on the bar, and Murtagh picked it up and tipped his drink toward Carter with a smaller, more genuine smile. He sipped from the glass and his brows rose as he swallowed. "You were right." He held the glass up to the light to examine the contents. "This is very good. I think my father would agree, too."

"Is Scotch the official Murtagh clan spirit?"

"No, Harry's just a fussy old bastard. He's eager to meet Bradley, by the way, after all the talking they've been doing this week."

For a second time, Carter's mood dipped and he fought to disguise his feelings. Aware of Murtagh's gaze, he forced a smile. "Brad was talking with a client in Japan when I left the office, but he'll be along. He's been looking forward to meeting you all, as well."

Murtagh hummed again. He signaled the bartender once more. "We'd better have another drink while we still can, then," he remarked. "I can already tell you're one of those business-as-usual types when the boss is around."

Carter couldn't help laughing. "And you're not?"

"Nope. I've never really tried to be, honestly." He grimaced. "If you want a model Murtagh, my brother, Eric, is your man—he's so perfect it's almost alarming. I used to have a hard time with all of that perfection when I was younger."

Carter met Murtagh's gaze and cocked his head. "You've obviously figured out how to work with them."

"Sure." Murtagh nodded. "I got out of town for a while. Went to school on the West Coast, traveled the country and the world for a few of years. I did some growing up and by the time I was ready to come back to New York, it was easier to fit in."

He smiled. "I don't suppose you've ever had to worry about fitting in, though, have you, Mr. Hamilton?"

"A year ago, I would have agreed with you. I was practically the poster boy for up-and-coming heirs to a family fortune."

Murtagh raised his left eyebrow. "You're capable of being even more straight-laced than this?"

Carter glanced down at his three-piece suit and bit his lip to keep from laughing. "I used to be."

"So, what changed?"

Images of Kate's face flashed through Carter's mind, followed by Sadie's and Dylan's and finally Riley's. He squeezed the nearly empty glass in his hand, an ache throbbing through his chest. It took him a moment to answer.

"I messed up my relationships and had to start over. I couldn't leave town, the way you did, so I've been rebuilding a lot of things back up from the ground level."

"How's that been?"

"Epically shitty." Carter met Murtagh's unwavering gaze and smiled at his soft laugh. "But worth it in many ways."

He thought again of Riley, of the time they'd been making for each other as they relearned how to be friends. Once they'd gotten over some of the initial stiffness, it had been so…easy, no matter what they were doing. Working out, catching up over dinner and drinks, playing stupid word games on their phones. Things had become comfortable between them. Until the other night, when they'd spoken on the phone, of course. Carter had pushed too hard. Now Riley's boyfriend was pissed and Riley wasn't answering texts or calls.

"It's been a rough year," Carter admitted, his voice gruff. "Probably the most challenging of my life. I'm hopeful things will turn out okay, though. Not perfect, but, like you, I've figured out I'm not cut out to be perfect anyway. That may be the better option when all is said and done."

Murtagh's gaze was speculative but not unkind. "Sounds like an interesting story, Mr. Hamilton."

Carter managed a smile. "Please, call me Carter."

Murtagh held out his hand again, his smile warm and open. "Jesse."

* * * *

Jesse Murtagh's considerable charm proved to be a family trait. His brother, Eric, and father, Harry, were equally captivating. All three were sharply intelligent and observant beyond their affable good looks — even Bradley Hamilton seemed almost smitten.

Carter savored his dinner, sipping his Bordeaux slowly and listening to the shifting dialogue around the table. He was having fun, something he hadn't truly done during a client dinner for some time. Yes, Brad's deep freeze act was still in full effect and, no, Carter didn't really care if Murtagh Media hired the firm to pimp out their television station. None of that seemed to matter in the face of good company and a superlative meal, though. He bit back a smile when Jesse leaned close to speak.

"You know, Carter, if we hire you to give our stations a makeover, you and I won't be able to hang out."

Carter shrugged. "I don't see why not."

"Mm-mm." Jesse shook his head. "I don't mix business with pleasure."

"Ah." Carter dropped his gaze, his cheeks warm. "I suspect you and I have different interpretations of 'hanging out.'"

Jesse let out a rumbling laugh. "Oh, I'm sure of it. And I bet you'd enjoy my interpretation far more."

"Are you always so bold?"

"Yes, when I know what I want." Jesse looked smug. "I see no shame in being assertive. Eric's the one with the soft touch—his sense of propriety and guilt are much keener than mine. Poor bastard got the lion's share of the morality genes in the family."

Carter didn't bother hiding his amusement, particularly after Eric Murtagh glanced up to focus on Jesse with what seems like an older brother's sixth sense. Like Jesse, Eric was handsome, urbane and very appealing. More reserved than Jesse, he seemed content to step back to allow his father and brother to take the spotlight most of the time. The brothers held obvious affection for each other and delighted in teasing and baiting. A smile lit Eric's gray gaze and he slowly shot his brother the middle finger.

Jesse tutted quietly. "Don't be crass, bro. It's a business dinner."

"I'm not your bro, Jes."

Jesse cocked his head. "Not to argue semantics with you, Eric, but you literally are my bro. Or is this some kind of big reveal where you finally disclose I'm actually adopted?"

Eric's jaw dropped slightly. "That's out of line." He flicked his gaze to Carter's. "I apologize, Carter — my brother's tendency to whistle in the dark gets away from him sometimes."

Carter waved Eric off, ignoring the feeling of Jesse's gaze on the side of his face. "Don't worry about it."

"He's not offended." Jesse shrugged while his brother frowned. "I know better than to joke about that in front of someone I don't know."

Eric stared. "You met the man two and a half hours ago, Jesse — you hardly know him at all." He huffed at Jesse's eye roll.

"Please. Carter's practically an open book — I drew a bead on him sixty seconds after we met."

Carter rubbed a thumb over his lower lip as he watched the Murtaghs. He was surprised by how much Jesse's cocky assertion stung, but he shook it off in the next moment and cleared his throat.

"I think that's as good an opening as any for a discussion about next steps, Jesse."

They spent the remainder of the main course deliberating strategies to increase Murtagh Media's public profile. Jesse behaved with a professional detachment Carter knew from other clients, though his behavioral one-eighty was unsettling after their earlier flirting. Especially when the glossy business veneer vanished after the cheese course.

"Come have a drink with me," he told Carter after the party began to break up.

Carter raised an eyebrow at the twinkle in Jesse's eyes. "Why would I do that?"

"Because ruining some more liver cells sounds like a good time?" He grinned and they followed the others toward the restaurant's exit. "Come on, it'll be fun. I promise you'll be home before the sun comes up and you turn into a pumpkin like Cinderella."

"Cinderella didn't turn into a pumpkin," Carter replied, "her coach did."

"I really don't want to know how you know that."

Carter smirked. "As it happens, I've got nothing but team meetings tomorrow, so —"

"So let's get the dads into their cars, grab Eric and get the hell out of here," Jesse finished. He reached past Carter to hold open the door. "The Old Town's right around the corner."

Carter nodded absently. He needed to watch his alcohol intake because of the meds he was taking and he'd had a couple of drinks already. Besides, the last time he'd been near The Old Town Bar, the sight of Riley and Will through the bar's window had sent his life into a tailspin. *What if Riley and his boyfriend are there again tonight?* Carter nearly cringed at the thought.

"You okay?"

Jesse's deep voice snapped him back to the present. "Sure," he replied, his smile only slightly stilted. "I think Pete's Tavern on East 16th would be the better choice, though. We'll have to grab a taxi, but I happen to know they stock Bulleit behind the bar."

Jesse clapped his hands together. "Sold. And screw the cab — I'll get my old man to drop us on his way uptown. He'll be excited to show off his new car to someone who hasn't seen it eighty-seven-hundred times already."

* * * *

Carter's tension faded as they sat at Pete's crowded bar and Eric talked about the house he and his wife were renovating in rural Vermont.

"It's taken way longer than we expected, but the bulk of the construction should conclude next spring," Eric said with relish. "We're planning to spend most of the summer there working on restoring the barn."

"You and Sara are both raving mad." Jesse smiled fondly at his brother, though Carter could tell he was mystified.

"I'm guessing rural homeownership isn't something you're interested in?" Carter asked, then raised a hand to the passing bartender for a refill.

Jesse mimed choking himself. "I prefer to spend my time off traveling, not buried under piles of drywall," he replied. "The way I figure it, there's a whole world out there to see before I need to get up close and personal with a house in the woods."

"Shut it." Eric's scolding words were at odds with his gentle smile. "You're just being a snob. You'd be more than happy to snap up a country house in Tuscany or the Alentejo if the opportunity arose." He pointed a long finger at Jesse. "Admit it—I'm right. All it'd take is one call from Isaac, that good-looking teacher you were dating last year—"

"Oh, Jesus," Jesse cut in, hands raised in surrender. "Yes, I admit it, okay? I, Jesse Thomas Murtagh, am a snob who would rather live in rural Europe than here in the country of my birth." He peered at his brother, his expression peevish. "Satisfied?"

Eric leaned forward and threw an arm around his brother, pulling him close and making Jesse grunt in surprise. "Yes," he replied, squeezing Jesse's shoulder.

"I'm satisfied and, what's more, glad you told the truth."

"Dude. Get off me before you freak Carter out."

"He hasn't run off screaming yet," Eric teased and swatted Jesse's head.

"You two remind me of my kids," Carter mused after Eric excused himself to use the men's room. "Minus the booze, of course."

"Well, that's reassuring." Jesse sat back in his seat. "A boy and a girl, right?"

"Did you read up on me?"

His frank gaze sent a wave of heat through Carter's chest. "Of course I did."

"So that line at the restaurant earlier, about not recognizing me?"

"Was just that—a line," Jesse replied, a small smile gracing his lips.

Carter shook his head. "Do you always come on to prospective employees?"

"Yes." Jesse's smile widened at Carter's chuckle. "Okay, maybe not come on so much as flirt a little." He shrugged. "It's an easy way to get to know someone and gauge the water temperature, if you know what I mean."

"But you had no idea if I'd be receptive," Carter countered. "What if I'd reacted badly?" Jesse looked askance at him and Carter raised his brows. "What?"

"I had some inside information on the temperature of your water, so to speak."

Carter swallowed, his mouth dry. "Oh?"

Jesse nodded. "Brewster Collier and I have the same trainer."

"Really." Carter blinked. He'd met Brewster through friends at his athletic club and they'd been out a couple of times. Brewster worked in arbitrage and though Carter had worried they'd have nothing in common, Brewster had been excellent company, as committed to enjoying life as he was to making money for his clients.

"We've known each other for years," Jesse told him. "We had lunch last week and got to talking about where things stand with the rebrand. I mentioned we were considering hiring Hamilton Advertising, Brew mentioned he knew you—"

"And you gossiped about me over club sandwiches."

"Sushi, actually."

Carter managed a smile, though his heart lurched, and he reached for his glass to occupy his hands. His face heated as he made another leap in logic. "I'm guessing you and Brewster spend time together outside of lunch dates…?"

Surprise flashed across Jesse's face, then quickly vanished. "We used to, yeah, but not for a while now—we're better suited to be friends. How did you know?"

"Seemed only logical," Carter replied, swallowing down a wave of nausea. "Given who you both are…and my shitty luck." He managed a weak chuckle, but Jesse frowned.

"Brewster didn't say much, if that's what you're worried about. Just that you'd been out a few times and he was looking forward to getting to know you better."

"I don't care about that."

"What then?"

Suddenly exhausted, Carter fought the impulse to lay his head down on the bar. "It's nothing…and everything. I'm getting divorced, working at dating again, though, most of the people in my life don't know I'm interested in guys and now I find out a guy I have been dating is involved with a client who made a pass at me."

"Prospective client," Jesse reminded, his gaze intense, "and I already told you Brew and I are just friends. I'm not apologizing for hitting on you, though. You're an attractive motherfucker and I haven't actually hired you yet." He grinned after Carter scoffed. "Come on, you know you're gorgeous. You can't hold it against me for acknowledging that."

"I don't." Carter lifted his glass and tossed back the last of his drink. "But you know this kind of shit can't go on if you and I are working together."

He watched Jesse draw a hand through his close-cropped hair. After a long moment, Jesse nodded, holding his gaze. "You're right, it can't," he agreed, smiling while Eric slid back onto his bar stool beside him.

* * * *

Carter made it home before sunrise, but only just. He'd only had one drink at Pete's, but he felt it and the lack of sleep the next day. Shaking it off, he concentrated on his work and before he knew it, it was after six p.m. He'd already packed his briefcase to leave when his office door whispered open and Brad Hamilton walked in. Carter blinked in surprise. "Something you need?"

"Murtagh Media declined our proposal." Brad's voice was even as he seated himself in one of the guest chairs.

"I see." Carter pulled off his glasses with a sigh. "I thought for sure they'd be on board after dinner last night. Any indication as to why?"

Brad tented his fingers under his chin and shook his head. "Nothing specific. Though, I wouldn't be surprised if you having drinks with Jesse Murtagh after dinner didn't have something to do with it."

"Why?" Carter drew his eyebrows together. "I had drinks with Jesse and Eric and we headed in different directions at the end of the night—we never even discussed business."

Brad cocked his head. "You never talked about the proposal?"

"Of course not. It was a spur-of-the-moment social outing and nothing to do with Hamilton Advertising. I know we haven't been seeing eye-to-eye lately, Brad, but I'd like to think you know me better than that."

"I see." Brad licked his lips and met Carter's gaze. "So, you turning Murtagh down has nothing to do with losing that job?"

Carter stared at his father. "What?"

"You heard me. Did Murtagh come on to you? Did you reject him?"

"No, he did not." Carter let the lie settle in his chest while he stared at his father. "We had drinks with Eric and swapped stories about life in general."

Brad scoffed. "Don't play stupid with me, Carter—it doesn't suit you. Are you really telling me you didn't know Jesse Murtagh is a fag?"

Carter mashed his lips together at the steel in his father's glare. "Jesse is bisexual. Anyone who looks him up knows it, and you know very well I research every prospective client."

"Bisexual." Brad's mouth twisted disdainfully. "What the hell does that even mean?"

A chill crept up Carter's spine—too much of this conversation hit close to home. "You know exactly what that means. Jesse partners with both men and women."

"And you don't think he's interested in pursuing you?"

"I don't know, but it wouldn't matter if he did," Carter exclaimed quietly. "Jesse and I knew the likelihood of our working together was high. If he expressed interest in me, neither of us would act on it." Carter recognized his mistake as soon as the words were out of his mouth and the flush of angry color in his father's cheeks only drove the point home.

"Did I hear you right?" Brad's voice was low and dangerous. "A potential conflict of interest is the only reason you'd have turned him down? Not your wife? Or your marriage?"

"You're twisting my words," Carter protested, his face burning. "I never said anything like that—"

"That has something to do with your split with Kate, doesn't it?" Understanding tracked across Brad's face. "Being attracted to men, that is. Because I've gathered you are."

Carter could only stare, struck dumb by his father's words.

"What's more, I thought you'd never met Murtagh before last night."

"I hadn't. The first time I ever spoke to him was over a drink at the Gramercy Tavern while we were waiting for the rest of you to arrive. Jesse has nothing to do with my marital problems."

"Someone like him does." Brad's voice was sharp and certain. "I know you are to blame for the split, Carter, but I'd rather you screwed women all over town than be a goddamned deviant—"

"You don't know what you're talking about," Carter ground out.

"I think I do." Brad stood, leaning over Carter's desk, his face twisting with disgust. "And I'd bet good money it's got something to do with Riley Porter-Wright, too. He's been dragging you down since the day you met him and he's doing it now."

Carter shoved back his chair to stand, too. "That is the most ridiculous thing you've said yet. You and Mom always liked Riley!"

"We approved of him as long as he was a good friend to you, but by the time you moved back to New York, we knew Riley had stopped wanting to be just your friend. Your mother and I could see he had designs on you even before you met Kate — you were just too naïve to see it."

Carter's breath left him in a rush. "Wh-why didn't you ever say anything?" he whispered.

"You got married and so did Riley." Brad shot back. "Any misgivings your mother or I had seemed unimportant once Kate and Sadie were in your life. Everything was perfect."

"Until it wasn't." Throat aching, Carter turned to stare at the skyline beyond his office windows. "I fucked up my perfect marriage and my perfect life just the same."

"So it would seem." Brad's cold voice frayed Carter's nerves. "Jonathon and Geneva suspected you played some part in the failure of Riley and Alex's marriage. Your mother and I did, too, but we defended you to the Porter-Wrights because we wanted to trust you."

Carter turned back to his father with a bitter laugh. "Gee, thanks."

"Don't be childish. You're my son, Carter, but you're also a grown man. There's not a hell of a lot I can do to stop you from ruining your own life. I can make sure you don't ruin Sadie and Dylan's lives in the process, however."

"Meaning?"

"It means I'm going to insist on something that I should have a long time ago. I want people like Murtagh and Riley kept away from my grandchildren. Sadie and Dylan are young and impressionable and shouldn't be exposed to men with abnormal habits and urges. It's not safe, especially with their goddamned father feeling the same way."

Carter's blood ran cold. "You're not serious."

"I'm nothing but serious when it comes to the well-being of my family."

"I am your family, Brad. I would never harm a child and neither would Riley, especially any child of mine. He loves Sadie and Dylan and they love him back. He's Dylan's godfather, for Christ's sake!"

Brad's eyes flashed with undisguised fury. "Are you sure you want to test me?"

"I'm sure I'm a good father." Carter was trembling with emotion, but he held his chin high in defiance. "And I'm sure the people in my life are good to my children."

Some of the anger went out of Brad's face then, though his features didn't soften. "If I were you, I'd put some serious thought into your priorities, Carter," he said quietly. "You need to decide if your friends mean more to you than your job or your family, and especially your children. If I think any of the things I hold dear are being threatened, I will do anything to ensure their safety."

"Even if you have to hurt me to do it?" Carter eyed the man who had raised him as he might an enemy. He wasn't surprised when Brad simply turned away and left. He was, however, surprised to find that his father's silence hurt almost more than his words.

* * * *

The next morning, Carter found the idea of getting out of bed completely overwhelming. Slitting his eyes against the sunlight leaching under the window shades, he felt more unsure than ever about...well, everything. Riley, Kate, his career, even his own ability to be a good father. Flattened by self-doubt, he pulled up the bedding over his head and willed himself back to sleep.

He surfaced a few times as the morning passed. The quiet chime of his phone woke him once and the pressure of his bladder woke him again a few hours later. He forced himself to get up after that, and made a lateral move to the couch, where he slouched down into the cushions watching *The Lord of The Rings* trilogy. It was past noon when his front door opened.

Bracing for a confrontation with Audrey or Max, Carter gaped after Riley appeared in the doorway. He held a pizza box and a paper bag and wore a smile that made a lump rise in Carter's throat. *I want this*, he thought. Carter wanted Riley in his home, in his life, weathering its ups and downs — and everything in between — together. In the next moment, he became aware of his rumpled hair and sweats and sat up with a grimace.

"Riley...what are you doing here?" he asked, voice hoarse with disuse. "How did you get in?"

"Your sister loaned me your extra keys and gave me the security code." Riley made his way into the room, laying the pizza box and bag on the coffee table before sitting down beside Carter. "I've been calling you."

"Sorry."

"I was kind of peeved you didn't at least text, to be honest," Riley replied, his voice light. "It's unlike you not to reply eventually." Carter moved to cover his face with his hands before Riley caught his wrists.

"Stop it, you idiot, I'm in the middle of a story." He looked down at their hands and gently brushed his thumbs over Carter's pulse points before letting him go. "You didn't answer, I got worried, I called Audrey. Turns out she's been trying to get hold of you today, too. The way I see it, you're lucky it's me checking up on you and not an angry sister or your ex."

"I'm...having a bad day." Carter leaned back into the couch cushions and closed his eyes. Warmth filled his chest when a hand came to lie on the crown of his head.

"You're having a bad hair day, that's for sure," Riley murmured, using his fingers to smooth down Carter's cowlicks. "I have pizza and beer if you're up for some company, though."

Carter cracked open his eyes to give his friend a sidelong glance. "Thanks. You don't have to stay, though. And I'm not drinking today, so you should take the beer, too. I'm sure you've got better things to do than watch me wallow."

"Are you kidding? Watching a grown man wallow in his pajamas is one my favorite things to do." Riley met Carter's gaze, his face filled with both fondness and concern. "You want to talk about what's got you holed up today? It's okay if you don't—just know I'll listen if you're in the mood to talk."

Carter shook his head and tried to smile. "I do want to talk about it, just not right now. Is it okay with you if we sit for a while longer?"

Riley slid an arm over Carter's shoulders, his smile warm. "Sure, we can do that."

Chapter Seven

"Thanks." Carter locked gazes with Riley for a long, suspended moment and Riley's breaths grew shallow.

When Carter licked his lips, Riley stood and cleared his throat. "I think we need to talk, Carter."

A brief expression of disappointment shadowed Carter's face, but he nodded. "Okay. So talk."

He cleared his throat again. "Will is pretty pissed about the way I acted at the wedding and I think he has every reason to be. I wasn't putting him first. I've always put you first, and now…I think that's going to have to change."

"So what does that mean? We can't hang out like this anymore?" There was an edge to his voice.

Riley spun to face Carter. "What? No, I don't mean that. Of course, we can still hang out and go running in the morning and play word games. I want to be your friend. I just need to—to make him the priority in my life. I think we need to set some boundaries." Riley's chest tightened. He paced, trying to keep the anxiety at bay.

Carter nodded. "Fair enough."

"I just..." Riley raked a hand through his hair, becoming more agitated by the second. "I don't want to be the guy who can't commit. The one who always wants someone other than the person he's with. I did it with you when I was with Alex and I'm done with that, Carter. I can't stand the thought of being that guy, you know?"

Carter stood and gently grabbed Riley's wrist. "Hey, I get that, okay?"

Riley stared at him. "I'm so conflicted, Carter. You know how much I care about you, but I don't want to hurt Will. "

Carter nodded and stepped back. "I know. And I don't want to be a dick about this and be the one holding you back from a great relationship. If you feel like our friendship is making this harder on you..."

"It's not your fault. I just think—I hope—talking about it will help so we both know where we stand. If I don't jump to answer your call or text, it's not because I don't want to talk to you, it's because I'm putting Will first."

"Sure, I understand that."

"And I think if I'm focused on where I'm at with Will and you're focused on your relationships, we'll find a way to make our friendship work."

Carter nodded and plopped down on the sofa. "Well, I guess Jesse will be pleased."

"That's the guy you mentioned, right? The one you thought was interesting enough to go out with again?"

"Uh, no. That's Kyle. He's nice enough and I'll probably go out with him again, but I was talking about

Jesse Murtagh. He's the son of the CEO of Murtagh Media Conglomerate. A couple of days ago, Brad and I had a dinner with Jesse, his brother Eric and their father, Harry Murtagh. After the pitch was through, Jesse, Eric and I went out for drinks."

Riley raised an eyebrow. "And…something happened between you two?"

"No, no, nothing happened." The flush on Carter's cheeks deepened. "We flirted a little, I suppose. That's all."

"You were interested, though?" Riley took a seat at the other end of the sofa, jealousy warring with his curiosity.

Carter hesitated. "Yes. He's the first man — other than you — who seriously piqued my interest, to be honest. I might have pursued that, but there's a conflict of interest with work. Although, I suppose that's moot now that Murtagh Media declined our proposal." Carter shrugged. "He texted me today."

"Okay," Riley said slowly, not quite sure where Carter was going with it.

"I haven't responded yet, but…I don't know what I'm waiting for. I mean, other than not wanting to give my father more ammunition."

The sadness in Carter's eyes made Riley frown. "What happened?"

"Yesterday, Brad came storming into my office, furious that Murtagh hadn't accepted our offer. He ranted and raved about Jesse coming onto me and me turning him down and that it ruined the deal." Carter closed his eyes. "We argued for a while and I…I slipped up. He figured out that I wasn't totally against the idea of being with Jesse and insinuated that you and I were sexually involved and that it led to our marriages ending. He doesn't know all of it, obviously, but he's figured out enough…"

Riley's heart sank — Carter appeared crushed. "I'm sorry."

"No, obviously, it needed to come out at some point. What hit me hardest was him threatening me."

"Threatening you how?" Riley asked, appalled.

"Telling me to keep the kids away from 'deviants' like you and Jesse." Carter's jaw was hard and a muscle there twitched.

"Jesus Christ, you know I'd never harm Sadie and Dylan!" Riley yelled. "He should know that, too!"

"Of course, I do," Carter said soothingly. "And, yes, he should know that too. He's so blinded by his narrow-minded little world he can't see reason anymore. I knew it was bad, but this…equating gay men with pedophiles is a new low."

Riley bit back a snarl. He'd always liked Brad and Eleanor and it hurt to think they honestly believed something so horrible about him. "How could they ever think I'd hurt your kids? Hell, I felt bad enough that I had any part in your divorce from Kate. Wondering what effect that had on Sadie and Dylan makes me feel terrible."

"I know, Ri." Carter let out a heavy sigh. "I have no idea how to deal with them right now. I'm just so overwhelmed. There's too much to cope with."

Riley gave Carter a sympathetic smile. "I was in a similar state last November."

"Although it's been difficult since you came out, you kept me from sleepwalking through the rest of my life. I owe you for that."

"Why the…unwashed, slovenly wallowing, then?" Riley asked, using Carter's own words for the emotional — and somewhat literal — funk he'd found his friend in when he'd arrived.

"Because I'm depressed. Everything's changed and I let my head get in the way. I'm still going to therapy, still taking the antidepressants, but sometimes it's not quite enough. I'll get there, though."

"It kills me to think I've made things so stressful for you."

Carter's voice was slow but steady. "I don't want you to blame yourself. This is what happens when you spend most of your life denying what you want and who you are. Yeah, I'm not going to lie, it *has* been stressful, but a lot of that is because of the choices *I* made." He sat back and gave Riley a long, searching look. "You never wanted to start the threesomes with Natalie at all, did you?"

Riley hesitated, unsure if he wanted to dredge up the feelings surrounding that situation. "I wanted to be with you."

"And you went along with it because it was the only way you could. I pushed pretty hard, too, didn't I?"

He shrugged. "I don't want to get into the blame game. Not to mention the fact that I genuinely like Natalie and value her friendship. Some good came of the situation."

"I know. And Natalie aside, I want to take responsibility for my part in what happened. Because when you came out, I was so in denial I couldn't see any of it. I blamed you for dropping this bomb on me when I was every bit as culpable. Don't get me wrong — I loved Kate. I will always love her, but there was something profoundly wrong with our relationship if I was willing to screw around behind her back with an escort just to be with you. At the time, it seemed like the only way I could have everything I wanted. That wasn't fair to either of you."

"And I feel guilty for disrupting your life like that. We're quite a pair, but I'm not going to spend my time dwelling on the mistakes. I'd rather move forward. "

"I was feeling overwhelmed and wallowing earlier, but I'm better now."

"Good. I'm glad to hear it. And how about we agree that the next time you're in a funk, you call me?" Riley asked lightly, although he meant every word of it. "I know I said I need to make Will a priority, but if it's truly an emergency, *tell* me and I'll come. Day or night."

Carter nodded. "I swear, I will. And I promise not to abuse the generous offer."

Riley gave him a smile, pleased that he and Carter had finally turned a corner in their relationship. Their friendship seemed back on solid footing again. "Deal."

"Can we eat now? I'm starving."

"Sure," Riley agreed with a laugh. "Pizza's probably cold by now, so I'll heat that up. But first, you *really* need to shower. You stink."

The rough bark of Carter's laughter and the look on his face made Riley grin, even though Carter shoved him away. "Thanks, jerk."

"Any time," Riley said.

The twist of Carter's lips when he stood didn't go unnoticed. He shot Riley the finger before he left the room and Riley laughed long and hard. Things were finally starting to feel normal with Carter again—no, *better* than normal, because they were finally honest with each other. *God, that's a good feeling.*

Riley hummed an aria from Verdi's *Rigoletto* as he slid the pizza onto a pan and put it in the oven. Carter hadn't done the dishes in the last day or so and Riley decided to empty the dishwasher of clean dishes and refill it with the dirty ones in the sink. While he cleaned, it occurred to him how comfortable he felt at Carter's new place. It was warm and masculine, filled with the eclectic collection of things Carter had acquired over the years. The sound of the shower running in the background was familiar from the times at Harvard when they'd shared a dorm room or apartment.

By the time Carter walked into the living room—his hair dripping onto the clean T-shirt and shorts he wore—Riley was sprawled on the couch, nursing a beer. Carter held out his arms. "Better?"

"Much," Riley teased. "I was about to start breaking out the gas mask."

"Oh, fuck off," Carter bantered back. "It wasn't that bad. Now, where's my pizza?"

"Demanding asshole, aren't you?" Riley asked with a snort. He set his beer bottle down and stood.

"How long have we been friends?" Carter asked. "There's no way you should be surprised about *that*."

Their banter continued while Riley pulled the pizza from the oven and slid a few pieces onto each plate. They spent the rest of the afternoon watching movies and relaxing together, like they'd done for years.

Riley left Carter's building early that evening, with a smile on his face and a bounce in his step.

* * * *

Once home, Riley made the decision to call Will. They hadn't spoken since the wedding and Riley didn't want to let the fight they'd had linger.

Will's tone was disappointingly neutral when he answered, however. "Riley."

"Hey, Will. First of all, I'd really like to apologize for my behavior at the wedding on Saturday. I know I acted like a thoughtless asshole and I'm sorry. It shouldn't have happened."

"I appreciate the apology." Will's tone still didn't give any clues about how he felt. He didn't seem angry, but he hardly sounded excited to hear from Riley, either.

"It's the least I could do," Riley admitted. "I was rude to you and to Gabe and Charles."

Will sighed. "I care about you a lot, Riley, and I think I've been very patient with you, but I'm not in the habit of letting men walk all over me and I'm not about to start now."

"I never meant to do that."

"I understand that, but I feel like that's what's been happening."

Riley took a deep breath and contemplated how to tell Will about his talk with Carter. "Would it help to know that Carter and I discussed it?"

"Discussed what, exactly?" Now Will's tone was wary. "My relationship with you?"

"Sort of." Riley tried to explain. "We discussed the fact that my friendship with him is impacting my relationship with you. And that we need to set some boundaries."

"Ahh."

Riley waited for Will to say more, but he didn't continue. Riley spoke instead. "You know I don't want to lose Carter's friendship."

"I know. And I don't want to be the guy who tells you he can't see his friends. That's not the way I operate. I'm just not sure I feel entirely comfortable with your relationship with him."

"Yeah, I know." Riley scrubbed a hand across his face. "It's my fault. I've been letting my attraction to Carter get in the way of things, but I feel like I got that squared away today. Carter is clear that you're my priority. He and I will continue to play word games and grab lunch occasionally. We'll go for our weekly run, but otherwise, my time with you will take priority. And if I don't answer his calls or texts while I'm with you, he knows not to push."

"That's fair." Will's voice seemed a little softer.

"He is going through kind of a rough time right now, though," Riley added. "I don't want to go into details, but let's just say his father is beginning to put the pieces together about his sexuality and the history Carter and I have. He doesn't know everything, but it's enough. It may be the final nail in the coffin for his relationship with his father *and* his job."

"I'm sorry to hear that." Will sounded sincere. "That's never easy."

"So, I told him that if he truly needed me...not because he was bored or just wanted to hang out, but if it got to be too much emotionally, he could let me know that it was an emergency. I hope that's okay. I promise I won't drop everything we're doing and run to him unless it really is dire, and he promised not to abuse it."

"Of course." Will let out a sigh. "I'm not a monster, Riley. I honestly don't want to be the jealous boyfriend."

Riley swallowed hard. "You have every right to be. I let my attraction to Carter get in the way. Not that I ever crossed a line physically, but mentally..." He thought of the times he'd ogled Carter in the locker room and winced.

"Hey, none of us are saints. We're going to have the occasional fantasy," Will replied gently. "I trust you to not stray and I believe you when you say you've never crossed that line."

"I don't like to think of myself as a man who cheats on my partner," Riley admitted. "But I did with Alex. It was easy to rationalize because of the circumstances, but it doesn't mean it was okay. I want to be honest with you."

"I appreciate that."

"So, we're okay?"

There was a brief pause. "Yeah, we're okay. If Carter needs you because of the shit he's dealing with in his life, I can live with that occasionally. I can live with you two still hanging out. What I can't live with is feeling like I'm not the man you want to be with."

"I want to be with you," Riley said sincerely. "Give me a chance to prove it."

"Okay."

They were both silent for a moment. "Have you had dinner yet?" Riley asked when it grew awkward.

"No, I haven't."

"Then why don't you give me about an hour or so? I'll stop at the store, pick up a few ingredients and I'll make dinner for you."

"I'd like that." Will's tone was warm for the first time that night.

"Me, too," Riley admitted. "I've missed you."

"I've missed you, too. In fact, why don't you pack an overnight bag?"

"I'd like that," he said, echoing Will's earlier words.

After he hung up the phone, Riley closed his eyes for a moment, relieved that he and Will had worked through the fight. For a little while there, he'd honestly thought he'd lost him.

And that mattered a hell of a lot more than he would have expected.

Chapter Eight

Carter fingered his phone for the fifth time since leaving his apartment. "Damn it." He ignored his nerves and trained his gaze out of the window of the Zimride carrying him along East 30th Street.

It had taken him a couple of days to shake off the dark cloud brought on by the argument with his father. But he'd gone to work, called the kids in the evenings and kept moving forward while he waited for his life to slide back into normalcy.

Riley kept in touch every day. He prompted Carter to continue their games and checked in with quick messages to ask how he was feeling.

Carter appreciated his friend's concern but knew his replies were hesitant and stilted. He wanted Riley to be happy, but it still stung to know Riley was willing to put their friendship on a back burner. Worse, Carter was hyperaware of the boundaries Riley had set. Worried he'd say the wrong thing or share too much, he'd searched for ways to avoid being around Riley, even begging off their weekly run in favor of going to the athletic club.

On Wednesday evening, he'd remembered to read Jesse Murtagh's message and flicked through the alerts on his phone as he rode the subway to Kate's for dinner.

Let's talk. We'll grab drinks and you can tell me I'm a terrible person. – J

Carter had stared at the words for a solid minute, trying to understand how they made him feel. Intrigued, certainly. Apprehensive, too...and maybe a little spiteful. His fight with Brad had been a long time coming, but losing the Murtagh account had been the catalyst. Spending some non-business time with Jesse certainly felt like a nice little 'fuck you' aimed at the old man.

Thursdays work for me, Carter tapped out, *and this time the tab's definitely on you. - C*

He'd pocketed the phone after hitting Send and put the whole thing out of his mind, sure Jesse wouldn't reply. Bright young things like Jesse Murtagh didn't wait almost a week for guys like Carter. He hadn't quite known what to do when his phone buzzed twenty minutes later with a message from that same bright young thing.

You're cranky when you lose money. Meet me at Wine:30 tomorrow at 9. – J

Carter had stood in Kate's foyer, re-reading the message, until Dylan had come to get him, scolding his father for spacing out while meatballs were waiting to be rolled.

Now, as Carter climbed out of the car in front of the wine bar on East 30th, he fought the urge to turn tail and run.

Why did Jesse make him so nervous? It wasn't as if Carter hadn't been dating. He stopped then, his hand hovering over the door's handle, and let out a breathless laugh. He had no idea if he was even *on* a date.

Jesse had been flirtatious at their first meeting, even provocative, but that had been a week ago. Carter really didn't know if the vibe he'd picked up that night had been genuine attraction or if Jesse simply enjoyed pursuing the forbidden. Hell, maybe he had a kink for fooling around with his employees.

And so what if he does? Carter wondered to himself and pushed open the door. Murtagh Media hadn't hired Carter's team and nothing was stopping him from enjoying an evening with Jesse. Drinks and dinner with a man he found charming were preferable to brooding at home over a bag of microwave popcorn.

He found Jesse at the bar with a glass of red wine. As during their first meeting, he radiated easy elegance, his tailored blue jacket and navy button-down shirt highlighting his pale gold skin. The stubble Jesse had been sporting the week before had grown in and the short, well-groomed beard set off his full lips beautifully.

Jesse glanced up to meet Carter's gaze, his eyes sparking with interest. "Carter," he said, turning to extend his right hand, his smile transforming his serious expression. "I reserved a table for nine-fifteen and I hope you don't mind that I had a bottle of red opened already. I remembered you drinking it the other night at dinner."

"Red's fine," Carter replied. He felt clumsy as he slid onto the bar stool and knew his dark wool suit looked stuffy and dated. "I'm not sure if I should feel fascinated or disturbed by your level of recall, though."

Jesse's smile turned impish. "You should feel flattered," he suggested, turning to gesture to the bartender. "I don't usually bother to notice details like that in people who don't interest me."

"I'll keep that in mind," Carter murmured. He turned to watch the bartender, who approached with a bottle of wine and second glass.

"That's a very fine pinot noir from New Zealand," Jesse told him as she poured, "though I should note the nice selection of bourbon behind the bar, too." He shrugged when Carter met his gaze with a raised eyebrow. "Seeing it on the list made me think of you."

Carter smiled. "I feel like I've done you a favor."

"Perhaps the first of many." Jesse waited until Carter had sampled his wine and nodded in approval before speaking again. "I'm glad you could make it."

The intensity in his gaze sent a jolt of nerves through Carter. "Did you think I'd blow you off?"

"I had no idea. I wasn't sure you'd even message me back, though, after the first couple of days."

"I got caught up with some things and lost track of my personal correspondence for a few days." Carter's smile felt stiff, though his words were true. "And, to be honest, Brad doesn't take rejection well. It's possible my brain made a strategic decision not to recognize the name 'Murtagh' for a day or two."

"Yeah…" Jesse ran a hand over his head, seeming uncharacteristically hesitant. "Harry, Eric and I argued through the decision for a good long while. In the end, Harry was on board, but Eric thought McKenzie the better option."

"Which means you were the tiebreaker and you sided with your brother." Carter studied Jesse's face. "Not that it really matters, but what put you off?"

"Nothing put me off—it wasn't anything you did or said, or Bradley did or said, for that matter. McKenzie is a bigger firm, with more experience in re-branding companies like Murtagh Media." Jesse shrugged. "They were the better choice for us."

Carter cocked his head, intrigued almost despite himself. "So the aggressive flirting the other night—is that how you do business?"

"In part, yes." Jesse cocked an eyebrow when Carter scoffed. "Oh, come on. You're a smart guy. You met my father and brother—charm is basically a family MO."

"I *had* noticed, sure," Carter replied. "The same can be said of almost anyone successful in business—seducing your audience is all part of the game." He watched Jesse sip his wine for a moment. "When I asked you a minute ago about the flirting, you said it was 'partly' about business...does that imply you were—?"

"Genuinely interested in you?" Jesse smiled. "It's true, and I continue to be."

Well...that answered Carter's doubts the evening wasn't a date.

Jesse raised his brows. "You seem surprised."

"I am, a little," Carter admitted, ignoring the heat crawling up the back of his neck.

"Maybe losing Murtagh Media as a client is clouding your judgement."

Carter shot him a look. "And maybe you're full of crap." He tried unsuccessfully to bite back a grin after Jesse burst out laughing. "In the interest of complete disclosure, I told my father Murtagh Media was not a good match for our firm. That said, we both know you're not being completely straight with me right now."

"Completely straight is something I haven't claimed to be in years," Jesse told him, his voice tinged with amusement. "But you're right—my own reasons for turning down Hamilton Advertising were partly selfish. I liked you too much to want to hire you, Carter. I knew your firm could do the job and that you and I would work well together, but...I knew we couldn't be friends if we hired you to work for us."

Jesse fell silent and ran a hand over his lips, seemingly in thought. "I wanted that—to be friends with you, and more. And I chose that over the work your firm was offering. Sounds selfish, but I really don't give a fuck."

"Now *that* I believe." Carter smiled. "I wasn't sure if you were trying to get a new brand or in my pants the other night, but it felt like more than business to me."

"Oh, I was *absolutely* trying to get in your pants." Jesse gave him a grin. "You didn't give me much to go on, though. Didn't have much to say about yourself unless you were talking about your kids."

"I wanted your company to hire mine, Jesse—I was trying to keep things on the level."

"Hmm...okay. I just figured you were involved with someone."

"I wasn't. I mean, I'm not. Involved with someone, that is."

Jesse snickered. "You sure about that?"

"Very."

"Well, good." Jesse's smile widened. "This seems like the right time to reiterate that I am interested in you, Carter. Like, get-in-your-pants interested."

Carter silently cursed the blush he felt on his cheeks.

"What is that about?" Jesse asked, his voice softer.

"What's what about?"

"Well, the red face, for one thing." Jesse reached up to graze Carter's cheekbone with a fingertip. "Have I embarrassed you?"

Jesse dropped his hand and Carter blinked, dismayed at how flustered he'd become at the simple gesture. He started to reply when the restaurant's host approached to let them know their table was ready.

Carter was silently grateful for the interruption so he could pull himself together. He followed Jesse and the host through the restaurant to the back garden. Votives lit the intimate courtyard space and there were lamps in each corner to brighten the evening's gloom. By the time they were seated and the server refilled their glasses, Carter had mostly composed himself. Meeting Jesse's gaze over the table didn't help, though, because now Jesse was frowning.

"Carter, I think maybe we should start over."

"What do you mean?"

Jesse licked his lips, appearing to consider his words before speaking. "I know you agreed to meet me here tonight—I mean, you messaged me back, which I took as a sign that you were willing to spend some time with me."

It was Carter's turn to frown. "I wouldn't be here if I wasn't."

"Are you sure?" Jesse asked gently. "Because I can't help feeling I'm making you incredibly uncomfortable."

Carter's chest ached at Jesse's earnest words. God, he was so fucked up.

"It's not you." He paused, then laughed with relief when Jesse grinned and broke the awkwardness between them at last. "I'm sorry. It's a bit early to be spouting relationship clichés, especially when we hardly know each other."

"Hey, I'm just glad you don't look like you're about to bolt," Jesse told him, head cocked as he sat back in his seat.

"I'm not," Carter assured, "and you're right. I wouldn't have messaged you back if I didn't want to see you again. I'm just out of practice with dating."

"What makes you think this is a date?" Jesse's eyes twinkled and he picked up his menu.

"Honestly, nothing. I'm a bit hopeless in social situations lately."

Jesse dropped one corner of the menu to reach across the table and lay a hand on Carter's. "Relax. I asked you to dinner because I enjoyed spending time with you last week. I thought there was something between us worth exploring. But whatever happens depends on you, too. Tonight isn't about business and I don't want you to feel as though you're being forced to be here."

"I don't." Carter struggled to smile through his lingering guilt. "I meant what I said before — I wouldn't be here if I didn't want to be."

Jesse's megawatt smile lit his face once more. "Then let me buy you dinner."

Things between them were easier from there. Carter and Jesse fell naturally into conversation, ranging through various topics rather than focusing on any one thing. They shared oysters on the half shell and tuna tartare to start, then moved on to NY strip steaks for the main course.

Carter relaxed as they ate and talked, even while his attraction to Jesse increased. The idea of acting on the impulse appealed, but it worried Carter too. He was out of his depth when it came to fooling around with men. He'd been dating, but hadn't gone beyond a few kisses with any of the men he'd seen. Jesse, so confident and assertive, was on a whole other plane from *any* of them, even when Carter included Riley in the mix.

Then again, he didn't really know Riley anymore, did he? When it came down to it, Riley had more in common with Jesse now than he did with Carter. *Maybe that has always been the case,* Carter thought, and his stomach dropped with the realization.

Jesse looked at Carter questioningly when Carter met his gaze.

"Sorry, I lost my train of thought." Carter drew the tines of his fork through the potatoes on his plate. "I wasn't exaggerating earlier when I said I was out of practice with this whole thing."

Jesse nodded. If he was puzzled by Carter's abrupt subject change, he hid it well. "That's understandable, considering you were married until very recently. Just remember, Carter — this doesn't *have* to be a date if you don't want it to be."

"It feels like a date, though." Carter reached for his wineglass with his free hand. "I think we both came here thinking it was. I certainly did." He pursed his lips at Jesse's sly smile. "Stop looking so pleased with yourself."

Jesse set down his fork and held both hands up in front of his chest in mock surrender. "I came here tonight to have dinner with a new friend. Possibly to engage in casual sex if things went as I'd planned." He smirked when Carter's jaw went slack.

"You have a plan, huh?"

"Not really." Jesse shrugged. "I mean, other than to finally find out what that sexy mouth of yours tastes like. I figured that'd be the best place to start."

Carter laughed. His nerves were rising again, but this time it felt less like anxiety and more like anticipation. The idea of kissing Jesse, who'd made no secret of wanting him, was undeniably exciting.

"I like the sound of that." A wave of heat spread through him when Jesse wet his lips with his tongue.

"I'm glad to hear it."

Something unfurled deep in Carter's gut then, a tension he'd been carrying for he didn't know how long. He felt...comfortable, even while flirting, and more at home in his own body than he had for a very long time. The electricity of attraction between himself and the beautiful man seated across the table felt *right*.

"Is there anything I need to know?" Jesse asked as he signed the bill for their meal.

Carter watched Jesse tuck his credit card back into his wallet. "Meaning?"

"You went out of your way to explain you're reacquainting yourself with dating again and I've seen photos of you with your wife. You made a smoking-hot couple, by the way," he added, his gaze sharp when it met Carter's, and they both rose to their feet.

"Thank you, I think." Jesse stood a few inches shorter than Carter, though his lean build gave him the illusion of being taller. In that moment, Carter used his height to his advantage and stared down his nose at Jesse. "Is there a point you're trying to make?"

Jesse gave him an easy grin. "Not really. I think *you've* been talking around something, though. I'm pretty good at reading people," he continued while they walked through the restaurant. "It's one of the reasons I'm good at my job. I hoped you'd tell me whatever it is that's got you thinking so hard, but you haven't, which means I have to guess."

Jesse stepped forward and pushed open the restaurant door, gesturing for Carter to move ahead of him. Carter waited until they were standing on the sidewalk outside before sliding his hands into his pockets.

"And what is your guess?"

"I'm still working on it." Jesse's brow creased and he looked as though he was puzzling through a problem. "If I had to *hazard* a guess right now, I'd say you're not entirely comfortable being out with a man."

Carter shook his head at once. "You're wrong. I have no problem being seen with a man. I'm nervous right now because that man is you."

Jesse's eyes widened. "Oh, wow. That's…really not very reassuring."

Carter resisted the urge to smack his own hand over his face. "That came out wrong."

Relief surged through him when Jesse laughed — at least he found humor in Carter's hopeless bumbling. A moment later, Jesse reached up to give Carter's arm a squeeze and his gaze warmed.

"What were you trying to say?"

"Dating men isn't something I'd ever done until recently. And you're the first I've been truly attracted to in quite a while."

He ignored the little lie in his own words as Jesse took another step closer. He studied Jesse's small smile, then forgot it completely after Jesse closed his fingers around Carter's right wrist, gently pulling Carter's hand from his pocket.

"Thank you for being honest with me." Jesse twined their fingers together. "I'd tell you not to be nervous if I thought it would do any good, but just remember what I told you earlier. I'm interested in you. Word vomit and all."

Carter ducked his head and laughed, glad the streetlights hid his embarrassment. "I hoped so, since I've been making an ass of myself all evening, Jesse. Amazingly, you're still here." He was vividly aware of Jesse, who smelled delicious, like citrus and cloves, his breath sweet as it gusted over Carter's cheek.

Jesse winked and showed a hint of that cocky attitude Carter found so appealing. His smile was kind, though, as were his next words. "Don't worry. You'll figure it out as you go, just like the rest of us."

He turned his head to gaze toward uptown before looking at Carter again. "I thought of suggesting we head back to my place for a drink, but maybe it's better for me to invite myself to your place instead."

"Why's that?" Carter's breath caught as Jesse slipped his fingers away from Carter's, then brought them to rest on Carter's hip.

"I want you to be comfortable, no matter what happens — or doesn't happen — tonight. You should know I'm planning on lots of things, though."

Carter bit his lip, desire zinging pleasantly through him, and nodded. "Okay. Let's get out of here."

* * * *

They walked a couple of blocks and hailed a cab on Park Avenue to bring them back to Murray Hill. Their attraction seemed to escalate after the car door closed behind them, though neither made a move to touch the other.

Carter's thoughts were spinning as he unlocked the door to his apartment and led Jesse inside. He waved Jesse toward the sitting area and swallowed when he met Jesse's heated gaze.

"Can I get you a drink?" Carter asked, then winced at himself — he sounded like a total cheeseball. "I've got some good bourbon if you feel like trying something new."

"Sure, if you're having one." Jesse headed for the balcony door at the far end of the room and turned back to glance at Carter. "Okay to go outside?"

"Absolutely — go on and I'll meet you in a minute."

Carter stepped into the kitchen, listening to the door snick open and the low hum of the city filter through the apartment. He pulled two glasses and a bottle of Widow Jane from the cabinet and went to the freezer for ice, his brain buzzing all the while. He wanted this, wanted to know what Jesse was like underneath all the flirting and joking. And as he poured two fingers of bourbon over the ice balls in the glasses, Carter understood that nothing — and no one — stood in his way.

Jesse glanced back over his shoulder when Carter came up behind him. "This is beautiful," he said, nodding toward the city lights before accepting the drink Carter held out.

"It's one of the reasons I decided to rent the place," Carter admitted. "I liked the idea of being able to get outside without needing to go anywhere."

"I know what you mean. There's a small terrace off the master bedroom at my place," Jesse told him. "I don't spend as much time out there as I should, but it's always a big hit when I have people over."

"I can imagine." Carter smirked. "Nothing like a little starlight to set the scene for seduction."

Jesse let out a laugh. "I wasn't being coy, but you do have a point. And this isn't exactly something to sneeze at," he added with a tilt of his head toward the scene before them.

"You're actually the first person I've had up here. Outside of family and friends, I mean. Not that you aren't a friend, too." He grimaced, his face hot. "Ugh."

Jesse shook his head. "Hey, you're doing fine." He reached out to link the fingers of his free hand with Carter's again, and that small contact eased the tightness in Carter's chest.

"You're nice to lie to me." Carter smiled at Jesse's broad grin before turning back to the view and lifting his glass to his lips. He savored the bourbon's deep cherry notes but looked to his side when Jesse let out a hum of pleasure. Carter found him staring at the drink in his glass and his breath caught a little as Jesse slowly licked his lips.

"Like it?" He swallowed when Jesse's gaze flicked up to meet his own.

"This is fucking delicious." Jesse smiled at Carter's laugh. "I'm serious."

"I know you are."

"So what the hell is it and where can I buy some?"

Carter told him about the Widow Jane chocolate factory and distillery in Brooklyn, excited by Jesse's obvious interest. "You know, they're talking about giving tours of the distillery starting this fall," Carter told him. "We could take one if you're interested."

"That is an excellent idea—count both Eric and me in," Jesse told him. "I brought a bottle of Bulleit to Eric and Sara's when they had me over for dinner last week and it was a smash hit. I'm under strict orders to pay attention to whatever you have to say about booze because it's clear we Murtaghs don't know a goddamned thing."

Good whiskey and pleasure made Carter warm. "A friend of mine tends bar at a place in TriBeCa that serves amazing craft cocktails. You should come with me some time. I've always been a bourbon drinker, but Kyle's been introducing me to a whole new world of spirits."

"Kyle's a friend of yours?"

"Yeah. We met through a mutual friend at my athletic club."

"And you and Kyle are dating?"

"Not really?"

Jesse chuckled. "You don't seem too sure."

Carter rolled his eyes with a smile. "Kyle and I have gone out a couple of times and I do enjoy spending time with him. I plan to see him again, but I'm not sure we're dating yet or if we're more just friends."

Jesse dropped Carter's hand to take his glass, then moved to set both glasses on a nearby cocktail table. When he stepped back, he slid one hand under Carter's jacket and gripped Carter's waist with his fingers.

"So, I don't have to worry about Kyle busting in here anytime soon?"

"Kyle's never been here. I told you, you're the first person I've brought up here." Carter's skin tingled under the heat of Jesse's fingers through his shirt.

"Well, good." Jesse leaned in close, his breath warm against Carter's lips and chin. "That means I get to kiss you out here first."

Carter's breath caught when Jesse's lips met his. The kiss was light, but the feeling of that mobile mouth on his own lit a fire in Carter's belly. The soft hairs of Jesse's beard scraped Carter's lips and he closed his eyes with a groan.

Carter savored the taste of the bourbon in Jesse's mouth as the kiss deepened. Jesse moved his hand from Carter's waist to the small of his back, pulling him close while he brought his free hand up to cup Carter's jaw. Carter mirrored the gesture, bringing a hand to rest on the back of Jesse's neck while he used the other to grasp Jesse's waist. Jesse slipped his tongue into Carter's mouth, sending arousal jolting through him.

He didn't know how long they stood on that balcony, groping and pulling each other close. Jesse groaned loudly as his groin brushed Carter's through their trousers and the sound made Carter's head spin.

"Jesus," Jesse muttered when they finally broke apart. He leaned in to suck lightly at Carter's throat, murmuring words into his skin. "I thought you were out of practice with all this stuff."

"Out of practice with the dating," Carter corrected breathlessly, "more up to date with the kissing." He nipped the line of Jesse's jaw with his lips and made his friend shiver. "Come inside with me?"

Jesse pulled back, his eyes glittering in the low light, and smiled. "Lead the way, handsome."

Carter should have felt nervous as they moved inside, their hands linked together. He didn't, though. Excited, yes. Aroused, definitely. And maybe…just a little bit guilty. It hadn't been so long ago he'd hoped to lead

Riley toward the big bed in his master bedroom. Carter shoved the feeling back, though, because Riley was out of his reach. Jesse, who had been watching Carter's cues so closely, was not.

Carter stood still when Jesse stepped forward to help him undress, then turned his attention to his own clothes. They fell away to reveal miles and miles of Jesse's perfect, golden skin and Carter's mouth went dry. At Jesse's urging, he sat on the bed so Jesse could straddle his lap, squeezing Carter's thighs with his long, lean legs.

Carter wound his arms around Jesse's waist and swallowed Jesse's gasp with a kiss. Jesse's hands were everywhere, his touch driving the heat in Carter's body higher. He pushed against Carter's shoulders, guiding him backward to lie down on the bed, and Carter's bones turned liquid as Jesse pressed against him.

"God," he gasped. "If I didn't know better I'd think you were trying to make me come in my pants."

Jesse swirled his tongue around Carter's Adam's apple and gave a low, filthy chuckle. "You're not wearing pants, Carter."

"Shit, you're right." He huffed a laugh against Jesse's shoulder. "Your fault for scrambling my brains."

"We need lube," Jesse told him with a grin.

"Oh—in the bedside table," Carter managed before reaching down to grab Jesse's ass. He smiled at Jesse's low curse, but swore himself a second later when Jesse snaked a hand between them to run his fingers over the flat plane of Carter's belly. Jesse drew back to rest his weight on his heels, his gaze intent, and Carter drank in the sight of him, his breath and pulse racing.

Jesse had a beautiful body, all long lines of muscles that rippled and flexed as he leaned up and over Carter to open the drawer of the bedside table. Carter held his breath when a bottle of lube landed on the mattress beside him.

Jesse stretched over him in the next moment, his body covering Carter's while he reached down to circle Carter's cock with his fingers. Jesse bit his lip as Carter bucked his hips forward, chasing Jesse's fist.

"Fuck." Jesse's voice was gruff.

Carter's heart pounded so his head spun. "Yeah," he muttered, and dug his fingers into the muscles of Jesse's back.

They fell to exploring, learning how to make each other squirm. Jesse kissed and licked Carter's nipples until he begged, then swore when Carter dragged his tongue over Jesse's ribs, raising goosebumps.

Carter moaned as Jesse cupped his balls with a slick hand. Jesse massaged the soft skin of Carter's perineum in slow, maddening circles and Carter forced his eyes open when Jesse made a hungry sound.

"This okay?"

"Yeah," Carter managed.

"You should see yourself, Carter. All spread out and perfect."

Carter whined. He was so erect his cock ached and, as Jesse trailed his fingers from Carter's balls to the cleft of his ass, Carter let his knees fall open.

"Oh, God, Jes."

"Damn." Jesse slowly pushed a finger into Carter. "You like this."

Carter's words and thoughts were lost in the rush of sensation. He closed his eyes and pressed his head back into the pillow, sweat breaking out over his skin. Pleasure curled around his spine as Jesse slid a second finger inside him.

"Fuck, *yes*," he breathed, opening his eyes and tracking lust and pride on Jesse's face.

"That's it." Jesse bent to take Carter's cock in his mouth, his gaze rapt.

Carter swore and reached up to grasp Jesse's head with both hands. Jesse curled his fingers, making Carter writhe, and used the short hairs of his beard to tickle the fragile skin of Carter's groin and balls, amplifying Carter's senses to almost unbearable levels.

Jesse swallowed around him and pressed a hand into Carter's hip, making Carter cry out, his voice faltering as he thrust up into Jesse's mouth. Carter's skin felt too hot and tight for his body and, when Jesse moaned around him, Carter unraveled.

He came so hard he lost his breath. Distantly, he heard himself call out and knew he'd wound his fingers tightly in Jesse's hair. Jesse rolled half on top of him, his cock like iron against Carter's hip.

"Jesus Christ, Carter."

Carter gasped as his brain came back online. He turned to meet Jesse's searing kiss and grunted at the taste of himself on Jesse's tongue. Somehow, he found the lube on the mattress beside them and quickly slicked his hands. He wrapped one around Jesse's cock and Jesse shuddered.

"Oh, fuck," Jesse panted, "I'm not...I'm gonna come." Quickly, he pushed himself up on his hands and knees, bracing his body over Carter's and driving his hips forward into Carter's fist.

Carter worked Jesse's cock with fast strokes, his chest tightening at Jesse's almost desperate expression. "Come on me, Jes," he murmured. "Come on, baby."

Jesse let out a hoarse shout as his cock pulsed onto Carter's skin. He was on Carter a moment later, pushing at his body until they were on their sides and their legs were tangled together.

"You've been holding out on me." Jesse pressed his forehead to Carter's, still breathless as he spoke. "Here I thought you didn't have lot of experience with men."

"I don't," Carter protested. He chuckled as Jesse nosed against his neck with a hum. "Hey, we're covered with six kinds of goo!"

"And I'm going to teach you to love it," Jesse promised, his lips vibrating against Carter's throat and making him laugh.

They lay together for a while, doing nothing more than catching their breaths and swapping lazy kisses, until Jesse finally pulled back to run a hand over Carter's side.

"So…'baby', huh?"

"Hey, you're the one who promised to teach me to love being covered in lube and spunk," Carter countered. He smiled at Jesse's goofy laugh.

"I tend to get loopy when I'm post-orgasmic," Jesse admitted, then pinched Carter and leered. "Something I suspect we have in common."

"Your secret is safe with me," Carter promised, before untangling himself to climb out of bed and head for the bathroom.

Carter washed his hands and was startled by his reflection in the mirror when he glanced up. He looked…happy and exceptionally well-fucked. His hazel eyes were bright and his cheeks rosy, his lips kiss-swollen beneath his smile. Carter raised a washcloth to his torso, eyeing the marks on his skin. He huffed out a laugh as it dawned on him that he itched wherever Jesse's beard had touched.

He straightened when footsteps padded closer, and met Jesse's gaze in the mirror.

Jesse leaned against the bathroom's doorframe with a satisfied smile. "You want me to head out?"

Carter turned to face him. "No." He didn't like imagining Jesse walking out of the door. "It's late... Stay, if you'd like to."

"Okay." Jesse stepped forward to join Carter at the sink, his gaze traveling over his body. "You are a hot mess, Hamilton."

"I'm *itchy*," Carter told him, voice trembling with laughter. "You need to do something about that thing on your face if you want to do anything like this ever again." He laughed at Jesse's noise of outrage, then let out an embarrassing squawk after Jesse grabbed him around the waist.

"The beard is another thing I'm going to teach you to love," Jesse told him. He leaned in to rub it over Carter's cheek and neck, squeezing tighter while Carter squirmed.

"Get off me," Carter gasped, unable to hold back his laughter, his skin tingling under the onslaught. "Stop or I'll shave you in your sleep! And no coffee tomorrow morning!"

"Ohhh, fine. Don't be so dramatic." Jesse lifted his head and gave Carter a wink. "Will you make me coffee if I *let* you shave it off tomorrow morning?"

"Maybe," Carter replied. "You have to help me change the sheets, too. All bets are off if I develop a rash from that fucking thing, though."

Their laughter echoed off the bathroom tiles as they moved to the shower to clean up.

Chapter Nine

"Why am I doing this again?" Carter asked under his breath, leaning in to speak in Riley's ear.

Riley chuckled. "Because you told me you wanted to learn to cook."

"It seemed like a good idea at the time. I'm having second thoughts."

Riley had been taking cooking classes twice a month for the last several months and he'd enjoyed them a lot. When Carter had told him he wanted to improve his cooking skills, Riley had suggested they go to the classes together. Carter had sounded willing at the time, but now he seemed less convinced. In fact, Carter appeared tense in general. It wasn't exactly what Riley had been hoping for.

Carter had been quiet on the cab ride to the cooking school on Amsterdam Avenue on the Upper West Side, not the light-hearted, relaxed man Riley had spent time with lately. Now that they were there, he seemed even more tense, if that was possible.

Class hadn't begun yet and they could still ditch it if it made Carter that uncomfortable. He knew Carter wasn't much of a cook, but he'd honestly thought it would be fun for the two of them. Something they hadn't done before. He couldn't quite figure out what Carter's hang-up was.

"We can leave if you want," he offered softly.

"No, it's fine."

Riley began to protest that he wanted it to be more than fine, but when a woman in a chef's hat stepped to the front of the room he shut up. Perhaps ten years older than him, she had a wiry, lean body and dark hair pulled up in a practical knot at the back of her head. She'd taught the knife skills classes Riley had attended the previous month.

"My name is Marisol King and I'll be teaching class today. I've been a chef for twenty-plus years, and believe me when I say that although this class should be fun, I'm not going to go easy on you. I want you to learn."

She scanned the room and nodded, smiling at Riley, then at a woman across the room. "I recognize a few familiar faces from previous classes. Riley, Linda, I see you've brought your partners" — out of the corner of his eye, Riley saw Carter jerk in surprise — "so welcome to our class. Perhaps you can show them what's been taught in previous classes. Tonight, we'll be cooking an eight-course meal. Now, we don't have time for everyone to make all eight courses, unfortunately. So, we'll divide into two groups and each group will focus on half of the menu. My assistant, Stuart, will help me with demonstrations." A tattooed, attractive hipster in chef's whites waved to the class. "Please follow me to the kitchen."

As the class stood, Riley shot Carter a quizzical glance, wondering why Carter had reacted that way to being called Riley's partner. Obviously, they had been mistaken for a couple, but he'd thought Carter was a lot more comfortable with being out about his sexuality. Carter waved off his questioning look as they trooped into the kitchen and he didn't have an opportunity to ask him any further questions.

Including them, there were sixteen people in the class. Riley watched Carter while they slipped on aprons and was relieved when Carter held out his right arm so Riley could help fold up the cuff of his gray shirt.

"Thanks, man," Carter said when it was neatly folded out of the way. "Need help with yours?" Riley relaxed a fraction. Maybe Carter just needed some time to acclimate.

After dividing the class into two groups and directing the couples to their stations, where ingredients, utensils and recipe sheets were all laid out, Chef Marisol began her lecture.

"Tonight's class is about aphrodisiacs. An aphrodisiac is a substance that increases sexual desire. Some, like chilies, chocolate and oysters, are obvious ones. I designed this menu with some less common choices. One of the dishes is honey-glazed salmon with chopped basil. Many of the ingredients are filled with compounds that help to enhance the sex drive on a physical level. Salmon is packed with omega-3 fatty acids, which keep sex-hormone production at its peak. Others, like the honey, aren't direct aphrodisiacs, yet their taste and texture heighten the senses, contributing to a more sensual experience. Use all of your senses tonight. Sight, smell, taste, feel, even sound can be arousing. Savor the textures, not just as you eat but while you're preparing the food."

Carter leaned in again. "Uh, Ri? What the hell kind of class did you sign us up for?"

"Shit," Riley muttered. "I didn't realize what the focus of the class was. They do special classes every so often, but I assumed this would be Italian or Thai night or something."

"Only you." Carter rolled his eyes and Riley gave him a sheepish look.

Chef Marisol directed the class to read through their instructions and recipes then had them begin prepping. While the class sliced and diced, she spoke again. "For a chef, or anyone who loves cooking, preparing food is a gesture of love. We cook for the people we care about, for friends, family and lovers. We cook to nourish them on every level."

Carter and Riley worked quietly for a while, taking instruction from Marisol and Stuart as they milled around the room, making suggestions and offering tips. Riley showed Carter the proper way to hold a chef's knife. When he stood behind Carter, reaching around him and cupping his hand around Carter's to demonstrate, Carter leaned back against his chest. Riley wondered if Carter was even aware that he was doing it. Now that they were both dating other men, they'd spent the past month walking a very fine line. Riley was always scrupulously aware of his actions so he didn't let himself get caught up in the familiarity of Carter and forget Will. Riley stepped back, both to give himself more space and to show Carter how to chop the herbs.

Carter shot him a grin. "You just wanted to take this class to show off, didn't you?" Carter teased after Riley julienned the basil and dumped it into a prep bowl with a flourish.

"Well, yeah," Riley replied with a laugh when he turned to face Carter. "Of course, I did. What did you expect?"

"How long have you been together?" Marisol asked from behind them, surprising them both. Riley blinked and glanced away from Carter's warm gaze.

"I'm sorry?" Riley asked, wondering if he'd heard her right.

"You two are dating, right? How long have you been together?"

Carter's laugh sounded strained. "We're not dating."

She blinked at them. "With the theme of the class and your closeness, I just assumed..."

"This is my best friend, Carter," Riley explained. "We've been friends for fifteen years. And I clearly didn't pay attention when I chose the class. I expected Italian night and got...something else entirely."

"Ahh, that explains it." She gave them an assessing glance. "Well, very nice to meet you, Carter. Glad you joined us." She peered at Riley's prep bowls. "Excellent knife work, Riley. Much improved."

After she walked away, Riley glanced at Carter, who shook his head. "Guess I should have seen that coming."

"Us being mistaken for a couple?" Riley turned back to the counter and de-stemmed strawberries.

"Yeah. I mean, I can see how people would do that."

Riley shrugged. "Sure. We're a hell of a lot closer than your average guys, I'd imagine."

Carter's laugh was sardonic. "No wonder Will hates me."

"Will doesn't hate you." Carter raised an eyebrow at him. "He *doesn't*. He's not entirely comfortable with our friendship, but he didn't have a problem with us taking this class and when I mentioned you were seeing Jesse, he relaxed quite a bit." Riley passed a bowl of de-stemmed strawberries over to Carter to slice. "How are things going with Mr. Murtagh, by the way?"

Carter let out a small choking sound. "God, please don't ever call him that. All I can think of is dating Murtagh Senior. Which is more or less like dating my father. *Jesse* is fine, however. It's going well."

"Fine, fine. I won't refer to your boyfriend as anything but Jesse." Riley paused and glanced over at Carter. "He *is* your boyfriend, yes?"

Carter shrugged. "We haven't exactly had that conversation yet. We're seeing each other a couple of times a week and I'm also seeing Kyle. Not sure if he is seeing other people or not. We haven't really talked about it."

"You're being careful?"

Rolling his eyes, Carter gave him a disgusted look. "You're kidding, right?"

"No."

"I've been having safe sex since I was seventeen. I think I can manage it."

"I'm just checking," Riley protested.

"We're good, I promise," Carter said.

Dinner was served in a small dining area. Normally, it was a more relaxed, casual atmosphere and everyone dined at a large table, but in light of the menu's theme, the lights had been dimmed and there were small tables set up with linens and candles. Wine was served along with dinner and when Riley reached for his wineglass, Carter stopped him. "This was a good idea."

Riley smiled. "I'm glad. I think Sadie and Dylan will be suitably impressed with what you've learned."

The smile Carter gave him in return was blinding. "You might never make a chef out of me, but at least I can say I'm not totally hopeless anymore. And seeing you so in your element...it was good. You sure you don't want to become a chef?"

Riley laughed and picked up his glass. "I'm sure. I love my job. This is just a hobby."

Carter took a bite of his food and made a happy sound of contentment. "A delicious one. Damn, this is good."

"You made half of it," Riley countered.

"I don't think I could have done it without you." Carter's tone was earnest and Riley smiled.

After class, they stood on the sidewalk in front of the building.

"Want to share a cab?" Carter asked.

"I'm actually heading over to Will's," Riley said.

Carter nodded. "Got it. Maybe I'll give Jesse a call, actually."

"If you see him tonight, give him my regards."

"Yeah, same to Will, if that won't be weird."

Riley shrugged. "To be honest, we're still figuring it all out, but I think he's getting more comfortable with things."

"Good, good." Carter flashed a smile at him. "Well, there's a cab coming. Why don't you grab it and I'll wait until I see what's going on with Jesse?"

"Okay." Riley leaned in for a brief hug. "Thanks for coming tonight."

"Thanks for inviting me. It wound up being pretty fun."

* * * *

"Hey, how was class?" Will brushed his lips across Riley's.

"Good. Carter managed not to cut off a finger and the food was edible," Riley joked.

Will chuckled and stepped back. "Is he really that bad in the kitchen?"

"Worse." Riley grinned and shut the apartment door behind him. "Nah, he's improving. I think he learned enough to impress his kids, which was his main goal."

"Good." Will walked into the living room and threw a glance over his shoulder. "Want a drink?"

"No, I'm fine. Thanks, though." Riley caught his arm. "Wait. Uh, I have a confession to make."

Will turned to him, a frown creasing his forehead. "What do you mean?"

"Well, the class I signed Carter and me up for was not the Italian cuisine one I planned. It was, ahh, all about aphrodisiacs."

Snorting, Will shook his head, his expression smoothing out. "Seriously?"

"Yeah, seriously. And everyone there was coupled, of course, so the Chef instructing the class assumed Carter and I were, too." What began as a joking confession had begun to feel real. "Not that we did anything inappropriate, but I figured, in the interest of full disclosure…"

"Hey, it's okay." Will's expression softened and he wrapped his arms around Riley's hips, pulling him closer. "Given the circumstances, I think that's to be expected. You don't need to apologize or explain to me. I can see how hard you've worked to make me a priority and now that Carter's dating someone, I feel better about things."

"I'm glad." Riley gave him a relieved smile. "I just wanted to be sure."

"We're good." Will leaned in and gave him a deep, searing kiss. His gaze was intense when he finally pulled back. "I just have one question for you."

Riley licked his tingling lips, then answered. "What's that?"

"Do you think the aphrodisiacs worked?" Will moved his mouth across Riley's jaw, sliding down to nip at his ear while he unbuttoned Riley's shirt.

"No idea," Riley said with a gasp. "I can't tell if it's them or you, or both, but I am really ready to take this to the bedroom."

"Couch is closer." Will muttered the words against the juncture of his neck and shoulder and Riley shuddered when he used his teeth on the sensitive spot.

"Couch it is."

Will walked them backward toward the couch and Riley groaned against his mouth. They tumbled onto it, Will pinning Riley beneath him with an eagerness that surprised him. As Will worked the buttons of his shirt loose and pushed the undershirt up to chest height, Riley vaguely wondered if Carter and Jesse were doing the same thing this evening.

Any rational thought was quelled by Will quickly opening Riley's pants. Will's lips were warm as he trailed them from Riley's navel to his cock, his silky hair brushing across Riley's stomach. Riley held his breath with anticipation as Will grasped the base and brushed his lips over the thickening shaft. His heart thudded at the first deliberate lick Will gave his cock. He closed his eyes, head spinning, as he threaded his fingers through

Will's hair and waited with breathless anticipation. He was disappointed when Will pulled away and sat up, but it was only to strip off his shirt. He tossed it to the floor next to the couch and removed his belt.

Will ran a hand across the fly of his pants and Riley got a glimpse of the outline of his hard cock. Riley reached down to grasp his own dick, watching as Will unbuttoned and unzipped his pants but left them on. Will leaned down again, batting Riley's hand away, and lowered his head. The gentle whoosh of air from his mouth made Riley jerk and he fought to keep from grabbing Will's head again.

Will's touch was sure and steady as he worked Riley over. Kisses to Riley's cock sent pleasure skittering through his body and made his skin prickle with goosebumps. "Will..." he whispered, at a loss for words.

"You like that?" Will asked quietly, his breath against the wet skin making Riley shudder.

"Yeah, God, you have no idea." Riley's tone was fervent. He glanced down and saw Will crouched over him, looking up at him through his lashes, his lips slightly parted. Riley ran an affectionate hand through his hair and pushed Will's head lower. "Please. I need you."

That seemed to be all the encouragement Will required, and when Will slid his mouth over Riley's cock, he groaned. He closed his eyes as Will sucked him, afraid he'd come too quickly. The wet swirl of his tongue and the firm suction made pleasure gather low in his belly, and he cried out when Will caressed his balls, then moved below. The sure, familiar exploration was so arousing he reached back and grasped the arm of the sofa. "Not going to last very long," he said through gritted teeth.

Will tightened his grip as he stroked Riley's shaft and teased along the seam of Riley's balls with his tongue. The low, aching pressure there built to an unbearable level and his body spasmed as he came. Will stroked him through it and cum spattered everywhere. Eyes clenched shut, Riley gasped, raising his hips in time with Will's slow strokes. He stilled Will's hand when it became painfully intense, then sagged back onto the cushions. He looked down and saw cum coating Will's hand and Riley's abs, and Will grinning at him from where he knelt between Riley's thighs.

"Oh, God, that was..." Riley didn't even have words.

"I'm a mess," Will said, but he still grinned. He was a mess, but he was clearly aroused, too, and Riley sat up and took both of his shirts off. He chucked the button-down onto the floor and used the undershirt to clean Will's hand, then himself, and discarded it. His skin was damp and slightly sticky as he shifted to tug off his pants. He knelt in front of Will. He was shirtless and Riley trailed his fingertips across the smooth planes of his chest, then skimmed across his nipples. He dropped one hand to Will's groin and felt the length of Will's cock under his undone fly and boxer briefs. He cupped it, enjoying the way it twitched in his hand through the soft, warm cotton. He kissed Will's shoulder and Will wrapped his arms around Riley as he groaned and pressed into Riley's touch.

He fished Will's cock out from his pants and underwear, stroking him in the space between their bodies as they made out. He felt the desperation in Will's touch. Will kissed Riley more insistently, rocking his hips as Riley teased him. Riley pulled away for a moment, pressing Will back. He shifted so Will sat, leaning against the arm of the sofa, and Riley knelt between his legs. Will's cock was warm and solid in his mouth and the taste of the salty pre-cum on his tongue made him speed up, hoping to coax out more. Will shook under him, clenching the back of Riley's head as he whispered Riley's name. Riley sucked him hard and fast, rolling his balls gently in his hand. Will gave him a brief, choked warning and came, filling Riley's mouth. He drank it down and it wasn't until Will gasped and shuddered that he let go with a slow swipe of his tongue.

Will grabbed his shoulder and shifted their bodies so Riley lay on top of him, their hearts thudding against each other. Will captured his lips, drawing him into a languid, sated kiss before pulling back. Will combed a hand through his hair and tangled their legs together. He closed his eyes and felt the gentle whoosh of Will's breath and the slow strokes Will's fingers made against the bare skin of his back.

* * * *

Riley awoke, confused and disoriented. He could hardly move and his left side was too warm, while his right was chilled. "The hell?" he muttered, words sliding together. Something — no, someone — shifted next to him and his brain finally put the pieces together. "Will?" he asked quietly.

"Huh?" Will slurred.

"We fell asleep on the couch."

"So we did."

Riley opened his eyes, grimacing when the lamp next to the table blinded him. They must have fallen asleep with the lights still on. He tried to move his arm, but it was pinned under Will's body and had gone numb. "C'mon, get up."

"Ugh. My mouth tastes like something died in it."

Riley finally managed to slide out from under Will. "I guarantee you, mine is worse." He rotated his shoulder, feeling blood begin to flow again, and the agonizing prickles of pain that shot through his arm woke him up a little. He held out his other hand to Will, who took it and let Riley pull him up off the couch with a grunt.

They brushed their teeth quickly and Will loaned him a pair of clean boxer briefs to sleep in. Riley climbed into bed and watched Will squint at his phone as he set an alarm and tossed it onto the nightstand. Riley let out a sound of contentment when Will slid into the bed and draped an arm around his waist. "Much more comfortable than the couch," he teased.

"Mmhmm." Will murmured the words against his shoulder and it was only a matter of moments before his breathing evened out and he was asleep. Riley lay awake a while longer, feeling the steady rise and fall of Will's chest against his back.

In the morning, Riley awoke with his underwear around his knees and Will's hand around his cock. He made an inarticulate sound of pleasure, not fully alert yet. The heat of Will's chest scorched Riley's back and the sensation of his lightly haired thigh between Riley's was arousing. Riley drew in a ragged breath and Will pressed a kiss to his shoulder. "You finally woke up."

Riley moaned. "And what a way to wake up." He stretched out, yanking the drawer open to grab a bottle of lube. He slicked his hand and reached back to coat Will's cock.

"You want me to fuck you?" Will asked.

"No time for prep, I'm afraid." Riley twisted to give Will a quick, hard kiss. "Between my thighs."

Once they were aligned, he coaxed Will to move. It was awkward at first, but they found a rhythm. Will groaned in Riley's ear and held out his hand for lube so he could stroke Riley's cock. They lay on their sides, Will fucking the space between his thighs, the tip of his dick occasionally nudging Riley's balls or the cleft of his ass if they got too enthusiastic. Will had a tight grip around his cock and the feeling made his head swim.

He came first and Will just a few moments later, panting and shuddering against him. Sticky and spent, Riley had to fight to keep from falling back to sleep.

"Shower before work?" Will asked. Riley smiled and nodded, finally beginning to believe everything was on track with his life. He had a great job and his friendship with Carter, and his relationship with Will was solid. *What more could I ask for?*

Chapter Ten

Carter glanced down at the pink bakery box in his left hand as he waited at Kate's door, then back up when the door opened and Dylan flung himself forward with a happy shout.

"*Dad!*"

Carter hung onto his things after Dylan collided with his legs, but wobbled dangerously as Dylan started climbing.

"Whoa, buddy, be careful of the cookies!"

Dylan shot backward at his father's words and Carter flailed, overcompensating for the abrupt change.

"Jesus!"

"Don't take the Lord's name in vain, Dad! And for Christ's sake, don't drop the cookies!"

Carter dropped everything and laughed. Kneeling down, he gathered Dylan into his arms, then peered up at Kate, standing in the doorway.

"What on Earth is going on out here?" she asked, her voice wavering with suppressed laughter as Carter got to his feet.

Carter dragged his briefcase back onto his shoulder while Dylan rescued the pink box from where it had fallen to the floor. "The usual—mayhem and destruction."

Dylan raced back into the apartment with a shout, while Kate and Carter followed behind, chatting. Sadie was at the counter when they all walked into the kitchen, and did a double-take when she spotted her father.

"Daddy, your hair is gone!" she exclaimed and hopped down from her stepstool, then ran over to meet Carter.

Carter laid his briefcase on a chair by the kitchen door. "Almost!" Squatting down, he bent forward slightly so Sadie could run her little hands over what was left of his hair. She patted Carter's head gently, her expression rapt.

"Do you like it?" Carter asked with a grin.

Sadie nodded vigorously. "Uh-huh! Your head feels like Remus' butt!"

Carter chuckled and straightened up again. "That's the first time anyone's ever told me my head feels like a stuffed hedgehog's bum, Sadie. Thanks!"

"You're welcome. We're having tacos for dinner," she added. "There's chicken and those orange thingies. Um…seafoods? They sorta look like bugs."

"Shrimp?" Carter guessed. He forced himself not to grimace as Sadie nodded eagerly. "Mmm, yummy."

Carter pulled off his suit coat and left it with his bag, then glanced around Kate's kitchen. There were things both familiar and strange in the bright space and an odd melancholy filled his heart. The kids' chatter was the same, as was Leo's tail battering Carter's shins, and the ponytail trailing over Kate's shoulder. New art hung on the refrigerator, though, Dylan was missing a front tooth and Sadie was wearing pink fingernail polish.

Stifling a sigh, Carter moved to the island to stand beside his ex while the kids pulled themselves up onto stools.

"Want some help?" He smiled when Kate raised her brows.

"You can't cook, Dad!" Dylan laughed when Carter raised an eyebrow.

"True, but I can chop vegetables like a pro, kiddo."

Dylan watched Kate hand Carter a bowl of tomatoes and a zucchini and his eyes grew round as Carter diced the vegetables. "Have you been practicing?"

"Oh, maybe a little." Carter winked broadly at his kids. "I thought I'd learn to cook more than grilled cheese sandwiches and spaghetti with sauce from a jar."

"Hey, I like those things, Dad!"

The family fell into easy banter. The kids talked about school while Carter oohed and aahed, and he caught up with Kate in quick snatches, too.

"I heard what Sadie said about your hedgehog-butt haircut," Kate observed when they finally sat down to eat. "I think this is the shortest I've ever seen it!"

Carter nodded and picked up a bottle of Tabasco. "I didn't mean for the guy who cuts my hair to go this short," he admitted and shook the chili sauce over his food. "But it's easy and I kind of like it."

"I like these bugs," Sadie declared abruptly and eyed the taco in her hand.

Dylan was quick to agree. "Bugs are yummy!"

Carter hid a smile behind his water glass while Kate cringed.

"Those are shrimp, honey. Please don't tell your grandmother that Daddy and I served you bugs."

"But I like them." Sadie stared at her mother and drew her brows together.

"I like them, too," Carter told her, "and I'm sure we'll make shrimp again sometime."

Sadie brightened. "This weekend?"

"Well, yeah, if that's what you want."

Kate raised her brows at him. "You think you can handle the recipe? No disrespect to your newly acquired knife skills, but there are a lot of ingredients…"

"I'll manage," Carter replied, trying to convince himself as well as Kate. "Just write everything down for me. I can always call in reinforcements if I need to."

"Like Auntie Audrey?" Dylan asked. "She makes the best cookies."

"Auntie Audrey's cookies are amazing," Carter agreed, "but if she's not around I can call your Uncle Dan—"

"He lives a million miles away!"

"—or Uncle Ri, or even my friend, Jesse. They both live right here in the city."

Dylan cut a narrow glance at him. "And they know how to cook?"

"They're better cooks than I am." Carter turned a withering glare on Kate, who was snorting with laughter. "Especially Jesse. Uncle Ri's been taking some cooking lessons, though—"

"Which means he's a much better cook than Daddy," Kate cut in, while Sadie turned a serious look on her father.

"You should take cooking lessons, Daddy. That way you won't need to call for help when you're cooking bugs."

"Stop telling me I'm eating bugs, girl!" Carter mock-glared at his children while they fell into each other, laughing. "And for your information, I have been taking cooking lessons."

Kate furrowed her brows. "Really?"

"Okay, one lesson. But I learned a lot."

Kate raised an eyebrow and Carter's stomach sank a little.

"Couples' cooking class?" she asked and smirked when Carter rubbed the back of his neck.

"No."

"That's...sort of sweet."

"It was a regular old cooking class, Kate—"

"And I'll have to send a thank-you to whomever convinced you to attend," she continued. "You never showed any interest in learning to cook when you and I were together, after all," she added and smiled brightly at Sadie.

Carter cleared his throat. "You're right, I didn't. I had fun learning the other night, though, and got to hang out with Riley for a change."

Kate appeared skeptical. "Haven't you and Riley been spending a lot of time together?"

"We were. Then we weren't." Carter put down his fork, feeling less hungry than a moment before. "His, um, friend, Will, thought Ri and I were spending too much time together. Asked Ri to back off a bit."

"Ugh." Kate pulled a face.

"Yeah. Ri doesn't want to mess things up between them, so we cut back on hanging out. The cooking class invitation came out of nowhere."

Kate's demeanor relaxed. "I'm glad you and Riley are reconnecting."

"Me, too. It was weird not seeing him or speaking to him." Carter sipped his water, then ran his fingers over the glass' edge. "We're still figuring out how things work between us. And with Riley's friend."

"The friend named Will." Kate's gaze lost focus for a moment, then met Carter's as her face brightened. "I met him!"

Carter remembered the paparazzi photos he'd seen in the paper. "The opera?"

"They were there for the *Giulio Cesare* gala. I bumped into Riley during the intermission and he introduced me to Will."

"Nice. Will's an opera aficionado?"

"Honestly, I didn't talk to him very much, but he seemed pretty excited to be there. More so than you would have been," she pointed out with a wink to soften the barb in her words.

"Hey, I am a great opera date. I don't complain or fall asleep, I'm polite when everyone plays Obscure Opera Facts and I look spectacular in a tuxedo." Carter smiled at Kate's chuckle. He'd never made a secret about not caring for opera over the years. He'd taken genuine pleasure in Riley's and Kate's delight, though, and missed those moments.

"Daddy, what are we doing for your birthday?"

Carter glanced at his son in surprise. "Well, some friends are taking me out for dinner on Sunday night to celebrate, but I thought you and Sadie and I could go apple picking this weekend. There's a lot of fall festivals going on around the city, too, so — "

Dylan cut him off. "No, no, no, that's not what I mean. I mean what are we doing?" He gestured meaningfully at his family seated around the table. "We always have dinner and cake for the family, Daddy."

Carter's heart squeezed and he floundered for something to say. He hadn't planned anything family-related for his birthday. His parents had no plans to acknowledge the day and goodness knew why Kate would arrange a party. He was still considering how to reply when Kate touched his forearm.

"We could all go out for lunch on Sunday afternoon if you like." She smiled at the children and Carter. "Daddy can pick a place and I'll come meet you."

Sadie's face pulled into a frown. "Can we get birthday cake in a restaurant? And what about Grandma and Grandpa and Auntie Audrey and Uncle Max?"

"I'm sure we can get one, honey, even if I have to bring one myself in a box," Kate replied. "Grandma and Grandpa are going out of town, but let's call Audrey and Max after dinner — if they don't already have plans, I'm sure they'll want to come."

Sadie and Dylan exchanged a look then turned back to their parents.

"That sounds fun," Sadie told them.

Carter nodded and gave Kate a smile. "It does sound fun, thanks."

"No one else can come, though," Dylan declared, his gaze shifting to meet Kate's. "This is a family party."

Carter wondered at the bubble of tension he sensed between his ex and their children, but kept quiet as the conversation turned to cake flavors.

"What did Dylan mean?" he asked after dinner. He carried plates to the sink, where Kate was rinsing them. "That 'no outsiders at the Hamilton family dinner' thing?"

Kate gave him a rueful smile. "You caught that, huh?"

"It was hard not to."

"Yeah, well. When Dylan decides something, it's like talking to a brick wall. He reminds me of...well, me, actually."

"Karma is a bitch," Carter joked, though he wondered why Kate's cheeks flushed pink. "What's got his dander up this time? Everything okay?"

"Oh, gosh, yes, it's nothing bad. It's just...different. For the kids, I mean. And well, for me, too."

Carter reached to turn off the water, gently taking hold of Kate's wet hands, turning her to face him. "What's different?"

"I went on a date," she blurted. "A couple of dates, actually."

"Oh." Carter blinked a couple of times before letting go of her hands. "Okay. With someone I know?"

"I don't think so, other than in passing." Kate furrowed her brow in thought and she turned back to the sink. "Robert's on the opera planning committee. I've known him for a couple of years. When he asked me to lunch, I thought, 'Well, at least we have something in common.' It seemed easier than a blind date, you know? So, we had lunch last week and again this week. It was nice and we thought we'd try dinner. We're going out tomorrow night while the kids are at your place."

Carter nodded slowly, handing Kate another plate to rinse before a thought struck him. "Has he met Sadie and Dylan?"

"No," Kate denied quickly. "Robert and I have only been out twice, for God's sake. I'm not ready to introduce him to the kids and they're definitely not ready to meet him. I told them I was dating, though, after that second time." She sighed. "They aren't particularly happy with the changes I've made in my social life."

Carter grimaced, though he felt relieved to hear Kate was being cautious with introductions. When they'd split, he'd known they'd both eventually begin dating. At the time, he'd hoped the new person in his life would be Riley. He suspected the kids would need time to adjust to a Riley who was more than just Daddy's best friend, but they'd also known Riley their whole lives and loved him. Now, with Riley out of the picture, the idea of introducing Sadie and Dylan to someone new was terrifying.

"Did they give you a hard time?" he asked Kate, angling his head toward the kids seated at the table.

"Oh, yeah. Dylan gave me the third degree. I swear I thought he was going to ask me for Robert's tax returns." She shook her head and Carter put a hand over his mouth to hide his smile. "And Sadie...well. She didn't talk to me for a couple of days."

Carter boggled. "You're kidding."

"Nope. She shut me out almost completely. She'd answer me if I asked her a question and while she never avoided being in the same room, she was like a different kid." Kate smiled sadly. "You and Sadie have always been close, but she really is her daddy's girl."

"Oh, come on." Carter wiped his hands on the towel while Kate shut off the faucet and closed the dishwasher. "I'd never tell the kids to give you a hard time about living your own life, Kate."

"Oh, I know." Kate crossed to the counter and picked up the pink bakery box, yanking at the knot of twine holding the box closed. "They still decided I was the bad guy in all this, basically because I decided to go out to lunch as a single woman for the first time in a decade."

With a flourish, she flipped the lid on the box up but stopped short at the sight of its contents. "Oh, man, these are Bow Tie cookies."

"Apricot and raspberry," Carter put in. "I saw them at the bakery near my office and remembered how much the three of you like them."

"I almost love you in a romantic way right now, though, I'll have to work out for an extra hour to burn off all the butter I'm about to eat. Will you make coffee?"

They waited until they'd finished dessert before resuming talking, sitting at the island after Sadie and Dylan wandered off.

"So, what about you?" Kate asked.

"What about me?"

"Are you seeing anyone? Making lots of new friends who are doing over your wardrobe?" She met Carter's gaze over the rim of her cup. "I've noticed some changes in the last couple of weeks, Carter. The haircut, the smiley face, the new clothes and new glasses...I mean, you're wearing blue plaid, for crying out loud, and it is not a subtle pattern."

Carter cleared his throat, conscious of the heat crawling up his neck. "It was time to update some of my things."

"Are you really telling me that you became a cool dude out of the blue?"

"Hey." Carter frowned. "I've always been cool," he declared and popped another raspberry cookie into his mouth.

"Carter, you've never been this cool," Kate countered. "You're dangerously close to being too hip to hang out above 59th Street."

Carter choked and nearly knocked over his coffee cup in the process. He glared at Kate as he coughed and spluttered, then finally managed to grunt out a raspy, "You suck."

Kate grinned. "And you haven't answered my question—are you seeing someone?"

"Someones, actually," Carter replied and shifted in his seat after Kate raised an eyebrow.

"Really?"

"Uh, yes?"

"I have no way of knowing if you don't tell me."

"I've been going out here and there," Carter managed, cursing himself for blushing and bumbling. "Most of the outings haven't gone anywhere, but a couple…have."

He shrugged at Kate's encouraging nod. "There's nothing serious going on—I'm not trying to find a grand romance or anything. Just learning things about myself. Trying to understand my life again, if that makes sense."

"It does, actually—what do you think I've been doing for the past six months?" Kate looked weary, but she waved Carter off when he tried to apologize. "So, there are special someones? Am I allowed to ask you that?"

"Of course, you are." Carter drained the last of his coffee before placing the cup back on the island. "And the answer is sort of."

"So you won't be introducing the kids to anyone soon?"

"I've been thinking of introducing them to a couple of my friends this weekend. Especially after hearing about their reaction to Robert, too. I don't want them to think I'm actively looking for a boyfriend."

Kate widened her blue eyes comically and Carter's confusion melted into dread. "Oh, shit."

"Language!" Sadie shouted from the couch in the corner and Carter clapped a hand over his mouth to stifle a wild laugh.

Kate grimaced. "Oh, my God. Honestly, this family some days...I don't even know what it's like to be normal anymore."

Carter cocked an eyebrow. "Did you ever?"

"Yes, I did, thank you. Or I thought I did, anyway." Kate made a face. "Maybe I was wrong."

Carefully, Carter placed his hand beside Kate's on the table, their pinkie fingers almost touching. "You weren't," he told her. "I just think we have a new normal."

Kate nodded slowly. "A new normal...where you're dating men."

"Yeah." Carter licked his lips. "I can't see myself dating women right now." He looked away, letting the unspoken 'after you' hang between them. "And as far as the guys go...there's something there I need to understand better. I used to think it was strictly a Riley thing, but it turns out that's not so."

"Huh." Kate rubbed her fingers over her lips in thought. "So, you're bi?"

"It would seem so."

"You don't know?"

"I'm still figuring everything out." Carter grimaced. "I'm definitely attracted to both male and female genders, obviously."

"Okay," Kate replied. "I guess that explains why I keep seeing photos of you hanging out with that hot beast, Jesse Murtagh. Is he one of the boyfriends?"

Carter lowered his head to rest against the island's countertop. "Oh, God. They're not my boyfriends. They're just good friends."

"Okay, fine. Do your parents know about your 'just good friends'?"

"Well, if you've noticed the paparazzi photos, then they certainly have. I don't speak to either of them about personal things, though, and I wouldn't give them specific details."

Kate hummed thoughtfully. "I see photos of Jesse Murtagh out with women, too, so the odds are they don't know what to make of any of it."

"Jesse's got girlfriends and boyfriends—he's not big on monogamous relationships," Carter added.

"Ah. And he's the one who's been giving you the makeover?"

"He and my other friend, Kyle, have been taking turns. Because, of course, Jesse and Kyle get along like a house on fire." Carter lifted his head enough to fold his arms and tuck them under this chin. "I suspect they've roped Malcolm in, too, somehow. Malcolm set me up with a new optician to pick out frames for my glasses and I don't remember asking him to do any such thing."

Kate laughed. "Well, the new frames are nice. And, for what it's worth, you look good, Car."

"Yeah?"

"Yeah. And I don't just mean the new clothes and haircut, either. You seem a little less like you have a stick jammed sideways up your ass."

Carter barked out a laugh and straightened in his chair. "Thanks. I'm still stressed as hell, honestly. And worried about everything. But I'm better than I was six months ago, so that's something."

* * * *

The kids approached Carter on Saturday while they were out shopping to talk about their mother's dating. Neither reacted well to realizing Carter not only supported Kate's decision but was also seeing people himself. Dylan in particular seemed sour and threw down the plastic bags of Halloween candy he'd been carrying in a show of temper.

"But, Dad, why?" He looked at his father, the hurt clear in his blue gaze. "If you and Mommy don't want to be married anymore, why can't you both just stay alone?"

Carter shrugged. "Your mom and I don't want to be alone forever, buddy. Eventually, we'll want someone else to share our lives with and to share with you."

"Well, I don't feel like sharing with anyone new." Dylan stuck out his lip in a sulk.

Carter's heart ached to see his son hurting. Carefully, he leaned over and scooped Dylan up, cuddling him close, and smiled down at Sadie, who bent to retrieve the fallen bags.

"You don't have to share anything right now, Dyl. If and when your mom or I think we've found someone special enough to introduce to you guys, we'll talk to you about it first, okay?"

"Okay," Dylan mumbled into the collar of Carter's gray field jacket. "Mommy said something kind of like that, too."

"Didn't you believe her?"

"I guess. I wanted to make sure you said the same thing, though." Dylan reached up to wrap his arms around Carter's neck. "'Cause you're my Dad, even if you live away from us."

"Mommy and I try always to check in with each other when it comes to you guys." Carter met Sadie's glance over Dylan's shoulder. "I promise we'll make an effort to be even better about that."

"But what's going to happen if Mommy likes someone who doesn't like kids?" Sadie wondered. "Or if you find a lady like Alex? She hates kids."

"Okay, first of all, Alex does not hate kids. She doesn't want to have any of her own and that's okay—not every woman wants to be someone's mommy, Sadie." Dropping one hand to Sadie's shoulder, Carter steered them toward the checkout lines. "But while you and Alex may not have been best friends, she did a lot of nice things for you over the years."

"I still wouldn't want you to marry her," Sadie grumbled, and Carter had to bite back a smile.

"I wouldn't go out with a person who didn't like children and neither would your mom. I'm going to put you down, buddy," he told Dylan and let out a heartfelt grunt as he set his son down on the floor. "What the heck have you been eating, rocks?"

He smiled at Dylan's laughter, then noticed Sadie's head cocked in thought. "What's up, Sadie?"

"So if you or Mommy really liked someone, but they didn't like Dyl or me, you would tell them to take a hike?"

"I...would probably use different wording, but, yes, basically." He laid the bags on the checkout belt, organizing his thoughts before he continued. "Honey, I don't think your mom or I would even get to the 'I like this person' stage if we knew they didn't want to share their lives with you and Dylan, too."

"So, if that guy Robert doesn't like us, Mommy won't go out with him?"

Carter could almost hear the wheels turning in his children's little heads. "Your mom wouldn't go out with someone who didn't like children, no. And that means she's already talked to Robert about you two and liked what he told her. Now she's trying to get to know Robert better, so she can decide if he is special enough to get to know *you*. If she decides he is, I want you to be nice to him."

Both children balked, complaining loudly while Carter paid for the candy and shepherded them outside. After half a block of their bitching, he led them out of the flow of pedestrian traffic to stand by the window of what he belatedly realized was a doughnut shop. Briefly, he considering using pastry to shut them up, then squatted down in front of them to hash it out instead.

"Guys, listen. Mom and I have never done this before and we're trying hard to get it right. A big part of what we worry about every day is that we're doing the right thing for the two of you." He stared from one to the other, recognizing anger in Sadie's gaze. He ignored the burn in his chest.

"This wouldn't be happening if you and Mommy were still together." Sadie folded her arms over her chest and Carter reached out to straighten the collar of her pink pea coat.

He drew a breath, to make sure he still could, before speaking again. "I know that, Sadie. You have no idea how sorry I am that I messed everything up between Mommy and me and that you and Dylan were part of that. That's why your mom and I are trying really hard not to make mistakes now. If Mommy decides that someone is ready to meet you two, it means she trusts them to be good to you. It also means she trusts *you* to be good to her friend. You get what I'm saying?"

Sadie and Dylan exchanged a long glance before turning back to their father. "Yeah. I guess so," Sadie told him.

"But we don't have to like Mommy's friends unless we want to," Dylan added. His eyebrows were drawn together in a way that reminded Carter abruptly of himself when he was feeling stubborn or unhappy.

"That's true, Dyl, you don't. But I can tell you right now that it'll make things a lot easier for you and Mommy if you try to like her friends."

"What about you?" Sadie asked, her face troubled. "Will it make things easier for you if we like Mommy's friends?"

"Don't worry about me, sweetheart." Carter's throat tightened without warning and it was a moment before he could speak. Carefully, he reached out to smooth back a tendril of hair from her forehead. "If you and Dyl are okay with Mommy's friends, then I will be, too."

* * * *

The kids kept at Carter through the rest of the weekend, asking questions and voicing their concerns. Unable to be completely honest with them about his dating, Carter felt on edge and guilty for lying by omission. By the time the family lunch had concluded on Sunday, he was emotionally raw and wrung out, and totally unwilling to celebrate his birthday.

He walked home with Audrey and Max after they'd bid the kids goodbye, putting serious thought toward rescheduling the birthday dinner as they approached his block. He had his phone in his hand when Max slung an arm over his shoulders.

"Don't do it, dude."

Carter turned to Max, his brows drawing together in confusion. "Don't do what?"

"Don't call your hipster squad to tell them you don't want to eat steak and drink booze with them tonight."

Carter blinked. His mouth fell open slightly and a smile broke out on Max's handsome face. "How the hell did you know that?"

"You had a 'don't touch me' look on your face while we were eating lunch." Max screwed up his face in a pained scowl.

"I did not."

"You looked constipated," Audrey added, slipping her arm through Carter's free elbow. "And really, sweetie, no one wants that. You should go out tonight." She nodded while Carter shook his head.

"I don't think I'm up to it, Aud. The kids really ran me ragged this weekend and all I want to do tonight is sack out on the couch with ice cream and Netflix."

"Oh, no." Audrey dropped Carter's elbow, sliding her arm around his waist. "You cannot stay at home and brood on your birthday. Especially not when a bunch of hot guys want to take you out! And Max, of course."

Carter laughed at Max's offended noise.

"You just need a couple of hours of kid-free quiet and a nap," Audrey continued. "And maybe a hot shower. A change of clothes wouldn't hurt, either."

"What's wrong with my clothes?" Carter glanced down at his jeans and black wool sweater—both new and rather nice, he thought—before he grimaced. A small handprint decorated the sweater's hem, lime green icing perfectly forming the palm and five fingers. "Ugh."

"Don't worry, it'll come out." Audrey gave him a squeeze while Max laughed. "Plus, now you have an excuse to wear something a little sexier when you go out tonight."

Carter grimaced. "Oh, yeah, because 'a little sexier' is what I was going for. No one gives a damn what I look like, Audrey."

"That's not true," Max told him. "I can't wait to see you in something daring tonight, Carter." He widened his eyes dramatically and caught his lower lip between his teeth. "Do you think you'll need a bodyguard to beat back the crowd?"

Carter sank his elbow into Max's ribs. "Get bent, doofus."

"Come on," Audrey chided. "Let's get you into a time out so you can start feeling human again."

* * * *

As Audrey predicted, several hours of quiet worked wonders for Carter's state of mind. By early evening, he was looking forward to going out again, though a bit on edge too. He thought he did a good job of hiding his nerves, until the Zimride door closed and Max turned to him.

"What's up with you?"

"What do you mean?"

"You're blinking like a Chihuahua on a hot date."

Carter's cackling bounced around the back of the car. "What the hell does that even mean?"

"I'm not really sure," Max admitted with a chuckle. "But you look a little, I don't know...incredibly fucking tense?"

"Yeah, well." Carter rubbed the back of his neck with one hand. "I'm introducing some of my oldest friends to a bunch of new ones. It feels a little weird."

"I'm not going to judge you."

The sadness in Max's gaze sent a pang of guilt through Carter. "I know that, Max—I'd never have thought otherwise."

"So, is this about Riley? Because I can't imagine he'd judge you, either, or your friends."

"I'm sure you're right," Carter agreed. "Still feels weird, though."

"Maybe because you're sleeping with a couple of your new friends."

Carter's face heated. "Dude. You've been spending too much time with my sister."

"Okay, fine, you don't want to talk about your fuck buddies." Max reared back in his seat with a laugh when Carter reached out to smack him. "Is it weird because Riley's bringing his boyfriend?"

"A little. I mean, hanging out with Will is just a new level of awkward, because he's not a fan of mine. He and I don't have to be friends, though. If we can hang out in the same room without arguing, Riley will be satisfied."

"So what's the problem?"

Carter ran a hand over his hair in thought. "I've sort of been living in two worlds since Kate and I split up. My job and my family are in one, then in the other —"

" — there's your big gay life," Max finished.

Carter pushed down a flicker of irritation. "Don't be glib."

"I'm not, Carter, I'm trying to talk to you."

"I know. Sorry." Carter blew out a breath. "And you're almost right. I do have this other life with men I've been meeting and dating and it's completely removed from everyone else."

"Until tonight."

"Until tonight," Carter agreed, meeting Max's small smile with one of his own. "I have no idea what I'm doing, you know. Or how to act. What do I do if you all hate one another?"

Max reached out to squeeze Carter's shoulder. "That's not going to happen." The warmth in his touch and demeanor a soothing balm to Carter's nerves. "We all tolerate you, right? So, there's one thing everybody already has in common."

Carter let out a laugh. "I dislike you so much right now."

"Good." Max sat back with a smug smile. "That'll take your mind off being nervous for a while."

Jesse and Kyle were at the bar in the Benjamin Steakhouse, with Gale, Jarrod, Henry and Miles, all men from their shared circles of friends. Carter introduced Max around while Kyle ordered drinks and Jesse slipped an arm around Carter's shoulders. He eyed Carter's tailored shirt, dark jeans and leather jacket with an appreciative grin.

"You're looking good, birthday boy. Hard to believe you spent the whole weekend running around after juvenile human beings!"

"We made bets on whether you'd show or cancel," Kyle threw in. His brown eyes were warm with laughter while Carter scoffed. "Naturally, Big Money over here won." He mimed throwing a cocktail peanut at Jesse, who bowed.

"You owe half your winnings to Max." Carter looked from Jesse to Max with a grin. "He and Audrey are the ones who talked me out of calling to cancel."

"Done." Jesse pulled a money clip from his trouser pocket, quickly peeling off three twenties to hand to Max, who laughed. "I still say Carter would have shown without any outside intervention," Jesse added. "Not even *you* can resist celebrating your birthday with steak and Scotch, sweetheart."

Carter was about to reply when a familiar voice cut through the buzz of the bar.

"Since when is Carter Hamilton a Scotch drinker?"

Carter met Riley's gaze with a rush of gladness. The two friends shared a grin before Carter extended his hand to Will. Another round of introductions began and Carter ignored his own discomfort under Will Martin's gray gaze.

"I started drinking Scotch after meeting these reprobates," he told Riley at last. Carter shook his head while Jesse preened. "Don't worry, though — I give as good as I get."

Max snorted. "He's probably talking about bourbon and cigars, but everything Carter says sounds disconcertingly sexual these days." Carter flicked the side of Max's neck and he let out a yip.

Riley gave him a wide grin. "This reminds me a lot of old times. It's good to see you, Max." He stared at Carter's shorn head with a furrowed brow. "Some of us had a lot more hair back then, though."

"I'm probably to blame for Carter's haircut," Jesse threw in. "He's surprisingly suggestible when he's sleepy, not to mention downright adorable." His smile was sly when Carter turned to glare and the others' laughter rang out around them.

"You're ridiculous," Carter shot back, "though I suppose that's part of your charm." He turned back in surprise when Riley brought a hand up to rest on Carter's shoulder.

"You've always been a sucker for charm, Car," Riley told him, his tone light. He had a strange gleam in his eye as he stared at the men flanking Carter and Max, but his expression softened when he turned to meet Will's gaze. "But, then again, aren't we all."

Carter kept a straight face while Riley and Will made eyes at each other. Will's cool gaze swept over Carter next.

"Thanks for the invite, Carter. It's nice to finally put a face with the name."

"It's not like you've never seen his photo," Riley chided, melting the chill in Will's gaze immediately.

"I don't count grainy newspaper photos, Riley, you know that."

"Well, that's good to hear, because there were a few cameras as we came in," Riley quipped. "So, you can ignore a new crop of grainy newspaper photos featuring not only Carter's face but your own."

Their playful sniping came to an abrupt halt when Jesse began handing out glasses of Scotch.

"We can argue over who's the prettiest girl at the party later, gentlemen. *After* we've finished ragging on the birthday boy."

Carter met Jesse's gaze with a laugh. His friend was really turning on the charm, drawing Riley and Will forward to make small talk with the others. An elbow in Carter's side caught his attention.

"Your boyfriend is something else," Max told him. "Kyle, too. It's like watching twin hurricanes in Armani."

"Jesse's not my boyfriend," Carter replied, "but he and Kyle are definitely something else."

Carter sipped his drink, gratitude surging through him as he watched Jesse and Kyle with the others. They expected nothing from Carter except that he be himself. And Carter was one hundred percent on board with being himself these days, even if it was still a bit scary to do so.

Chapter Eleven

"Fuuuuuuck." Exhausted and wrung out from an orgasm, Riley rested his forehead against the slick shower tiles and struggled to catch his breath. Will pressed a kiss to his shoulder before he slid carefully out. He stepped away to dispose of the condom and water hit Riley's back with a pleasantly warm sting. A few moments later, Will returned, molding his body around Riley's, caressing his chest as he nuzzled the side of his neck.

"You're incredible."

Smiling, Riley turned his head to give Will a quick kiss. "You're not so bad yourself."

Will rested his chin on Riley's shoulder. "God, tonight was exactly what I needed. I swear there's some sort of amnesia that comes over professors every year. We seem to forget just how much work goes into grading papers and scoring exams."

"You'd think you'd at least remember what it was like to be a student," Riley joked. "I never understood why

I'd have papers and exams for all of my classes crammed together in a three-day period."

"No such luck, unfortunately. We're all bastards who assume our class will be every student's priority." Will squeezed him a little tighter. "Tomorrow, it's back to the grindstone for me, but I am glad you talked me into coming over tonight. I needed a break." He pressed another kiss to the top of Riley's shoulder. "And to see you. That always helps me."

Riley's smile widened. "I'm glad to help."

Will's voice was intense when he spoke. "There's something that's been on the tip of my tongue for a while now and I'm going to just blurt it out before I talk myself out of it again." He touched Riley's chin and turned his head so they could look each other in the eye. "I love you, Riley."

Riley froze, his heart beating hard. For a long moment, there was only the sound of water splashing on tile. "Will...I..." He tried to formulate words as his brain whirled, attempting to process what he'd heard.

Will straightened, his touch disappearing from Riley's body. He turned away to face the showerhead on the opposite wall before dunking his head under the stream of water. He reached for soap and washed his body without another word.

"I don't know what to say," Riley finally managed.

Will rinsed off and slicked back his hair from his face. When he turned back to Riley, his expression was blank and his high cheekbones and serious gaze gave him an unfamiliar, stern expression. "I guess that says everything, then."

"I'm not saying I won't get there, Will," Riley said softly. "I'm just not there yet." Riley reached out to touch Will, but he shrugged off the gesture then reached for the shower door. "Please, give me some time," Riley pleaded.

Will stepped out onto the white bathmat and turned to face him. "I'm trying, Riley, but it's been nearly a year since we started seeing each other. I've tried to respect that you're at a very complicated point in your life and still trying to figure out what you want, but how much more time do you need?"

He reached for a towel and wrapped it around himself without drying off. Will disappeared from the bathroom and Riley stared at the empty doorway, feeling helpless and guilty.

By the time Riley dried off and stepped into the bedroom, Will was in bed and the lights were out except for a dim lamp on the nightstand. Riley slipped into a pair of boxers before crawling into bed. He clicked off the light and reached for Will, but he faced away from Riley, his body stiff and unyielding.

Riley sighed and pressed an apologetic kiss to the spot between his shoulder blades. At least Will hadn't left. That had to mean something.

"I'm sorry, Will," he murmured, but there was no reply beyond the quiet, steady sound of his breathing.

* * * *

"I got the wine. Is there anything else you need me to pick up?"

Riley wedged the phone closer to his neck and wrestled the plastic wrap around the tray of *hors d'oeuvres*. Tonight, a handful of friends were coming over for a holiday cocktail party and Carter had offered to help him prepare. "No, I think I'm all set now. You're a lifesaver."

He chuckled in Riley's ear, the sound low and warm. "All part of my duties as best friend and your own personal superhero."

Riley laughed and grabbed the phone with his left hand before he opened the fridge door and surveyed the interior. The fridge practically overflowed and he wasn't quite sure where to put the tray. "You might be overselling things a bit. I only asked you to pick up some wine."

"No, no, get this right. Your best friend is a bona-fide superhero. I'll expect you to laud my praises at the party tonight."

Riley snorted and managed to balance the tray on several other containers. "I'll see what I can do."

"Are you sure you don't need anything else?" Carter's tone turned more serious. "I'd be happy to help. The kids are with Kate tonight and I don't have anything else going on before the party."

Riley closed the fridge door and surveyed the messy kitchen. "I wouldn't mind some company while I finish prepping and cleaning. Will is grading exams and won't be here until later."

"I'll be there in twenty," Carter promised.

"See you then." Riley hung up with a smile on his face, but it fell when he contemplated his relationship with Will.

In the week since Will's 'I love you' they'd hardly seen each other. Although he knew Will *was* exceptionally busy with classes at the moment, Riley couldn't help but feel it was a convenient excuse for avoiding him.

The morning after Will's admission, he'd woken Riley up with a hell of a blowjob and a smile. Riley had tried to talk to him about what had happened the night before, but he'd assured Riley that it wasn't necessary and that he should stop worrying and forget about it. Riley couldn't shake the feeling that it continued to hang over them, however, and the longer they went without discussing it, the more that feeling deepened. With Christmas only a few days away, Riley hoped they could figure out how to enjoy the holidays together. Will wasn't planning to go to Long Island to visit his family and Riley certainly hadn't received any invitations from Jonathon and Geneva, so he'd been looking forward to spending Christmas alone with Will. Certainly better than his drunken, lonely Christmas at the beach house the year before.

Riley shook himself out of his ruminations and reached for his iPad to skim the planning document for the party. He'd considered having the party catered, but work was relatively slow this time of year and Riley had more accumulated time off than he'd ever been able to use, so he'd spent much of the past week Christmas shopping and preparing for the party. If not for the fight with Will, it would have been the perfect week.

All he had left to make was the wild mushroom-goat cheese phyllo triangles. He'd just finished slicing the mushrooms and mincing the rosemary and thyme when he heard a brisk rap and the sound of a key in the lock. Carter came in, juggling a case of wine and a brown paper bag with a handle, his cheeks pink from the cold. Riley quickly rinsed his hands and dried them on a dish towel before hurrying over to Carter.

"Let me get that." He took the wine from Carter's hands and smiled at him.

Carter grinned back and set the bag on the floor. "The good news is, the white should be adequately chilled already. It's been cold and windy all day and the temperature just keeps dropping."

"Is this when I'm supposed to call you a superhero?" Riley teased. "Braving the icy Manhattan wind to bring me wine?"

Carter—who had been unwinding a black cashmere scarf from around his neck—paused and gave Riley a serious look. "No, see, you're getting this all wrong. Save the effusive praise for the party tonight."

Riley snorted and set the wine on the dining room table. "Well, wow me with your ability to put the whites in the wine fridge and the reds on the bar there and I'll see what I can do."

Carter shot him the finger before Riley headed back into the kitchen. A glance at the clock told him he needed to finish the appetizers quickly so he could hop into the shower before his guests arrived. He lit the burner and waited a moment for it to heat. He dropped a few tablespoons of butter in the hot pan. It sizzled and popped when he dumped in the minced shallots and garlic.

"The place looks great," Carter said and Riley glanced over at him. The kitchen was semi-open, with a decent amount of space between the upper and lower cabinets that allowed him to see into the open dining and living rooms, but he'd been contemplating meeting with an architect and contractor about opening the space up so it would be easier to socialize while he cooked. "Very festive."

"Thanks, I had fun with the tree." He glanced over at the Christmas tree near the balcony door and smiled. Alex had always hired a professional decorator around the holidays and he'd been disappointed by the artificial tree and ultra-modern look she'd been fond of.

His favorite trees had been the live ones at the Hamilton home—when Carter and Kate had still been together—filled with colored lights and ornaments handmade by the kids and collected over the years.

His current tree was less homey, but the warm white lights, along with the silver and red bulbs, were festive and cheerful. He'd spent several evenings reading and drinking wine with the soft glow of the tree and the scent of spruce in the background.

Now, the smell of cooking onions brought him out of the stupor he'd been in and he hastily stirred the contents of the pan. Thankfully, the food wasn't burned, only beginning to brown and stick to the bottom. He added the mushrooms and watched Carter carefully arrange the wine bottles. "Thanks for coming over," Riley said. "Aside from appreciating the help, it's nice to just hang out."

"It is." Carter shot him a smile over his shoulder as he placed the last bottle on the bar cart, and an odd sense of déjà vu washed over Riley.

Carter broke down the wine box and stashed it in the pantry closet near the kitchen. Riley stirred the mushrooms and dropped in the herbs. Carter approached, leaning in to inhale the steam coming from them. "God, that smells amazing."

The low rumble of his voice and his proximity made Riley's heart beat a little faster. He cleared his throat. "It should be."

"Is there anything you need me to do?" Carter asked, stepping back.

"Just pour us some wine and keep me company while I cook."

"This reminds me of nights with Natalie," Carter said a few minutes later. He handed Riley a glass of dry riesling. "I keep expecting her to walk in the door."

Their fingers brushed as Riley took the glass from him and sipped the wine before he spoke. "That's funny you said that. I had a weird moment of déjà vu earlier. That must be why."

"It's not bad," Carter said, leaning against the counter across the kitchen from the stove, "just odd."

"True." Honestly, it made him a little nostalgic. Not that he wanted to go back to the days of cheating on Alex and furtive encounters with Carter and Natalie, but he missed the easy camaraderie they'd had. There was always an undercurrent of tension when Riley tried to navigate his relationship with Will and his friendship with Carter.

Riley stirred goat cheese into the mushroom mixture and sipped his wine. The only noise came from the sizzle from the pan and the Christmas carols playing on the sound system. "Natalie will be here later, actually," he said and moved the pan off the burner, replacing it with a small saucepan to melt butter in. "She and Julian are coming."

"That'll be nice to see her," Carter said.

"Creating the guest list was interesting," Riley admitted, swirling the pan to melt the butter. "I contemplated inviting Kate, but I wasn't sure where the two of you were at."

"We're doing okay. I wouldn't say we're quite ready to socialize together, though."

"That's what I figured," Riley said, turning off the burner. "And I had already decided to invite Natalie and I realized *that* would be disastrous."

Carter shuddered and grimaced at him. "Yes, it would be. I feel guilty enough about what I did to Kate. Although she has no idea Natalie was the woman I slept with, I know she's shrewd enough to pick up on my discomfort at seeing them interact."

"True." Riley scraped the mushroom mixture into the food processor and let it whir for a moment. He spoke again once the appliance was off. "How are you feeling in general? Now that the divorce hearing is over and everything."

Carter exhaled and scrubbed at his face. "Okay, I guess. I am glad it's final and that the hearing went smoothly, but it was emotionally taxing."

Riley gave him a sympathetic smile before he laid out the phyllo dough. "I'm sure."

"Kate cried after, and seeing her cry made me feel like shit, even though I know we're doing the right thing." Carter dragged a hand through his hair, which had grown out a little since the last haircut. Although Carter had been handsome with shorter hair, Riley was glad to see him looking more like his old self. "We went out to lunch after—I can't imagine that's usually how people wrap up a divorce—but it seemed weird to just walk out of the courthouse and go our separate ways."

Riley brushed the phyllo with melted butter. "How are the kids doing with it?"

"Okay. Sadie was extra snotty to me after and Dylan was really clingy, but overall they seem to be handling it. They knew it was coming for a while. I would have preferred it didn't come during the holidays, but it seemed pointless to drag it out into the new year."

Riley gave him a sad smile. "It's hard to believe it's been over a year since I dropped the bombshell on you."

"No kidding." Carter swirled the wine in his glass. "I still regret the way I reacted."

"No hard feelings," Riley said lightly, although he meant every word. "We've moved past it. Speaking of which, is Jesse coming tonight?"

The conversation segued into less heavy topics as Riley formed the mushroom triangles and placed them on a baking sheet. He wouldn't bake them until the guests arrived.

He glanced at the clock and frowned when he saw he was short on time. "Could you clean up while I hop in the shower?"

"Oh, I see, make a mess of your kitchen and leave it to me," Carter joked, but he'd already set down his wine and begun to roll up his sleeves.

"The dishwasher is empty and the only things that need to be hand-washed are the pans, knives and cutting board," Riley assured him and turned to leave the kitchen.

"Think about my superhero name while you shower," Carter called out. Riley disappeared down the hallway, Carter's voice and laughter following him.

Fifteen minutes later, Riley heard the sound of the front door opening as he stood in his bedroom, wearing nothing but a towel. "Shit," he muttered under his breath, wondering who on Earth had arrived so early.

"Carter." The surprise in Will's voice made Riley wince. Leaving Carter and Will alone seemed like an especially bad idea at the moment, although they'd been cordial enough to each other the few times they'd interacted since Carter's birthday.

Hastily drying off, Riley tossed the damp towel on the bed and reached for the clothes he'd laid out before he got in the shower. He listened to Will and Carter's conversation while he dressed.

"Hey, Will. How are you?"

"What are you doing here?" Will's tone was clipped and there was an uneasy note in Carter's answering laugh.

"Oh, just hanging out. Riley asked me to pick up some wine and I came over a little early to keep him company while he prepped for the party."

"Ahh. And where is he?" Riley could hear the tension in Will's tone as he dragged trousers up over his still-damp skin.

"Uh" — Carter cleared his throat — "he just got out of the shower. I'm sure he'll be out in a few."

Riley heard the sound of footfalls and a tentative knock on the door.

"Come in," he called.

Will peered inside, a frown marring his brow. "It's me."

"I know." Riley smiled and crossed the room to him, leaning in to brush his lips across Will's. Will's posture remained stiff and he barely returned the kiss. "I heard you and Carter talking, so I assumed you were the one knocking on my bedroom door. You're here early."

Will frowned and closed the door behind him. "Is that a problem?"

"No," Riley said slowly. He pulled a sleeveless undershirt over his head. "Why would it be? I was just surprised since you said you'd be running late."

Will's tone was terse. "Well, it seemed like I interrupted something. I mean, Carter's made himself comfortable here and you just got out of the shower…"

"What exactly are you implying?" Riley asked, yanking on his shirt and fastening the buttons.

"I am not implying anything. I'm just not comfortable with this situation."

Riley's sigh was tinged with irritation. "Honestly, Will, it was perfectly innocent."

"Well, I'm sorry, Riley, but it puts me on edge to walk into my boyfriend's apartment and find him half-naked with another man here. Especially *him*."

Riley dropped his voice but couldn't disguise the irritation in his tone. "You told me you would be late, so I asked Carter to pick up wine. He wanted to know if I needed help with anything else and offered to come over. I prepped appetizers and he cleaned the kitchen while I hopped in the shower. That's all. End of story."

Will crossed his arms over his chest. "It just seems a little too intimate."

"The most intimate thing that happened was Carter telling me how his divorce hearing went and discussing his relationship with Jesse."

"You can hardly blame me for being a little on edge, given your feelings for Carter."

Riley took a deep breath, trying to be patient with Will. He knew Will was sensitive about it and that he was probably extra vulnerable after he'd confessed his feelings and Riley hadn't returned them. He was tired of having to defend himself constantly, however. "There is nothing Carter and I did today that we wouldn't have done in front of you."

"I know you're sick of having this argument, Riley, but I'm struggling. You yourself admitted that you weren't over Carter, and given the fact that you weren't exactly faithful to your ex-wife, I have some pretty valid reasons to be concerned about trusting you!" Will's voice rose.

The words hung in the air as Riley tried to put his thoughts together before he lashed out and said something he'd regret. "So, once a cheater, always a cheater? Is that it, Will?" he snarled.

Will's jaw clenched. "You have to admit that's pretty common."

"Well, it's not the case for me, that's for sure. Yes, I cheated on Alex and I have spent a lot of time beating myself up over that. Despite the fact that Alex and I had a sham of a marriage, it was inexcusable for me to sleep around without her knowledge and agreement. I have to live with that. But I made a choice to be in a relationship with you and I have done everything I can think of to make it work. I have never cheated on you — not with Carter or anyone else — and I resent the accusation."

Will sighed. "Riley... I..."

The *ding* of the doorbell interrupted their argument.

"Carter, will you answer that?" Riley yelled through the door. "We'll just be a minute."

"Sure!"

"Look, I have to get out there," Riley said to Will, reaching out to grasp his shoulder in the hopes that Will would actually meet his gaze. "I need to greet my guests. I'd like to talk to you more about this when the party is over, okay?"

Will wouldn't meet his gaze. "Are you sure you want me to stay?"

"Of course, I do." Riley softened. He slid a hand across Will's shoulder and up his neck to tangle in his hair. "Let's try to pretend this didn't happen, okay? We'll have a good time tonight then talk after, yes?"

"Okay." Will sounded weary, but he finally met Riley's gaze. Riley gave him a half-smile and pressed their lips together, glad to feel some of the tension leave Will's body.

"Hey, we'll figure this out," Riley said quietly after he drew back. "I'm committed to you, Will. No one else."

Riley gave himself a quick, critical glance in the mirror and reached for the watch in the leather valet tray on top of the dresser. He owned several, but the one Carter had given him for his twenty-fourth birthday was the one he wore daily. He slipped on the watch and clasped it, but paused as he considered Will's earlier statement about him not being over Carter. Was he fooling himself by pretending he was? Carter was woven into every moment of his past and current life. There was no escaping his presence in Riley's life and Riley was unwilling to end his most important friendship.

"Riley?" The sound of his name made him turn his head. Will stood by the door with an expectant, brittle smile. "Ready?"

"Ready," Riley echoed and followed him out of the bedroom and down the hall. He plastered a pleasant smile on when they reached the living room.

"There you two are!" Natalie greeted them, a warm smile lighting up her face. She gave Will a peck on the cheek and leaned in to give Riley a hug. He hugged her back, feeling a warm wash of affection for her. Other than the occasional yoga class they could both manage to attend at the same time, it had been a while since they'd been able to socialize. "I hope you boys were up to something wonderfully naughty."

Riley's mood lightened at her good-natured teasing and he offered a genuine smile in response. "No, I'm afraid not. Will got here just as I stepped out of the shower and I only had time to dress. There's always tonight, though." He glanced over at Will, who managed a faint smile.

"We were a bit early, I'm afraid." Natalie glanced over at the handsome, older man who stood talking to Carter. "Will, you know Julian, but I'd like you to meet him, Riley."

"Of course." Julian turned at the sound of his name and Riley smiled at him and held out a hand. "It's a pleasure to meet you. Natalie told me you're a choreographer?"

"I am." When Julian smiled back, Riley felt momentarily dazzled. Although a good twenty years older than Riley and Carter, Julian was extremely handsome. His smile was bright against his lightly tanned skin and silver hair. "With the New York City Ballet."

"It's been years since I've been to a performance," Riley admitted. "Most of my time is spent at the opera, but I'd love to come to one of your shows."

Natalie's face lit up and she slipped a hand into the crook of Julian's arm. "Oh, that would be wonderful, Riley. Perhaps you and Will could join us sometime."

"That sounds nice, Nat," Will said with a smile, and a little of Riley's tension evaporated.

"I'd like to talk to both of you more, but I have a few things to do before the rest of the guests arrive," Riley admitted.

"Please let me help," Natalie said. "I do miss the cooking we used to do here."

Riley glanced at Julian, wondering if he knew about what the evenings had entailed, although he knew Natalie had been open about her previous career. Riley was impressed with how well he had apparently handled it. He knew most men weren't so understanding. If Will had been an escort, Riley wasn't sure he could have been quite so comfortable with it. Riley's thoughts returned to Will's earlier jealousy. He could hardly blame Will for being so on edge about his relationship with Carter.

"You can preheat the oven and pop the mushroom triangles in, Natalie," he said. "The recipe is on my iPad in the kitchen."

"Ooh, yummy." Natalie squeezed his arm as they walked toward the kitchen.

"Will, could you open a bottle of white wine and put it on ice while I put the food on the table? I'm going to set everything up on the dining table and kitchen counter."

"Sure."

Riley had just finished neatening the final platter of food when the next knock on the door came. He was halfway to the door when Will called out, "Where is the ice bucket?"

"Oh, I can show you," Carter said.

Riley's step faltered when Will muttered, "Of course you can."

His smile was forced as he opened the door to reveal Gabe and Charles. *Maybe it wasn't such a good idea for Carter and Will to be at this party together.*

* * * *

A few hours later, with several glasses of wine and some delicious food in him, Riley had finally relaxed. Audrey and Natalie stood near the tree, chatting, and Will was immersed in conversation with Julian, Jesse and Gabe while Riley discussed the holidays with Charles and Carter. Carter's sleeves were still rolled up and he'd loosened the top buttons of his shirt. Slightly buzzed from the wine and enjoyable party, Riley found himself distracted by the sight of Carter's bare throat and the tiny peek of chest hair below.

Carter—who sat next to him on the couch—nudged Riley's thigh with his knee. "By the way, what are your plans for Christmas?"

Riley shrugged. "I assume Will and I will just be relaxing. We're going to a big dinner at Gabe's restaurant on Christmas Eve, but that's all we really had planned."

"You should come over to my place that afternoon. Audrey, Max and I are planning a small dinner and the kids will open gifts. Kate and I agreed it would probably be best if they slept in their own beds Christmas Eve and woke up to open gifts from Santa with Kate."

Riley saw the disappointment in Carter's eyes and winced, realizing how difficult Christmas would be for him this year.

"The kids asked if Unca' Ri would be at our Christmas celebration and Dylan sounded especially excited to have you there."

Riley smiled at the thought. It had been a while since he'd seen the littlest Hamilton. "I'd love that. Let me check with Will and see if that works for him."

Carter flashed him a brief, guilty smile. "Ah, I was just thinking it would be family. Not that Will isn't great, but..."

"You weren't planning to invite Jesse, I take it?" Riley asked. He knew Carter hadn't introduced Jesse to the kids yet and he couldn't really see Carter picking Christmas to do that.

Carter laughed. "No. Definitely not. I'd considered asking Malcolm because the guy doesn't have any family around here, but Dylan put his foot down about that. This Christmas is going to be rough on all of us so I don't mind following Dylan Hamilton's 'family only' rules this time."

"Understandable," Riley said. A quick glance at Will showed that he'd been listening from his spot on the chair a few feet away, his lips pressed in a thin, tight line, and Riley amended his statement. "Let me talk to Will about it first before I make any decision. I need to see what he had planned for Christmas Day. Maybe I can just come for a short time or something."

Carter's glance was knowing as he glanced between Will and Riley. "Sure. No problem."

Riley had just reached for his glass of wine when there came a knock on the door. He frowned in confusion and stood, wondering who was on the other side. Everyone he'd invited was in the room already. He doubted it was a neighbor complaining about the noise, since the building had excellent soundproofing.

He opened the door to reveal Dan and Melanie Conley.

Riley grinned at his friends. "Dan, Mel! What on Earth are you doing in Manhattan?"

"Surprise!" Dan grinned back and yanked Riley in for a hug. Riley returned it wholeheartedly and gave Mel an equally heartfelt embrace.

"So, what are you doing here?" he asked. He drew back and gestured for them to come inside. "I'm thrilled to see you, of course, but I had no idea you were in town."

It must have begun to snow, because Dan brushed a few snowflakes from his short, tight curls. "Carter and

I talked the other day. I whined about the fact that I never see you guys anymore and he told me to put up or shut up. Despite his crude humor, he had a good point, so I talked to Mel, booked a flight, left the kids with Mel's mom and here we are!"

Riley turned to Carter, who stood with his arm around Mel, grinning proudly.

"You shit," Riley said with a laugh and pulled Carter into a hug. "I can't believe you arranged this and managed to keep it a surprise."

Carter chuckled and his chest vibrating against Riley's combined with his familiar woodsy cologne sent a sudden and unexpected surge of arousal through Riley. Uncomfortable, he stepped back.

Jesse appeared at his elbow.

"Please do introduce me," he murmured to Riley. He raked an appreciative gaze over Dan. "I assume you live out of town because I make it my business to know all of the gorgeous men in Manhattan."

"And Brooklyn and the Bronx," Carter chimed in with a laugh.

"I'm thorough." Jesse's grin was wolfish.

"Well, my wife, Mel" — Dan pulled her close — "and I live in Chicago," he said with a grin. "But I appreciate the compliment."

"Jesse Murtagh." He stuck out his hand to Dan, but trailed his gaze over Mel. "And don't worry, your wife is included in my appreciation. I'm willing to ditch Carter for a night to spend it with you two." He winked. Riley laughed at the entire interaction and Carter let out a quiet huff.

Dan glanced over at Riley. "Where is the famous Will I've heard so much about, Ri?"

Riley glanced around, looking for Will, who approached carrying a glass of wine and wearing a tight smile that didn't quite reach his eyes.

"Sorry about that." Will held out a hand to Dan. "You must be Dan Conley. You roomed with Riley in college, right?"

"Yeah, I was stuck with those two fuckers," Dan gave him a hearty handshake. "Which is why I hightailed it for Chicago after we graduated. It's beyond me why I felt so nostalgic I decided to fly back here, but we'll chalk it up to holiday-induced psychosis."

Everyone laughed and Riley gestured toward the dining area before he clapped Dan on the shoulder. "Come on in. We have food and wine. Have a seat and get comfortable. We can catch up later."

* * * *

"...and they stumbled in together, drunk off their asses, and fell into bed together. The next morning I found them snoring off-key and drooling on Carter's pillow." Dan finished telling a story from college that Riley had completely forgotten, and everyone laughed uproariously. He'd been reminiscing and entertaining the crowd with stories from Riley and Carter's past for the better part of an hour and his audience was rapt.

Riley turned to Will to say something about not being able to get a word in edgewise at his own party, but Will abruptly stood and disappeared through the door onto the balcony. Riley watched him for a moment while he paced, stopping only to toss back the contents of his glass. Concerned, Riley followed him.

He closed the door behind him and shivered when the icy wind hit, snowflakes pelting his cheeks. "What are you doing out here in this weather?" he asked Will.

Will turned to look at him. "What the hell are *you* doing, Riley?" His tone was weary.

"What do you mean?" Riley asked, the wine making his head a little muddled.

"Am I the only one who watches you and Carter together and sees that you two love each other?" he shouted. Riley startled and took half a step back. "How much longer do you expect me to sit here waiting for you to let go of him and want to be with me?"

The words hung in the cold winter air for a long moment and Riley's stomach tumbled to his toes. Was Will right? They'd been dating for almost a year. Will was in love with him. And while Riley cared for Will, he couldn't say that he loved him. After a year, shouldn't he?

Will had been nothing but patient with him, but it was clear Riley couldn't give Will what he needed.

Riley swallowed hard, sad and disappointed in himself. He'd tried his best to focus on Will in the last few months, and yet it clearly wasn't enough.

There was only one person Riley was in love with and it wasn't Will. It was Carter.

Even Will saw that.

God, he'd been a shitty boyfriend. No matter what he did, he seemed to hurt Will, and that wasn't fair to him at all. What choice did he have but to end the relationship?

In the long run, it would be better for both of them.

"God, Will, I'm so sorry," he said hoarsely.

Will offered him a sad smile. "Yeah, me, too."

"You have nothing to apologize for," Riley said. "You've been amazing. I'm just...we're not..." He couldn't find the words to explain. "I don't think I can be what you need," he finally managed. "I want to be, but you're right, it's been almost a year. I can't keep asking you to put your feelings aside and wait for me to catch up." He laughed sadly. "Maybe I'm just not capable of it."

Will shook his head. "Don't you see it, Riley? It's *Carter*. It's always been Carter for you. I never doubted that you cared about me or that you tried, but when it comes down to it, there is no man — *no person* — you will ever love as much as your best friend. For a while, I thought maybe that would fade, but seeing the two of you together in the past month...there's no denying it. I don't know if you guys can make a relationship work, I know it's hellishly complicated, but I do know there's nothing I will ever be able to do to compete with the bond you two have. *No one* will."

Before Riley could respond, Will spun on his heel and disappeared into the apartment. A cold gust of wind prompted Riley to follow. The party had broken up — clearly aware of the problem between Will and Riley. Carter and Natalie were in the kitchen, cleaning up, and Jesse, Max and Audrey had already left.

Unsure of what to say to the remaining guests who were clustered in the living room, Riley sighed and continued down the hall where Will had disappeared. Riley found him in the bedroom, packing his bag. Over the past few months, Will had gradually begun leaving more and more of his belongings. It hurt to see Will open the drawer Riley had given him and empty the contents into his leather weekender bag, but Riley knew it was even harder for Will. Sadness tightened the lines of his face and his eyes were red-rimmed. Riley's heart ached. He knew he'd hurt Will deeply.

Will disappeared into the bathroom and returned with his dopp kit and toiletries. He dropped it into his bag, zipped it and hoisted it on his shoulder. He finally met Riley's gaze and Riley stepped forward.

"I'm so sorry, Will," Riley said miserably. "I never wanted to hurt you."

"I know." Will's voice was gruff. "But it does hurt and I'm going to need some time. I'm not saying we'll never talk again, or that you shouldn't continue your friendship with Gabe and Charles, but give me some space for a while, okay?"

"Of course." Riley would agree to anything that would help Will.

Will cleared his throat. "Look, I'll pack up your stuff in my apartment and have Gabe or Charles get it to you."

"Whatever's easiest for you."

Will reached out with a sad smile and rubbed his thumb along Riley's jaw. "Be happy, Riley. You deserve it."

He disappeared out of the door before Riley could respond and Riley stood in his bedroom, feeling like he'd been hit by a wrecking ball. When he emerged, Natalie and Julian stood by the front door, putting on their coats and talking to Gabe and Charles, who were doing the same.

"Gabe? Charles?" Riley asked. "Would you mind…?"

He wasn't sure what he was even asking, but Gabe nodded and gave Riley a sympathetic smile. "I'll check on Will tonight and see how he's doing."

Charles gave him a terse nod. "We'll look after him."

They disappeared out of the door and Riley turned back to his remaining friends.

"I'm so sorry about this," Riley said, embarrassed that his fight with Will had ruined an otherwise great party.

"Hey, it's okay." Natalie hugged him around the middle and glanced up at him. "I take it you and Will…?"

Riley finished her thought. "We ended things. It just…wasn't working anymore." He wasn't comfortable going into more detail and she nodded as if she understood.

"Take care of yourself then." She pressed a kiss to his cheek and he accepted it gratefully. "And you can always call me if you need to talk."

Riley nodded and numbly said goodbye to Julian. Dan and Melanie stood to leave and Dan gave him a searching look once he was bundled up against the cold. "Let's grab lunch tomorrow, okay?"

Relieved, Riley agreed. If there was anyone who could help him sort through the mess in his head and his feelings about Carter, it was Dan. He hugged his friends and promised to call the next day.

After they left, Riley turned to face Carter, who stood in the living room with a worried expression.

"What do you need?" he asked quietly, and Riley shrugged. It didn't feel right to tell Carter how he felt, when he wasn't sure himself. He needed a few days to sort through things and talk to Dan before he made any decisions about what he wanted to do next.

"I don't know," he said honestly, feeling exhausted and stripped raw.

Carter closed the distance between them and pulled Riley into an embrace. For the longest time, they stood in Riley's living room, foreheads pressed together,

Christmas carols playing in the background the only sound.

Despite the turmoil in his head and his heart, with Carter's arms around him, a sense of peace settled over him.

Will was right.

In the end, Carter was the only one who had ever made him feel this way.

Chapter Twelve

"So, what happened after everybody left?" Jesse asked. "Was there more yelling? Did anyone cry? Did you suck Riley's dick?"

"Charming," Carter muttered, simultaneously annoyed and entertained by Jesse's blatant curiosity.

It was a week before Christmas, and Jesse had offered to cook dinner. The luscious smell of coconut curry and lime filled the air and Carter watched with a fond smile as his friend bustled about. His mouth watered as Jesse set their plates on the table.

"Holy hell, Jes. This looks fantastic."

Jesse slid into the seat opposite Carter with a grin. "Thank you. And don't change the subject."

"Would you stop?" Carter shook his head. "I'd much rather talk about this idea you and Kyle are hatching to open a bar together."

Jesse made a face. "Yeah, yeah, Kyle and I are opening a speakeasy uptown. I don't have to let anyone in that I don't want to and it'll be awesome."

"So tell me about it!"

"No, because I want to gossip about your former BFF and his crazy party. I mean, we barely got through dinner before he and his boyfriend started fighting—"

"Jes—"

"And the next thing I know, I get tossed out on my ass and end up going home with no dessert, half-drunk and very much alone. The end," Jesse finished with a scowl.

Carter burst out laughing. "That's...you are ridiculous!"

"And you still haven't answered my question. Did you or did you not suck Riley's dick?"

"I did not." Carter reached for the wine bottle on the table, ignoring the heat creeping up the collar of his dress shirt. "I listened to Ri bitch and moan about Will and how he hated to be single at Christmas again. Then he had some more wine and we shared a plate of brownies, I poured him into bed and took a cab home."

Jesse went still, his gaze jewel-bright over his plain white T-shirt. "That is incredibly boring, Carter."

"The guy had just had his heart stomped on, for crying out loud—what did you expect?"

"I expected you to offer him solace in your arms and mouth!"

"Oh, God."

"Listen, we both know you want him and now that you're both finally *available*—"

"Please, shut up."

"I'm being serious, Carter."

"So am I." Carter shook his head. "Look, I know you have no interest in monogamous norms, but Riley isn't like you. He wants to find someone to share his life. *One* person, not a roster of willing bodies."

"That's because Riley is a lame ass," Jesse muttered.

"To you, maybe, but he's also my friend."

"Okay, fine. Who says you can't be Riley's one person?"

"I say," Carter told Jesse. "It's way too soon for Riley to even be thinking that way. About anyone," he added, shoving aside the ache in his chest. "Riley cared about Will, Jesse. He worked really hard to give Will what he wanted."

Jesse nodded and used his chopsticks to stir his food. "So, what happened?"

"I'm not sure." Carter picked up his wineglass. "Riley admitted they'd argued a few days before, but I get the feeling he didn't see the break-up coming at all. He's hurting, you know? What kind of friend would I be to ignore that?"

"A shitty one," Jesse conceded. "It sounds like your boy's better off without the bitchy boyfriend, though. And frankly, the idea of having to bend over backward to make someone happy makes me queasy."

Carter picked up his chopsticks again and trained his gaze on the vibrant plate in front of him.

"Relationships can be like that. I mean, there's always some give and take, a concept you might recognize as compromise." Jesse stuck out his tongue and Carter smiled, but quickly sobered. "In Riley's case, though...I think he's just used to it."

Jesse's brow furrowed. "Used to what?" he asked before taking a bite of food.

"Used to putting his own needs second. He did it for his parents, then his ex-wife. Hell, he even let me have my way when I asked him for things he didn't want to do." Shame made Carter's stomach tighten. "Riley's been putting other people's needs first for so long, it's probably second nature."

"Well, shit." Jesse watched Carter closely. "You keep telling me things like that and I won't be able to sustain an appropriate level of disdain for the guy."

Carter fished a piece of shrimp from his plate. "Why do you dislike him at all?"

"Well, he did his level best to act like a douche when I met him at your birthday dinner," Jesse pointed out. "Plus, his boyfriend was rude to us and Riley never said a word."

"I didn't find Will rude," Carter countered mildly. "He wasn't particularly friendly, I'll admit, but I wouldn't say he was rude, either."

Jesse scoffed. "And Riley?"

"I suspect he feels threatened by you, honestly. Riley doesn't know you or Kyle or the other guys well, but knows we're all close and that I spend a good chunk of time with you. I think it's weird for him, not sharing that part of my life."

"Then Riley needs to learn to share his toys."

Carter hummed in agreement. Jesse was right — Riley did need to get used to Carter having other friends. It felt wrong to throw Riley under the bus, though, especially when his friend was hurting. Carter put a bit of food in his mouth, then nearly dropped his chopsticks.

"Oh, my God." Carter let out a low moan of delight. "This is possibly the best thing you've ever cooked in my presence."

"Ugh. Don't talk with your mouth full, you pig." Jesse laid his foot over Carter's under the table in a gesture of affection. "I thought you'd like it. Especially after your daughter told everybody at school you served her bugs for dinner."

Carter inhaled rice and choked. "It was a mistake to tell you that story," he gasped out.

"Make sure Sadie knows your friends serve you bugs, too." Jesse picked up his glass and swirled his wine, his eyes gleaming with mischief.

"They'll like that. Particularly Dylan," Carter replied. "He's really into pranking people these days, you know. Max took him to a comic book store in the East Village and now our lives are all about whoopee cushions and trick gum."

"I love it."

"Mmm, my mother doesn't — she ate a piece of gum that turned her mouth black last week. She was at a luncheon."

Jesse's eyes went wide. "An important luncheon?"

"A fundraiser for one of her pet charities," Carter replied with a straight face. "She was a key speaker." He finally grinned as Jesse threw his head back and cackled with laughter.

"Yes, that is fantastic — go, Dylan!"

An image of his children and Jesse struck Carter from out of the blue and he slowly laid down his chopsticks, turning the idea over in his head. He wasn't sure introducing Sadie and Dylan to Jesse was smart, because God knew what heights of evil genius the three could achieve together. Something about it seemed right, though.

"Hey, do you want to meet them?" Carter asked while Jesse wiped his eyes with his napkin.

Jesse quirked an eyebrow at him. "Meet who? Sadie and Dylan?"

"Sure. I have them this weekend and promised I'd take them back to the comic book store on Saturday. I'd introduce you as my friend," he clarified, fighting not to squirm at his own ridiculous words. "Which is what you are, obviously."

Jesse tapped his foot against Carter's under the table again. "I think we can both agree we're a little more than friends, Carter. I mean, I plan to have your cock in my mouth as soon as the dishes are in the washer."

"Yes, I know." Carter picked up his glass, ignoring the lust that shot through his groin. "The kids aren't ready to meet anyone I'm dating, though, and since this thing between us is casual—"

"You figured you'd wiggle through a 'just friends' loophole." Jesse gave him an oddly tender smile. "I get it."

"That's okay, right?" Carter swallowed against a sudden pulse of nervous energy. "I mean, I do love you dearly, but we both know we're not going to end up together. You're *definitely* not looking to be anyone's husband or stepfather."

"True." Jesse grimaced. "What about what *you* want, though?"

"What do you mean?"

"Are you really going to sit there and tell me you're not interested in settling down someday? Especially now that Riley's single again—"

Carter shook his head. "It doesn't matter how I feel about him, Jes. Riley needs to figure out what he wants first."

A frown settled over Jesse's features. "Explain."

"When Kate and I split, I told Riley I wanted to see where things could go between us. Unfortunately for me, he'd already met Will."

"And Riley chose Will over you," Jesse murmured, a knowing expression on his face. "More proof he's not very smart."

Carter smiled weakly and played with his food until he trusted his voice to be even. "On the bright side, it proves Riley can put himself first when he wants to. I think that's something he should do for a while."

"Okay." Jesse kept quiet until Carter met his gaze. "So you'll be okay if Riley goes out and screws half the city?"

Carter shrugged off the sting of Jesse's candid words. "Yeah. For all I know, he and Will could be back together by New Year's."

"Don't bother inviting me to their next dinner party, then," Jesse teased. "But if you're okay with it, so be it. I'm glad we're slightly more than friends, you know. Even though you haven't let me fuck you yet."

He grinned when Carter dropped his head in defeat. "Aw, don't pout. I'll tell you about the speakeasy Kyle and I are going to open if you like," he offered. "It's actually in a basement space under a crappy pub in Morningside Heights. We're hoping to open this summer."

"Can I see it?"

"Of course you can. And I'd love to meet your tiny terrors, by the way."

Carter blinked in surprise then grinned. "Okay, great! Come for breakfast at my place on Saturday."

"Why don't you guys come here instead?"

Carter glanced around at the sleek loft and shuddered. Just imagining Sadie's and Dylan's voices bouncing off the brick walls made his ears ache.

"I'm not sure you want to witness my kids' energy levels first thing in the morning—they can be pretty loud."

Jesse scoffed. "I've been around young children before, Carter—I know what they can be like. Plus, I'm closer to the East Village, so if you all come *here*, I can sleep in an extra half-hour."

"Nice. I'll pick up some coffee and bagels on the way then." He cocked a brow when Jesse waved him off.

"Nope. Just relax and leave the details to me. Trust me."

"Okay. I do, actually. Trust you, I mean." Jesse smiled and Carter's faced heated again. "I'm glad we're slightly more than friends, too."

"Well, good."

They ate in silence for a moment before Carter gave Jesse a slow, evil grin.

"We'll be here by eight a.m. on Saturday, by the way." He chuckled at Jesse's noise of protest.

"Son of a bitch."

* * * *

Six days later, Carter knelt in front of his Christmas tree with two presents covered in cat and rainbow wrapping paper. His doorbell chimed and Carter watched Audrey place a tray of snacks on the side table before heading for the door.

"It's probably Kate and the kids," he called after her. "They were supposed to leave Brad and Eleanor's place around three-thirty."

Carter laid the gifts under the tree while excited voices filled his apartment, then looked up as a sharp bark rang out. His jaw dropped as the family's Border

Collie, Leo, streaked toward him, nearly knocking Carter over a moment later.

"Who the heck let you in?" he demanded, wrapping his arms around thirty pounds of wriggling dog, and laughed while Leo frantically licked his face.

"Surprise, Dad!" Dylan and Sadie called over the noise, clambering forward when Carter held out his hands.

"Leo wanted to see you for Christmas," Sadie told him.

"Well, Merry Christmas to Leo!" He spotted Riley standing beside Kate over the kids' heads. "Hey, guys!"

"You need a hand there, Carter?" Riley asked.

Carter lost his balance and went toppling over in a heap of children and dog. "Yes!" he grunted as Dylan flopped onto his stomach and Sadie latched her arms around his neck. "Help me, Uncle Riley, you're my only hope!"

A few minutes passed before Carter, the children and Leo were vertical again. Carter swiped at the dog hair on his blue cashmere sweater and guided Kate and Riley into the kitchen area. Dylan and Sadie stayed by the tree with Leo, exclaiming to Audrey over the pile of presents.

"Did you guys come up in the elevator together?" Carter asked while Max handed glasses around.

"Yes. We actually ran into Riley on the sidewalk outside, though." Kate handed Carter a brown paper bag. "And I mean that quite literally, because Leo almost knocked him over. Are you okay, Riley?"

Riley laughed and waved her off. "Don't worry about it. You guys surprised me more than anything else and it's not like anything I was carrying broke." He examined the drink in his hand with interest. "This looks fun."

"It's a citrus-cinnamon punch," Carter told him. "Something Kyle and Jesse dreamed up last night at dinner. It's good, I promise," he added after Riley looked askance at him. "Orange and grapefruit juices, grapefruit soda, grenadine, cinnamon sticks and Cognac."

"There's a virgin mix for the kids, too, with a little food coloring to make it stand out," Max threw in. "I figured they'd be a fun change from Shirley Temples."

"Holy Hannah, this is delicious," Kate murmured after a long sip. "Please give my compliments to the mixologists when you see them next."

"I'll do that." Carter held up the bag she'd given him. "Is this something that needs refrigerating?"

"Nope. Sadie wants to make S'mores after dinner tonight." She shrugged and Carter opened the bag. "She got the idea after spending the weekend with you, so I picked up the ingredients and told her we'd make them here. You don't mind, do you?"

Carter laughed. "Of course not. I'm a little mystified as to how we can make S'mores without a campfire, though."

"Use the toaster oven," Kate and Max said at the same time, meeting each other's gazes with a laugh.

"You could use a kitchen torch," Riley mused then gave Carter a sly grin. "Though I don't suppose you have one of those, do you, Car?"

Carter shot him a withering stare. "Not unless you brought one in that bag of yours."

"I'm afraid I did not." Riley placed his glass on the counter so he could rummage through the bag. "I do have presents for the kids, however, and some very fine

chocolate from Mast Brothers for the adults. Oh, yes —
a bottle of bourbon just for you, too."

Carter accepted the bottle Riley held out to him with
an appreciative whistle. "Booker's. Merry Christmas to
me. Thank you, Ri."

Carter noted the shadows under Riley's eyes and his
heart squeezed a little. Despite his perfect hair and chic
clothes, Riley looked worn out and there were fine lines
of strain around his eyes and mouth. His smile was
genuinely happy, though, and for a moment, Carter
lost himself in Riley's gaze.

"There's something under the tree for you," Carter
told him, inclining his head toward the living area.

"Excellent." Riley reached into the bag again. "Should
I put the kids' presents under the tree, too, or does it
make more sense for them to open them now?"

"Let's open them now!" Dylan shouted from his seat
next to Audrey.

"Yes, now, now, now!" Sadie agreed. Hopping to her
feet, she then executed a smart little dance while Leo
barked and Audrey simply laughed.

Carter groaned. "Riley, what are you doing? You
can't say things like that around children. What is
wrong with you?"

"I forgot about the bionic hearing!"

"Well, now you've done it." Carter shot him a glare.
"Better give them whatever's in that bag before they go
from gleeful to angry mob. Just one!" he called out and
the children surged forward to wrap themselves
around Riley's legs. "The rest have to wait until after
dinner!"

With some coaxing, the children settled down and, as
the evening progressed, Carter kept an eye on his
friend. Although Riley showed occasional hints of

melancholy, he appeared relaxed and even seemed to enjoy himself.

"I missed this, you know," he told Carter. The adults had gathered to watch Sadie and Dylan open their gifts and he and Carter were sitting on one of the couches, nursing glasses of the cinnamon-citrus punch.

Carter raised a brow. "You missed being incapable of finishing a complete thought and spending every meal talking with your mouth full?"

Riley snorted softly with laughter. "Well, no, neither of those. Dinner was fantastic, by the way."

"Thanks. Audrey and Max did the cooking, but I chopped every goddamned vegetable they put in front of me."

"Atta boy." A gleam lit Riley's eyes. "Hey, what would you say to taking another cooking class?"

Carter raised a brow in interest. "Another class with you, you mean?"

"Sure. We had fun the last time, right? And you can't deny the food was fantastic."

"Oh, I agree." Carter smiled as he remembered the evening they'd spent cooking sumptuous foods. He'd been out of his element, but Riley's confidence had been contagious.

He cocked his head and met Riley's gaze. "I have considered trying another class, actually."

"Really?"

"Yeah. It's humiliating being incapable of cooking anything more complicated than boxed mac-n-cheese. I think it'd be nice to be able to cook more for Sadie and Dylan. Plus, I could return the favor for all the meals Audrey and Jesse and Kyle have fed me." The sudden tension in Riley face gave him pause. "What's wrong?"

"Nothing." Riley's smile didn't quite reach his eyes. "I'm just surprised to hear you've been thinking about taking another class, that's all. But great! I can check the course catalog and see what's coming up."

"Sure, that sounds great. Are you really willing to sit through another night of cooking for dummies with me?"

"Why wouldn't I?"

Carter shrugged. "You already know how to cook — it must be boring watching me blunder through basic things." A thought occurred to him and he raised an eyebrow. "Or is my bumbling part of the appeal?"

"Of *course*, your bumbling is part of the appeal." Riley smirked. "You make me look like a superstar."

"Oh, well, anything for your ego."

"I was joking." Riley nudged Carter's shoulder with his own. "I don't mind hanging back a little while you get your feet wet. I'm hardly a master chef, you know — I learn new things every time I take a class."

"Okay, then. Let's do it. Nothing too crazy, though, okay? I'd like to avoid injury and accidental poisoning if at all possible."

"Okay," Riley agreed with a laugh. "You're definitely more adventurous about this than I expected."

"Well, it beats yoga class," Carter joked. "And I never thought I'd say this, but…"

Riley's brows drew together. "Never thought you'd say what?"

"I actually enjoy cooking class over opera." Carter bit his lip against a smile at Riley's loud laugh.

"I'm sorry I dragged you to all those performances, you know," Riley told him. He nodded as Carter's eyes widened with surprise. "No, wait — that's a lie. I don't regret taking you, because I liked having your company. I do feel badly you didn't enjoy them as much as I did, though."

Dylan and Sadie swarmed them in the next moment, waving the gifts Riley had given them. Carter sat back and watched while they chattered and Riley listened, his gaze soft and open in a way that Carter hadn't seen in a long time.

Swallowing against a sudden tightness in his throat, Carter excused himself to take his and Riley's glasses to the kitchen. He left them in the sink, then he pulled two more from the corner cabinet and picked up a decanter he'd filled before dinner. He'd poured two fingers of bourbon into each glass when Kate ambled up, looking slim and especially blonde in a deep mulberry sweater dress. Carter automatically slid one of the glasses her way.

"Hang on one sec and I'll get you some ice."

Kate frowned. "Isn't that against the rules?"

"What rules?" Carter pulled another glass from the cabinet.

"Carter Hamilton's Rules for Enjoying Good Booze." Kate batted her eyelashes and Carter moved to the refrigerator.

"I don't have rules," he muttered. He opened the freezer, then pulled out a special mold, leveling a glare at his ex. "I have *guidelines*."

Carter cracked open the mold, exposing four small globes of ice. "There's no wrong or right when it comes to enjoying a drink," he told Kate as he moved back to her side. "Remembering a few simple things is worth the effort, though. Give your booze air, don't water it down too much and use the right glass." With care, he extracted one of the ice globes from the mold and slipped it into her glass. "Try that."

Kate lifted the glass to her lips. "You're such a nerd," she murmured, then sipped, pausing to let the liquor roll over her tongue the way Carter had taught her. She shook her head and smiled. "This is delicious, though."

Dylan's wild laughter drew their attention then and Carter and Kate stood quietly for a moment, watching their children with Riley. He'd given them dress-up gear for Christmas and the kids were trading items as they saw fit. Dylan had donned a blue-stoned tiara while Sadie wore a pirate's eye patch.

"How's Ri doing?" Kate asked quietly.

Carter shrugged. "Not too bad. He seems a little down, but…not as bad as I expected. I think being here with us takes his mind off Will and everything." He paused a moment before asking, "How are you?"

"I'm okay." Kate sipped her drink again. "Not really happy or sad, if that makes sense. I suppose I've been more focused on making sure the kids are okay than on how I feel, but that's okay. You probably know what I mean."

Carter extracted another ice globe from the mold for Riley's glass. "I do, indeed."

The kids had resumed their attack on the pile of presents when Carter sat back down, while Riley appeared concerned.

"Everything all right?"

Carter blinked and handed Riley the glass of bourbon and rocks, uncertain of where the question was coming from. "Sure…why wouldn't it be?"

"You were talking with Kate," Riley explained, cradling his drink in one hand. "I didn't know…"

"It was nothing," Carter assured him. "I mean, it wasn't *nothing*, but we were just chatting. We've learned how to do that pretty well these days. We were talking about bourbon, actually," he added with a nod at Riley's glass.

Riley's brows rose in interest. "Oh, look at you with the fancy ice ball, hah," he murmured, then sniffed delicately at the glass's contents. "Is this the Booker's?"

"Mm-hm, and Kate says it's fantastic, so thank you again." Carter raised his glass, tapping it against Riley's with a grin. "Merry Christmas."

"Merry Christmas, Car."

Carter sipped his drink, the bourbon's sweet, pleasant burn spreading through his gut. "Damn, that's good."

"Natalie helped me pick it out." Riley nodded. "We had lunch and went shopping last weekend."

"She doesn't blame me for what happened with Will?" Carter wondered.

"Oh, no—she blames me for that. She's not super-excited about your influence over me, though. She thinks you should find someone else to spend your time with."

"Yeah, she said as much during your party," Carter replied. "I told her we *hadn't* been spending a lot of time together, but I don't think she believed me. Or maybe she didn't care."

Riley grimaced. "Ugh."

"It's fine." Carter shook his head. "Will's her friend, I get it. Plus, I know she's angry about how I handled things after you came out. Not that I blame her, of course." He bowed his head and Riley rested his hand on Carter's shoulder.

"That's the past." Riley's voice was a low, soothing rumble. "No sense dwelling on it now that we've moved on."

Carter gave Riley a shaky smile just as Sadie bounced up with a package in her hands.

"This one has your name on it, Uncle Ri," she piped, thrusting it at Riley. "It's from Daddy!"

"Well, thank you very much, Sadie." Riley winked and made Sadie giggle before she dashed back to the tree. "Thanks, Carter."

"You're welcome," Carter replied. "It's not quite on par with a bottle of small batch bourbon, but I think you'll like it."

Riley pulled the book free of its wrappings and he ran his fingers slowly over its cover, his mouth falling open a little. "*The Metropolitan Opera Cookbook*. This is great! Where on Earth did you find this?"

"One of Kyle's friends is a book dealer — she put out some feelers and it didn't take too long to find one for sale." Carter smiled and Riley let the cookbook fall open. "I figured opera stars sharing recipes was right up your alley. Just, uh, don't show it to Kate right now because I will never hear the end of it."

"Got it!" Riley closed the book and folded his hands over it. "Thanks for including me tonight, by the way. I'm really glad I didn't have to spend a second Christmas without all of this."

Carter glanced around. His low-key decorations seemed drab in comparison to what he and Riley were used to. "It's not much compared to Kate and Alex's big parties, but it's all right, I suppose."

"It's great." Riley nodded solemnly. "Really. I've always liked spending time with you during the holidays, ever since we were back at school. Remember that first holiday concert at the Baptist church?"

"And the Szechuan food feast that followed. God, we got so wasted." Carter grinned. "That was a great night."

"Yeah. The big family parties were fun, but I love just hanging out like this." Riley's expression turned wistful. "I missed seeing the kids and the chaos last year. It's nice being back here, you know?"

Carter remembered the hole Riley's absence had left at Christmastime the year before and his heart ached to know his own thoughtless actions had caused it.

"Yeah, I do. The kids missed you, too. *I* missed you and I'm glad you could join us tonight."

"Dad!" Dylan called, getting to his feet and running over with Sadie by his side. "Dad, look at these!"

"What have you got there?" Carter nodded at the presents in the children's hands, though he easily recognized the garish wrapping paper.

"They're from your friend, Jesse!" Dylan told him. "I read his name on the tag!"

"Uh-oh... I'll bet he found something for you at the comic book store." Carter bit his lip and suppressed a laugh at Dylan's wide eyes. "Better open them and find out!"

Both children sat on the floor, tearing at the wrapping paper, and Max crossed the room to join them, lured by the call of comic book store purchases. All four burst out laughing as the paper fell away to reveal the fruits of Jesse Murtagh's unerring eye for detail and zany sense of humor.

"What is that?" Kate asked, squinting at the small white figurine in Sadie's hand.

"It's a unicorn," Sadie cried. The unicorn had a multi-colored horn, mane and tail and when Sadie shook it over her empty palm, tiny bits of candy fell out of the animal's rear end. "It's a unicorn that poops rainbow sprinkles!"

Kate groaned. "Lovely," she muttered, though Carter could see she was trying not to laugh. "What on Earth did he give you, Dyl?" She gasped aloud when Dylan turned around sporting a lush, very orange pencil mustache under his nose.

"I got mood mustaches!" Dylan waved the package over his head, nearly whacking Max—who laughed helplessly next to Sadie—in the face. "There's a different color for every feeling! This one is sassy!"

Several minutes passed before the hilarity subsided enough for Carter to wipe his streaming eyes. Using his phone, he snapped a photo of the kids with their gifts and sent it to Jesse with a quick note of thanks. His phone buzzed almost immediately with a reply, but Carter's smile faded as he glanced up to meet Riley's hard gaze.

"What's up?"

Riley's lips thinned and he moved his gaze to the doors leading out to Carter's balcony. "Can we step outside a minute? I, uh, need to ask you something."

"O-o-kay." Carter recognized anger in his friend's face and apprehension bubbled in his gut. He pointed at Riley's glass. "Why don't you give me that and go grab your coat? I'll pour you another drink and meet you outside."

Riley didn't seem any less stressed when Carter joined him five minutes later, though he murmured his thanks after Carter handed him a drink. They turned to look out at the city skyline and the silence between them lengthened, growing heavy. Carter bit his tongue in an effort to wait his friend out.

At last, Riley cast a glance over his shoulder at the little party still going on inside. "Sorry to drag you out here in the middle of everything. What did you tell them?"

Carter shrugged. "Just that we needed some air. Audrey's brewing coffee and putting together a cheese platter. We have time to talk, if that's what you want." He turned his head to meet Riley's gaze. "*Is* that what you want?"

"I don't know." Riley sipped from his glass, then leaned forward to rest his forearms on the balcony's stone ledge. "I'm not sure I'm ready to hear the answers you might have to my questions."

Mirroring Riley's stance, Carter leaned forward, taking a moment to digest his friend's words. "Well, I'll try to answer honestly."

"That's what I'm afraid of." Riley twisted his lips in a wry smile. "Though I suppose it's too late now to pretend there's a way out of this mess."

"What mess, Riley? What are you talking about?"

Riley shifted his gaze back to the city lights and he blew out a long breath. "How deep are you in with Jesse Murtagh?"

"How deep am I—?" Carter drew up short. "I don't know what you mean. Jesse's my friend."

"Come on, Carter," Riley scoffed. "You don't really think anyone's buying that, do you?"

Carter almost laughed at the feeling of déjà vu. "Okay, sure. We're friends and a little extra. You know this," he added, while Riley shook his head.

"You've told me that before. I didn't believe it then and I definitely don't believe it now."

The dry skepticism in Riley's tone set Carter's teeth on edge. "Why would I lie?"

"I have no idea." Standing straight, Riley turned, his whole demeanor screaming distress. "Especially since you've already introduced Jesse to Sadie and Dylan."

"Yes, as my friend. The kids aren't ready to meet anyone Kate or I are dating—in fact, they've flat out refused to do so. They're fine with meeting people we call friends, though." Carter nearly flinched when Riley muttered a curse.

"You make it a habit to introduce your kids to friends who you fuck?"

"That is none of your goddamned business, Riley!" Carter's voice rang through the chilly air and he raised a hand to his mouth.

Great, more yelling on a balcony, he thought, then swallowed hard. "I know you don't approve of Jesse and Kyle," he continued more quietly, "but they've been good to me."

"I don't care how you spend your private time—"

Carter sneered. "Come on."

"I don't!" Riley protested. "Okay, fine. It's weird that you went from being happily married to sleeping with multiple partners. I thought I knew you better, Carter. Thought you'd be against open relationships after everything we went through, honestly. But, hey, it's none of my business. I do hope you're being careful when it comes to Sadie and Dylan's feelings, though."

Riley swallowed as Carter stared at him. "What's that face for?"

Carter raised his free hand to rub at the nape of his neck, weighed down by a sudden wave of sadness. Riley had no idea how far off he was in his assumptions about Carter's sex life. And while Carter had gotten used to other people assuming the worst of him, even misjudging how much Carter cared for his children, it rankled to know that Riley had misjudged him too.

"Honestly, I don't even know what to say. You don't know me at *all* if you think I'm anything but careful about protecting Sadie and Dylan. Their well-being means more to me than my own. If you want to judge me, that's fine, but leave my kids out of it. I'm not a perfect father, but you truly have no idea what you're talking about."

Riley seemed to deflate all at once. "Jesus. I'm really sorry."

"Okay."

"No, I mean it. None of that came out the way I meant. I know you're a good dad."

"I try to be." Carter worried his lip with his teeth at the remorse in Riley's face. "Look, let's just forget it. Unless…you want to tell me what's bothering you? I mean, it's obvious you don't like my friends. I don't expect you to be buddies with everyone I know, but you could at least try to get along with them. I tried with Will," he added, before ducking his head a little in embarrassment. "I know it didn't go well, but I did try."

Riley waved him off. "I know. You and Will never hit it off because he didn't want to like you." His tone was resigned. "He was jealous of the time I spent with you, resentful of the history you and I shared. The worst part was knowing I'd have to end my friendship with you to satisfy him."

Carter nodded, considering his friend's words for a long moment. "So why are you making things hard on me when it comes to Jesse and the other guys?" He reached out and squeezed Riley's shoulder when Riley looked sheepish. "Jesse's a good guy—I think you'd actually like him if you just got to know him. What did he ever do to you?"

"He got you," Riley made a face and Carter let his hand fall away. "You spent Christmas Eve with him."

"And a bunch of other friends," Carter countered. "Jesse knew I wasn't going to see the kids or my parents and invited me over for dinner."

"He makes you happy. I can see it on your face when you talk about him." Riley shook his head. "Hell, he's even got your kids singing his praises."

"Sadie and Dylan spent one day with Jesse. He fed them waffles, ran around a comic book store with them, then let Sadie put barrettes in his hair while we watched an *Iron Man* movie marathon. He called Dylan 'Dyl Pickle' for the whole day. Of *course*, the kids like him."

Riley chuckled. "Did Sadie get the idea for S'mores from him?"

"Yeah." Carter glanced over his shoulder at his family behind the windows. "He mentioned making them a couple of weekends before at his brother's house."

Carter turned his gaze on the lights as Riley stayed quiet beside him.

"Making friends doesn't come as easily to me as it does you, Ri. Jesse and Kyle…they're good for me. Especially Jesse. He *is* fun and I *do* like spending time with him. Especially fooling around with him. A lot. But he hasn't 'got me', or not in the way you might think. There's no great romance happening between us."

"That's…surprising." Riley's brow was creased when Carter met his gaze. "That's enough for you?"

"For now, yes."

"You don't want more? Someone more permanent in your life?"

Carter exhaled slowly. "I think I would, yes. Sometime. I'm not sure I'm ready for it yet, though. I mean, I don't know what the fuck I'm doing most days—I'm still a big mess."

"Stop selling yourself short, Car—you're doing just fine." Riley's eyes were bright. "I think all you need is some practice dating with someone who's not just your friend."

"Huh." Carter's chest ached almost painfully. "Do you have someone special in mind for the job?"

"I might." Riley took a step closer, bringing his free hand up to brush his knuckles against the coat covering Carter's chest. "If you want to try, that is."

A lump rose in Carter's throat, making it impossible for him to speak for a moment. He stared at his best friend instead, wanting desperately to pull him close. He wanted to breathe in Riley's scent and feel Riley's warmth against him. It was a bad idea, though, no matter what Riley thought or Carter wanted. Riley wasn't ready to jump into another flirtation, especially one with the potential to become serious. If they tried and Riley pulled away because he changed his mind...well, Carter wasn't sure his heart could handle it. And if Carter had learned anything in the last two years, he knew he needed his friendship with Riley to be solid.

His voice croaked when he replied. "I'd like to try. Soon. For now, though, I think we need to get back on track as friends before we can know what else is there between us. We were headed that way for a while," he added hastily when Riley's face fell, "before you put things on hold—"

"Because I needed to focus my attention on making things work with Will."

"Yeah."

Riley nodded and his throat worked. "Will's not here now, Carter."

"So, we start again. I think we both finally know what we want, now. Let's try it out and see what happens."

"Okay." Riley's face lit up with a smile. "I can do that."

Carter's heart practically soared.

"Okay, good." Glancing over his shoulder again, he jerked his head at the door to the apartment. "Now come back inside with me—you need to make sure I don't burn the house down making S'mores with my kids."

Chapter Thirteen

A snowball hit Riley square in the chest, spraying snow into his face. Laughing, he sputtered and wiped it off. "You are dead, Carter Hamilton," he called.

Carter snickered and fired another shot, which clipped Riley on the thigh.

"You're supposed to be making a snowman, Daddy!" Dylan called.

"Yeah, Carter," Riley teased. "I thought we were here to build a snowman, not start a snowball fight."

Carter glared at him, narrowing his eyes, but he grinned after a moment and bent down to roll the snowball he'd been making in the snow. "Then I guess we'd better make the biggest, best snowman *ever*."

Sadie and Dylan's enthusiastic cheer made Riley smile.

Manhattan had gotten a good six to eight inches of snow dumped on it in the past forty-eight hours and the city was a winter wonderland. When Carter had suggested taking the kids to Central Park on Saturday,

Riley had wholeheartedly agreed. He couldn't remember the last time he'd played in the snow and was enjoying himself immensely.

Half an hour later, a slightly lopsided snowman stood in front of them, decked out in a red hat Dylan had outgrown and a carrot Riley had brought, along with a few branches they'd found to use for arms.

"Hamiltons," Riley called, "go stand by the snowman and I'll take a picture."

Dylan threw his arms around the snowman on one side, while Sadie took a spot on the other and Carter stood behind. Riley used his phone camera to snap a shot of them and chuckled at the cheesy grin on Dylan's face.

"Looks good!" Riley called out.

"You get in one, too," Sadie said.

"I think I can do that," Riley said. He knelt in front of the snowman and the Hamiltons crowded around him. He lined it up so the snowman's head was still in the shot. "Okay, everyone, on three. One, two, three—"

"Cheeeeeese!" Dylan yelled and they all dissolved into giggles. The shot Riley got with his phone was one of them laughing, and Riley showed it to Carter, who grinned.

"You'll have to send that to me. I'll set it as my lock screen on my phone."

"I will when I can feel my fingers again." Riley tucked his cell phone into his pocket before he stood and brushed off his knees. "Brr. Remind me to buy some better outwear. I haven't been skiing in years and I think I donated all my warm outdoor gear to a shelter years ago."

"God, I haven't gone in years, either," Carter said. He glanced over at the kids, who were now pelting each other with snowballs. "What do you think about taking the kids sometime? They should learn to ski while they're still little and Kate was never that fond of skiing. She turns into an ice cube after twenty minutes outside."

"Sure," Riley agreed. "I don't know if the weather will cooperate this year, but if we can figure out a time to take a long weekend in Vermont or New Hampshire, that would be fun." He tried to brush off more snow, but his jeans were damp underneath. "Are we just about done? Unfortunately, I'm not very well-dressed for this."

"Time to head back home, kids!" Carter called to them.

"Do we have to, Daddy?" Dylan whined.

"I promise hot chocolate!"

"Okay." Dylan dropped his snowball and scampered over. "C'mon, Sadie. Hurry! Hot *cocoa!*"

They piled into a cab for the trip back and, once inside the apartment, they all disappeared to change into dry clothes. Carter loaned him a pair of too-long sweatpants and Riley was the first to finish dressing.

He went straight to the kitchen, poured milk into a saucepan and turned it on to simmer. He'd just finished stirring the chocolate into it when Carter reappeared. His cheeks were still pink from the cold and his hair was wind-tousled. The sight made Riley's heart race.

Carter skimmed a hand along Riley's lower back as he leaned in. He peered into the pan and smiled. "Mmm, you made it the good way."

"With milk? Yes. Dear Lord, don't tell me you're a heathen and make it with water?"

Carter shrugged.

"I am exceptionally lazy in the kitchen — you should know this by now."

Riley shuddered. "There's lazy and then there's just wrong. Good thing you Hamiltons have me around."

Carter tightened his grip on Riley's hip and coaxed him to turn. "I would have to agree with that sentiment. The past month has been so good."

Riley glanced toward the hallway to be sure the kids weren't coming before he smoothed a hand over Carter's chest. The wool of his cream-colored sweater was soft under Riley's palm, a contrast to the firm planes of muscle beneath. "It has."

It was late January and since his breakup with Will, Riley had spent a lot more time with Carter. They'd kept it platonic, but with every day, their friendship seemed to strengthen, along with the attraction.

"How are you feeling about Will?"

He shrugged. "Still a bit guilty that things ended so badly. But a part of me is relieved and I can see that it was for the best. I always felt like I had to push myself to take the next step with him, where it's pretty effortless with you." He chuckled and stepped a little closer to Carter. "Well, if you can call over a decade and a half and being married to other people effortless…"

Carter chuckled. "I know what you mean." He grew more serious. "Does that mean you are ready for more with me?"

Riley nodded. "I think taking this time was good. I've had a chance to think about what happened with Will and I know what I want now."

"What's that?" Carter's voice turned husky.

"You, Carter. A relationship with you. If you're ready to end things with Jesse and Kyle, that is. I don't think I can handle an open relationship. If we're together —

finally—after all this time, I don't think I can share you with anyone. I need to know you're mine."

"Oh, God, Ri." The look in Carter's eyes heated Riley's blood. Carter cupped Riley's face with his hands and brought their foreheads together. "I want that. You and me. No one else. If you're ready, I'm in. All the way."

Riley felt dizzy as Carter brushed their lips together. "I'm ready."

The sound of small, chattering voices interrupted their embrace and Carter sprang back, brushing his mouth with his fingertips before he gave Riley an apologetic grin.

"I want three marshmallows, Daddy!" Dylan said as he appeared in the kitchen.

"I think that can be arranged!" Carter replied.

Riley cleared his throat and turned back to the stove. He clicked off the burner, hoping he hadn't scorched the milk. He took a few deep breaths, trying to slow his rapidly beating heart.

"Don't forget the purple mug," Sadie said. "It's my favorite."

"Aww, man, I was going to use it," Carter said as he reached into the cupboard near Riley. "I guess I can let you have it."

She giggled. "It's *my* mug, Daddy."

"Oh, that's right," Carter said. "I always forget."

Riley poured chocolate into mugs for Sadie and Dylan and turned to face them with a smile. "If you come over to my place, I can make you really fancy drinks with shaved chocolate and real whipped cream."

Sadie's eyes lit up, but Dylan gave him a skeptical look. "I like marshmallows better."

"I think I could probably get some of those for you," Riley answered.

Carter handed two more mugs to Riley. "Since I can't use the purple mug, I guess I'll have to use my other favorite one." Riley smiled at the sight of the *Eat, Sleep, Study, Row* mug Riley had bought him in college. It was coffee-stained and there was a small chip in the rim — it was obviously well-used and well-loved. Riley filled it with hot chocolate and handed it back to Carter. Rather than take it from him, Carter wrapped his hand around Riley's grip on the handle and squeezed.

"Sorry," he mouthed.

Riley shrugged. He couldn't wait to kiss Carter later, when they were alone, but for now, he was perfectly content.

He poured the remainder of the hot chocolate into the plain white cup Carter had given him and carried it to the table, where Carter was occupied dropping marshmallows into the kids' drinks.

Carter bumped his shoulder as he passed and they exchanged a lingering glance.

We're together now, Riley thought, the knowledge thrilling him. *Finally. After all this time, we've finally managed to be ready for a relationship at the same time.*

The idea warmed him to his toes.

* * * *

"Mmm. You spoil me." Carter's moan was nearly pornographic. Riley glanced at him across the table and was struck dumb by Carter's smile. It was slow and warm. It heated Riley's blood and he tugged at the collar of his midnight-blue shirt.

"I enjoy it."

Carter lifted a forkful of pasta and crab to his lips and chewed slowly, his eyelids fluttering with pleasure. "God, you're going to have to teach to me how to make this."

Riley smiled and dug into his plate of seafood linguine. It was Carter's favorite. "What fun is that? I'm all for you learning to cook, Carter, but a man has to have some tricks up his sleeve. I'm not above seducing you with food."

"I'm not above being seduced."

A smile played at his lips as he sipped the Pouilly-Fumé Carter had brought. "I'll keep that in mind."

They continued to flirt throughout dinner and stole a few kisses as they cleaned up after. After Riley slid the Santoku knife into the block on the counter, Carter wrapped his arms around Riley's midsection, pinning him against the cabinets. "God, I don't want to leave."

Riley attempted to hide his frown. "I don't want you to leave, either."

"Damn the dentist," Carter grumbled in his ear.

The kids both had dentist appointments at an unholy hour the next day, which was why he couldn't stick around.

"Kate has a meeting for one of her charity boards tomorrow morning, or I'd ask her to take them." Carter nuzzled Riley's neck, the soft scrape of his stubble sending a jolt of desire through Riley's body.

"I understand." Riley tightened his grip on the edge of the counter. "God, Carter! You're killing me."

"Call it payback for seducing me with my favorite dinner when you knew I had to leave." He gently bit at Riley's throat.

Riley's chuckle dissolved into a moan. "Am I going to have to kick you out before you drive both of us insane?"

"Possibly." Carter pressed a kiss to the spot he'd bitten, then stepped back with a heartfelt sigh.

Riley turned and smiled at him. It was probably best that Carter had to leave. It had only been a few weeks since their discussion about starting a relationship and they were still feeling out the transition as they moved from being friends to *more than friends*. They had both agreed it was best not to rush things, but it was difficult not to want to when Carter stood in front of him, appearing handsome and practically irresistible. *'Damn the dentist' is right.*

"Fine. I'm going, I'm going," Carter grumbled.

Riley followed him to the entryway and handed him his leather coat. Once it was on, it took all of Riley's willpower not to run his hands across the smooth, supple fabric molded across Carter's chest.

At first, Riley had been a little unsure of Carter's makeover. The new clothes and different haircut had thrown him for a while, especially since they'd come about because of the influence of Jesse Murtagh. But now that Jesse was firmly relegated to *friend* and Riley had slid into the place of *boyfriend*, he could be a bit more magnanimous. He'd begun to enjoy Carter's new style.

Carter wrapped the black cashmere scarf around his throat and leaned in, his mouth inches from Riley's. "You make it very hard to go when you look at me like that."

"How do I look at you?"

Carter straightened. "Like you never want me to leave."

Riley shrugged and gave him a half-smile. There was some truth to that. "I wasn't planning to kidnap you, I swear," he said teasingly.

"It's difficult to kidnap the willing." Carter's smile was blinding.

"I'll keep that in mind."

Carter wrapped a hand around the back of Riley's head and drew him in for a thorough, lingering kiss. Despite the other changes, the scent of Carter's woodsy cologne had remained the same and, along with the scent of rich leather, it made Riley's head spin. Carter's mouth tasted of the chocolate torte they'd had for dinner and Riley teased Carter's tongue with his own, chasing the flavor.

Carter groaned deep in his throat and, reluctantly, Riley ended the kiss. They were still pressed together, chest to toes, and, when Riley tried to draw back, Carter tightened his grip. He dove in for another kiss, this one even deeper and needier, and by the time he finally pulled away, they were both panting. He could feel Carter's cock—half-hard and rapidly growing—pressed against his own. It took all of his willpower to step back instead of pushing Carter against the door and dropping to his knees.

"Thanks for dinner." Carter's smile was devilish.

Riley laughed, aroused and befuddled by the kisses. "Any time."

"G'night, Ri." He stepped back and was out of the door before Riley managed a reply.

"Night, Car," Riley whispered as he locked the door behind him, a smile on his face.

* * * *

The dishwasher hummed quietly in the background as Riley stretched out on the sectional and reached for his iPad. He turned it on and brought up the novel he'd been reading, but after a while, he found his mind drifting.

It had been a very pleasant evening. Although they'd had little time for more than the meal and all-too-brief kisses, Riley felt a quiet sense of contentment. Seeing Carter across the table from him, enjoying the dinner he'd made, was enough.

His phone vibrated on the coffee table beside him. He reached for it with a smile, wondering if Carter had sent him a 'good night' message as he climbed into bed. Riley was surprised to see Dan Conley's name flash across his screen.

"Hey, Dan," he answered a moment later, after he'd set his iPad aside.

"Hey, Riley. I called to see how you were doing, but maybe I don't need to ask. You sound good!"

"I feel good," Riley admitted, a smile stretching across his face. "But I'm glad you called."

"Of course. You sounded a little unsure about where you were headed when we talked last and I wanted to see how it was going with Carter."

"Carter and I are…trying."

"A relationship? That's fantastic, man. It's about damn time!"

Riley smiled wider at Dan's enthusiasm. "We talked about it at Christmas, actually. We're taking things pretty slow for now, but it feels good. It feels right this time," he admitted.

"Slow as in not hopping right into bed? I hate to point out the obvious, but you two have been dancing around this for nearly two decades now," Dan teased.

Riley winced at the reminder. "I know. But all the more reason to take it slowly. There's a lot at stake here. Neither of us want to screw this up."

Dan's tone grew serious. "I know. And I respect that. But if you two *haven't* been fucking like bunnies, what *have* you been doing?"

Riley chuckled. "Let's see. We went to a cooking class, a jazz concert and out to dinner several times. We spent a few nights in watching movies. Tonight, I cooked dinner for Carter. Oh! And we took the kids to the park to build snowmen after that snow we got a few weeks ago."

"How are Sadie and Dylan dealing with the fact that Dad and Uncle Riley are dating?"

"They don't know yet. Hell, Kate doesn't know about us yet. Like I said, we're going slowly," Riley said with a sigh. "It'll happen in time, but the ink on Carter and Kate's divorce papers is barely dry. We don't want to make the situation any more difficult than it has to be. Kate and the kids have been hurt enough."

"Of course." Dan hummed thoughtfully. "How do you think Kate'll take it?"

"Fuck, I don't know." Riley ran a hand through his hair and stretched. "She seemed okay with Carter dating other men, but I'm worried she'll take the idea of Carter and me together hard. I hope it'll go okay, but I can't be sure. And I can't say that I'd blame her if she was upset."

"It's a difficult situation. At least the kids are relatively young. That helps."

"God, I hope so. The last thing I want to do is be the guy who stole their dad away from their mom."

"Hey, don't be so hard on yourself," Dan chastised him gently. "Sadie and Dylan love you. They'll adjust and see that you are good for Carter."

"Am I?" Riley asked, voicing the fear that had nagged at him for the past few weeks. "That's what scares the hell out of me. That we'll go through all of this and find out we're not a great couple."

Dan's bark of laughter was incredulous. "You're kidding me, right?"

"No."

"Riley, I have known you and Carter for over a decade and a half, and I can honestly say that you two are *made* for each other. When you said you wanted to focus on your relationship with Will and Carter started seeing other guys, I understood, but I doubted it would last."

Riley snorted quietly. "I appreciate your faith in our ability to hold down relationships."

"Oh, fuck off." Dan's tone was affectionate, despite the harsh words. "What I have faith in is your bond. I wish I'd taken a video of you and Carter interacting at the party. It's no wonder Will lost his shit, because your feelings were written all over both your faces. Hell, you two mirror each other's movements and finish each other's sentences. Sure, some of it can be chalked up to a long-term friendship, but that's not all of it. The two of you have this incredible connection. It was like that in college and it's only deepened. And now that you're relaxed around each other and not trying to hide your feelings…it's pretty awe-inspiring, to be honest."

Riley was silent for a moment while he absorbed Dan's words. A stab of guilt chased them. "I just wish Will hadn't been hurt in the process."

"I know. Have you two talked at all since the party?"

"Once. It was awkward, to say the least." They'd spoken on the phone and Will's responses had been clipped and terse. He was hurting and Riley was the cause.

"Well, that's to be expected."

"He had Gabe drop off a box with my stuff. Gabe seems as though he wants to continue to be friends, although it puts him in a terrible position. Charles won't speak to me at all and Will's only speaking to me through Gabe."

"Are you going to try to stay friends with Will? Or let it go?"

Riley shrugged. "I'd *like* to remain friends. I don't know that it's realistic, though. And I don't feel like I have any right to ask anything of him after what happened."

"Riley." Dan sounded a little exasperated "Don't be so damn hard on yourself. You didn't lie to Will, you didn't cheat on him. You were very upfront about your feelings for Carter from the beginning. It's unfortunate that Will got hurt in the process, but you weren't deliberately cruel."

"I know. I just feel like I wasn't fair to him."

"It's never easy to hurt someone you care about, even if it's unintentional."

"No, it's not." Riley swallowed past the lump in his throat. "And I have wanted Carter so much and for so long that I'm always worried that I let that get in the way of treating people decently. I hurt Alex more than I ever realized, I hurt Kate, I hurt Will, and I just don't want to be the guy who runs roughshod over the people in his life to get what he wants."

"The fact that you're so concerned about the hurt you could cause is enough to reassure me that being that callous isn't in your nature, Ri. Apologize to Will again, take things slow with Carter and allow yourself to be happy." Dan cleared his throat. "You are allowed to be happy. Remember that."

* * * *

"Finally alone," Carter said with a smile as he walked into the living room. "I didn't expect to take so long. Dylan did not want to go down."

"It's fine. They're finally asleep now, though?" Riley asked.

Carter nodded. "In theory, anyway. Dylan tried to fight it, but he finally passed out after the third story and Sadie's either asleep or better at hiding the flashlight than she used to be. I couldn't see any light under the door."

Riley chuckled. He remembered reading under the covers by flashlight as a kid. His parents certainly wouldn't have noticed, but Sarah, his nanny, had. She'd sternly told him to turn it off and go to bed. She'd never told Geneva and Jonathon, though. He smiled at the memory.

Carter dropped onto the couch beside Riley and draped an arm around his shoulders. A pleasant thrill ran through him at the gesture. Riley, Carter, Sadie and Dylan had made pizzas and watched *How to Train Your Dragon* on DVD that evening. It had been enjoyable, but he looked forward to some alone time with Carter. Riley grabbed the remote and cued up the movie he'd picked earlier.

When he'd asked Carter what he'd wanted to watch, he'd shrugged and requested *'anything not animated.'*

Riley had debated between a Tarantino flick and a legal thriller before finally settling on the latter, in case one of the kids came out. He didn't want to be responsible for their nightmares after accidentally seeing a blood-soaked scene.

"Thanks for being so flexible about plans tonight," Carter said with a half-smile. "I'm sorry we had to cancel dinner reservations."

Riley shrugged. "You could hardly anticipate Kate's plane being grounded by a snowstorm in Baltimore. I am just glad you didn't cancel altogether." Kate had flown to D.C. to visit her college roommate and a freak snowstorm had caught everyone by surprise. She was safe in a hotel in Baltimore for the night, but unlikely to get home for another day or two.

Carter shrugged. "I know pizza and animated movies aren't your idea of high entertainment."

"Carter!" Riley said, feeling exasperated. "I had a great time tonight. Making pizza was fun. The kids had a blast stretching the dough, you got to show them your knife skills and the picture I got of Dylan covered in flour is going to be excellent to display at his high school graduation party."

Carter snorted. "True."

Riley nudged his thigh with his knee. "So, stop apologizing. I had fun tonight."

"I'm glad." Carter brushed his lips across Riley's hair. "I just want to be sure you don't feel neglected."

"Stop worrying." He craned his neck to look Carter in the eye. "We have a couple of hours of alone time right now. Let's enjoy that."

Carter's eyes lit up and he pressed a light kiss to Riley's lips. "I like the sound of that. Let's get comfy."

He manhandled Riley until they both lay full length, with Riley wedged between the couch cushions and Carter's body. Carter lay on his back and Riley was on his side. Riley froze when Carter wrapped an arm around him and pulled him close.

"What if the kids get up and see us?" he asked.

"It'll be fine. They're both sound asleep, I promise," Carter said. "I just really need to feel you in my arms right now." There was a gruffness to his voice and an intensity in his eyes that Riley couldn't resist. To be honest, he needed it, too. Since Christmas, he and Carter hadn't managed much beyond some very steamy kisses, and he wanted to be as close to him as possible.

Riley reached for the plush, oatmeal-colored throw blanket on the back of the couch. He drew it over both of them, cocooning them together. He settled his head on the spot where Carter's shoulder and chest met and draped an arm across his torso.

The sound Carter let out went right to Riley's chest. He smoothed his thumb across Carter's ribs. He couldn't manage words at the moment, but he knew exactly how Carter felt. He'd wanted a night like this for the better part of fifteen years. Half of him expected to wake up and find out he was dreaming.

"I honestly never thought we'd get here. I wanted it, but I thought it was impossible," Carter said softly, echoing Riley's thoughts.

"Me, too."

"God, we wasted so much time." There was a melancholy note to Carter's voice.

Riley smiled sadly and tilted his head to look at Carter. "I have to believe it was for a good reason. Call it practice so we'd be ready when we finally got here."

"I hope so." Carter dipped his chin and brushed his lips across Riley's. With a sigh, Riley closed his eyes and returned it. The warmth of Carter's mouth and the rasp of his whiskers sent a shudder through Riley. He flicked his tongue against the seam of Carter's lips. He opened to Riley and returned the kiss with a staggering passion. Riley groaned against his mouth and grabbed Carter's shoulder, bracing an elbow on the couch so he lay half on Carter's chest and they could kiss more easily.

Carter slid his large, strong hands down Riley's back and came to rest on the swell of his ass. Riley shuddered and threaded his hand through Carter's hair, the kiss growing needier and more aggressive.

Riley tore his mouth away, gasping for air, and Carter moved his lips to Riley's jaw and the side of his neck. He whimpered when Carter took his earlobe between his teeth and he tilted his head to allow him better access.

"Ri..." Carter murmured against his skin, his low, needy voice making his chest rumble against Riley's. Carter kneaded his ass, pulling them tightly together. "God, I need you. I know we were going to take it slow, but..."

Riley opened his eyes and gazed down at Carter. Carter's eyes were bright, his hair mussed from Riley's hands and his lips were damp and shiny. He could feel Carter's erection against his thigh and his own throbbed against Carter's hip.

He didn't lose eye contact with Carter as he reached down, shifting just enough to touch Carter through the denim of his jeans. "How's this?" He ran his palm across the fly, watching Carter's pupils dilate and his cheeks flush when he passed over the ridged head of his cock.

"Good." Carter's voice came out strangled. "Oh, God."

Riley smiled down at him, beginning a rhythmic stroking motion that made Carter's eyelids flutter, then close, before he threw his head back. The quiet sound of his panting in Riley's ear made Riley continue despite the awkward angle and clothing in the way. He thoroughly enjoyed Carter's reactions. When he slid his hand down to cup Carter's balls, Carter let out a strangled gasp.

Riley ran his palm up and over the thick bulge of Carter's cock, pressing harder with the palm of his hand. Every tiny sound Carter made aroused him and the whimpers and bitten-back moans spurred Riley on.

"You're gonna make me come in my pants," Carter hissed.

"Do you want me to stop?" Riley asked.

"No." The word dissolved in a moan and Carter lifted his hips in time with Riley's firm strokes.

Riley toyed with the fly of Carter's jeans, struggling for a moment before he managed to open the button. He lowered the zipper, inching it down painfully slowly. He slipped his fingers underneath the fly, finding the soft cotton of Carter's boxers, sticky-wet in one spot.

Carter clutched the back of Riley's shirt when he slid under the flap on the front of his boxers and their skin made contact.

"Oh, fuck, Ri." Riley wrapped his hand around Carter's cock and smoothed his thumb across the leaking head. Carter made a quiet whimpering sound.

"You don't know how much I've missed having you touch me."

Riley smiled down at him—a brief moment of tenderness in the midst of desire—and pressed a kiss to Carter's lips. "I think I do," he murmured. He stroked—slowly, teasingly, wringing every single reaction he could from Carter. There was enough pre-cum to slick his movements and when Carter's thighs trembled, Riley ducked his head under the blanket and slid down Carter's body.

He'd barely gotten his mouth around Carter's cock when he came, his muffled sounds music to Riley's ears. Riley swallowed, then took Carter in his mouth again. He licked and teased, making Carter shudder and twitch. Carter rested a hand on his head, stroking his hair while Riley prolonged his pleasure.

A gentle tug from Carter made Riley stop. He pressed a kiss to Carter's hip and shifted so he was stretched out beside Carter again. Carter gave him a dazed half-grin before he pulled him in for a kiss.

"How hard are you?" Carter asked quietly when he pulled back.

Riley pressed his cock against Carter's thigh in answer.

"Let me see if I can do something about that," Carter replied. His hands disappeared under the blanket and Riley assumed he was zipping up again. "I want to taste you."

"Daddy?"

The sound of a small, sleepy voice jolted them both into action. Carter sat up, his forehead making contact with Riley's chin as they struggled to right themselves. Riley grabbed for the blanket to cover his rapidly wilting erection before he had time to think that Carter might not have managed to zip up his fly.

Riley gulped and looked over at Dylan. He stood in the hallway leading to the living room, sleepily rubbing his eyes.

"You okay, Dyl?" Carter asked. He stood — and to Riley's relief — appeared fully dressed, although his shirt was untucked. His fingers shook as he smoothed it down. Carter crossed the room to his son. Dylan nodded and held out his arms.

Riley took a few deeps breaths, trying to calm his racing heart. How long had Dylan been standing there? Had Dylan seen something? The room was dim, except for the glow from the TV and a lamp in the far corner, but he wasn't sure if that was enough to hide what they'd been doing.

Carter scooped him up and patted his back. "Bad dream?"

"Thirsty." Dylan yawned and buried his head against Carter's shoulder. "Were you and Unca' Ri building a fort?"

Carter's wide eyes met Riley's and Riley could see the wheels turning while he tried to figure out exactly what Dylan had seen.

"Uhh." Riley cleared his throat and racked his brain for a plausible explanation. He grabbed the blanket to fold it and his phone came tumbling out. Relief washed over him. "We were watching a movie and my phone fell out of my pocket. Your dad was helping me find it."

I'm not in the habit of lying to small children, but under the circumstances… Riley thought.

"Oh." Dylan yawned again. "A fort sounds more fun."

Carter's relief was palpable. "Maybe we can build a fort soon. How about we get some water and put you back to bed?"

"'k." Dylan's eyes closed. "Can Unca' Ri help?"

"With the fort? Sure. We can do that next time he's over." Carter pressed a kiss to the top of Dylan's head before they disappeared into Dylan's bedroom.

Riley let out a sigh of relief and sagged back against the couch cushions. Although he'd enjoyed sucking Carter's cock, there was no way they would risk that again. Dylan was young — and sleepy — enough to not question their story, but Sadie would never have believed it. In the future, he and Carter needed to be a hell of a lot more careful.

While he waited for Carter to return, Riley grabbed the remote and rewound until he found the place in the movie where they'd stopped paying attention.

"God, I am so sorry about that."

Riley glanced up from his phone to see Carter dragging a hand through his hair, a chagrined expression on his face.

"Why?" Riley asked, mystified by the apology. "I'm the one who—" He lowered his voice then changed his mind about what he was about to say, "Took things too far."

Carter dropped on the couch with a groan and Riley shifted to meet his gaze. "Yeah, but I certainly didn't try to stop you. I should have been paying more attention. Dylan doesn't get up often, but…" He shook his head. "They're my responsibility. I let myself get carried away."

Riley shrugged and reached for Carter's hand. Reluctantly, he took it. "Hey, now we know."

"We may need to tell Kate and the kids a little sooner than I planned."

"Whenever works best for all of you," Riley said. "I can be patient."

"I am sorry, Ri. This is my life now." Carter sounded apologetic. "I wouldn't blame you if you ran screaming in the other direction."

Riley reached out with his other hand and grabbed the back of Carter's head. Not to kiss him, but so they were eye-to-eye. "You don't need to apologize. I know this is all part of being with you and I'm not going anywhere. I want to be included in this life, if you'll let me."

Carter nodded, his shoulders sagging with relief. He glanced toward the doorway, then leaned in to lightly brush their lips together. Carter skimmed his along Riley's jaw when he pulled back. "Didn't mean to clock you like that. Dylan really scared the crap out of me."

"You do have an exceptionally hard head," Riley teased. Carter snorted and reached for the remote.

"Want to finish the movie?"

"Definitely."

Although they stayed upright this time, they were close enough to touch and Riley spent an equal amount of time marveling about the fact that he could hold Carter's hand as he did watching the movie.

"Thank you for staying," Carter said quietly after the movie ended. It sounded heartfelt.

Riley squeezed his hand. "There's nowhere I'd rather be."

Chapter Fourteen

Carter glanced at his watch when the train jerked to a stop, then stepped into the stream of passengers pushing toward the door. His last meeting of the day had gone over and now he was running late for dinner with the kids and Kate. His phone buzzed in his pocket as he stepped onto the platform and when he pulled it out, he smiled.

You are officially very tardy. The children want gelato as penance.

Carter waited until he'd reached the sidewalk outside the station before replying.

You realize a gelato run will make me later than ever?

How long?

30 minutes.

Get your ass in gear, Kate replied. *I'll do my best to hold them off.*

Carter slid his phone back into his pocket and headed down the block, feeling grateful for the friendship he'd been able to build with his ex. He'd been nervous to tell Kate about his and Riley's decision to begin dating, but had finally taken the plunge one night after a family dinner while the kids were immersed in a Pixar movie. Kate had given a long-suffering sigh and given Carter some good-natured shit about taking forever to get his act together. She'd handled it well, though, and together they'd agreed to wait a while longer to tell the kids — Sadie and Dylan had finally come around to the idea of their mother being involved with Robert, which was more than their parents had hoped for.

Unfortunately, Carter failed to anticipate long lines at the gelateria, and nearly forty-five minutes passed before he rang Kate's buzzer. He'd jogged the two blocks from the shop and felt overheated in his suit under his leather coat. His discomfort disappeared the moment the door opened to reveal his children's smiling faces.

"Dad, I have a terrible joke to tell you!" Dylan told him while Sadie pulled Carter inside by the hand.

Carter set his things down on the floor while Dylan closed the door behind them. He waited until Dylan met his gaze again before nodding. "Okay, let's hear it."

"What do you call a fish that's missing an eye?"

"Um…" Carter raised his hands to unbutton his coat while Dylan and his sister grinned broadly. "I don't know — what *do* you call a fish that's missing an eye?"

"A FSSSHHHH!" Dylan cried. He immediately erupted in raucous laughter so contagious Sadie and Carter joined in.

Carter followed the kids back into Kate's kitchen. Stepping into the good-natured chaos Sadie and Dylan generated still made him melancholy. It hurt to realize how much he was missing by living apart from them. He knew the wound would never truly heal, but it had become easier as his life away from Sadie and Dylan slowly became whole.

"Something smells delicious," he declared after they'd sat down to a meal of pasta, bread and green salad.

"There's bacon in the spaghetti, Daddy," Dylan told him before taking an enormous mouthful of bread that muffled his next words.

"He's saying there's butternut squash in it, too," Kate translated when Carter met her gaze across the table. "Dylan, please take human bites—pigs are not permitted at this dinner table."

Carter bit back a smile and he held out a hand to Sadie for her plate. "Bacon and butternut squash sounds fantastic. This is the second pasta meal I've had this week, though, so I'm going to have to run some extra miles or I'll look like a pig. Riley made linguine and a mess of seafood on Sunday night," he added after Kate raised her eyebrows in question.

"A mess of seafood sounds pretty gross," Sadie observed serenely over a forkful of spaghetti.

"It does sound gross when I say it like that," Carter agreed, "but it really was delicious."

"How come Uncle Ri knows how to cook?" Sadie asked suddenly. "Didn't Alex cook for him when they were married?"

"I'm not sure if Alex did any kind of cooking, sweetheart. Your mommy likes to cook and she's really good at it, but not everyone enjoys it," Carter explained. "Your Uncle Ri has always liked fooling around in the kitchen, but he wasn't very good at it until recently."

"I haven't seen Aunt Alex in a long time," Dylan observed, his tone thoughtful.

Sadie turned to her brother before Carter could answer. "Alex and Uncle Ri aren't married anymore, remember? They got divorced like Mommy and Daddy and Alex went away."

Carter's stomach tumbled to his feet. He glanced at Kate, who had paled, before turning back to his daughter. "Alex didn't go away, honey. She still lives in the same apartment she used to share with Riley."

"But they got divorced like you and Mommy," Sadie countered. "And Nana told me Riley and Alex don't see each other anymore."

"That's probably true, Sadie." Kate licked her lips and set down her fork. "Riley and Alex aren't friendly right now, but that doesn't mean they won't be sometime soon."

"How come they're not friendly?" Dylan frowned. "You and Daddy are divorced, but you're still friends, right?"

"Yes, but Daddy and I aren't in the same situation as Uncle Riley and Alex. We made a decision to stay friends, *plus* we have you two to make sure we don't mess that up," Kate added with a wink.

Sadie looked at Carter, her expression doubtful. "So, no one's going away like Alex, right?"

He paused a moment to steady his voice. "Of course not, Sadie."

"We don't all live together anymore, but Daddy isn't going anywhere and neither am I." Kate's face was sober. "Daddy and I are your parents and we're going to be with you for a long, long time."

"What's a parent?" Dylan wondered aloud.

"It's like a mom or dad," Sadie told him, "or, like, a stepmom or stepdad, I guess."

Dylan considered his sister's words, his face scrunched up in thought. "Like Cinderella's stepmother?"

"Yes, but without the wicked part," Carter agreed hastily, "that was just in the story. Parents are people who take care of children, the way Mommy and I take care of you and Sadie."

Dylan nodded, seeming satisfied with Carter's explanation, and began talking about a project for school. Sadie's piercing gaze told Carter his daughter had more on her mind. She'd inherited his own analytical nature on top of Kate's tenacity and he knew she wasn't finished with the topic of parents. They'd nearly finished eating before she spoke up again.

"Are Dylan and me going to have a stepdaddy someday? Because my friend Becca said we would."

Carter covered a smile with one hand while Kate shifted uncomfortably in her chair.

"That's possible, honey, but not for a while," she told them. "Daddy and I are, ah, still working out the best things for our family and we're happy the way things are for now. No one is getting married to anyone else for a long while."

"What about Unca' Ri?" Dylan piped.

Carter frowned. "What about him, sweetheart?"

"He doesn't have a family like ours. He doesn't have any kids and Alex went away. Isn't he lonely?" Dylan's earnest concern warmed Carter.

"That's a very thoughtful question, Dylan. Uncle Ri's doing great. He's got a lot of friends who look out for him and make sure that he doesn't feel lonely."

"Maybe he'll find a new lady to marry." Dylan drew his eyebrows together after Sadie emphatically disagreed.

"Uncle Ri doesn't like girls," she told her brother. "That's why Alex left."

Carter froze in his seat. He sat silent for several long seconds before meeting Kate's wide-eyed gaze. He wasn't surprised when Kate slowly shook her head — he knew she'd never discuss the details of Riley and Alex's divorce with the children and especially not without checking with Carter first.

Turning to Sadie, he smiled. "Who told you that Uncle Riley doesn't like girls, honey?"

"Grandpa," Sadie replied, her tone casual. "He said Uncle Riley doesn't like girls and it's his fault Alex went away."

Sadie's demeanor changed and Carter felt a sharp ache at her obvious confusion. "Grandpa also said that Uncle Riley is a bad person and that he got what he deserved." She shook her head. "That doesn't seem right, though, because Uncle Riley's really nice."

"Yes, he is," Carter said hoarsely. "Riley does like men — he even had a boyfriend for a while. He still likes women and girls, too, though. And more importantly, Riley loves you and Dylan very much. He would do anything for you guys and that's why Mommy and I asked him to be Dylan's godfather. Riley is a good person, Sadie. You know that, right?"

"Yeah, I do." Sadie studied her father's face and the tension in her body lessened. "I dunno...I guess Grandpa kind of confused me."

Carter nodded and looked at both of his children. "Will you do me a favor, guys? Talk to Mommy or me if people say things that confuse you. You can ask us anything."

Sadie raised her brows. "Really?"

"Absolutely. We'll always try to answer your questions and if we don't know the answer, we'll do our best to find out, okay?"

Sadie nodded, but Dylan simply seemed irritated.

"Who cares if Unca' Ri doesn't like girls?" he scoffed. "I don't like girls, either. I mean, you're okay most of the time, but I have to like you."

"Dylan—" Kate began, falling silent when Dylan spoke over her.

"Besides, Taylor Goode's dad doesn't like girls, either, and he's nice."

Sadie sneered. "I know that, Dyl."

Carter didn't know how to react to the abrupt turn in conversation. "Who is Taylor Goode?"

"She's in Dylan's class at school," Kate told him.

"Taylor's dad has a boyfriend and so does her mom," Dylan broke in again. "It's not like it's a big deal—no one cares!" He turned back to his sister. "Also, Aunt Alex wasn't very fun. *And* I've known Unca' Ri for practically my whole life! I think I'd know if he wasn't nice, Sadie, jeez."

Carter let out a strangled laugh as Sadie launched into arguing with her brother about who had known Riley longer. He glanced up when Kate's chair scraped against the kitchen floor, though, and heard her muttering about dessert.

Carter stood and gathered their plates, his gaze on Kate, who was pulling the gelato from the freezer. Bracing himself for sharp words, he put the dishes in the sink, then walked to the counter and opened the cabinet where the ice cream bowls were stored. He set the bowls on the counter and Kate stepped up beside him. When he glanced up, the tears streaking her face startled him.

"Oh, shit." He waited until she'd dropped the gelato containers on the counter before catching her left hand in his right and squeezing it tightly. "I'm sorry, Katie."

"What for?" She sniffed, knuckling the moisture out of her eyes with her free hand. "It's not your fault your father is a judgmental douchebag."

Carter glanced over his shoulder to make sure the kids hadn't noticed their mother's distress. "True, but it's my fault he thinks he can talk to Sadie and Dylan about things they can't possibly understand."

Kate pulled her hand from Carter's with a sniffle and reached for one of the gelato containers. "You're no more responsible for the old man's behavior than the rest of us, Car. I just… I've been so caught up in my own feelings about you having left, I sometimes forget how hard it must be for you to be around him."

"Imagine how much fun it will be when he actually knows what kind of son I am," Carter joked, then smiled to cover up the dread that swept through him.

Kate shook her head. "Stop. It's not funny and I don't like to hear you talk about yourself that way." She waited for Carter's nod of acknowledgement before she spoke again.

"As far as our kids go…I think they do understand what your father's talking about. Probably better than we realize and *certainly* better than your father ever will. You heard Dylan—he can't imagine why not liking a girl would be a problem."

"That's Dylan for you. It's just like Sadie to question what Brad told her, too, even if she hadn't worked herself up to voicing her disagreement."

"They really don't care about any of that shit."

"I know."

"I don't care, either, Car," Kate told him, her voice low and fervent. Carter swallowed hard and peeled the lids off the gelato containers. "I know I haven't been the easiest person to be around since we split up. I'm still angry about a lot of things and angry with you. I can't promise I won't have the occasional bitchy meltdown from time to time." She shrugged. "I'm human and it's a given that I'm going to fuck up."

"Kate, we've talked about this—" Carter closed his mouth when she held up a hand.

"And we'll talk about it again, Carter. I won't always be happy and I won't always agree with you, but please know that I'm on your side." Kate's lips pursed for a moment. "Even when I'm acting like an asshole because I'm still really fucking pissed at you."

Carter blinked against the sting in his eyes. "Thank you. Call me naïve, but I'd never expect anything less."

Kate's nod was jerky. She finished scooping mango gelato into the bowls before speaking again. "You've always believed the best about people. That's something I liked about you from the very beginning."

"You'd think I'd know better by now, though." Carter picked up a scoop and added raspberry to the servings. "I've been holding out hope my dad would come around, at least a little bit," he admitted, knowing he sounded bitter but no longer caring. "I know that's pathetic, but that's why I've been putting up with his bullshit for so long."

"He's your father—you have every right to expect more from him," Kate said simply. "Besides, he didn't always act like an asshole."

"No, he didn't," Carter replied. He reached for the container of chocolate. "It's as if finding out about Riley set off some kind of switch in his brain and he keeps on getting worse every day. I thought I was the only one dealing with it, though—I didn't think he'd say anything to them." He put the ice cream scoop down and laid his hands flat on the countertop. "Actually, that's not true. I *hoped* he wouldn't say anything to them. I still can't believe he did."

"He is a monumental jackass," Kate agreed.

"I can't let him push me around through them, though," Carter murmured. "I need to make sure Sadie and Dylan are better protected from his toxic attitude." He met Kate's gaze. "Do you have some time to talk after the kids are in bed tonight? I've been making some plans that I'd like to go over with you."

Kate nodded, then picked up the fourth container of gelato and examined its pale-yellow contents.

"What this?" she asked with a frown. "Did you buy extra?"

"It's Key Lime—I got that for you." Carter gave her a crooked smile. "And you don't even have to share."

* * * *

All of the good feelings Carter had experienced spending time with his family drained away during his three-block trek uptown to Brad and Eleanor's. He thought of calling Riley, just to hear a friendly voice, but quickly talked himself out of it. Riley was having dinner with clients and the idea of subjecting him to more Hamilton family drama made Carter cringe.

He let himself into his parents' building and signed the guest book, nodding at the doorman while a cold sweat gathered on the back of his neck. He boarded the elevator and stared unseeing while it carried him upward to his parents' home.

The blend of familiar and strange struck Carter as he stepped into the foyer. He knew the rooms around him almost better than any other, but knew he was no longer welcome within them. Then he caught sight of his mother descending the stairs in her nightclothes and started forward.

"Carter? Nelson called from downstairs to let me know you were on your way up—is everything all right?"

"Everything's fine, Mom."

Carter couldn't remember the last time he'd seen Eleanor without makeup, but concern marked her brow. He thought she looked tired as she crossed the foyer. Her deep blue dressing gown set off the subtle silver streaks in her hair and the fine lines around her expressive green eyes.

"Your father mentioned you were coming by, but I daresay he expected you earlier—are Kate and the children well?"

"They're fine, and so are Audrey and Max."

Carter hitched the strap of his briefcase higher onto his shoulder and forced himself to smile. He thought of the last time he'd been in these apartments, nearly a year before, to tell them he and Kate had split, and his heart ached. Who knew how much deeper the rift between them was about to become?

"I had dinner with the kids and Kate and we went longer than I expected," he explained, stepping closer. After a moment's hesitation, he laid one hand along his mother's shoulder. She met his gaze openly and warmth sparked through Carter's chest. "I just need to go over a few things with Dad and I'll be out of your hair."

With a sniff, Eleanor's face closed off again. "I don't see why it couldn't wait until tomorrow. The two of you are together all day at the office, after all."

Carter shrugged, letting his hand fall away. "I've put some things off for longer than I should. I don't want to put them off any more."

"You're like your father that way." Eleanor's tone was dry. "Once you get an idea in your head, there's no talking you out of it." She raised her eyebrows meaningfully at Carter before glancing in the direction of Brad's study. "He made some calls earlier, but I imagine he's finished by now."

"Thanks. This shouldn't take very long — you should get on back to bed." Carter kept his tone light, though every word he spoke seemed to weigh him down. He had no way of knowing when he'd speak to his mother again, outside of intermediaries.

After she'd gone back upstairs, Carter made his way toward Brad's study. He knocked at the door, then waited out of habit for his father's call to enter before stepping into the room.

Brad had seated himself behind the big mahogany desk in the center of the study, surrounded by his work, a tumbler of bourbon by his left hand. Unlike Eleanor, who had seemed softer in the late hour, Brad's gaze was stony as he glanced up over his reading glasses.

Carter slid his hands into his trouser pockets and stepped forward.

"Thanks for seeing me on such short notice."

Brad made no effort to hide a sigh. He pulled off his glasses, tossed them down and laid aside his pen.

"Your mother wants to know why this couldn't wait until tomorrow, Carter," he observed, his tone cool. "I wondered the same. You could have made an appointment to see me in the office and saved yourself the trip over here."

Carter glanced down at his shoes before withdrawing his right hand from his pocket and opening the clasp of his briefcase. "I know. I thought it would easier this way."

Brad raised an eyebrow. "How the hell does having a meeting at ten o'clock on a Wednesday night make anything easier?"

For a moment, Carter stood silent, thinking about his parents' cold behavior over the last twelve months as the blood roared in his ears. He'd been afraid, for so long and of so many things—losing his job, his colleagues' respect, his family's love. He needed to stop being afraid, for himself and for his kids, and he needed to start now.

Carefully, he withdrew an envelope from his briefcase, fingering the fine-grained ivory paper for a moment.

"I didn't want to do this in the office," he explained. "I didn't want to cause a scene or make the people we work with uncomfortable, or walk out feeling like they were gawking at me."

"Walk out? Walk out of where?"

"I'm resigning, effective in thirty days." Carter's voice was quiet but clear and he met the shock in his father's gaze without flinching. Placing the envelope flat on the desktop, Carter pushed it forward with his fingertips.

"My letter of resignation is enclosed. I can leave sooner, of course, if the board feels it's in the firm's best interests. God knows I've got a hell of a lot of vacation time on the books."

Brad reached to cover the envelope with one broad hand, his gaze hard.

"Are you out of your goddamned mind? The board won't stand for this — you know that. They'll strip you of everything and ruin your reputation — you won't be able to get a job in the industry for the next twenty years."

Carter shook his head. "I don't think so."

"Bullshit." Brad glared at his son, his lips pressed thin. "Who the hell do you think you are?"

"I'm a Senior Vice President of Hamilton Advertising." Carter ignored his own racing heart while his father's face flushed an unattractive red. "And starting today, I'm coming out of the closet. See, you may have a bigoted attitude toward the LGBT community, but I know you're aware of the company's non-discrimination policy. It includes a section regarding sexual orientation and gender identity and that policy is part of the Employee Handbook. What you don't know is that I recently had a meeting with the Director of Human Resources. I voiced concerns about making my own sexual orientation public knowledge. In return, I received repeated assurances my job and reputation at Hamilton are safe."

The muscle jumping in Brad's clenched jaw brought a grim smile to Carter's lips.

"Everyone knows civil liberties violations cases tend to attract a lot of bad publicity." Carter nodded at his glowering father. "The firm doesn't need that. I think the board will be very okay with letting me go without a fuss in exchange for my signature on a non-disclosure agreement regarding the terms of my departure with a non-compete clause on the side."

When Brad spoke, his voice was eerily even. "How long have you been lying to us about what you are? Lying to everyone? Has it been your whole goddamned life or is this...gay thing something you're trying out because you're fucking *bored*?"

"Oh, yes, that's it," Carter retorted. "I blew up my whole life and my family's because I couldn't find anything better to do."

"You can't be gay," Brad seethed.

"I assure you, I can," Carter countered, his tone icy, before he clenched his eyes shut and counted to ten before he spoke again. "It's more likely I'm bisexual or something else altogether, but I doubt you care about the specifics."

"What the hell does that mean?"

"It means it doesn't matter to me if my partner is a man or a woman."

"Meaning you want to *fuck* men and not just women."

"Jesus. If that's how you need to look at it, then, yes. It's not something I can control or even predict," Carter persisted while his father scoffed. "I didn't even realize I was attracted to men until I went to college and it took me years to be curious enough to act on it. I'm still trying to figure everything out."

"You should have repressed those urges."

Carter barked out a laugh. "Yeah, well, it's a little late for that."

"So, your marriage, the kids, your life — everything about you is a sham." Brad's disdain was palpable.

Carter swallowed down a wave of nausea. "No. My relationship with Kate was real. It still *is* real, even though it doesn't work anymore."

"Why the hell not?"

"It just *doesn't*. I can't do it anymore, can't pretend I'm someone I'm not."

"What a load of bullshit." Brad shook his head. "You're soft, Carter, and your head's always been in the clouds. You've needed pushing from day one. If I'd left you to your own devices, you'd have been a goddamned failure at whatever you decided to do. That is something this family will not tolerate."

Carter set his jaw and ignored the sting of his father's insults.

"I'm not going to let you do this. It's bad enough you left your wife and kids — I am not going to let you leave the business. Not after all the goddamned time and money I've invested over the years turning you into a money-maker for my company." Brad rose to his feet, his eyes shining with disgust. "My great-great-grandfather started this business with next to nothing. Hamilton men have spent the last ninety-five years making sure that it's not only succeeded in this city but thrived. The *last* thing I'm going to do is let you tarnish the reputation of the most important thing in my life."

"That's the thing though, Brad." Carter gave a hoarse laugh. "The firm is the great love of *your* life, not mine. Why would you want me to stay? Knowing your son has a thing for men certainly won't improve our working relationship."

Brad sneered. "So, what, you've got a boyfriend now? Or do you fuck around with any guy who'll pay you some attention?"

"That's none of your business."

"The hell it's not." Brad's gaze narrowed. "I have every right to know what kind of behavior and people you might be exposing my grandchildren to—"

"And that's another thing that's off limits, right there." The steel that ran through Carter's voice cut his father's ranting off cold. "You don't get to bring the kids into your hate, *ever*. I know better than to expect you to be tolerant of me, but whatever you think about my lifestyle or my friends is on *you*, not Sadie and Dylan. You keep your poison to yourself when you're around them."

"How *dare* you speak to me like that—"

Adrenaline rushed through Carter, making his nerves sing. He drew himself up and stared down his nose at his father, using his height to his advantage.

"I'll speak to you any way I like—I'm not going to lie down and take it anymore." Carter gave a jagged laugh. "Hell, we both know you don't even consider me your son at this point, so there's no reason for either of us to go on playing happy families in front of other people. You and I are finished."

For a moment, Brad seemed startled into silence. Carter nodded, sliding his hands into his pockets once more, ignoring the way they trembled.

"As I said, I'm under no illusions that you or Mom are capable of change. You're too comfortable in the world you've built for yourselves to recognize your own narrow-mindedness. But that's not my problem— your thoughts and opinions are your own. Sadie and Dylan are mine and Kate's. *Ours*, Brad, not yours. And if I hear that you or Mom are feeding the kids lies about Kate or me, it will be a very goddamned long time before you see them again."

Brad lunged forward suddenly, dragging his arm over the desktop, sweeping everything from the surface on to the floor with a curse. There was fire in his gaze when he turned back to Carter, rage saturating his features, though Carter simply watched in silence.

How differently he would have reacted to this level of fury only a year and a half ago. The rift with Riley and the split with Kate had cost Carter almost everything he valued. He was damned if he'd let his old man ruin things after Carter had busted his ass to build it all back up.

He held up a hand as Brad began to speak. "I don't want to hear it. I've said my piece. I'm cutting ties with the firm and you. It's up to you to decide which means more to you— your pride, or seeing your grandchildren."

Carter stared at his father, taking in his mottled color and grim expression, aware Brad had only the barest control over his emotions. "You think hard before you do something stupid like go after Kate, by the way. She and I are on the same side—she's not going to let you go through her or the kids to get to me."

"Everyone can be bought," Brad all but growled. "That's something you've never understood."

Carter gave him a cold smile. "You're wrong about that—you always have been. And that's something *you've* never understood."

He turned to go, acutely aware neither of them had anything left to say—for all he knew, they'd had nothing to say to each other for years. Carter paused at the door with his hand on the knob, his voice so flat he hardly recognized it.

"I'll expect to have access to my office tomorrow as well as my staff so I can begin working on the separation process with Human Resources. If that's not possible, I'll have Malcolm pack up my personal items and deliver them to my place. You can reach me through my attorney — her card's in the envelope."

* * * *

"Hey, buddy...you gettin' out here, or you want me to drive you somewhere else?"

Carter started at the cabbie's gruff voice. The driver met Carter's gaze in the taxi's rearview mirror, before Carter squinted at the meter's display.

"Oh, right." Carter reached into his coat pocket for his wallet with clumsy fingers. "Sorry — been a long day."

He hardly remembered the taxi ride downtown. He'd walked for a little while after leaving his parents' and texted Kate to let her know that the deed had been done. He'd plodded on until his legs tired, then finally flagged down a taxi and ridden home in a daze.

His fatigue deepened after he paid the driver and climbed out of the cab, becoming a dark lethargy Carter knew well. For the first time, he welcomed the depressed feelings. He wasn't ready to examine those blistering moments in his father's study — who and what he'd left behind as he'd upended his life for good. He was more than ready to take his meds and crash for a couple of hours, though.

When his phone chimed, he pulled it free of his pocket out of reflex and an ache spread through his chest when Riley's name flashed across the display.

It's late — you up for a drink? I'm wired from the drive back.

Carter waited until he'd locked his front door behind him before replying.

Not tonight — really wiped. You in town tomorrow? Would love to talk.

The phone chimed almost before Carter had his coat off. He took a few minutes to get his medication from the bathroom before reading Riley's message.

Dinner? I'll cook, you take notes and pay me compliments.

Carter sank onto the foot of his bed with his pills and a glass of water, trying to decide whether to reply. Placing the glass on the floor near his feet, he let himself space out until the phone buzzed in his hand again with another message from Riley.

Or we can order sushi and you can pay me in compliments instead.

The tight knot in Carter's chest loosened and he let out a weary chuckle. He toed off his shoes, intent on replying and putting off thinking about his life for a little while longer.

Chapter Fifteen

"I hope you've had adequate time to prepare your compliments," Riley joked loudly as he stepped inside Carter's door and dropped his keys on the hall table. "Oh, and I grabbed spicy tuna rolls for you."

His steps slowed when he realized there was silence from inside the apartment. He frowned, wondering if Carter was out. After he'd left the sushi restaurant, he'd texted Carter to let him know he was on his way, and hadn't thought twice about using the spare key to let himself in, even though he hadn't received a response. "Carter? You here?"

As Riley rounded the corner, he was relieved to see Carter sitting on the couch. Carter turned and stared at him blankly for a second before he roused himself with a shake of his head and stood. A ghost of a smile lit his face. "Ri."

"You okay?"

"Yeah, it was just a…strange day. I'm glad to see you, though. And did I hear something about spicy tuna rolls?" Carter had begun to seem more like himself, but Riley set down the bag of takeout on the floor and frowned at him.

"You sure?"

"Yeah, yeah." Carter waved off his concern. "I'll be fine. We can talk about it over dinner. Seriously, did you get me spicy tuna?"

Riley scoffed. "Of course. Do you really think I'd forget your favorite?"

For the first time that night, Carter's smile was warm and genuine. "No, of course not."

"You ready to eat?"

"Yeah, I'm starved." But rather than reach for the bag of food, Carter reached for him. Riley didn't argue when Carter grasped his hips and drew him in for a slow, lingering kiss.

"Am I on the menu?" Riley asked, amused, after Carter drew back.

Carter's smile was wolfish. "You taste good to me."

"Flatterer."

"I thought that was repayment for my dinner? Don't I owe you obscene compliments?"

Riley chuckled. "Mmm, I suppose you do. Keep talking. Or kissing me—I'm fine with either."

"Can I eat first? I skipped lunch today. I can't adequately flatter *or* kiss you on an empty stomach."

"Sure. What did you want to drink?" Riley asked. He unbuttoned his suit jacket and draped it over the arm of the sofa. "I figured you'd have something that'll work so I didn't pick up anything on the way. Maybe a chenin blanc or a dry riesling if you've got it?"

He took a seat on the sofa, unbuttoning and rolling up his sleeves while Carter walked toward the kitchen.

"I have something better," Carter called out. "It's been chilling for the last few hours."

"Gruner veltliner?" Riley asked, intrigued. He and Carter had discovered how well it paired with sashimi years before, but few restaurants had it on their wine list.

"No, although that would have been good. I should pick up a few bottles."

Riley unpacked the bag of takeout. When Carter returned from the kitchen, carrying two plates, a dark, heavy bottle and a dish towel, he raised an eyebrow.

"Champagne? What are we celebrating?" Riley grinned at Carter. "I mean, I know getting to spend time with me is always worth celebrating, but…"

Carter laughed and took a seat next to him, handing over the plates. "We are celebrating the fact that I put in my official resignation at Hamilton Advertising today. I delivered it to my father last night and I have thirty days to wrap up my work before I hand it off to the other VPs. No doubt Brad's already searching for my replacement, but I don't expect they'll have anyone hired before I leave."

"Holy shit, Car. That's huge."

He shrugged, seeming nonchalant, but Riley saw the tension in his shoulders as he untwisted the wire cage over the Champagne cork. "It was long overdue."

"How did Brad take it?"

Carter snorted, but there was nothing amused about his expression. "Let's see, he tried to bully me into staying with the company and disparaged my sexual orientation. When he understood that I wouldn't be swayed, he lost his temper and—in a move that would make Dylan's tantrums look well-behaved—shoved everything off his desk."

"Wow."

Carter shook his head. "It's more or less what I expected, but…" He swallowed hard. "He also implied he could go after Kate and buy her off."

"Oh, Car." The thought made Riley's chest ache and he was unable to speak for a few moments. He carefully arranged sushi on the plates and set out pieces of pickled ginger and wasabi. Not that he believed for a moment that Kate would take Bradley up on it, but the thought that his father had even suggested trying to turn his former daughter-in-law against his own son was painful. Riley had held Brad and Eleanor in high regard and, for many years, had considered himself closer to them than his own parents. He'd been deeply hurt by Jonathon and Geneva cutting him out of their lives, but he'd never expected it from Carter's parents.

"How do you feel about it? About walking away from the ad agency, I mean."

"Shit, I forgot glasses," Carter muttered. He stood and disappeared into the kitchen again. Riley frowned — the deflection was obvious — but he didn't push. Carter would tell him when he was ready.

Carter returned and they worked their way through half of the sushi and the better part of the Champagne before he spoke.

"I wasn't ignoring your question earlier."

Riley glanced over, chopsticks and a piece of salmon nigiri frozen in front of his face. "Okay."

"I'm still trying to figure it out, to be honest."

"Fair enough. It's a huge change," Riley pointed out, then realized what an asinine statement that was. Of course, Carter knew it was a huge change.

"On the one hand, I'm relieved to have it over with so I can move forward, but it's kind of depressing." Carter let out a huge sigh. "What the fuck have I been doing for the last twelve years?"

"Are you going to miss the job?" Riley asked.

Carter shrugged. "I don't think so. I was good at the work and I liked my staff, but I never really loved my job. I suppose you could say it challenged my head but not my heart."

"What comes next?"

"After the thirty days to get everything wrapped up...I guess I'll figure out what I want to do next with my life."

"What do you really love? Well, other than music and anything combining chocolate with peanut butter."

"You're right about those two things, but there's one other thing I love." Carter smiled at him and, for a moment, Riley wasn't sure if it was the wine or the look on his face that made his head swim.

"What's that?" Riley teased.

Carter deftly snagged a piece of sushi and winked at him. "Spicy tuna rolls, of course."

Riley shot him the finger. "Fuck you."

"Maybe later."

The heat that roared through Riley at the thought had nothing to do with the fiery wasabi that hit his tongue. *Is Carter just playing around or does he mean it?* Riley wondered. He set down his chopsticks and tugged at his tie, loosening it and popping open the top two shirt buttons. Given the way Carter followed his movements with his gaze, he would bet it was a little of both.

He was lost in thought, imagining what he wanted to do with Carter later as he snagged an avocado and shrimp roll, when Carter spoke again, changing the subject.

"So, Sadie has taken to calling shrimp 'bugs'. No idea where that came from, but, of course, Dylan decided it was a great idea to imitate her."

"Bugs?" Riley tried not to gag. "That's... unappetizing."

Carter's grin was wry. "That's children for you."

Riley nodded and inspected the bite of food he held in his chopsticks. Thankfully, the shrimp was peeled and without legs or tail, because he wasn't sure he could choke it down after hearing about Sadie's new name for them. He had to suppress his gag reflex as he chewed and swallowed the bite, though. *Maybe no more shrimp tonight*, he thought. "I know you want Sadie to find a career she's passionate about, but perhaps you should steer her away from becoming a food critic," he suggested.

Carter laughed and held his glass out to Riley. "I'll toast to that."

They clinked glasses and after Riley finished his, he set the flute on the coffee table. "I have a question for you." Ever since Carter had told him about the possibility of quitting his job and confronting his father, Riley had been thinking about where their relationship was headed. It was clear Carter was committed to rebuilding his life and including Riley in it. It took away the wary, anxious feeling Riley'd had since they'd begun exploring the idea of a relationship together, even with the hurdles they still had to face.

Carter gave him a questioning look and he set aside his plate. "Yeah, of course. What is it?"

"You came out at work and we've been out in public together, but are you ready for the big hurdle?"

"What's that?"

"Going with me to the Met."

Carter groaned and leaned back against the arm of the sofa. "You're asking a lot."

"Look, if you're not ready for that level of exposure yet, I understand. No pressure. I want to go to the final performance before the summer break, but I can go by myself if you aren't ready. It's Bellini's *I Puritani*."

"For the record, the only Bellini I like are the ones I drink at brunch" — Carter grinned at him — "but I was referring to you asking me to go to an opera, not about going public with our relationship. It seems no matter who I'm with, I can't get away from the damn opera."

"Hey, I dragged you there first," Riley teased.

"You did." Carter snorted. "How I didn't realize how I felt about you then is beyond me."

"Denial is a powerful thing."

Carter nodded, his smile wry. "True. But to answer your question, yes, I will go with you. I can't say I'm not anxious about the exposure, but I can handle it."

"Thank you. For what it's worth, I don't think it will be that bad. Even if my parents are there, they'll ignore us. Well, assuming we don't run into the Finches. They forced Jonathon and Geneva to meet Will."

"How did that go?"

"Oh, it could have been worse. It was frosty politeness until they could make their exit. The evening went fine until I ran into Kate and found out you two were separated. Poor Will." Carter made a face but didn't comment, so Riley continued, "The performance is Saturday night."

"I'll ask Kate if she can watch the kids — if she's busy, I'll talk to Audrey."

Riley winced. "I'm still getting used to the idea of factoring them in. You sure you want to be away from them?"

"Yes. But only if you agree to take them to the park with me on Sunday."

"Deal."

* * * *

Carter appeared tense as they took their seats in Riley's box at the Met, and Riley wondered if coming had been such a good idea.

Carter glanced at the senior Porter-Wrights' box. "Oh, good," Carter said under his breath, "Jonathon and Geneva are here."

"Trust me, they'll go out of their way to ignore us," Riley reassured him.

And they did. They so very obviously and pointedly avoided eye contact with their son and his date during the first act. And during intermission, somehow, no matter where Riley and Carter stood, his parents stayed on the opposite side of the room. It would almost have been amusing if not for the fact that it stung. It was exactly what he'd expected and he didn't see it ever changing, but it didn't stop hurting.

Unfortunately, he was so focused on them that he failed to notice the willowy redhead until they were face-to-face. "Alex!" he said, blinking in shock. He tried to school his expression into a more neutral one.

"Riley." Her tone was frosty and dropped even lower as she swept a glance across the two of them. "Carter."

"Hello, Alex." Carter's tone was bland, but Riley could feel the tension in his body. "How are you?"

"I've been better." She looked beautiful, elegant in a black sheath dress that left one shoulder bare. A man hovered behind her and he seemed vaguely familiar, but Riley couldn't place him at first. He was a good ten or fifteen years older than both Riley and Alex, with silver hair and a distinguished face.

"Riley, I'm sure you remember Joshua Hartman. Joshua, my ex-husband Riley." Alex's voice was cool.

It was strange to hear himself called anyone's ex-husband and it took him a moment to place the man standing with his arm around Alex. It suddenly clicked. They had moved in the same social circles before the divorce and Riley had seen Alex flirting with him at opera events before. He was on the board of some company Riley could never seem to remember. For a while, he'd wondered if Alex had been having an affair with Joshua. According to her, she hadn't and, oddly enough, he believed her. Either way, the man hadn't wasted any time once she was single.

If Alex was happy with him, good for her, though. Riley wished her nothing but the best.

"Good to see you again," Riley said politely, holding out a hand to Joshua who gave it a firm shake. "Do you know Carter Hamilton?" Joshua's gaze glanced between him and Carter and a flicker of recognition appeared.

"Not officially, no."

Alex narrowed her eyes. "Are you two here *together*?"

Riley nodded and Carter pressed his palm against the middle of his back, the warmth and pressure reassuring.

"I knew it," Alex snarled. "I was right all along to think there was something going on between you two."

"Alex," Joshua chastised. He put a hand on her arm. "Not here."

"No, I think *here* is perfect. If Riley wants to humiliate me publicly, I might as well say my piece."

Joshua frowned. "I'll be at the bar."

Riley glanced at Carter who also appeared ready to bolt. Riley took pity on him. "Why don't you grab drinks for both of us, Car? I'll meet you there shortly once Alex and I have a chance to talk." Carter nodded and squeezed his elbow before walking away.

Alex crossed her arms over her chest and fixed her gaze on him, her jaw tightening as she clenched it. "Did you absolutely *have* to come here and flaunt your relationship with him?"

"I'm not flaunting anything," Riley said calmly. "I came because I love the opera — you know that — and Carter was willing to come with me. I never expected you to be here and I apologize if our being here makes you uncomfortable."

"It's not fair," she snarled. "You cheated on me with your best friend for years and you come out of this smelling like roses! How am I the bad guy here, Riley? Tell me that. Tell me why I deserve to be humiliated while everyone thinks you're so brave for being 'true to yourself'? I was faithful in our relationship and I know that's more than you can say."

Riley pitched his voice low. "Will you please at least keep your voice down? Let's go find somewhere more private to discuss this."

"Fine." Alex spun on her heel and stalked away.

Even after they had found an alcove where they could talk, Riley struggled to find the right words. Alex was right — there had been something between him and Carter since long before he'd met her and he certainly couldn't ignore what they'd done together with Natalie.

"Look, Alex, I should have been honest with you from the start of our marriage. The problem was, I wasn't being honest with myself. I thought... I thought I could ignore how I felt."

Her anger turned frosty. "What I don't understand is why you couldn't continue to ignore those feelings."

"You would honestly have rather had a sham of a marriage?"

"Yes."

A profound sense of sadness filled Riley. He was aware he'd made horrible mistakes in his marriage and he was more than willing to take responsibility for them, but he had a difficult time understanding where Alex was coming from. "I'm sorry I hurt you. I'm sorry I wasn't honest with myself and I'm sorry I lied to you. I'm not saying that what I did was right or fair. Trust me, I wish I'd figured this out in college."

"You had no right to do this to me."

"I can't undo it, though, and although I truly regret hurting you, I wouldn't want to. I'm not asking you to be happy for me. I just don't see the point in making a public spectacle of ourselves." He gestured around them and, for the first time, Alex seemed to become truly aware of the clusters of people watching them. Not overtly—that would be tacky—but out of the corners of their eyes. Although they were no longer in the middle of the crowd, there were plenty of people observing their every move. Two bright spots of color appeared on Alex's pale cheeks. "If you want to sit down and talk about this more privately, I'm willing, but this isn't the time or place."

She pursed her lips. "No, I'm done with you. Go bend over for Carter like you've wanted to do since college." She spun on her heel and walked away, leaving Riley feeling exhausted. He stood there for a moment before he shook off his stupor and went to find Carter at the bar.

Carter took one look at Riley, frowned and slid a hand across his lower back. "You okay? I'm guessing that didn't go well."

Riley's laugh sounded hollow. "Not at all. And now we've made enough of a scene to keep tongues wagging for weeks."

The lights dimmed in warning that intermission had ended and Carter leaned in. "You want to head out?"

"No, not unless you do."

Carter shook his head. "We can stay."

Riley found the touch of Carter's hand reassuring as they returned to their seats, shaken by the encounter with Alex. Although he had no regrets about making such drastic changes in his life, there was no denying the guilt over how badly he'd hurt Alex. Apparently, he'd never really known his ex-wife at all, and that was a horrible realization.

Carter threaded their fingers together and rested their intertwined hands on his thigh. "You sure you're okay?"

"I will be." The lights dimmed and he squeezed Carter's hand. *I have you,* he thought. For the first time, the tentative, fumbling attempts they'd been making toward a relationship had finally coalesced into something solid. He and Carter were in this together.

* * * *

When Riley awoke in the morning, Carter lay sprawled on his stomach, his head half-buried beneath a pillow. Riley smiled and ran a hand across Carter's bare back, pressing a light kiss to his shoulder. He didn't stir.

Riley got up and slipped on a robe before quietly leaving the bedroom. They had a few hours before they needed to pick up the kids and Riley thought he'd make breakfast in bed for Carter. He hummed to himself while he started the coffee maker and heated a skillet. He thought about the night before and smiled. The scene at the opera with Alex might have been a nightmare, but everything after…well, Carter had seen to it that Riley enjoyed himself. He cracked eggs into the skillet and his cock stirred as he remembered the wet heat of Carter's mouth. Sex with Carter was really damn good. Being able to freely touch and taste Carter the way he'd wanted to for years was the best feeling in the world.

He mashed ripe avocado and spread it on toast, smiling at the sound of water running in the bathroom. He hoped he and Carter could shower together after they ate breakfast. Breakfast, shower, then a trip to the park with Sadie and Dylan. Today would be a good day. He topped the avocado toast with fresh mozzarella and tomato, sprinkling on slivers of basil before he slid a sunny-side-up egg on top. He whistled while he fixed Carter's coffee and placed everything on a tray.

"I made you breakfast," Riley said, carefully balancing the tray as he pushed open the bedroom door. "Hope you like it."

Carter glanced up from his tablet, eyes wide. He was propped against the headboard, still naked, and he appeared shell-shocked.

"What's wrong?" Riley placed the tray on the dresser and took a seat on the bed beside Carter, his hip pressing against his lover's thigh.

"I got an email from Audrey telling me to check the gossip column."

"Oh, Christ." Riley closed his eyes for a moment. He knew where this was going.

"Yeah." Carter's tone was flat. He handed over the tablet and Riley stared at the photos of the two of them. Some from outside of the Met, a few of them laughing together early in the evening, others of Carter's hand on Riley's back, one of Riley whispering in Carter's ear. They were intimate and — under other circumstances — Riley might have enjoyed the sight of the two of them together. It certainly wasn't the first time they'd had paparazzi photos taken of them, or even the first time they'd been in the gossip columns. It was the price of being a part of powerful families in Manhattan, but it felt even more invasive than usual. He scanned the blurb, mood plummeting with every word.

It looks like the rumors were true! Riley Porter-Wright — son of Jonathon and Geneva Porter-Wright — and Carter Hamilton — son of Bradley and Eleanor Hamilton — were spotted at The Met last night. Mr. Porter-Wright came out last fall and was spotted about town with NYU law professor and author Will Parker — the son of conservative state senator William Martin, Sr. The romance ended just after Carter and Kate Hamilton's divorce was finalized. Coincidence? Clearly not.

Rumors about their closeness have dogged the friends for years, but it looks as if they've both finally stepped out of the closet. Although neither man has confirmed that they're dating, this columnist saw plenty of evidence that confirms that theory.

It appears Alexandra Porter-Wright was less than pleased to see her former husband with his new lover, however. A run-in led to a heated encounter between the two. Looks like there's no love lost between them. We have to wonder if the former Mrs. Hamilton feels the same.

Riley rubbed his forehead, dread making his gut churn. He looked up at Carter. "Shit. How…how are you feeling about this?"

Carter sighed heavily and let his head *thunk* back against the headboard. "Christ. I don't know. I said I could handle being out, but this" — he gestured toward the tablet — "this kind of gossip isn't good and I worry about my family."

"About your parents or your kids?" Riley asked, tone gentle.

"Fuck my parents — especially my goddamn father. I don't care what he thinks. But Sadie and Dylan…"

"I know."

"I'm not sure you *do* know, Riley. You're not a parent," Carter snapped, throwing back the covers.

Riley reached for Carter's forearm to stop him from getting up and tried to keep his voice level. "No, I'm not, but I care about you and I care about your kids. I *want* to learn."

Carter stilled, but he frowned at Riley. "You don't know what kind of things they're going to hear at school. What it's going to be like for Kate to deal with…"

"You think there won't be fallout for me, too? Jonathon's going to be even more of a nightmare at work. Look, we're in this together, or at least we're supposed to be. After a decade and a half, two failed marriages and nearly ruining our friendship, are you really going to let some pap photos and a blurb in a gossip column come between us?" Riley stared into Carter's eyes, sick with worry. "Are we together or not, Carter?"

Chapter Sixteen

Carter's breath caught as he read the uncertainty in Riley's expression. He covered Riley's hand with his own, shoving his anxiety away to deal with later. He had no doubt that the gossip pages would be problematic, no matter how hard he tried to tell himself otherwise. For now, while Riley needed reassurance, Carter put his feelings aside.

"Of course, we're together," he murmured. "I'm with you, Riley—right here, right now. I'm not going anywhere."

Riley nodded, relief plain in his gaze before he glanced back to the tablet that lay on the duvet between them. "God, I'm sorry about this."

Forcing himself to smile, Carter reached with his free hand to smooth Riley's dark hair back from his forehead. "What are you apologizing for? You didn't call the paparazzi."

"No, but I did have an argument with my ex-wife in front of some of New York's biggest gossips.

Photographers being present to capture the moment for posterity was just a bonus." Riley sighed. "I hate to say it, but a part of me thinks we should have been prepared for something like this. It's not as if we've never been pap'ed at the opera before."

Carter shrugged. "Maybe that's why it never occurred to us to expect it. We're used to seeing photographers at the performances, used to seeing photos of ourselves in the papers. They've been following me around a lot more this year because of my friendship with Jesse, too. The opera crowd, though…we've known a lot of those people for years — hell, you've worked with some of them to plan special events. The opera's always seemed, I don't know…like a safe place, somehow."

Riley furrowed his brows. "Meaning you normally feel vulnerable when we're out together?"

"No, not exactly. It's not feeling vulnerable so much as…exposed? Like we're under a microscope."

"And you don't normally feel that way when you're at the Met?" Riley looked dubious. "I would have thought the complete opposite to be true. Those so-called friends and acquaintances of ours pay far more attention to the things we do and say than strangers we run into on the street."

"I know, I know." Carter raised a hand to rub at his lips and tried to find the words to explain himself. "Events at the Met are about people-watching, especially if you're interested in society types. I suppose I thought that no one would really care that we were there together. Outside of the first ten minutes of shock and awe, I mean." Carter ignored the heat on his cheeks as Riley stared at him blankly. "Sounds kind of stupid now that I say it out loud, though."

Riley's laugh was quiet but kind. "No, it doesn't. Your ability to expect the best of people still surprises me after all this time." He leaned forward, pressing a lingering kiss to Carter's lips before speaking again. "Honestly, I don't know how you do it, especially after the year you've had."

Carter leaned into Riley, pushing away thoughts of wagging tongues and paparazzi photos. He focused instead on Riley's warmth and touch. Riley's lips were soft at the corner of Carter's mouth and on the apple of his cheek, lingering over Carter's eyelid and temple. Something inside Carter turned over when Riley drew him close, wrapping his arms tight around Carter's waist.

"We'll figure this out, Car." Riley's rumbling voice sent a shiver of desire through Carter's body. "It's just gonna take a little while."

"I know," he murmured, pushing his fingers under the hem of Riley's T-shirt to brush against his warm skin. "I may not always say it, but there's nowhere I'd rather be."

The words were hardly out of Carter's mouth when his cell phone's chime pierced the fragile bubble hovering over them. Riley's exasperated groan when Carter pulled away was heartfelt enough for both of them.

"That's my sister." Carter reached for his phone. "Probably checking to make sure I got her email and we've seen the photos."

"Half of New York's probably seen the photos," Riley grumbled. He got to his feet and crossed the room to pick up the breakfast tray from the dresser.

Carter swiped at his phone's screen to scan his texts and Riley came to sit beside him, arranging the tray of food between them on the bed and handing Carter a cup of coffee.

Carter examined their plates and smiled. "Eggs and avocado, huh? You trying to sweet talk your way into something?"

"If I wanted to bribe you with food, I'd fry up a couple of pounds of bacon and leave you alone with the plate." Riley grinned when Carter sat back with a laugh. "I just felt like eating eggs today." He nudged a plate toward Carter before picking up the other. "A little extra protein always seems like a good idea before we spend any time with your kids, too."

Carter hummed and reached for his plate. "You've got a point there."

They ate in silence for a minute or two before Riley nodded at the phone still resting on Carter's lap. "What did Audrey have to say?"

"About what I expected—she saw the photos this morning and wanted to be sure we had, too. Good advice, considering we've got to pick up the kids at Kate's in an hour and a half." Carter shook his head, his thoughts racing as he considered how to gain some control over the situation.

"You know, I think it would be better if you stayed here," he mused, then smiled when Riley raised a brow in question. "Sorry—that didn't make much sense. I meant that I'd call Kate first and tell her what happened, then go over to see the kids a bit earlier than we'd planned. I want to tell them about what's going on before we meet up with you."

Riley's expression darkened. "You don't think it's a good idea to talk to them about this together?"

"Oh, I do think it's a good idea and I'm sure some kind of conversation like that will happen, Riley—

please don't think otherwise." He moved a hand to squeeze Riley's thigh. "The kids like you—a lot—and the last thing they'll want is to do or say anything that they think might hurt your feelings. I want them to have a chance to react to what I tell them without feeling like they're under pressure."

Riley nodded and dropped his gaze to his empty plate. "That makes sense, actually. Do you…you think they'll be upset?"

"Maybe, yeah, but not for the reasons you'd think."

Riley's gaze snapped up to meet Carter's. "What does that mean?"

"My father let it slip that you 'like boys'," Carter explained, drawing quotes in the air with his fingers. "He also told the kids that your preference is the reason Alex left you. Kate and I talked to them about it and they were pretty nonchalant. It was sort of a non-issue after we hashed out their grandfather's comments."

"I can only imagine what your father might have said. So…the kids know I'm bi?"

"Yeah. Well, sort of. They know you like men and that you had a new boyfriend as opposed to a new girlfriend."

"And they don't care?"

"Not that I could tell. They have friends at school who have gay parents, so the whole idea seems pretty mundane to them."

"Huh." Riley sipped his coffee, taking a long moment to swallow before speaking again. "That's not the worst news I've ever heard."

Carter chuckled. "Well, that's good to know. I planned to tell them about *myself* after I'd wrapped up everything at work, but these photos mean I'll have to move my plans up a bit." He fingered the tablet's screen.

"Think Kate's seen the photos already?"

"I'm guessing no — she'd have texted or called by now if she had." Carter reached for Riley's empty plate, then piled it and his own on the tray. "And that is definitely a sign from the universe that I should call her first and get it over with. She shouldn't have to hear about it from anyone other than me."

Riley looked at him solemnly. "How angry is she going to be?"

"I'm not sure," Carter admitted. "She knew we were going together last night but she probably expected us to lie a little lower than we did. Definitely lower than paparazzi photos. Not that we did anything to call this kind of attention to ourselves."

He put his cup on the nightstand and picked up his phone again. "At any rate, Kate hates being surprised, so she's bound to be a little snotty. Let's hope she's already had her coffee."

He'd already pulled up Kate's number when Riley laid his hand over the nape of Carter's neck. Glancing up, Carter was surprised by the tenderness on Riley's face. "What's that look for?"

"Nothing," Riley replied, the intensity of his gaze belying his easy tone.

Carter watched him, frowning when Riley seemed to hesitate before quickly leaning over to press his lips to Carter's. The kiss was brief but passionate and sent heat curling through Carter's gut.

"Damn, Ri, no fair," he mumbled.

"You're right — I almost feel bad." Riley cupped Carter's face in his hands for a moment, leaning to kiss him again before he let Carter go and climbed out of bed. He smiled shyly and bent to pick up the breakfast tray. "I'll get out of your way."

"You don't need to leave," Carter protested. "It's your bedroom!"

Riley tutted and headed for the door. "And you need some privacy to make this phone call. I'll grab a shower in the guest room—just let me know if you need anything."

Carter watched Riley leave, then turned his attention back to the phone in his hand, his mood darkening. For a moment, he quailed, nearly giving in to the temptation to send a text to Kate in lieu of calling. Shaking his head, he initiated the call before he could chicken out. He climbed out of Riley's bed to stand by the window, silently counting the rings before Kate's voice rang out on the other end of the line.

"Hey, Carter."

Carter drew a calming breath—knowing he had to break the news to Kate was different from actually speaking the words. "Hey, Kate, good morning."

Kate paused before she spoke again. "What did you do?"

"What do you mean?"

"You only get stiff and formal like that with me when you've either done something wrong or have something difficult to tell me. Do you need to cancel your day with the kids?"

"No, no, nothing like that," he assured. "In fact, I thought I'd come over a little bit earlier so I could talk to the kids for a bit."

"Okay, sure. I'd like to know about the topic of discussion beforehand, if you don't mind."

"Of course—that's one of the reasons I'm calling you." Carter closed his eyes, his desire to live life freely tempered by the instinct to protect his family. "Riley and I got more attention last night at the Met than either of us anticipated."

"Did something happen?"

"Well, we ran into Alex, which was pretty fucking awkward, as you might imagine."

Kate let out a low whistle. "Oh, boy."

"Yeah, well...turns out that two old friends showing up together at the opera is a much hotter topic than any reasonable person might expect."

Carter could almost hear the penny drop on Kate's end of the line. "Oh, hell. The gossip columns."

"Got it in one," Carter murmured, rubbing his fingers over his forehead. "I'm sure you've already guessed there are photos, too."

"Yeah, well, that figures." Kate sighed. "I haven't checked my phone this morning, but I'm sure the texts and emails have begun. Were the photos, um, you know...suggestive?"

Carter winced. "No. No, nothing like that. Riley and I are mindful of ourselves when we go out and we were especially so last night. We didn't do anything romantic. The photos look like any of the others that have been taken of us over the years—just a couple of white guys in tuxedos."

"So, the pictures are no big deal, but the gossip column copy is provocative, right?"

"Right." Carter turned his back to the windows and leaned against the glass. "Kate, I know we planned to wait until I had things wrapped up at work to talk to the kids, but I think we should go ahead and do it today. Chances are half of New York's already buzzing with the news and Sadie and Dylan's friends at school are going to hear all about it."

He tried not to hold his breath, worrying his bottom lip with his teeth while Kate stayed silent.

"I hate that I'm being pushed into this." Kate sounded strained. "I thought I still had some time to get used to the idea of telling them. I'm not...I don't feel ready to do this today."

Carter steeled himself. He was painfully aware that Kate could withhold his visitation rights with Sadie and Dylan if she thought it best. "I know. I feel terrible about the timing—you have to believe that. I won't feel badly about having to tell them, though."

Kate stayed silent for another long moment. "Okay, come on over."

"Thank you." Carter let out a breath, his head spinning slightly. "I'll just grab a quick shower and be there as soon as I can."

"I'll figure something out to keep them busy until you get here, then."

"Okay. Listen, Kate," Carter had to stop then, his whole body practically sagging with relief. "I didn't mean for any of this to happen the way it has."

Kate made an unhappy noise. "I know. Doesn't mean I have to like it. Just...get over here and we'll figure out what to do."

Carter cut the call and hurried into the shower. When he darted out of Riley's bedroom twenty minutes later, his hair still damp, he found Riley at the kitchen counter with his tablet and another cup of coffee. When Riley turned to meet him, Carter's mouth went dry. Riley's faded chambray shirt and ancient jeans were stretched tight over his lean body and, with his wry half-smile, Riley was almost too beautiful to look at.

"Everything all right?" He reached up to straighten Carter's glasses. "You seem stressed."

Carter nodded. "It's fine. Kate is pissed. She agreed that we can't wait any longer to tell the kids about me, though. About us," he clarified, licking his lips nervously. "So, I'm, uh, gonna go do that now."

"C'mere." Riley pulled Carter into a hug, his low voice steadying Carter's jittering nerves. "Are you okay?"

"Yeah. I'm okay." For a moment, he leaned into Riley, relishing the warmth and press of lips against his hair. Those few moments calmed him enough to draw back to meet Riley's gaze. "I thought I'd bring the kids back here after the big talk."

Riley's brow furrowed. "Okay. Whatever you want. Should I do anything?"

"Nothing that you wouldn't normally do. The kids just want to spend time with us — doesn't really matter how."

"Okay. I'll be here."

Tenderness bloomed in Carter's chest as he watched uncertainty settle over Riley's face. "Listen to me for a second. Sadie and Dylan already know you and like you — they've loved you for as long as they can remember. If they have questions for anyone about why this is all happening or whose fault it is, it'll be me." Carter expected Sadie, in particular, to pose the hardest questions, though he didn't tell Riley, who frowned.

"That seems unfair — why should you have to take the brunt of whatever happens?"

"I'm their father, Ri. I should be the one to answer for those things. I'm the one who broke up the family, and today I'm the one with a new person in my life." Carter shrugged. "Just trust me on this, okay?"

"I do trust you." Riley's ears turned pink as he looked down at their joined hands. "I just want to make sure you guys have as much time as you need to get through this." His gaze was achingly earnest. "I know how important your family is to you, Carter, how hard you've been trying to protect everyone and make this work. I don't want you rushing through this, not even for me."

Carter had to close his eyes against the crush of emotions Riley's words set loose. He leaned in and kissed Riley with sweet longing. "I love you, Ri."

Riley stilled. He leaned back slowly, his face blank for a moment when Carter opened his eyes before his face lit up with a blinding smile. "I love you, too."

Carter kissed him again, harder this time, pulling a little groan from Riley before Carter leaned back. "I'm not rushing," he added. "And you're part of that family now, too, you know — always have been, to tell you the truth. I'm just really fucking eager to live my life without having anything hanging over me and I'm so close, Ri. So close."

Riley pressed his forehead gently to Carter's and closed his eyes, holding Carter close. "I know you are. You'll get there too."

Carter gave him another squeeze before letting go. "We'll be back in a couple of hours."

* * * *

Just before lunchtime, Carter ushered the kids back through Riley's front door and Riley came to meet them with a smile.

For a while, the chatter of excited children filled the air and Carter let himself relax into easy talk of what to make for lunch and how to spend the day. Watching Sadie and Dylan set the table for lunch, Carter knew his intuition had been spot on.

Dylan's interactions with his godfather were completely unchanged. His boundless enthusiasm and affection were as obvious as they'd ever been.

Sadie was more subdued. While still clearly happy to spend time with Riley, she appeared to be seeing the people around her with new eyes, which Carter supposed was accurate. He met her gaze over the counter, his heart cracking a little at her serious demeanor. He smiled encouragingly at her before placing a plate of quesadillas down in front of her.

"We didn't have all of the ingredients for your mom's tacos, but I think you'll like these, too."

Sadie lifted the corner of a tortilla, glancing down at the chicken and cheese before meeting Carter's gaze again. "No bugs, huh?"

"Not enough for everyone, no." Carter folded his elbows onto the counter, leaning forward and lowering his voice. "You have to feed Riley a lot," he confided, "otherwise he turns into a big cranky-pants whiner, just like your brother."

Sadie's eyes widened with surprise and Carter winked, making her laugh before she turned to carry her plate to the table.

It wasn't until after lunch and the kids were settled on the couch with a movie that Carter had a few moments to himself. A part of him craved the distraction of a book or even some work to take his mind off the events of the day, but he instead sought out Riley. He'd read insecurity in Riley's face that morning and no matter how 'okay' he appeared at the moment, Carter knew he needed reassurance.

"I feel as though this is going pretty well," Riley told him, his voice quiet. They stood at the kitchen counter, facing out into the open living space where the kids had set up camp. "Is it too much to hope things went just as smoothly at Kate's?"

"Smoothly is not a word I'd use, no, but I think you're just getting starry-eyed in your old age." Carter grunted when Riley nudged his ribs with an elbow.

"That bad, huh?"

"It was tense," Carter admitted, folding his arms over his chest. "Our fucking phones kept pinging with messages and calls from people who had seen the photos. My mother called, and Kate's, though, neither of us answered. Jesse messaged me, too, by the way," he added. "He's seen the photos, of course." Carter schooled his face and Riley narrowed his eyes.

"And what did Mr. Murtagh have to say?"

"That you looked good enough to eat in your tuxedo." Carter watched Riley raise his eyebrows.

"Did he really say that?"

"Of course, he did," Carter replied. "Jesse is going to make friends with you—you need to accept that. And with Jesse's friendship comes flirting. He also said he wanted to undress you with his teeth and promised to do all manner of things to the both of us if we'd let him," Carter continued as Riley laughed. "I think it's a safe bet he'll be prowling around the Met performances now, by the way, so watch your back."

Riley shook his head, his eyes merry. "Your friend is a special snowflake."

"You don't know the half of it," Carter agreed. "He's happy for me, though. For both of us. He's always said he would be if you and I got it together. Unlike some of the other people in my life."

Riley made a soft sound of sympathy and Carter rubbed a hand over his eyes for a moment, fighting off a sense of exhaustion. Right now, he reminded himself, he cared only about the opinions of a very small number of people, three of whom were in this very room.

He turned to meet Riley's gaze. "The kids had a lot of questions. Sadie's more concerned than she's letting on, though she and Dylan took things pretty well overall. They're both reacting to the news a lot better than they did to Kate telling them about Robert."

Riley cocked his head slightly. "What kind of questions did they ask?"

"Oh, you know — am I going to stay in my apartment or move in with you, where are they going to stay when they come over to visit..." Carter paused, leaning his hip against the counter. He lowered his voice. "Are you still okay with having them stay over? Do you still like them? Those kinds of things."

Riley leaned against the counter, too, his posture mirroring Carter's, and somberness settling over his handsome face. "Did they really ask you that? If I still like them?"

"Yeah." Carter nodded slowly. "At the risk of sounding self-centered, I think it was their way of asking how I feel, too. They're trying to understand whether the relationship you and I have has changed the way we feel about them. Whether we're still...if the four of us are a family, per se, or if you and I want to start over without them."

Riley's face fell. Carter had been similarly crestfallen earlier, but he understood how his kids absorbed and processed information. He took Riley's hand in his own, words of comfort crowding onto his tongue.

"This is all new for them and not something they'd ever expected to go through. They're still trying to figure out how things work between Kate and myself, between Kate and Robert and now between you and me. We tell them all the time we're still there for them, but it's pretty obvious they're wondering what's going on and where they fit in."

Riley's brows drew together abruptly. "What's Kate up to today?"

"I set her up with a spa day, actually — she'll be there with my sister for the rest of the afternoon." Carter ran his free hand over his hair. "I asked her to come here to pick up the kids at around five to take them out for dinner. I hope that's all right."

Riley stared. "She's coming here?"

"Just to meet us in the lobby," Carter reassured. "She's using the car and driver today and if we take the kids out to the car together, it'll give anyone who might be watching a good look at all of us being friendly. You don't have to be there unless you want to be," he hastened to add.

Riley said nothing for a long moment, his face pensive when he turned to watch Sadie and Dylan. "I forget sometimes," he murmured, "how many moving pieces there are in your life."

Carter's lips thinned. He wondered sometimes if Riley regretted becoming involved with someone carrying so much baggage. After struggling for years to find himself, was it worth it to Riley to stay with Carter?

"I'm just so used to dealing only with myself," Riley told him. "What I need and want and never being held accountable for the things I do. Even when Alex and I were married, we led almost totally separate lives. As long as I showed up to escort her to events and didn't embarrass her or hurt our bank accounts, she didn't take much interest in what I did."

He shifted his gaze to meet Carter's. "I'm not always very good at understanding how this all works. And I know for sure that I don't tell you enough, but it means a lot to me that you're letting me into your life."

Carter let out a startled little laugh, his chest tightening with emotion. "Riley, if anyone should be grateful, it's me. I wake up most days not believing you're still talking to me."

Riley made a face, but Carter could read the emotion behind his friend's bluster. "That's because you're a bit of an idiot, you know. You have been since the day we met, and I still have no idea why I wanted to make friends with you."

Carter raised an eyebrow. "You had your chance to get away."

"God knows I should have taken it."

"And yet here we are." Carter's breath caught when Riley tightened his fingers around his own.

A slow smile worked its way across Riley's face. "Yeah. Here we are."

* * * *

As much as Carter enjoyed spending time with his kids, he handed them back over to Kate at the end of the afternoon with a true sense of relief. Kate appeared relaxed from her day at the spa, but she also hadn't removed her sunglasses. Carter knew she wanted to avoid direct eye contact with not only Riley but also himself.

"You feel like grabbing some dinner and drinks?" Riley asked as they walked back into the apartment, settling a hand at the small of Carter's back. "I thought we could try to find that little wine bar we used to go to, back before I bought this place. Do you remember? The food was really good there."

Carter hummed. "It might not be there anymore," he replied, "or maybe it's become another hipster hangout."

"Shit, I hope not." Riley shuddered. "The last thing this neighborhood needs is another specialty coffee shop." He smiled at Carter's chuckle, though his brow pulled down into a crease. Coming to a stop beside the couch in the living area, he turned to face Carter and brought his hands to rest at Carter's waist.

"Are you okay? You look pretty beat."

"I feel it, to be honest. It's been kind of a weird day and I guess it's catching up to me. I think" — Carter paused, grimacing — "I hate to say it, but the only thing I really feel like doing right now is taking a nap. I'm getting old."

Riley inclined his head toward the bedroom with a chuckle. "Come on, Grandpa — we can order in some food and just hang out here tonight."

Carter glanced at Riley, searching his face for signs of impatience but finding none. "You don't mind? You don't have to stay in, you know. I'm sure you had better plans for tonight than — "

"Carter, please shut up." Riley's glance was both fond and exasperated. "The only plans I have tonight involve spending time with you. I don't much care what we do as long as we do it together."

Carter grinned and rested his head on Riley's shoulder. "You're surprisingly sappy, you know that, right? You give me so much blackmail material every single day. So much." Riley's bright laughter filled him with delight.

"Yeah, well, no one will believe you. My reputation as a heartless bastard is already firmly established."

They bantered back and forth and a pleasant warmth settled over Carter. Riley steered him toward the bed and pushed Carter down to sit, kneeling to remove his shoes and socks. Carter sprawled back onto the mattress, grumbling good-naturedly while Riley unbuttoned his shirt. The tension in the room shifted as the fabric fell away from Carter's body, becoming charged with an energy that raised goosebumps on his skin.

Riley swept his gaze over the bared skin beneath his hands and met Carter's eye. "You still sleepy, Car?"

Heat pooled in Carter's groin. Mute, he shook his head. Riley skated his fingers down Carter's torso, sliding them over his skin before he reached for Carter's belt buckle. Riley paused, teasing his fingertips under the waist of Carter's jeans instead. He bent down to kiss Carter deeply, the wet slide of their tongues making Carter's heart race and his cock stir. He bit back a gasp as Riley pulled away.

"I want you," Riley told him, unbuckling Carter's belt, his cheeks flushed with color.

Carter could only nod. His jeans fell open and Riley slid one hand under the waistband of Carter's boxers, making him gasp. Riley wrapped his fingers around Carter's cock and smiled at the groan that rolled through Carter's chest.

Carter surged up to sit, grasping Riley's shoulders with his hands and pulling him close. "Want you, too," he managed between kisses, and relished Riley's greedy sounds.

They pulled at each other's clothes, peeling away the layers until there was nothing left between them. Carter shivered as Riley stroked his skin. Riley leaned to press deep, wet kisses into Carter's neck, driving him to distraction.

"God, Ri...feels so good."

"I love the way you sound when we're like this," Riley told him, "like you're gonna lose it just from my hands on you."

With a soft grunt, Carter pushed Riley back onto the mattress. He lavished attention on Riley's lean torso, licking and sucking the flushed skin, desire coiling in his belly.

"Jesus, Car."

Carter worked his way lower, running his teeth gently against Riley's ribs. Riley shuddered out a rough laugh and brought one hand up to rest on the top of Carter's head. He let Riley guide him, trailing kisses over Riley's flawless skin until he was nosing at the crisp hair at the base of Riley's cock. He hummed to feel Riley's thighs trembling under his touch.

Carter took Riley in his mouth, sucking hard, and closed his eyes as Riley twined his fingers in Carter's hair. He reached down with one hand to palm himself when Riley swore. Carter opened his eyes and looked at Riley, humming at the expression of awe on his face, and the vibration in his throat made Riley gasp.

Riley reached for him, panting. "Come here, please."

Carter crawled up his lover's body to meet Riley's lips in a searing kiss before Riley swiftly pushed him on to his back. Riley reached between Carter's legs, taking his cock in one hand and tugging at his balls with the other. The sting of pleasure pulled a whine out of Carter and he arched up against Riley, heat racing under his skin.

"Ri," he managed, unashamed of the waver in his voice. "I need you. Need you inside me."

Carter had never had penetrative sex with a man. He'd had plenty of sex since coming out to Riley, and had completely re-learned his own body and the way it responded to pleasure with men. He'd never been ready to take the final step, though, until tonight. And he wanted it with an intensity that stole his breath.

Riley brought his hands back up to frame Carter's face, his eyes burning. "Is that what you want?"

Carter's heart clenched painfully. "Yeah. Want you, so much. So much," he whispered, his pulse thundering in his ears when Riley kissed him again.

Riley broke away to turn to the nightstand and Carter rolled onto his belly, his stomach fluttering with nerves. He listened to the click of the lube bottle and the sound of tearing foil, and bit his lip. His dick throbbed as Riley reached between his legs, using one hand to spread Carter's thighs and trailing the other up the cleft of his ass. Carter held his breath, his body tense, and Riley pushed a cool, slick finger inside him.

Riley pinned him down, his free arm cradling Carter's neck in a loose embrace. "Easy, Car."

Carter exhaled and a fine sweat broke out over his skin. He grasped at the strong arm around him and willed himself to relax. Riley slipped a second finger inside him and Carter turned his head to press his face against the pillow.

"God. I love you like this," Riley rumbled.

Carter hadn't known it was possible to feel so much. The drag of hot skin against his own, the scrape of teeth on the shell of his ear, the pain razoring through his pleasure. He bit back a whine and fought not to lose himself in the overwhelming sensations rolling through him.

"Oh, Jesus," he choked out.

Riley drew Carter against him more tightly. "I know," he soothed, slowly pumping his long fingers until Carter bucked mindlessly against the mattress.

"*Riley*—I need you."

Riley slipped his fingers away and Carter tensed again when he felt the head of Riley's cock instead.

"Never done this, y'know," he murmured then. He closed his eyes and Riley went still. "Not with Jesse or Kyle. Or anyone. I know you thought—"

"Oh," Riley hushed, his breath warm against Carter's face. "Why didn't you tell me?"

"I didn't know how," Carter admitted, his face hot. "Wasn't sure...you'd care after everything that happened." Something inside him loosened as Riley pressed a kiss against his temple.

"You can tell me anything," Riley promised. "I always want to hear you."

Riley pressed forward, breaching the tight ring of muscle, and Carter inhaled sharply. He slid into Carter's body in a long, slow push. Carter dropped his head forward, his eyes clenched shut, breathing through the stretch and burn.

"Okay, Car?"

Fire raced through Carter's gut. He fisted the sheets, aware of Riley curling over him, his arms wrapped tight around Carter's shoulders and waist.

"Yeah," Carter got out. He gasped when Riley rocked back and forward again, whispering praise and encouragement.

Blindly, Carter reached back, clutching at Riley with one hand. As Riley moved, the sharp ache in Carter's body changed, deepening into a throbbing pleasure.

"Oh, fuck. Fuck, Riley."

Riley made a broken sound. He drove into Carter, moving the arm at Carter's waist and shoving it under Carter's body to fist his cock. Carter surrendered, losing all sense of time as they moved together, until his voice caught on every exhalation. Riley pushed deep, scraping his cock against Carter's prostate, and Carter jolted and gave a strangled shout.

Riley swore, thrusting rapidly until his movements stuttered then slowed and he curled his body into Carter's when he came. Riley moaned as he rode out his orgasm, his breaths gusting over the damp skin of Carter's shoulders.

Carter let out a noise of protest when Riley finally drew back, the sudden loss of sensation making him shake. He let Riley ease him onto his back and push his knees up toward his chest. Riley was smiling when Carter opened his eyes.

"Look at you," Riley murmured. "So fucking beautiful."

Carter jerked when Riley wrapped a hot hand around his cock. He stopped breathing altogether when Riley slid the fingers of his other hand back inside Carter. Those fingers filled him again, turning his bones to water, and when Riley crooked just right, sparks ran over Carter's nerves.

He unraveled without warning. Carter's world narrowed down to sensation and Riley's cool, blue gaze under the roar of his orgasm, waves of pleasure wiping his mind clean.

Carter drifted as he slowly came back down, the sounds around him plucking at his consciousness. Quiet footsteps padded around the room, followed by the sound of running water. He stirred when the bedding tangled around his body was pulled free and sighed at the sensation of a warm, wet cloth wiping down his body. He forced his eyes open at last when the weight beside him on the bed shifted.

"Stay for a minute," he murmured, reaching out to catch hold of Riley's arm.

Riley's eyes were shining. "Of course." He bent to press a chaste kiss to Carter's lips then held up the washcloth. "This is going in the bathroom, though, otherwise I'll end up tripping over it in the middle of the night and it'll be all your fault."

"Things usually are." Carter's words were slurred with fatigue. He watched Riley stand and stride toward the bathroom, the light of the room moving beautifully over his naked body.

Carter fell into a light doze while Riley finished washing up, but roused when the mattress beside him dipped again.

"Love you, Ri," he murmured sleepily.

Riley pressed kisses against his shoulder and spooned in close. "Love you, too, Car. So much."

Carter's body thrummed with contentment before the soft tendrils of sleep finally dragged him under.

Chapter Seventeen

"I am appalled by your taste in music, Riley Porter-Wright."

Riley snorted and put the Audi in park. He glanced over at Carter. "Liar. You've been singing along, mister. Out of tune, I might add. You don't get to pull the full name and disapproval bit over this one. You're equally culpable."

Carter unbuckled his seat belt. "You're the one who rolled the windows down. We're in the *Hamptons*. One simply doesn't sing at the top of one's lungs. I'm fairly sure you gave at least three old ladies heart attacks."

"That's a disturbingly good impression of Alex there." He popped open the car door.

Carter shuddered and got out of the car. "Please never compare me to your ex-wife. My point is, I don't know why you were in charge of the tunes. As navigator, that is *my* job."

"I don't remember agreeing to those rules. Do you have a signed and notarized copy of that agreement?"

Riley asked, stretching. What should have been less than a two-and-a-half-hour drive had been well over three thanks to a minor accident and rubberneckers. His relief at getting off the I-495 had been the reason he'd put down the windows and cranked up the music. He smiled at the memory of Carter's laughing face and the wind in his hair. Despite his teasing, Carter had enjoyed himself.

"No, Riley, it's an unwritten human law," Carter said, exactly the way he sounded when he explained something to Dylan. "Everyone in the world recognizes…what are you smirking at?"

Riley grinned at him over the top of the R8. "I'm not smirking. I'm happy."

Carter's expression softened and he rounded the rear of the car, drawing Riley in for a warm kiss. He lingered his hand on Riley's cheek. "Me, too."

"Who's the one doing things to give old ladies heart attacks now?" Riley murmured. "I don't think that's allowed in Southampton. I think they'd prefer if we kept to Fire Island."

"Fuck the old ladies of The Hamptons," Carter said, skimming his fingers along Riley's jaw. "If I want to kiss the man I love in his driveway, I'm going to damn well do it."

"Carter Hamilton! I've never heard you talk that way. I'm shocked." Riley's tone was teasing, but there was some truth to it. Carter had relaxed a lot in the five months since they'd begun officially dating. "But I'm not complaining," he amended.

Carter's mouth stretched into a wide smile. His eyes were hidden behind sunglasses, but Riley could picture his hazel eyes behind the polarized lenses, crinkled at the corners. "You like Carter 2.0?"

"You know I do. The question is, do you?"

Carter slung an arm over Riley's shoulder and his voice was quiet and sure. "Yeah, I do."

"This looks fantastic," Carter murmured twenty minutes later, as they finished the tour of the beach house in the living room where they'd begun. "Truly. Everything about it is *you*. I hated when Alex stripped out all the charm your parents put into it. But this is far better than what they had. Warm, modern, a bit eclectic. I love it."

Warmth kindled in Riley's chest. "It's definitely become a sanctuary for me."

"I understand why."

"What do you think about bringing the kids here some this summer?" Riley asked. "Assuming Kate is fine with it, of course."

Carter grinned at him. "Oh, Kate'll be fine with it, and I think Sadie and Dylan would love it. The question is, are you sure you're willing to risk the fabric of that gorgeous new sectional and what I'm sure is a very nice wool rug?"

Riley laughed. "It'll be fine. I had the store include a fabric protector with that in mind."

Carter furrowed his brow. "But you decorated the place when we weren't even talking."

Riley shrugged. "I guess I always hoped you'd come around. Besides, it's a beach house — it should be lived in. Alex was the one who wanted to live in a museum, not me. I want it to feel homey. Nothing here is irreplaceable. Except you." The look on Carter's face brought a lump to Riley's throat and he had to swallow around it before he could speak. "Look around. This place has pictures from all the most important moments of my life. And you're the biggest part of that."

He watched Carter step toward the bookshelf and pick up a photo of them at graduation. Riley knew it was the companion to the one Carter had at his place. He set the frame down and gazed at the other photos with a half-smile on his face.

"Will can't have liked the timeline of our history together," Carter said. He reached for the one of them at Dan and Mel's wedding.

"That's part of the reason I kept the photos here," Riley admitted.

Carter glanced over, surprise written across his face. "Will never came here with you? I assumed he had."

Riley shook his head. "I never invited him. I kept putting it off for some reason and I could never figure out why." He smiled sadly. "I could never quite let him in all the way, I guess. It's no wonder things didn't work out."

Carter set the silver frame on the shelf and turned to face Riley. "Do I hear guilt?"

"Maybe a little," Riley admitted. "Things are getting better with Will. We managed to have a brief, civil conversation at that benefit held at Gabriel's restaurant a few weeks ago, so that's something. But I still wish I'd handled things differently."

"Yeah, you mentioned that you talked to him there. Sorry I couldn't make it, by the way."

Riley waved off his apology and walked toward the wall of glass that overlooked the ocean. "Sadie was sick. Of course, you needed to take care of her. Besides, it was probably just as well. I doubt Will would have been terribly eager to talk to you."

Carter hummed and followed behind him. "I suppose it would have been in poor taste if we'd gotten in a fistfight in the middle of a fundraiser for cystic fibrosis."

Riley laughed and pushed open the French doors. "We certainly didn't need another write-up in the gossip column, that's for sure."

"Ugh, don't remind me." Carter kicked off his shoes and Riley followed suit. "The one after our visit to the Met was bad enough."

"Not to mention the tongues wagging about the fact that neither the Hamiltons nor the Porter-Wrights approve of our relationship." Riley felt perversely pleased.

"Mmm, there is that," Carter murmured.

For all the stodginess of the Upper East Side crowd, where it seems like nothing would ever change, it's no longer fashionable to shun people for being gay, Riley thought with no small amount of satisfaction. Times *were* changing, albeit slowly, and it reflected badly on both families that they'd cut Carter and Riley out of their lives. Riley tried not to dwell on it any more than necessary, but their families' concern with appearances had begun to backfire on them and Riley couldn't help but feel a small sense of relief.

Anna — Riley's assistant — had recently passed along the information that a noted lesbian author who published mysteries through Porter-Wright had dropped them and hinted on her blog that she was shopping around for a more LGBT-friendly publisher. Through Audrey, Carter had discovered that Hamilton Advertising's board of directors was less than pleased with Brad over his treatment of his son. Carter, who had stayed in contact with his assistant Malcolm, had also found out that there had been an unexpected wave of employee departures shortly after Carter left. It appeared that karma had worked its magic. As far as Riley was concerned, there was no better revenge.

They were both silent for a few minutes. In the distance, Riley could hear the sound of gulls squawking and the roar of the ocean. As he stared out over the stretch of sand that led to sparkling blue waters, the stress that always accompanied thoughts of his parents slipped away in the warm, salty breeze. He breathed deeply and closed his eyes for a moment. Content.

The weather had been unseasonably hot lately and the water called to him. He opened his eyes and gave Carter a mischievous grin. "Want to take a dip with me?" Riley stripped out of his shirt and tossed it onto the lounge chair, which was still covered in heavy canvas. He'd remove the covers later so they could enjoy a fire in the fire pit he'd purchased for the deck. Less charming than the bonfires they used to have on the beach, but far more convenient.

He reached for the button on his shorts and undid it.

"I didn't exactly wear my suit under my clothes." Carter sounded faintly apprehensive but amused.

Riley grinned at him and lowered his zipper. "Who said anything about a suit?" Carter's startled glance made him laugh aloud. "We used to skinny dip all the time."

"We were eighteen!"

Riley shrugged. "I think you look even better than the first time I saw you naked." Carter's shoulders were broader and firmer than ever now that he had more time to devote to working out. One of the perks of no longer being with Hamilton Advertising, Riley supposed. Carter seemed to be enjoying his sabbatical, although Riley knew he itched to find a career that was the right fit.

"Thank you, but I wasn't referring to my body," Carter said with a laugh as he stripped his shirt off. "I meant that we were idiots at eighteen and not thinking about the consequences of getting arrested for indecent exposure."

Riley sobered. Carter had brought up a good point. He had children and a court-approved custody arrangement. Kate had been supportive, but Carter getting arrested for indecent exposure — especially now that they were in a relationship — was a recipe for disaster. "God, I didn't even think about that. I'll go grab our suits." He turned to go, but Carter grabbed his hand to stop him.

"You know, boxer-briefs seem like a safe compromise."

"You sure? I don't mind getting our suits."

Carter glanced around before he took off his khakis and dropped them onto the lounge chair beside Riley's. "We'd *probably* be fine stripping down completely, since this beach is pretty deserted, but just to be safe, we'll go for boxer-briefs." He nudged Riley with an elbow. "Come on, I bet I can beat you to the water."

Riley yelped in surprise as Carter took off and he was a few steps behind when he hit the sand. He probably could have caught up, but he enjoyed the flex and play of Carter's back and thigh muscles as his long legs ate up the distance between the deck and the waterline. Carter plunged into the water without stopping, diving under the white-tipped waves as Riley followed suit.

The water hit with an icy slap and stole the air from Riley's lungs. He gasped as he surfaced and saw Carter's equally shocked expression.

"Holy *fuck*, it's cold," Carter said, shaking his hair like a dog.

"It *is* May," Riley said with chattering teeth, wrapping his arms around himself. It had been an unusually hot month already, but it was still early in the season. And the northeast Atlantic Ocean never really got that warm. It seemed as though he had amnesia about it every year and forgot just how truly icy it could be.

"Now, he tells me!"

"You're the one who dove in without testing the water, you idiot." Riley playfully shoved at his chest.

Carter gave him a broad grin as he slicked his hair back from his forehead. "The guy who wanted to go in in the first place calls *me* an idiot." He swam closer Riley.

"But you're my idiot."

"Hey!" Carter wrapped an arm around his neck and Riley tried to shove it off, their wet skin sliding together and sending a pleasant hum through his body.

They wrestled for a moment, bobbing in the waves as they playfully grappled for control. Riley felt like his heart would burst from the sheer joy bubbling up inside him. This was what he'd wanted at eighteen, when the first stirrings of attraction to Carter had begun to appear. This was what had been missing from his marriage to Alex.

The open, unbridled happiness at being with the person he loved was exactly what he'd spent his entire adult life searching for.

He grabbed the sides of Carter's face and pulled him in for a desperate kiss, allowing the waves to drag them toward the shore. The cool wind and the hot sun played over his body as he stood in chest-deep water, kissing Carter like he'd never stop.

When he finally drew back, Carter's expression was solemn while he brushed away the droplets at the corner of Riley's eyes, as if he knew the salty liquid hadn't come from the ocean. From the look on Carter's face, Riley was certain he knew everything Riley was thinking without having to put it into words.

He was so happy it *hurt*.

* * * *

"This is the life," Carter said later that evening, as he pulled a throw blanket over their bodies. They lay on their sides, legs twined together. Carter draped an arm over his midsection and pulled him closer.

Riley stared into the flickering fire and nodded. "It really is," he murmured sleepily.

After the bracing swim, they'd used the outdoor shower to rinse off. Riley had dropped to his knees to suck Carter off and the sight of Carter gripping the top of the open-air shower enclosure with his hands had made Riley shoot onto the tile. Some part of him had wanted to do that since he'd first brought Carter to the beach house. They'd laughed breathlessly after, when they'd dried off and dressed in clean, warm clothing.

Although the caretaker had prepped for their arrival, Riley had only asked him to do a minimal amount to get the place ready. He liked being the one to take the canvas cover off the grill and pull out the cushions on the deck furniture. Opening up the beach house for the summer was joyful, especially with Carter working beside him.

That afternoon, they'd gone for a long, leisurely stroll on the beach. Carter had taken his camera to get shots of the water and Riley had borrowed it long enough to take a few shots of them together. He planned to frame them and add them to the collection in the living room.

Back at the house, they'd made grilled chicken with green goddess sauce, roasted carrots and potatoes. Now, they were curled up together on a wide lounge chair. Riley's eyelids were heavy with contentment after a full meal and an excellent beer.

The fresh sea air and exercise hadn't hurt either, and the rhythmic lull of the waves and the crackle of the fire threatened to send him straight to sleep. He yawned and stretched. "I could nod off right here."

"Sleeping under the stars sounds nice, if chilly. The temp is dropping."

Riley nodded, eyes beginning to close. He could feel the cool, salty breeze on his bare face and hands, but the rest of him was warm from Carter's body and the old, ragged Crimson sweatshirt he wore with a hole in the cuff. Carter had burned it, long ago, lighting a bonfire on the beach, and Riley had kept it all these years. Carter had smiled faintly when he'd seen the scorch mark and rubbed his fingertips across the fabric. "I'd wondered where that thing ended up," was all he'd said about Riley's theft of his sweatshirt.

"Bet I can find a way to keep you awake and warm, though," Carter whispered against his ear, his tone low and seductive. The promise of what was to come sent a pleasant jolt through Riley's body.

"Oh, you think so, huh?" Riley asked, turning his head toward Carter's.

"I *know* so." Rather than kiss his mouth, Carter dipped his head and brushed his lips across Riley's jaw, sending small sparks of pleasure through him. Riley's eyes drifted shut as Carter moved to his neck, his lips brushing, feather-light, across the spot where his pulse thrummed. His heart rate leapt as Carter gently lapped at the skin then grazed it with his teeth. "In fact, I think it's working already," he teased.

"You might be right," Riley said, feeling a little breathless. He was getting warm. "But don't stop."

"Oh, I have no intention of stopping." Carter slid his hands up under Riley's sweatshirt and tee. His fingers were cool against Riley's stomach. He moved with maddening slowness, reaching up to tease Riley's nipples before he moved his mouth down Riley's neck. Carter tormented him until he thought he'd go out of his mind. He gasped with relief when Carter finally slid a hand down to cup the fly of his jeans. Despite the earlier orgasm, he was achingly aroused and so was Carter. God, he needed to be in Carter *now*.

Carter's hand on his dick disintegrated any thoughts of sleep. Riley groaned and shifted, pushing Carter onto his back. He settled over him, parting his long legs as he dropped his head down to kiss him. After all the years spent wanting to kiss Carter, he still never felt like he could get enough of it. Carter responded with equal enthusiasm, sliding his fingers into Riley's hair and deepening the kiss. Carter let out a tortured sound of pleasure when Riley ground against him. They stopped to gasp for air, panting against each other's mouths.

"I brought stuff with me," Carter said, gripping Riley's hips. "It's in my pocket. But I'm afraid of freezing my balls off."

Riley laughed and kissed him again before drawing back to respond. "All that talk about keeping me warm…"

"I've decided to save outdoor sex for July," Carter responded.

"Plus, there's that whole indecent exposure issue," Riley joked. "Let's go inside." He stood and tossed the blanket onto the nearby lounger. He reached down to help Carter up. Riley glanced at the firepit to be sure they weren't going to burn down the deck while they went inside, but it had died down from the earlier roaring fire to a few smoldering coals. No wonder they'd been getting cold.

Riley pushed Carter toward the French doors, then into the living room. The bedroom seemed too far away. Carter kissed him deeply and for a few desperate moments Riley could do nothing but hold on and enjoy it.

"You said you brought stuff," he asked when he couldn't take another moment of foreplay. He fumbled for the button on Carter's jeans, fingers suddenly clumsy, as if he no longer had enough blood in his brain or his hands to work them. "Where?"

"Front right pocket." Carter stripped off his own shirt, flinging both layers across the room.

Riley dug in Carter's pocket, pulling out a condom and a small packet of lube. "I like the way you think ahead."

Carter just grinned and reached for the hem of Riley's shirt. They wrestled the remainder of their clothes off and Carter fell back onto the couch, pulling Riley down with him. Riley braced himself on one arm long enough to toss the lube and condom on Carter's taut stomach. "Will you?"

Carter reached between their bodies and in a few moments had Riley's cock covered with a condom and slicked with lube. Riley groaned as he watched Carter push slippery fingers into his own ass. The room was dim, with only a lamp on the dresser across the room and the faint light of the fire outside, and he wished it was brighter to see Carter better. "Fuck, that's hot."

"Just give me a minute and I'll be ready." Carter's voice sounded strained and Riley could see a drop of liquid pooling on the head of Carter's cock. He wanted to lick it off, but he wanted to be inside Carter more.

Carter removed his fingers and reached for the discarded shirt to wipe his hand. Riley sat back and Carter gazed up at him, lips parted with anticipation. Riley pushed Carter's knees up to his chest and positioned himself at Carter's entrance. Carter's face was in shadow, but even in the dim light he saw Carter's brow furrow as he pushed forward. He heard the hitch of Carter's breath and felt the momentary tightening of his body before he relaxed and Riley slipped inside. Riley set as steady and slow a pace as he could manage, but he wanted to give Carter time to acclimate. Carter grabbed at Riley's forearms, urging him into a faster rhythm.

"Harder."

Riley didn't answer, but he did speed up. Sweat slicked his skin and the cool air coming through the open door sent a shudder down his spine. The heat and pressure of Carter's body, combined with the breeze blowing across his skin, heightened his arousal. He groaned as he fucked Carter more forcefully, trying to wring out every ounce of pleasure for both of them.

Carter reached down and grasped his own cock, stroking it in time with Riley's thrusts. He watched

Carter jerk himself and the sight sent him hurtling toward an orgasm.

"Are you close?" he asked.

"Almost." Carter's body went rigid under him a moment later and he threw back his head, panting as he stroked even faster.

Riley gripped him tighter as he thrust with deep, desperate strokes. The hot wet splat of Carter's cum painting his belly and the sudden clench of Carter's muscles sent him over the edge. He gasped out something — maybe Carter's name — and shuddered as he came into the condom.

"Holy. Fuck," he managed before he collapsed onto Carter's chest, panting with exertion.

"You've got that right." Carter seemed to be having an equally difficult time catching his breath. He lifted a hand to Riley's back, stroking the damp skin there, and Riley hummed with pleasure. "We're making a mess," Carter muttered.

"Fabric protector," Riley mumbled against Carter's chest.

Carter shook with quiet laughter for a moment, and after it faded, Riley heard the steady thump of Carter's heart beneath his ear. He heard the roar of the waves through the open door as well and together they made a soothing rhythm. Riley sighed with contentment, his entire body feeling loose and relaxed. This position would be both messy and uncomfortable in a few minutes, but for now, he wanted to savor the moment. This was the life he'd dreamed of.

It had been over a decade and a half since he'd sat in this living room and imagined kissing Carter. It had been a furtive, guilty desire, but here he was, sated and content, lying in Carter's arms.

The realization brought him a profound sense of relief and gratitude. Despite the rocky road they'd traveled, he honestly believed he and Carter were finally on the right path.

Chapter Eighteen

Carter had few financial worries as an unemployed ad man. He struggled with being out of work, however, unsure what to do with himself or even how to feel about being without a job for the first time in his adult life. He'd been anxious when he'd turned in his ID badge and keys to Hamilton Advertising security at the end of May and he'd wondered if he'd recognize his life without the structure and pressures of a corporate identity. Carter had effectively run the family's firm for over a decade, after all — who was he without that job?

Unsurprisingly, Carter's departure from the firm became a hot topic in the gossip pages and, while both friends and business contacts reached out to him, most seemed more interested in details of the split rather than in Carter's well-being. Things heated up even more after Hamilton Advertising issued a press release detailing its search for the right person to fill Carter's job without mentioning Carter by name even once.

As the days passed, Carter became restless. He fell prey to dark moods during the day with everyone at work or school and he was most at loose ends, though he tried to keep his discontent under wraps and took care to take his medications regularly. He knew from the looks his family gave him he wasn't fooling anyone, though. Even Sadie and Dylan seemed to take extra care to behave around Carter whenever he spent time with them.

Things came to a head one spring evening while Carter sat in Riley's kitchen and Riley prepared dinner, talking about the publishing house. Riley was so handsome, still wearing his suit trousers and dress shirt, though he'd removed his jacket and tie by the time Carter arrived. Carter felt underdressed in his jeans and crew-neck sweater and more than a little superfluous overall. Riley kept busy, after all — he had purpose and drive and *direction,* while Carter was still spinning his wheels and trying to figure out what the hell to do next. He couldn't even be trusted to cook a decent dinner, for God's sake.

"Carter, are you all right?"

Carter glanced up from the glass of wine he'd been eyeballing and not really drinking to meet Riley's gaze. "Sure. Why?"

"Because in the last twenty minutes you haven't said anything beyond, 'red wine sounds good' and 'I like these olives.'" Riley gave Carter a crooked smile. "I'm trying not to take it personally, but it's starting to feel like you don't want to be here tonight."

"Shit." Carter slid his glass onto the counter and ran his hands through his hair. "Of course, I want to be here. I *am* distracted, though, and for that I apologize."

Riley laid aside the knife he'd been using to chop fresh dill and turned to face Carter fully. "What is it? Will talking about it help?"

"I don't know," Carter admitted. "I'm not sure talking about it will make it any easier to deal with, but—"

"Try me."

For a long moment, Carter simply watched his lover. He wasn't sure Riley would be happy to hear the truth he was asking for, though they'd promised they wouldn't hide things from each other. But Carter did know he had to stop his dejected behavior before it drove a wedge between them.

"Hearing you talk about work is sometimes hard for me to listen to," he said slowly. "I realize that must sound…well, ridiculous, but I feel resentful you've got something to do every day when I don't. It's my own fault I don't have a job and I know it was the right thing to leave Hamilton Ad, but I can't help the way I feel."

Riley frowned. "I'm not sure I understand, to be honest. I mean, it's not as though you and I have ever had similar careers—in fact, one of the things we've always agreed on is that neither of us would want the other's job." He cocked an eyebrow and Carter chuckled in agreement. "So, why do you resent the work I'm doing when it has nothing to do with you specifically?"

"It's not the work you do, Riley—it's that you have it to do at all." Carter worried his lower lip with his teeth. He bowed his head and inhaled deeply, his chest tight with unnamable concerns. His breath caught as Riley stepped forward and drew him into a hug. "I never thought I'd say this, but I think I turned into my father somewhere along the line, at least when it comes to working. I'm not sure I know who I am without a career."

"Do you regret leaving?" Riley rumbled close to Carter's ear.

"No. I don't belong there anymore." Carter leaned into Riley's touch, drawing comfort from his warmth and silent strength.

"And do you miss the job?"

"I liked the work, you know that — it could be fun. But I miss the people more. I keep waiting for Malcolm to show up on my doorstep with his pad of paper and a box of pilfered baked goods." Carter managed a smile after a laugh rolled through Riley's chest, and brought his hands up to rest on Riley's waist. "I feel directionless, Ri. Like I'm supposed to be doing *something*, even if I don't know what that something is. I feel useless…like a failure. And I have no idea where I belong." Carter closed his eyes and Riley went still against him.

"Oh, Carter. You are not useless and you are *not* a failure. Is that what you've been telling yourself?"

"More often than I'd like to admit. The really shitty part is that the voice in my head kind of sounds like my old man."

"Oh, Jesus, no." Riley's pained groan dragged a laugh out of Carter.

"I know."

"Is that really how you see yourself?"

"Sometimes. I know I'm more than that job. I was good at it and I enjoyed the creative aspects, but it stopped being a challenge a long time ago. To be perfectly honest, I've been functioning on autopilot for about five years," he admitted and Riley pulled back to meet his gaze. "The problem is that the job was a part of my life for so long, I don't know how to see past it."

Riley watched Carter for a moment longer before kissing him softly, a sweet press of lips that soothed some of the rough edges of Carter's heart. When Riley finally stepped back, he gently pulled Carter over to the counter.

"Come here and help me."

Carter scanned what appeared to be a huge array of ingredients with a frown. "Oh, I don't know —"

"Come on now," Riley persisted. As he'd done months ago during cooking class, he stepped up behind Carter, threading his arms around Carter's waist and resting his hands over Carter's to guide his movements. "We both know you've picked up some passable skills in the kitchen and we're not making anything super-complicated here. With a little guidance, there's nothing on this counter you can't make into a meal."

Carter let himself relax into Riley's loose embrace. "Okay. What are we making, anyway?"

"Smoked salmon salad sandwiches," Riley replied and smiled when Carter turned to meet his gaze. "Bet you can't say that five times fast."

"I'm starting to think I shouldn't *eat* it, never mind say it," Carter snarked before he turned back to the food and Riley chuckled in his ear. "Show me what to do."

Riley led him through the recipe which, after a fair amount of vegetable and herb chopping, wasn't hard to put together at all. Carter's mood had lightened by the time Riley finally slipped out from behind him to set out a basket of home-style potato chips while Carter assembled the plates.

"Where do you find time to make all of this stuff?" Carter wondered as they sat down to eat.

"I really don't have that kind of time," Riley told him. "I try to leave the office at a decent hour, but it'd be a lot easier to just order delivery."

Carter leveled a look at Riley. "That wasn't a rhetorical question, you know."

"Oh! Well, I roasted the salmon fillets the other day while I was also making chicken for dinner," Riley explained. "I bought the rest of the things I needed on my way home after work."

"So, you plan out what to cook for the week?"

Riley shrugged and reached for the bottle of wine. "I try to. Otherwise, I really would get takeout every night. Try it the next time you've got the kids. Just make sure it's things you can throw together without a huge amount of effort."

"Avoiding a huge amount of effort goes without saying, Ri, but you know I don't know how to put any of this stuff together." Carter picked up a sandwich half. "I suppose I could go take another class now that I have nothing but spare time."

They ate in silence for a few moments and a thoughtful light came into Riley's blue eyes. "I think that's a good idea, Car. You need some time off."

"Time off?" Carter scoffed. "I'm unemployed — all I have is time off."

"I mean time off from...well, from being this guy you're describing as having no life outside of work. You need to step outside that life so you can figure out what happens next. *Without* Bradley breathing down your neck every goddamned day, *without* the work and definitely without that huge staff always looking to you to get them through the year. Go do all that stuff you've never had time for before."

Carter gave Riley a slow smile. "Like learn how to be less of an idiot in the kitchen?"

"More like learn how to be *you* again," Riley replied with a sweet smile of his own. "I think if you do that, you'll figure out where you belong, too."

* * * *

Though he didn't come right out and admit it, Carter immediately took Riley's advice to heart. Instead of holing up in his apartment, he forced himself to spend most of every day out and about, seeking both new and familiar ways to spend his time.

To Kate's great delight, Carter began picking up the kids from school. He put in extra time with them to go over homework assignments and work on projects and took them to the park to burn off extra energy before dropping them home for dinner.

In addition to his regular workouts at the athletic club, he fell in with a rowing team on an eight racing shell, spending more time out on the water than he had since his days at Harvard. Carter even let Jesse persuade him to train to run in the next year's New York City Marathon and laughed at Riley's horrified reaction to their plan to run over thirty miles every week.

While Carter put time into strengthening his body, he also took care to indulge his mind. He went to cafes to read books and listen to music. He dug out his camera equipment and roamed around the city taking photos and discovering new neighborhoods. He spent time working with Kyle and Jesse, gutting and rebuilding their speakeasy in Morningside Heights. He even attended the recreational cooking class he and Riley had joked about and relished the pleasure that crossed Riley's face each time Carter served him dinner.

Steadily, Carter's spirits improved. One afternoon, he was teaching Sadie how to use his camera and realized that somewhere in the middle of the things he'd undertaken in an effort to keep busy, he'd begun to enjoy himself. Carter still wasn't sure what he wanted to do now that he no longer had his father's firm hanging over his head, but he didn't feel quite so lost anymore, either.

* * * *

"This is going to sound sappy, but it's nice to see you smiling again," Jesse told Carter one Saturday while they were out running. They'd left Carter's at ten a.m. to follow the Five Bridges route for eleven-and-a-half miles, aiming to finish before one p.m. Jesse's cheeks were flushed and his hair and skin damp with sweat, but his grin was as bright as Carter had ever seen it.

Carter threw a rueful smile of his own at his friend. "Was it that bad?"

"I think even you would admit you were pretty cranky after you quit your job," Jesse chided. "But the worst thing was you being sad. There is nothing more pitiful than a bummed-out Carter."

Jesse pulled his features down into an exaggerated pout and Carter scoffed. "Come on, man."

"I'm serious! You were definitely pitiful, even under all the bitching. I felt bad about it, too. It's not like you're perky generally, but seeing you down is not a fun thing."

Carter fell silent for a few moments. "I'm not sure what to say beyond 'thank you.'"

Jesse furrowed his brow. "Thanks for feeling bad for you?"

"For caring," Carter clarified. "I apologize for being such a drag, Jes. I knew I was being insufferable, but it was like being in a hole I couldn't get out of."

"That's not what I meant—"

"I know what you meant," Carter countered, taking care to keep his tone gentle. "I meant what I said, too. I shouldn't have given you or Kyle a hard time when you guys were trying to be supportive." The two friends slowed to a fast walk as they turned on to Carter's block. "I'm grateful you both care so much, even though I sometimes wonder why you do."

Jesse scowled. "Jesus. You're our friend—of course, we care."

"This is coming out all wrong." Carter reached out to grasp Jesse's elbow, tugging until he stopped and turned to face Carter. "You know a lot of people have basically stepped out of my life in the last year and half. Friends *and* family. It started around the time Riley came out and only got worse after Kate and I split. There have been times when I've looked around me and wondered where the hell so many people disappeared to. My parents, for example," he added, shrugging at Jesse's expression of sympathy.

"My point is I was kind of a mess when I met you and Kyle, but it didn't seem to matter to either of you. You guys never seemed to care about any of that."

Jesse raised a hand to rest on Carter's shoulder. "In all fairness, Kyle and I had no idea you were a wreck, Carter—we just thought you were worried about coming out of the closet...and maybe a little neurotic, just like everyone else. But you were already on the outs with Brad and starting to act like a proper gay man. Kyle and I know how to deal with that—we've never really known the preppy guy born with a silver spoon up his ass."

Carter pressed his lips together in an effort to hold back a laugh, but gave up after Jesse batted his eyelashes. "There is something so wrong with you."

"Said the pot to the kettle," Jesse countered, then slung his arm over Carter's shoulder. "C'mon. I'm too sweaty and thirsty to be standing around for a heart-to-heart. Especially since I'm pretty sure we blew the time limit we set."

"In fact, we did not." Carter held up his wrist so Jesse could read the face of Carter's GPS running watch. "We've still got ten minutes on the clock."

"That's ten minutes I will gladly spend soaking in your shower," Jesse shot back before slapping Carter's ass. He took off for Carter's building at a run, while Carter followed behind, laughing in his wake.

A half hour later, Carter walked into his kitchen with an armful of damp running gear to find Jesse dressed in worn-out jeans and a gray Henley, using Carter's blender to make post-run drinks. "You put your stuff in the washing machine, right?" Carter called out over the noise of the whirling blades.

"Yes!" Jesse called back then cut the machine's power. "Thanks for washing my sweaty shit, by the way. I know it's not far, but I feel like everything totally reeks by the time I can get it home."

"No problem," Carter replied. Adding his own clothes and detergent to the machine, he got the cycle going and crossed the kitchen to stand next to Jesse. "You always wash my stuff when we shower at your place, plus you offered to make lunch. These are a particularly violent shade of red, by the way," he added, eyeing the drinks Jesse had poured with interest.

"Tart cherry juice, almond milk and ground chia seed." Jesse slid a glass across the table to Carter with a satisfied smile. "All the superfood, carbs and protein a handsome boy like you needs after pounding pavement all morning."

Carter took a sip and hummed. "Not bad."

"Plus, the cherry juice means you won't need to take any painkillers for sore muscles or joints." Jesse set down his glass and moved to the fridge. "I brought stuff to make salad, too. Is it just me and you or should I make enough for your boyfriend?"

Carter grimaced. "Riley should be along in a while, but he told me not to wait — he knows how I get after a long run."

"Yes, hungry and bitchy." Jesse's opened the refrigerator door with a grin. "What's with the face?"

"I need a better label for Riley than 'boyfriend,'" Carter replied. "A more grown-up word, I mean," he amended when Jesse cocked an eyebrow. "We've been friends and more for a lot of years, Jes. I don't even know if a word exists to describe what Riley means to me, you know? But 'boyfriend' seems...not serious enough, somehow. And, honestly, it makes me feel like a really, really overgrown teenager."

"Hmm, I get you. How about beau? Or suitor? Ooh, paramour!"

"I am not a Southern belle!"

"You sure act like one when the mood strikes you," Jesse muttered, then let the refrigerator door fall closed. His blue eyes were wide when he turned back to Carter. "Wait, I've got it."

"Oh, God."

"Swain."

"*What?* No!"

"Yes! Come on, Carter, it's perfect, especially for you." A devious smile lit Jesse's entire face. "Who else do you know that can say they've got a coxswain both on and off the water?" he managed before erupting in laughter.

Carter laughed so hard he came close to spilling cherry juice smoothie all over his black track pants. "I dislike you so much right now," he finally managed.

"Oh, girl, please." Jesse scoffed at him over handfuls of fresh produce. "You love me more every single day."

"I suppose I do," Carter admitted with a smile. "Need some help with that?"

They made a salad using beets, roasted asparagus, walnuts, red onion and tangerine, talking while they worked. They shared news about Sadie and Dylan and the other people in their lives before Carter asked Jesse about Isaac, someone he'd resumed seeing after a long break.

"You know, I don't really want to talk about Isaac," Jesse declared and sprinkled feta cheese over the finished salad.

Carter raised his brows. "Since when? Isaac is all you ever want to talk about, Jes. Not that I blame you, given the man is pretty damned delicious."

"Ugh, I know — he's so hot I sort of want to punch him in the face," Jesse confided before going to the fridge again for a bottle of salad dressing. "I think he's actually hotter than me, for fuck's sake, and that is a feat in itself."

"Your modesty is truly stunning, you know."

"I know this, just as I know Isaac will still be dead gorgeous tomorrow. In the meantime, there's something else I think you and I should talk about."

"Oka-a-y…" Carter frowned. It wasn't often Jesse sounded so serious and Carter examined his friend's unsmiling face, a tickle of dread in his chest. "What's going on?" he asked while they took their seats at the kitchen island.

"You need to find a job, buddy. And soon."

Carter blinked. "Excuse me? Did Riley put you up to this?"

"No." Jesse looked affronted. "I don't think Riley would go behind your back like that, frankly, though, I wouldn't blame him if he did."

"Neither would I," Carter admitted.

"Okay, I know we're all glad you're away from Brad and you definitely seem less pissed off at life than you did a couple of weeks ago. But this whole man-of-leisure thing you've got going isn't going to work forever." Jesse paused for a moment as he dressed the greens, but his gaze was intense when he met Carter's eyes. "You're not built to do nothing all day. I'm actually surprised you haven't gone crazy from boredom already."

Carter shrugged then reached for the salad servers. "Well, I sort of took care of the going crazy from boredom thing during those first few weeks. You know, when I was being a miserable fuck who made people walk around on eggshells," he added, heaping food on their plates.

"Ah, yes. And now?"

"Now? Well, I've been working on figuring out who I am without that job." Carter put the servers back in the salad bowl and ran a hand over his damp hair.

"Riley thought it would be a good way for me to figure out what the hell I want to do now that I'm finally growing up."

"How's that going? Because while you definitely seem happier in general, you haven't said a thing to me about a job search or career change or anything."

"I know I don't want to just go back to work for another ad firm." Carter picked up his fork and speared some beets on the tines. "The last thing I want to be doing is going up for jobs against the old man's firm. I don't care what kind of separation agreements were signed when I left, he will find a way to sink me at every turn."

Carter put the food in his mouth and chewed, thinking through what he wanted to say. "I feel like I should be doing something worthwhile, you know? Not just helping big businesses schmooze their customers to generate even more revenue."

Jesse pressed a hand against his chest. "As a big business owner who schmoozes money out of my customers, I'll try not to take that personally," he declared, eyes gleaming with amusement while Carter laughed behind one hand.

"My bad."

"Eh, it's fine—it's not like it isn't true." Jesse considered his salad for a moment. "So, if you could use your ad man wizarding powers for good, would you do it? Like for an NGO or other non-profit?"

"That's...an interesting idea," Carter admitted slowly. "I like where you're going."

"Think about it. Taking a pay cut wouldn't be a problem for you," Jesse continued. "I know you're good at what you do, Carter, and you could really benefit an organization that would otherwise be unable to afford someone with your experience."

"Says the guy who didn't hire me," Carter reminded.

"And you know *why* I didn't hire you," Jesse shot back. "I couldn't become your client and screw you at the same time."

"Says the guy who didn't screw me, either," Carter added, his dry tone breaking into laughter after Jesse tossed his fork on to the countertop with a curse.

"Will you stop trying to change the subject? I'm trying to give you valuable life advice here!"

"And I appreciate it," Carter soothed, reaching to lay a hand on his friend's forearm. "I do, Jes. And I know you're right—I can't just sit around doing nothing forever. But I'm not going to jump into just anything because I'm bored. Whatever I do next, I want it to be right."

Jesse covered Carter's hand with his own. "I would never suggest you do otherwise. In fact, I might be able to help, if you'll let me."

"How? Hire me to work in your bar?"

"No, dumbass, by networking with you. Believe it or not, Murtagh Media does more than generate revenue for itself. My parents are big believers in philanthropy and the family donates a lot of money and time to non-profit organizations." Jesse spread his hands and showed the same winning smile that had intrigued Carter from their first meeting. "Let me introduce you to some of the people I know, Car—maybe something will come of it."

Carter didn't hesitate. "Okay," he agreed. "Let's see what we can do."

Chapter Nineteen

One evening, Riley found himself at Carter's place with two kids and neither Carter nor Kate around. That hadn't been part of the plan — Carter was supposed to be home from running errands — but he'd gotten stuck in Midtown traffic and had called Riley. "You don't mind, do you?" Carter had asked when he called. "It'll just be you until I get there. Kate has plans this evening. I hate to ask her to cancel them when you're on your way right now."

"No, no, that's fine," Riley had assured him, but his stomach clenched.

Carter must have detected something in his voice, because his tone had softened. "It'll be fine, Ri. Just keep the kids from destroying the apartment. I should only be about twenty minutes late. I hope."

"See you then," Riley had said and muttered, "If I survive this," under his breath as he hung up.

He paced anxiously until Kate arrived. When he opened the door, she gave him a polite smile, but he could see the tension around the corners of her mouth.

"Hi, guys," Riley said and Sadie rushed past him without answering.

Dylan, however, clamored for his attention. "Unca' Ri, Unca' Ri, I made a picture for you today."

Riley smiled at him, aware that Kate watched their interaction. "I can't wait to see it, buddy. Why don't you go put it in the living room while I talk to your mom, then you can show me?"

Dylan scampered off and Riley turned to face Carter's ex-wife.

"Thanks for doing this, Riley," she said, handing over a bag — presumably filled with the kids' stuff. "I appreciate you getting here early and watching the kids this weekend with Carter. I've had plans to spend Memorial Day weekend on Martha's Vineyard with some girlfriends for a while."

"Glad I could help." Riley tried to give her a reassuring smile. "Anything I need to know before you head out?"

"The kids have had a snack but not dinner yet." Her voice dropped. "Sadie had a rough day at school. I didn't mention it to Carter when I spoke to him because I didn't want to bring it up in front of her, but can you pass that along?"

"Of course." Riley frowned. "Is she okay?"

"I'm sure she will be, but she hasn't talked to me about it, so see if Carter can get her to open up."

"Sure," Riley agreed. "Carter said he'd be home soon, so you don't have to worry about me screwing up too much in the meantime," he joked.

Kate softened. "Hey, I know you're trying and this is an adjustment for all of us. We'll get there."

Relieved, Riley thanked her and she called out her goodbyes to the kids. "Have a good weekend! Be good for your dad and Uncle Riley!"

Once Kate was gone, Riley took a deep breath and joined the kids in the living room. He oohed and ahhed over Dylan's picture but watched Sadie nervously. She had her nose in a book — which wasn't unusual — but she seemed more serious than normal and her lower lip was chapped from where she'd been biting it. Carter texted him to say the traffic had just cleared, but he was another twenty minutes away or so.

"You okay, Sadie?" Riley asked, when Dylan was occupied with toys.

"Yeah." She barely glanced up from her book.

"How was school?"

"Dumb," she muttered.

"Lots of homework?" he offered, and she gave him a scornful look.

"No. Casey Garner is a loser. She's not my friend anymore." Sadie scowled.

"Why?" Riley asked, wondering if he would regret asking the question.

"She was supposed to invite me and my friend Jenna to her birthday party but she didn't and now she's talking behind our backs." Riley's eyes widened as Sadie got started. He threw in the appropriate sounds of sympathy, but she was on a roll and it didn't let up until Carter got in through the door and rescued him.

That had been a turning point for him, however, and although often out of his comfort zone when the kids needed his help, it gradually became a bit easier.

Right now, Carter was on the phone with his sister Audrey and Riley was attempting to get the kids ready so they could go to the farmer's market. It was too warm for coats, but he had a nagging feeling he'd forgotten something important.

"Everyone has shoes on?" Riley asked. Dylan nodded and Sadie stuck out a purple shoe.

"Yep. See!"

"Excellent."

Sadie beamed at him. She had been quiet and thoughtful for the first few weeks while she processed the news that her father was dating Riley, but she'd seemed to come to terms with it. And over the next two months, as he'd slowly become more of a part of the kids' everyday lives, Sadie had opened up.

Dylan seemed bored as he scuffed his sneaker on the wood floor and Sadie stared at him with an expectant look on her face.

"I'm forgetting something, aren't I?" Riley asked her and she nodded.

"You forgot Dylan's bag. Daddy always packs a bag with snacks and a change of clothes."

"Shi—shoot. Thanks. I don't know what I'd do without you, Miss Sadie." Riley winked and she rolled her eyes, her expression so much like Kate's it was disconcerting. "Wait right here, guys. I'll grab some snacks and we can go. Your dad can talk to Aunt Audrey on the way there."

"Okay." Sadie flopped onto the sofa, fishing a book out of her small backpack. Dylan pulled a small toy truck out of what appeared to be thin air and raced it along the coffee table, zooming around the decorative bowl. No doubt there were several more toys stashed in Dylan's pockets—along with pennies, bits of paper, rocks and other odd things. Riley swore every time they came home from taking the kids to the park Dylan brought back half the rocks there. He found the little collections amusing and he supposed he had probably done the same thing as a kid. Too bad he couldn't ask his parents.

Then again, they wouldn't know, anyway. He would have had to ask his former nanny for information like that. He scowled as he crossed the room to the entryway. He grabbed the bag Carter had stashed in the coat closet the night before and rummaged around in it. There was a change of clothes but snacks were lacking.

Riley still couldn't understand how his parents had been so cavalier about their relationship with him. He couldn't fathom feeling that way about Sadie and Dylan. He was already far more invested with them than his parents had ever been with him. Some days he wondered if he'd have any hair left by the time the kids were adults, but it was worth it. All of it. Even the fact that it brought up issues with the way he'd been raised that he was continuing to work through.

He opened the pantry cupboard and his annoyance disappeared at the sight of the kids' — and Carter's — favorite snacks mingling with his. There was little space in his apartment that hadn't been invaded with something belonging to Carter, Sadie or Dylan, but he didn't mind one bit. They were going to need to discuss the possibility of moving in together at some point, but whether that meant Riley moving into Carter's place, Carter moving here, or them buying a new place he wasn't sure. *No point in rushing things, though.* Going back and forth between their places worked for now.

He pulled out a container of animal crackers and put some in a zippered bag. He filched a cookie and popped it between his lips just as Carter stepped into view.

"Stealing food from my children's mouths?" Carter teased, shaking his head in mock horror. "What am I going to do with you?"

Riley chewed the snack and swallowed before grinning at Carter. "Whatever you want."

"Thought I did that last night." Carter leaned in and kissed the side of Riley's neck above the collar of his shirt. "Or did you forget?"

Riley shivered at both the kiss and the reminder of Carter driving him out of his mind in bed the night before. He could still feel the scrape of Carter's stubble across his hipbone and the tease of his tongue against his inner thigh.

"I didn't forget. Although I'm looking forward to taking a turn teasing you, too, you know." He grabbed the back of Carter's neck to pull him in for a quick, deep kiss before he gently pushed him away. "You know what they say about turnabout being fair play."

Carter grinned and filched a cookie for himself as Riley continued to fill the bag. His voice dropped to a whisper. "We might want to invest in gags, though. You're loud."

Riley smirked and zipped the bag closed. "Like you should talk." With a nonchalant shrug, Carter turned away to grab juice boxes and Riley opened the refrigerator to pull out containers of grapes he'd packed earlier that week. "I know we're not there yet, but at some point, when we decide to move in together, maybe we should search for a place that has some good soundproofing. The kids will thank us when they're teenagers."

Carter froze, then turned back to stare at him. "You think about that?"

"Moving in together? Yeah. I'm not trying to rush anything, but…" He shrugged and stuffed the food into the bag. "We are headed in that direction. And I only have two bedrooms here. The kids don't care at the moment, but at some point, they're going to protest sharing a room."

"No, I meant what our life will be like when the kids are nearly grown."

Riley paused and gave Carter a puzzled smile. "Well, of course, I do. I told you I'm in this for the long haul. You don't think I'm going to get sick of you or the kids and leave, do you?"

"No, no, of course I don't think that." Carter set the juice boxes down on the counter and stepped close to Riley. "I don't know. I suppose I haven't heard you talk about our future like that until now and it surprised me. I like it, though."

Riley opened his mouth to reply, but was cut off. "Are we *ever* leaving?" Dylan hollered.

"Right now, buddy," Riley called out and Carter grinned as he helped Riley finish packing the bag.

Sadie was engrossed in her book when they went into the living room, but Dylan looked like he was about to explode. Riley scooped him up, turning him upside down and making him shriek. "We were waiting for you, Dylan," he joked. "What took you so long?"

"Noooooo, it was you, Unca' Ri!" Dylan giggled. "You're slow."

"Me? No, it was definitely you. I had everything packed—you just would not stop playing with that truck."

That set Dylan off into another fit of giggles and Sadie rolled her eyes as she pulled her nose out of her book. "Are we leaving now?"

"Yes," Carter said, herding them toward the entryway. "Sorry about that. I had to talk to your Aunt Audrey." He held the door open and Riley set Dylan down when they were in the hallway.

"How come?" Sadie asked, contorting herself as she attempted to put the book in her backpack without taking it off. Riley gave her a hand as they walked down the hall toward the elevator.

"Because your Aunt Audrey is having a dinner party and invited Riley and me," Carter explained, pointing at the Down button for Dylan to push. He glanced at Riley. "Do you want to go? It's next Friday."

"I should check my calendar for work conflicts, but yes, I'd love to go." Riley smiled at him as the elevator opened. Once again, Dylan was in charge of pushing the button.

"She also wanted to know if I thought she should invite Kate," Carter added quietly, leaning against the back of the elevator as it descended.

"Oh. What did you say?"

"That as far as I knew, you'd be fine with it, but I'd run it by you and let her know."

"That was nice of her," Riley said. He knew Kate and Audrey had always been close and it was considerate of her to be sure he'd be comfortable before he invited Carter's ex-wife. "Of course, I'm fine with Kate being there, as long as you think *she'll* be comfortable with it."

Things were better between him and Kate, but he could hardly blame her for needing some time to adjust to seeing him and Carter together. Carter, Riley, Kate and the kids had managed a slightly awkward but fairly successful outing to the zoo, namely to show the paps that things were fine amongst the three of them. The photos certainly hadn't shown the tension he knew they'd all felt. Still, Riley had been grateful when a nineteen-year-old heiress had decided to sleep with her much older, married professor and had gotten caught. Riley and Carter's relationship had been relegated to old news and Riley had jokingly suggested they send her flowers or at least a fruit basket as a thank-you. Carter had made a face but they both had been grateful to be out of the spotlight.

"I'll check with Kate, but yes, I think she'll be fine. You two have been working together well at the opera board meetings, yes?"

Riley nodded as the elevator doors opened into the lobby and the kids raced ahead of them to the door onto the sidewalk. Carter lengthened his stride to keep up with them.

"Someday this will be less complicated, right?" Riley asked.

Carter shot him a grin as he held the door open. "Theoretically, yes."

"Oh, that gives me hope."

* * * *

The Union Square Greenmarket was only about a mile from Riley's apartment and the weather was perfect. Dozens of vendors were there, selling fruits, vegetables, flowers, bread and handmade products.

They explored the market leisurely, letting the kids set the pace. Riley bought a few things for the upcoming week's dinner, but mostly they browsed.

They stopped midway through for small cups of gelato. Most of Dylan's ended up on his face and hands, but Sadie managed to keep hers fairly contained. They stopped to pet every dog they saw and Riley briefly contemplated the idea of getting one. He'd have to talk to Carter first. There was a lot to consider. For one, it might be too much on top of everything else they had going on and for another, the kids already had Leo—who still lived with Kate—but he was tempted. Riley had always wanted a dog growing up. He could picture the four of them at the beach house, walking along the water's edge, the kids and a dog playing in the waves. The idea brought Riley more happiness than he'd had in all the years he'd gone there with Alex.

There had been good moments, of course, but all of it paled in comparison to the images of his future with the Hamiltons.

"Is there anything else you want to pick up?" Carter asked, brushing a hand across Riley's lower back in an unconscious gesture of familiarity and affection that never failed to make Riley's stomach flip. "We're nearly done and I think the kids are getting restless."

"Let me grab some fresh herbs and we can head out," he said. Carter nodded, going to wrangle the kids while Riley walked to the nearby booth overflowing with fresh produce.

"A bundle of basil and one of parsley, please," he asked the woman running the stall.

She smiled at him as she plucked the herbs out of the buckets they were displayed in, and wrapped them with paper towel before putting them in a plastic bag. "Lovely family you have."

Riley briefly glanced over at Carter and the kids, then nodded at her with a small smile. "Thank you. I think so. They mean the world to me."

He paid for the herbs and she handed them to him with instructions. "Now, if you put a small amount of water in a jar or drinking glass, put the herbs in there and stick them in the fridge, they should last a week."

"Thanks for the tip." He smiled at her. "Have a nice day."

He re-joined Carter and the kids and Carter stuck a hand into his back pocket. "All done?"

"Yes. I thought we could take the food back to the apartment, then go to lunch. Sound good?"

"Works for me." Carter turned to Sadie and Dylan. "Any requests for lunch?

Of course, they both wanted pizza, so after dropping the food off at Riley's apartment, the four of them went to a nearby brick-oven place on Bleeker Street.

Lunch was messy but delicious and, when everyone was stuffed with pizza and they were on the sidewalk in front of the restaurant, Riley turned to glance at Carter. "I left some papers at work on Friday. I need to review them before Monday's meeting. Do you guys want to head home or do you want to come with me?"

"I wanna go," Sadie said. "Can we?"

Carter shrugged. "Sure, we can take a trip to visit Riley's office. It has a great view."

Riley grinned. That it did. "Sure, we'll all go then. Subway or cab, Carter?" He was better at anticipating how much energy and patience the kids had in them, although Riley had begun to recognize signs of impending meltdowns and crankiness.

They took the subway into Midtown and walked a block to Riley's office building.

"Push the number twenty-three please, Dylan," Carter instructed when they were inside the elevator. Dylan pressed it with a serious frown that made Riley want to laugh. He and Carter exchanged amused glances and Carter reached out, brushing Riley's chin with his thumb. His gaze was soft and warm, making Riley flush at the attention. When the doors opened, Riley noticed that Dylan appeared sleepy, so he scooped him up.

"Getting tired, bud?"

"Yeah." Dylan yawned.

"We can take a nap when we get back to the apartment, okay?"

"'K." Dylan tucked his head against Riley's shoulder and sighed.

Sadie would no doubt consider herself too old for naps, but Riley wasn't. Crashing on the king-sized bed with Dylan and Carter sounded like a nice way to spend a lazy Saturday afternoon and Sadie had no trouble amusing herself with a book. Usually, getting her out of the book was the real problem. She even managed to brush her teeth and read at the same time.

The floor was relatively deserted, with just a few people working away in their offices. When they reached his, Riley unlocked the door and flung it open. "Ta da!"

Sadie ran over to the window and pressed her nose to the glass. "Wow! That's so cool. Daddy, where do we live?" Carter and Riley joined her at the window and Carter pointed out a few familiar spots, although the building faced the wrong direction for her to see her home at either Carter's or Kate's places.

Sadie seemed suitably impressed by the view out of Riley's window but Dylan glanced around and put his head back down with a yawn. Riley bit back a smile and kissed his hair.

Sadie climbed into Riley's desk chair and spun, giggling as the men stepped back from the window.

"You know, this might be the most fun this office has ever seen," Riley commented, nodding at her.

Carter chuckled. "I can believe that." He glanced at Dylan, who was nearly out. "Maybe sometime we can stop by on the weekend without the kids."

With a quiet snort, Riley shifted Dylan a little higher on his hip. "My father would have a heart attack if he found out."

"Is that a no?"

"No." Riley grinned. "Not at all."

Carter's gaze heated Riley all the way to his toes. "I'll keep that in mind then."

Riley fished his keys out of his pocket with his free hand and clumsily fumbled through them to get his desk key, holding it up to Carter. "If you open the bottom left drawer, the file I need should be in the very front. I was in such a hurry to leave on Friday and see you guys, I forgot to grab it."

"Sure." Carter knelt, carefully avoiding Sadie's flying feet as she continued to spin in Riley's chair, and unlocked the drawer, pulling out the folder.

"This?" He held it up for Riley to inspect.

Riley peered at the label. "Yep, that's it. Just tuck it into my briefcase and we can head out once Sadie's done."

"Want me to take Dylan?" Carter offered. He stepped closer and reached for the leather satchel Riley wore across his body before deftly unbuckling it. Thankfully, it was on the opposite hip from Dylan. Carter lifted the top flap and slid the file folder in.

"Nah, I'm fine." Riley craned his neck to glance down at Dylan. "And he's out. I don't want to disturb him."

"Okay." Carter secured the buckle on the satchel, but he didn't step back. Instead, he threaded a hand through the back of Riley's hair. "You don't know what it's like seeing you hold him."

"No, but sometimes I think I can tell how you feel about it from the way you look at me," Riley said huskily.

Carter nodded, combing his fingers through Riley's hair. "I never thought we'd be able to be like this. You, me, the kids—a family."

"I didn't know how much I wanted it."

Carter frowned. "I don't know. I think maybe on some level you always wanted it. Wanted the kind of family you never had with your parents. You knew Alex couldn't give that to you, but I think deep down you always wanted this."

Riley let the words sink in for a moment, then nodded. "Maybe you're right. I certainly never thought I'd have it with you, though."

"No, me, neither." Carter smiled. In the last few months, he'd relaxed and become more like the man Riley had gone to college with. He seemed confident, happy and content with who he was. He leaned in, brushing his lips against Riley's. "I love you."

"I love you, too." Riley reached out with his free hand, snagging Carter's belt loop to hold him in place as he kissed him again. Briefly, because the kids were right there, but trying to show Carter how he felt.

Apparently, it wasn't brief enough for Sadie's tastes, though. She made a gagging noise. "Gross. You're *kissing*. Did you know that there are billions of germs in spit? Blecch."

The kids had taken remarkably well to the concept that their father liked girls *and* boys. They'd even taken well to the idea that the boy their dad kissed was their 'Uncle' Riley, although Riley wanted to encourage the kids to find a new title for him at some point or they'd find themselves getting stared at in public. The kids were, however, fairly grossed out by any display of affection. Riley knew not to take it personally. It was the act of kissing and the fact that it was their father doing it that bothered them. Riley could live with that.

Carter gave him a rueful glance and turned to face Sadie. "Yep. I did know that, but thanks for reminding me. Now, are you ready to go?" Sadie nodded and staggered up out of the chair, weaving like a little drunk. Riley choked back a laugh as Carter crossed the room and put a hand on her shoulder to steer her toward the door.

"Is your stomach feeling okay?" Carter asked, sounding doubtful.

Sadie nodded vigorously and giggled. "Yup, just dizzy."

Riley relaxed. He was sure cleaning up vomit was a very real part of his future, but he was okay if today wasn't that day. He glanced around the room to make sure he had everything he needed before he left. Satisfied, he followed Carter and Sadie out of the door.

"Someday I want an office with a big window and a chair like that," Sadie announced, and Riley grinned down at her.

"If that's what you want, I'm sure you'll have it someday, Sadie Bug," he said. "But I know your dad would be proud of you no matter what you do."

"I would." Carter's smile was soft as he locked the office for him and slid the keys into Riley's pocket. "We all set?"

"Yeah, I think so. Let's head back to my place and have a relaxing afternoon and evening in."

"Sounds good."

"Can we watch *Brave*?" Sadie asked. Riley bit back a groan. He'd lost count of the number of times he'd seen the movie and he would bet Carter had seen it far more than that.

"Did you pack it? I don't own a copy." He temporarily ignored that it was available for instant streaming on the TV and the fact that if Sadie turned her big eyes—which looked an awful lot like her father's—on him, he'd have no hope of saying no. He'd buy the damn thing in a heartbeat.

"I did." She bounced excitedly. "It's in my suitcase."

"Oh, good," Carter said, sounding more funereal than excited. "I'm *so* thrilled that you're so well organized."

Riley chuckled, but his laughter abruptly stopped as they rounded the corner and came face-to-face with a furious Jonathon Porter-Wright.

"What on Earth are you doing here?" Jonathon's tone was clipped.

Riley tightened his grip on Dylan. "I came to pick up a file I need for Monday's meeting," Riley said calmly. Carter pressed a hand to the middle of his back, warm and reassuring. They were united against his father, but if it got too heated, Riley would send Carter and the kids downstairs. Neither the kids nor Carter deserved to have his father's vitriol directed at them.

"Must I be subjected to seeing you and Carter together?" Jonathon asked, a flush creeping up his neck into his face. "And do you really think it's appropriate to parade your relationship around in front of children?"

Carter's voice was low and measured, but something in it made even Jonathon shrink back. "With all due respect, sir, what I choose to expose my children to is between me, my ex-wife and my current partner. And we are all in agreement that there isn't a damn thing wrong with my children seeing me in a relationship with the man I love. You are completely out of line."

"I'm out of line?" Jonathon scoffed. "Maybe I can't stop you two from being out in public, but I have a say in what I'm willing to tolerate in my own office. It's bad enough that I can't fire you, Riley. I don't want to ever see this" — he gestured to Carter and the kids — "again."

"Actually, you don't have a say," Riley reminded him, his tone low but furious. "Believe me, I have no compunction about taking this to HR, to the board, to the media if that's what it takes. Can you withstand pressure from the board and the press when it's revealed you won't accept your son's relationship with another man? That you won't accept the only grandchildren you may ever have?"

Jonathon blanched. "You can't be serious."

"Serious about *what*? Protecting the rights given to me by the State of New York or committing to a relationship with Carter? Because the State of New York gives me *those* rights, too. I've never been more serious about anything. I've spent my whole life bowing to your wishes, but if I'm no longer your son, I no longer have to consider that. Think of me as any other employee. If my rights are being infringed, I'll take it to the highest authority available. And the media."

Jonathon sputtered while Riley turned to Carter. "Let's go. We're done here."

"You can't do this!" Jonathon protested.

Riley turned back to face his father. "Oh, you'd better believe I can. I let you run my life for far too long, but I won't budge on this. You can expect to see Carter at the holiday party and we'll bring the kids to the company picnic next year. You and Geneva can learn to live with it. Ignore us or choose to be a part of our lives, but I won't give an inch on this. Maybe your relationships with my mother and me were no more than business transactions to you, but Carter, Sadie and Dylan are my family. No one, absolutely no one — not even you — will interfere with that. And that's final."

"Daddy, can we go?" Sadie asked Carter. Riley looked down in time to see her face go a sickly pale color. "I don't feel so — "

Riley winced when she doubled over, puking, but he didn't hide the smile when it splashed onto his father's custom-made suit and Italian leather shoes. Carter bit back a cough that Riley expected was actually a laugh as he knelt by his daughter and rubbed her back.

Riley turned his attention away from Jonathon sputtering angrily over the mess and focused on the people who really mattered to him. "There's a bathroom down the hall. Sadie can rinse her mouth out there while I call someone to get this cleaned up, then let's grab a cab home. It's been a long day for all of us."

Chapter Twenty

Carter kept a straight face as he made his way out of the offices of the Corporate Equality Campaign. He headed for the building's elevator, walking easily, though inside he felt a jumble of excitement and nerves. While his mind was a million miles away from the city of Manhattan when he disembarked on the ground floor, he forced himself back to reality and walked through the lobby, exiting onto East 44th Street. Feeling the warmth of the late-afternoon sun on his face, Carter let himself smile and, as he turned to walk toward downtown, he marveled quietly at how much his life had changed.

He started when his phone chimed, the vibrations in the pocket of his summer suit pulling him from his musings. He read the name scrolling on the phone's screen and a frisson of nerves bubbled up in his chest.

"Hey, Ri."

"Carter, hi! Where are you? How did it go? Everyone's been asking for you."

"I finished up a few minutes ago, and I'm on my way now." Carter glanced up to get his bearings, his cheeks heating after he recognized the landmarks. "I've got an errand to run at the wine store on 42nd and Second first, though. I promised Audrey I'd pick up a couple of bottles."

Riley made an impatient sound on the other end of the line. "Dude, we do not need any more fucking booze," he muttered. "There's enough here for everyone to get drunk twice over, Car—I'm sure Audrey won't care if you turn up empty-handed for once."

"Then I'm afraid you're still vastly underestimating my sister's ability to make my life miserable when she's in the mood."

"And you are definitely overestimating my ability to remain patient right now—you need to be here and tell me how the meeting went!"

"Aw, come on." Carter waited at the crosswalk for the light to change. "I'll be in and out of the store in five minutes."

"We both know that's an impossible task for someone who can spend twenty-five minutes agonizing over lip balm."

"That happened one time!"

"That happens every time!" Riley argued, his voice rich with amusement. "You are incapable of shopping for anything quickly unless the kids are there to keep you on track."

"And you need to learn to have a little more faith in me, Mr. Porter-Wright," Carter told him as he crossed the street. "One of these days, I just might surprise you." Reaching for the handle of the wine store's door, he paused when Riley didn't reply. "Ri? You there?"

"I'm here," Riley replied, his voice quieter but no less warm. "Always faithful and often surprised."

Carter stepped back from the door, delight blooming in his chest. "Okay, then," he murmured. "I promise, I'll be done in five minutes…ten minutes, tops, and in your face in less than an hour. Anything I can pick up for you while I'm here?"

"Well, since you're offering, could you find something to go with the cheese platter? I'm thinking something dry and appley."

Carter smiled and pulled open the door. "I know just the thing."

* * * *

The sky was twilit purple by the time Carter let himself into Audrey and Max's apartment. He closed the door behind him and made his way toward the kitchen at the opposite end of the ground floor. He looked around eagerly, taking in the familiar surroundings with new eyes. Light and music warmed the space and the echoing hum of voices and laughter drifted through the air.

Carter dropped his briefcase by a sideboard just inside the kitchen door and carried the bag of wine to the counter. He set it down, peeled off his suit jacket and loosened his tie, letting out a soft noise of pleasure when the extra layers fell away and the cooler indoor air hit his skin. The door on the other side of the room swung open and Carter's sister stepped inside, a grin brightening her face.

"Hey, you made it!"

"Finally," he agreed, catching Audrey in a hug after she'd crossed the room. Affection surged through him as he breathed in the smell of vanilla and bergamot. "Sorry, I'm late."

"No worries, bro." Audrey gave him another quick squeeze and stepped back, keeping one hand on Carter's waist. "Riley's been telling everyone that your appointment came up at the last minute and you'd be here as soon as you were able. I'd ask you how everything went, but I know you'll want to tell your boyfriend first."

Carter made a noise in agreement. "How's it going out there? Everyone enjoying themselves?"

"I certainly think so." Audrey's eyes gleamed. She looked pretty and relaxed in a simple rose-pink dress that flattered her figure and summer tan. "You know, I don't remember you having so many insanely attractive friends."

Carter raised a brow. "You've met half of the people we invited — Jarrod and Gale are from the opera, just like Peter and Meghan. You know Jesse and Kyle, *and* Dan and Melanie, and I'm pretty sure you met Riley's friend, Will, before tonight, too."

"Actually, I hadn't. Nor the unnervingly beautiful people Jesse and Kyle brought along, nor the brunette with the big guy in tow." She cocked her head thoughtfully. "You and Riley made a lot of new friends, huh?"

"Some new friends, sure. Not everyone we knew before we came out was comfortable with the…changes, if you will. Some friends cut off all ties, some backed off at first then reached out again. As we started living different lives, we met different people. Riley makes friends easily — he's always been the charmer." Carter smiled when Audrey's expression turned dubious. "I do okay, too. It's easier now than it was in the beginning."

Audrey gave his hip a brisk pat. "The party going on out there tells me you do just fine." Frowning, she turned to the bag Carter had set on the island. "What did you bring, anyway? Riley told me you stopped to pick up wine."

"That's because I told him you asked me to pick up a couple of bottles."

Audrey furrowed her eyebrows. "Why would you say that? I told you we were set for booze when we talked on the phone yesterday."

"I know you did, but I thought I'd bring something, anyway—something special." He smirked as he opened the bag. "Do you have glasses for sparkling wine? Doesn't need to be flutes, but they're nice if you have them."

"Oh, sure." Audrey jerked to a stop and her gaze fell on the bottles he'd pulled from the bag, then lifted to meet Carter's. "Oh! Is that—will we be toasting a proposal or something?"

"What? No!" Carter exclaimed. "I'm not proposing anything, to anyone. Or not tonight, anyway." He cringed after Audrey's mouth fell open a little in surprise.

"Oh, my God—you're thinking about it, aren't you?" She grinned after Carter made a violent shushing motion. "Admit it, you're thinking about proposing to Riley!"

"Would you shut the hell up?" He scowled and Audrey leaned against him in a fit of laughter. "How old are you?"

Audrey straightened, still giggling, while Carter turned back to the wine bottles with a huff.

"I wish you could have seen your face — you looked like you were about to pee your pants." She grimaced comically and mimicked Carter's panic.

"I swear to God, Audrey, Dylan is more grown up than you and he's not even in first grade."

"That's because Dylan's *father* has a stick wedged sideways up his ass. The poor kid's getting old before his time."

The siblings gathered the glasses and a tray, swapping insults the whole time. Audrey watched Carter work the foil off one of the bottles and finally cleared her throat to speak.

"Do you ever think about getting married again?"

Carter's throat tightened at his sister's overly gentle tone. He'd heard it too many times after he'd moved out of Kate's, when he'd been struggling not to fall apart. He shrugged and wrapped his fingers around the bottle's cork.

"Yes, I do," he admitted. And he did, more often than he liked to admit. "But nothing's going to happen for a while, if ever."

"I don't mean to be a pain, but why not?" Audrey pressed. "You two are perfect for each other."

"We're also still new at being together."

"Oh, Carter, come on — you've known each other for half your lives."

"And we were with other people for a lot of that time." Carter ran a hand through his hair, pushing down a flare of frustration. "Riley and I are taking things as they come. Don't get me wrong, things are really, really good between us, but it's been less than six months since we came out as a couple." Carter's smile was rueful.

"I have no idea how Riley feels about the idea of marrying again, let alone marrying me. Think about it, Audrey—we're divorced, our parents have disowned us, I've got two kids and been unemployed. We're not ready for rings or vows or legally binding documents right now."

Audrey face softened with sympathy. "You're always so hard on yourself. If you ever *do* decide you want to get hitched, Riley will be thrilled, trust me. I expect to be on the guest list, of course."

"Of course." Carter picked up the tray of glasses, then nodded at the opened bottles of wine on the countertop. "Can you give me a hand?"

His friends cheered when he and Audrey stepped through the kitchen door. Carter made his way down the narrow staircase that led into the garden, admiring the white fairy lights that had been strung along the ivy-covered stone walls that sheltered the space.

"It's about time!" Dan called out. He waited until Carter had set down the tray of glasses on one of the patio tables before wrapping him up in a bear hug.

Carter's ribs creaked under Dan's grip. "Jesus," he gasped out, "you need to stop working out, Danny."

"Be quiet, you big baby." Dan pushed Carter back, his hands still wrapped around Carter's shoulders, and his handsome face split in an enormous grin. "Riley won't tell us where the hell you've been, so do we finally get to know why you're so fucking late?"

"Yes, of course," Carter exclaimed, then looped an arm around Melanie, who had sidled in for a hug, too. "Hey, girl. I'm so glad to see you guys!"

"I told Dan on the flight down that it's been too long since our last visit to New York, let alone since we last saw the two of you in person." Melanie leaned up to kiss Carter's cheek. "The kids send their love, by the way, and made us promise they could come along next time instead of staying with my folks. We really need to start some kind of reunion schedule that isn't based around weddings, christenings or housewarmings."

"This particular housewarming notwithstanding, of course," Dan added and stepped back. "Nice place, by the way—I can't believe your sister's letting it go."

"Neither can we." Riley stepped closer and knocked shoulders with Dan. "We haven't moved our stuff in yet, though, and Audrey and Max still have time to change their minds."

Audrey scoffed. "We're moving three blocks uptown, Ri—we probably won't even notice the change of scene."

Riley grinned, then turned to Dan and Melanie. "I really like the idea of a yearly reunion, you know," he said. "We could take turns, switching between Chicago and New York every other year."

Melanie's eyes lit up. "I like that! It'd have to be during the summer, of course, because of the school vacations."

"Makes sense to me. We can talk to Kate and her boyfriend about working something out with Sadie and Dylan," Riley suggested, his tone colored by the slightest hesitation when he met Carter's gaze.

"Kate and Robert would *not* turn down a chance for kid-free time in the middle of the summer," Carter replied with a laugh. "We'll be lucky if they let us give Sadie and Dylan back at all."

Riley gave him a warm smile. "Sounds good to me."

Carter returned the smile, even though he was very aware of Dan's and Melanie's attentions. This was the first time their oldest friends had seen Carter and Riley together as a couple. Dan and Melanie had been incredibly supportive every step of the way, but Carter still needed a moment to push aside his anxious feelings.

Clearing his throat, he turned his attention to the wine and tray of glasses.

"Okay, I apologize for being tardy," he told them, pouring wine. "I had a last-minute appointment come up that I didn't feel right postponing, even though it meant being a little late to my own party."

Carter handed the bottle to Riley and grabbed two glasses, scanning the faces of the other guests drifting closer until he found Jesse's broad grin.

"As you all know, I quit the ad business earlier this year, which was an excellent if long overdue decision. *This* guy has been after me to get another job." Carter stepped forward to hand the glasses to Jesse and the woman at his side. "I put Jesse off and put him off, told him that I was having too much fun enjoying my summer off to go back to work just yet. Especially after he and Kyle opened a bar uptown and I started learning how to mix drinks."

Jesse mimed choking himself. "Oh, my God, stop being so dramatic."

Carter turned back to the table, enjoying his friends' laughter and taking the wineglasses Riley had filled to hand off to their friends.

"Okay, fine. I did enjoy the time off, though, once I remembered how to, like, actually relax," Carter insisted. "Jesse just wouldn't let it go, though. He made it a project to figure out what the hell I wanted to do next. And once a Murtagh gets an idea into their big brain, you literally have no choice but to see their crazy schemes through." He grinned at Jesse's snort of laughter.

"A couple of weeks ago, we found out that Corporate Equality Campaign was looking for a new Communications Director and for the first time in a while, I really wanted a job again."

"Probably for the first time ever," Riley added, handing Carter a glass for himself.

"I think you may be right." Carter took hold of Riley's free hand before glancing at Jesse, waiting for his friend to make a smartass remark that never came.

Jesse's eyes were bright and he practically bounced on the soles of his feet. "All I did was pass along the information, Car," he said. "You got yourself the job interview."

Carter nodded, his smile wry. "Did I thank you?"

"Yeah, you did." Jesse gestured toward Carter with his glass. "You're welcome, no problem, yadda yadda yadda. So?"

Carter shrugged, aware of Riley's soft laughter. "So?"

"So, are you gonna tell us how your fucking interview went or what?" Jesse exclaimed while the others broke up laughing.

"Fine." Carter glanced around at the others. "I contacted the CEC and they told me they'd retooled the position. They moved it from the Washington, D.C. offices to New York and added a digital media component." His heart seemed to beat a little faster as he met Riley's gaze.

"Turns out the position is the kind of job any media nerd would kill to have—all the flash and bang of hardcore marketing communications with an actual purpose built right in. It's a job with a heart."

"And perfect for you," Riley added. "Now, I think this sparkling wine is a pretty major spoiler, but I'm going to ask, anyway. Did you get the job?"

"They offered me the position this afternoon. I start in two weeks." Carter chuckled and Riley embraced him, their friends' congratulations ringing through the air.

"I knew you'd get it," Riley told him, the fierce conviction in his murmured words making Carter's heart squeeze.

For a long moment, the summer evening around Carter disappeared. He pressed his face into the side of Riley's neck and Riley pulled him close, their hearts seeming to beat as one. Enthusiastic hands slapping Carter's back and shoulders quickly broke the spell, however, and he pulled back with a shaky laugh.

"Thank you." He met Riley's too-bright gaze and his breath caught.

"It was all you—you're the one who did the hard work to get here," Riley told him. "Remember to thank yourself while you're patting the rest of us on the back, okay?"

Carter nodded, blinking against the sting in his eyes, and laughed when Dan crowded in for a group hug. Dan gave Carter and Riley a tight squeeze before he let them go, though he had to prop Riley up after he staggered a little.

Carter's nerves melted slowly away as he caught up with his friends, warmed by their congratulations and obvious affection. He caught Riley's gaze frequently as they each moved around the party and, while Riley busied himself refilling people's drinks and organizing platters of food with Audrey and Max, he paused frequently by Carter's side for a brief word or touch.

Natalie appeared at his side. "I've never seen Riley like this," she observed.

Taken off-guard by the remark, Carter raised his glass and sipped his wine. A certain coolness still existed between him and Natalie, though Riley counted Natalie and her boyfriend amongst his close friends.

"How do you mean?" Carter followed her gaze across the patio and found Riley immersed in conversation with his ex, Will. Catching Carter's eye, Riley winked before turning back to Will.

"I mean that Riley is mooning around like a teenager with his first crush," Natalie replied. She was smiling when Carter turned to look at her, her gaze still fixed on Riley and Will.

"It's not like that," Carter told her.

"Oh, come now — don't tell me you can't see how much he cares about you." Natalie tapped the rim of her glass with one finger. "I used to think Riley was simply far too jaded to fall in love. You know I adore him, but he's always been just a little bit detached. Always controlled, rarely a hair out of place. Hooking up with Will brought him out of his shell a bit," she added, her tone casual, "and Riley needed someone to do that at the time. Someone outside of the circle you two had built as friends. Will didn't judge Riley for the man he used to be or the one he was trying to become."

Unsure of how to respond without sounding petulant, Carter nodded, forcing himself not to look across the patio again to where Riley and Will were standing. Natalie's words came as no surprise. Riley had been open about his time with Will and how much he'd learned about himself during those months. Hearing it from a third party was a different experience for Carter, however, and not particularly comfortable given Natalie and Will were good friends.

"Riley never really let Will in, though." Natalie turned back to Carter. "Probably because of his connection to *you* — you are the one person Riley seems completely comfortable with. He only let go when the three of us were together, and particularly when he was with you. I always suspected you had feelings for each other," she mused.

Carter swallowed. Natalie had never broached this topic with him or spoken candidly of the three-sided relationship she'd once shared with him and Riley. "Really?"

She nodded. "It should have been obvious to anyone who really watched the two of you together. I'd like to say I'm surprised no one else in your lives picked up on it, but that would be a lie."

"Well, you have to admit you had an unfair advantage over our friends and families," Carter offered, shrugging at Natalie's laugh.

"I suppose that's true. I *am* the only person here who's been naked in bed with both of you at the same time." Natalie sobered then. "I wasn't sure how deep things went between you, of course, or if the two of you would ever figure out how to deal with it. There were times when I thought I was wrong about you, in particular…that the feelings were one-sided on Riley's part, especially after the two of you stopped speaking." She gave him a sympathetic look when Carter winced. "I don't mean to be hurtful, though, and I know that getting here wasn't easy for either of you."

Carter nodded. "It's still challenging at times. Weird dealing with my ex-wife, weird *not* dealing with my parents. Relearning your own life isn't a simple thing…at least not for me." His smile felt stiff. "Though I suppose you have some experience with that yourself, don't you?"

"Oh, more than enough." Natalie gave a dry laugh. "As difficult as it was, changing my life was right. For you and Riley, too, obviously. I mean, last year he was moaning about the apartment on 77th Street being too big for one person and now he's moving into a three-story house with you."

"That's how Riley and I met, you know," Carter murmured. "Moving into a set of rooms on the Harvard campus. It took us a while to get here, but we did." His skin prickled as Natalie narrowed her gaze at him.

"Is that your way of saying you'd do it all over again?"

"I'd like to say no, because I'd do things differently instead of all over again. Doing things differently might mean I wouldn't have my children, though, and I can never regret that they're in my life." Carter watched Natalie widen her eyes in understanding and rubbed the back of his neck with his free hand. "Shit, that's probably not what you want to hear."

"Relax, Carter." Natalie smiled gently. "It doesn't much matter what I want, particularly when I can see how much happier Riley is now."

"What you think matters to Riley."

"And Riley knows I'm more than okay with the two of you being in a relationship." Natalie reached up to squeeze Carter's shoulder with one hand. "You're a good man. A little cracked in the head and definitely oblivious to the world around you, but we all knew that, anyway. You're doing fine."

"Thank you." Carter's chest tightened. "I'm happy to know that you think so," he told her, then glanced up when a low whistle echoed through the warm air. He caught sight of Riley waving everyone toward the tables of food they'd set up near the stairs, and smiled.

"I guess that's our cue," Natalie observed as they headed for the food. "Your boyfriend's been bragging about his new cooking prowess again — it's time for him to put up or shut up."

Carter hadn't even picked up a plate before Will stepped up beside him. Swallowing a sigh, Carter put on another smile and traded hellos. Things were easier between Carter and Will, particularly since they'd started seeing each other at least once a month during Jesse and Kyle's private parties at the speakeasy in Morningside Heights. Carter wasn't sure he and Will would ever be truly close, but they'd built enough of a friendship to please Riley, which in turn made Carter happy.

"Riley's been telling me a bit about Corporate Equality Campaign," Will said, "and the work they do to ensure the rights of LGBTQ employees in the corporate workplace. It sounds pretty fascinating."

Carter nodded. "It is. It's very necessary work, too. They're one of the only advocacy groups in the country that focuses on corporate policies and practices pertinent to people like us. Being out in the workplace isn't something that should kill a person's career."

"Like it did yours?" Will eyed him coolly, though his tone was kind.

Carter dipped his head. "Yes, though, coming out wasn't the only reason my career at Hamilton Ad ended. I could have fought to keep my position at the firm, maybe even won, especially if I'd had someone at the CEC helping me. It didn't seem worth it, though. I wasn't really content there, for many reasons. By the time I felt ready to come out, I was also ready to leave the firm. Being disowned by my parents made it a hell of a lot easier to leave, too."

Will said nothing for a beat, his fine features drawing into a slight frown before he nodded. "That takes some kind of balls. Good to hear that you'll be loaning yours out to other people in the same position who need them."

Carter huffed a laugh, glad to see a new warmth in Will's gaze. "You've certainly got a way with words, Will. I may just add that to the skillset on my resume."

"Feel free." The twinkle in Will's eyes hinted at amusement.

"How are you doing?" Carter asked more seriously. "Riley mentioned that someone in your family was ill and that you were spending a lot of time on Long Island."

Will nodded. "Please don't repeat this to anyone, but my father has cancer. The prognosis is…not good. His staff are trying to keep it from the media until they're ready to make a formal announcement."

Carter frowned. "I'm sorry, I feel like I should know who your father is, but Riley's never mentioned him. Or if he did, it's slipped my mind."

Will waved off his apology. "My father is New York State Senator William Martin."

Carter made a small 'o' of surprise with his lips. "I understand the discretion, then. The information about his health won't travel any further than this conversation."

"I appreciate that." Will sighed and raked a hand through his hair. "It's been a difficult summer. My father and I have been estranged for years, you see. I went to Long Island to support my mother and sister, but my father seems like he's softening a little. Or maybe it's just the painkillers." His laugh held a touch of bitterness.

"I really am sorry you're going through this," Carter told him. "I can't imagine how difficult this has been for you all. I know we've had our differences, but please, if there's anything Riley or I can do…"

"Thank you. I appreciate that. I'll be fine, though. Believe it or not, seeing you all at the bar every couple of weeks has been a real sanity saver. David's also been a huge help and—" Will cut himself off with a grimace.

"David?"

"David Mori." Will sighed, his face suddenly lined and tired. "This is also off the record. David's a first term senator who works with my father. He's a great guy, but on the other end of the political spectrum from me. It's…complicated."

"I would imagine." Carter looked over at Riley, who was chatting with Audrey. "But, hey, some people are worth the complications."

Will nodded and Carter was surprised by his serious tone. "I'll keep that in mind."

* * * *

"I'm on to you, Carter."

A lean body settled on the bench beside Carter and he smiled down at the glass between his hands. "And what is it I've done, exactly?"

"Audrey didn't ask you to pick up bottles of wine for the party." Riley held up a dark glass bottle and caught Carter's eye.

Carter shook his head. "Is that what she told you?"

"Oh, no," Riley told him, filling his own glass. "Audrey's being strangely tight-lipped about the whole last-minute-errand thing. Which just so happens to involve one of my favorite sparkling wines, which can only be purchased at four stores on the island of Manhattan." He set the bottle down on the ground by his feet. "One of which is two blocks from the CEC offices."

"Well, you did ask me to pick up something dry and appley," Carter reminded. "The Michelle Brut was the first thing that sprang to mind."

"You are a terrible liar."

"I'm not lying!" Carter broke up laughing after Riley cocked his right eyebrow. "Not about the Michelle Brut, anyway. I remembered how much you liked it the last time we had it at the beach house. I had the idea to buy something bubbly as soon as they offered me the job this afternoon, though." He shrugged, pleasure fluttering in his chest at the soft light in Riley's gaze. "I wanted to tell you the news in person, of course. Wanted to thank you in person, too."

Riley lifted his free hand to stroke the soft hair above Carter's shirt collar with his fingers. "I don't know why you keep thanking me. You got yourself that job, Carter—the rest of us were just your cheerleaders."

"You guys are more than cheerleaders. Especially you." Carter shrugged. He suspected Riley would never understand how profoundly he'd changed Carter's life, simply by being willing to listen.

"I don't know where I'd be without you." He leaned close to press a kiss to Riley's lips, his voice rough when he spoke again. "And I know you don't want to hear it again, but thanks. For being here. For being my friend."

Carter kissed him again, lingering just long enough to make his lover hum and his own heart race. As he drew back, Riley let out a soft groan.

"You are driving me crazy."

Pressing his forehead to Riley's, Carter smiled. "That's a short trip."

Riley stuck out his tongue. "Think anyone would notice if we snuck out?"

"Of our own party? Where would we go?"

"Upstairs, of course. The master bedroom on the second floor, more specifically, which will soon be ours."

Carter laughed, reaching up to run his index finger over Riley's lower lip. "Tempting as that sounds, I think we should wait for Audrey and Max to move out before we get comfortable at *that* level, if you know what I mean."

Riley's face turned down in a playful pout. "You're no fun."

"That's not what you said last night when I did that thing with my tongue that made you —"

"Oh, my God. You are a horrible person."

"Well, that doesn't sound good," a deep voice teased.

Carter met Jesse's laughing blue eyes with a smirk. Jesse stepped forward, followed closely behind by Ingrid, the slim blonde he'd brought with him to the party.

"Trouble in paradise already, boys?"

"Just a difference of opinion." Riley winked at Carter before letting go of his hand and reaching for the empty wine bottle on the ground. He leveled a knowing glance at Jesse. "You know how Carter can be."

"I do, indeed," Jesse replied. He slung an arm over Ingrid's shoulders. "Carter's from the Upper East Side," he confided.

"Ohhh, I see. Lady in the streets, freak in the sheets." Ingrid's pretty features turned up in a smile when Riley and Jesse burst out laughing.

Carter's mouth fell open in outrage. "I hate you all."

"That's nice, dear." Riley patted his hand before standing. "I should put out the cheese and dessert platters before I forget."

"I'll help you," Ingrid offered and took Jesse's empty glass.

"Well, thank you very much, Ingrid, I appreciate that." Riley glanced back to Carter and turned toward the house. "Do you boys want more wine, or can I get you something stronger?"

"A finger of bourbon, please," Carter mumbled. He glowered after the others had moved away and Jesse had dropped into Riley's empty seat.

"What the hell is that face for?"

"Just wondering who or what I pissed off in this world to end up with you in my life." Carter grunted, and the corners of Jesse's eyes crinkled with mirth. "I'm really beginning to regret introducing you to Riley."

"Ah, don't be like that. You need people like me in your life to keep you on your toes. Besides, I told you it was a bad idea for me to make friends with your boyfriend," Jesse pointed out, "but did you take my advice?"

"You are the last person I'd take relationship advice from, dude."

A pang shot through Carter's chest as a shadow flickered across his friend's face. Jesse covered quickly, though, laying a hand over his heart with an exaggerated grimace.

"Ouch."

"I'm sorry—I'm out of line."

"Eh, you're not entirely wrong." Jesse's handsome features relaxed and he adjusted the rolled-up sleeves of his chambray shirt. "We both know I'm not the kind of guy someone takes home to meet the parents."

"Only because you want it that way. You're charming as hell, smart, funny and gorgeous." Carter gestured at Jesse. "You're sort of infuriatingly perfect, really. I'm sure that you could have any man or woman you wanted, within reason."

"I couldn't have you."

"You didn't want me," Carter pointed out. "Not really."

"I was totally honest with you about wanting to get into your pants. And I had a lot of fun getting there, let's be honest." Jesse grinned and Carter put his face in his hands.

"Dude, come on."

"I did! And so did you."

Carter peeked out from behind his hands. "Yeah, I did."

"Even while you were pining for your boy. Actually, you were more than pining, even if you didn't know it at the time." He nodded after Carter dropped his hands and raised an eyebrow. "You tried to act like a single guy, but I'm not sure your heart was in it."

"Well, I was out of practice being single. And I had next to zero experience with guys." Carter chuckled. "It took me a while to figure out how it all worked."

"No, that's not it." Jesse sounded thoughtful. "You knew what you wanted—you just had to figure out if it was ever going to happen." He waved a hand at the garden around them and the shadowy facade of the brownstone. "You wanted this kind of life with someone like Riley."

Carter frowned. "I know you think it's sort of boring, but is that so weird? To want to build a life with someone?"

"No, not at all." Jesse paused, seeming surprised by his own words. "I mean, I know it works for you and Ri, but it's not something I want. I'm not cut out to be a husband."

"Are you sure about that?"

Jesse's brow creased. "Why wouldn't I be?"

"I know you love this carefree-bachelor thing, but I get the feeling something's going on with you lately." Carter watched Jesse's normally open expression darken. "You've been dodging my calls and texts for weeks now and Kyle said the same. I'd started to think you'd gone out of country before you called to tell me about the job at CEC. You even skipped out on the last get-together at the bar and you're the host! Then tonight, you turn up without Isaac, even though you *and* Isaac told me he'd be here." Carter became concerned when Jesse's gaze slid away. "Did something happen between the two of you?"

"Isaac and I…experienced a difference of opinion." Jesse's smile was thin as he echoed Riley's earlier words.

"About what?"

"About seeing other people, what else?" Jesse murmured. "Isaac's been pushing me to make a commitment—to be exclusive—and I've been pushing back. So, he told me he can't see me anymore because I'm hurting him."

Carter shook his head. They'd discussed Jesse's disdain for monogamy on many occasions. Isaac wasn't the first of Jesse's partners to walk away after developing feelings Jesse was unwilling to explore. The grim set of Jesse's face, though, told Carter this might be one time it bothered his friend to be left behind.

"I'm sorry." Carter laid a hand on Jesse's shoulder. "I know you liked him."

"I really did. *Do.* Isaac is fun. Different from the kind of people I usually date. Kind of like you, now that I think about it. More of a grown-up with a real life."

Carter eyed him. "You need to think long and hard before you get involved with someone like me again, because real life can be a serious pain in the ass. Last week, Kate and I had almost a full day of meetings at the kids' school." He laughed when Jesse stared at him.

"It's August. Why the hell is anyone even there right now?"

"They're implementing a new arts program," Carter explained, "and this was our opportunity to meet the new staff who, by the way, are kids themselves. If I had to guess, not one of them was over twenty-five." Carter shook himself and grimaced, making Jesse snort.

"Oh, shit, I wish you could see your face."

"I'm not kidding. The guy who'll be teaching the kids music is practically a fetus."

"Was he hot?"

"Definitely, and smart and funny and wildly talented, but still my kids' teacher, and therefore, out of bounds. Plus, he's got two first names, which automatically makes him untrustworthy."

Jesse stared at Carter for a long moment before he broke up laughing. "What the fuck are you talking about?" he managed to get out.

"I don't know," Carter admitted with a smile—he was happy to play the clown if it lightened his friend's mood. "But the guy's name is Cameron Lewis, which sounds like some kind of Girl Scout Cookie from hell."

"That's it, no more booze for you." Jesse sighed when Carter dragged him in for a rough hug.

"At least I made you laugh. You were pouting pretty hard a minute ago, and that's really not like you."

Jesse pulled back and laid a loud, smacking kiss on Carter's cheek. "I'm okay—really. Isaac and I are still in contact. I'm sure we can be friends, if he's willing to try." Jesse grinned and glanced toward the house.

Following his gaze, Carter watched Riley and Audrey descend the staircase, carrying trays loaded with a variety of colorful bowls, while Ingrid followed behind with a bottle of wine in each hand. Riley's smile sent a thrum of pleasure through Carter's body and he held out a hand to Jesse.

"Come on," he urged, pulling Jesse up to stand beside him. "You'll feel better with some sweet treats in your belly."

Carter busied himself pouring wine while Riley arranged slices of pavlova on dessert plates, heaping fresh blackberries and whipped cream onto each serving and smiling at their friends' reactions while the plates were passed around. As Carter took a plate for himself, though, Riley pulled it just out of his grasp, an unfamiliar expression crossing his face.

"You doing okay, Car?"

Carter blinked. "Yeah, of course," he replied. "Why do you ask?"

"We've been lying pretty low for the last couple of months, taking it nice and easy. This has been an intense week in comparison, especially the last forty-eight hours. New house, new job—even a few new friends." He smiled at Carter's amused snort but looked at Carter closely, his gaze kind. "You've been a little quiet tonight. I just wanted to be sure you're feeling okay with all of this."

Carter took the plate from Riley's hand, laid it on the table beside them and stepped forward to wind his arms around his lover's waist.

"I'm more than okay," he replied. He stayed quiet for a moment, soaking in the comfort of Riley's touch. His sister's earlier questions about Carter's future with Riley kept coming back to his mind, though, and Carter knew he had to speak up or he'd go crazy turning those questions over and over in his head.

"You know, when Audrey saw the sparkling wine tonight, she asked if..." He paused and bit his lip, his cheeks burning.

"What did she ask?"

"If we'd be celebrating a proposal tonight. You know how my sister is," he hastened to add when Riley's eyes went wide. "She's always looking out for us and trying to make sure we're happy."

Riley nodded, moving his gaze over Carter's face. "She thinks we'd be happy if we were married?"

"Yeah."

"And what do you think?"

Carter shrugged. "Some days, I'm not sure I can answer that." He swallowed when hurt flashed across Riley's face. "Ri—"

"It's okay if you think the answer is no," Riley told him and the love in his gaze made Carter's heart squeeze. "Because I'd love to do that with you—make that kind of commitment to you—but I'm just not sure I *should*."

Carter frowned and reached up with one hand to smooth back the hair from Riley's forehead. "What do you mean?"

"Well, I tried being married once and look how spectacularly that all turned out."

Carter huffed out a laugh. "Hey, I tried it, too, and didn't do any better. But we both know we were with the wrong people back then. Who's to say we wouldn't do better if we were with the right people? Namely, each other."

"Maybe we'd just crash and burn again." Riley's voice sounded hollow. "Carter, I really don't want to lose what we have together. Everything feels right. Everything *fits*. Or almost everything, anyway. You know I love you. So maybe we don't need to be married to be happy. I'd be totally okay with continuing on just as we are, if that's what you want."

Carter stared at Riley for a long moment, his chest burning with emotions. "And if I want more someday? Because I really think I do. I want everything you're willing to give me, today and every day."

He held his breath, letting Riley absorb his declaration, and could have sworn his heart stopped beating when Riley shook his head. He nearly gasped a moment later when a grin transformed Riley's face.

"Jesus. You sure know how to pop a not-proposal with style." Riley reached up to slide his arms around Carter's neck. "You've thought about this, haven't you?"

"Yeah, I have. Especially since you told me you thought about your future with me and the kids. I knew you wanted to be with me but hearing that made me understand how much you wanted to be in my life, too, the messy parts included."

Riley leaned in to press a scorching kiss against Carter's mouth, turning his bones into water. "I can't remember a time I didn't want to be in your life," Riley murmured. "And I can't tell you how fucking grateful I am that we're finally here."

"God, I know." Carter's heart soared. "As of this month, we've known each other half our lives — did you remember that?" He gave Riley a squeeze. "It took me almost that long to understand who you are to me, Ri, and I nearly lost you in the process. Shit, I nearly lost *myself*. But here we are, moving into a new set of rooms, and I'm not going to let anything stop me from making the most of it."

Riley's eyes gleamed with unshed tears but his smile was radiant. "You're crazy, you know that? But you've got me, today and every day. If you ask me to marry you someday, I promise I'll be ready with an answer."

Carter pressed his forehead to Riley's. "I'll keep that in mind," he murmured and smiled.

About the Authors

K. Evan Coles is a mother and tech pirate by day and a writer by night. She is a dreamer who, with a little hard work and a lot of good coffee, coaxes words out of her head and onto paper.

K. lives in the northeast United States, where she complains bitterly about the winters, but truly loves the region and its diverse, tenacious and deceptively compassionate people. You'll usually find K. nerding out over books, movies and television with friends and family. She's especially proud to be raising her son as part of a new generation of unabashed geeks.

Brigham Vaughn is starting the adventure of a lifetime as a full-time writer. She devours books at an alarming rate and hasn't let her short arms and long torso stop her from doing yoga. She makes a killer key lime pie, hates green peppers and loves wine tasting tours. A collector of vintage Nancy Drew books and green glassware, she enjoys poking around in antique shops and refinishing thrift store furniture. An avid photographer, she dreams of traveling the world and she can't wait to discover everything else life has to offer her.

Our authors love to hear from readers. You can find their contact information, website details and author profile page at http://www.pride-publishing.com.